CW00499603

DON'T LOOK BACK

by

DAVID BLACKDENE

Edited by Alison Snailham

Published in 2012 by Blackdene & Snailham Publishing

British Library C.I.P.

A CIP catalogue record for this title is available from the British Library.

To Alison

Thank you for every day, every hour, every second

I couldn't have written this without you

Chapter One

As Jade slid into bed beside me, I savoured the sensation of her warm flesh pressing against mine. I couldn't remember the last time I felt that wonderful feeling of a woman's flesh fusing with my own. Okay, I could. I could remember the exact day and hour actually. But for my own sanity I had to push all thoughts of the past out of my mind. They had no place here. Jade was a good woman. She deserved my full attention. This was a turning point in my life. Time to let go of the past and give this new love a chance.

Jade is twenty-five, five eight, slim and athletic. She has long, tanned, well-toned legs. Her abs are like steel. She puts me to shame. She cycles, she swims and she surfs. Well, not for a while, not since Amber's accident. I don't think she'll ever surf again. I know I never will. But she still cycles to work everyday. She isn't just fit; she's super fit. Bursting with energy. Her zest for life is infectious. Her face does not immediately strike you as pretty, but she's always got a smile there and her eyes make you feel happy inside. Her posture, her demeanour, her whole manner is attractive. You can't help but look at her and keep looking at her. Like I said, she isn't pretty. But she is damned attractive.

Tonight was the sixth night that I'd gone across to Jade's for dinner in these past two months. Dinner, usually prepared courtesy of M & S; a bottle of red, usually Spanish and cheap, and an evening in front of the TV moaning at X Factor and Strictly Come Dancing. I'd always known that she liked me. The whole time I was seeing Amber, Jade had tried to tempt me, but it was always very subtle. An innocent touch of my hand when she passed me a drink, or leaning forward over my desk so that I had nowhere else to look but at her cleavage. Nothing ever happened of course. She knew how much Amber and I were in love and as her closest friend, she loved Amber herself. But it's been almost two years since we lost Amber and I guess I've known for some time that we might end up like this. And here we were.

I like Jade. Maybe if I'd met her before Amber we might have dated. Maybe more. As she cuddled up to me under the cool satin sheets in her bed I felt my heart quicken. I wasn't aroused, but I couldn't deny her eyes were drawing me in. Her flesh, pressed firmly against my own, felt silky, smooth and warm. Her breasts were small, maybe a B cup, but as I cupped one in my hand it surprised me how firm it felt. She kissed the tip of my nose and then quickly dropped her lips down on to mine. I could feel my heartbeat in my throat. Palpitations. Her lips were warm, wet and tasted of red wine and spearmint. The spearmint was most likely toothpaste; she had popped into the bathroom before coming into her bedroom. I could taste the wine, because I had decided to drink lager instead. One can of Kronenbourg 1664. Jade had offered me another, but I had told her I was limiting myself to one as I was still taking antidepressants. It was a lie. I hadn't taken the Fluoxetine for maybe three months.

Her fingers glided lazily over my chest, combing through the curly hairs there. It should have felt good, but that fluttery feeling in my throat was distracting me. Nerves. Her nails were long, immaculately manicured and painted a subtle shade of pink that matched her lip-gloss. They scored my skin sensuously as she let them wander south. She kissed me again. Soft. Sexy. Our lips parted, but she hovered millimetres from my mouth and spoke softly as her fingers continued their journey.

"I love you, Brendon. I think I always have."

I've known Jade maybe four years. I've never known her date anyone more than six months. Maybe she was speaking the truth. Then her fingers reached their destination and I gasped at her touch. She put her mouth over mine and I felt her tongue slide in between my lips. It felt hot. It had been almost two years since I had last made love and I hadn't even touched myself in all that time. Jade stroked me lightly and I felt my sex start to stir. I missed the intimacy. I missed the touch of a woman. I missed the release that sex provided. But most of all I missed Amber.

"What?" Jade stopped. She had noticed my expression change. I wanted to do this. I really did. Jade is a wonderful girl that any man would be overjoyed to be in bed with. But as attractive as she is, as wonderful as she felt and no matter that I had lain awake dozens of nights thinking about this, the feeling in my heart right then was overpowering all other emotions.

"I'm sorry, Jade." I reached down and grabbed her wrist. I didn't need to say any more. As I released her wrist, she let go of me and slid across to her side of the bed. We lay silent, motionless for an awkward ten, maybe fifteen seconds. She sighed heavily, then got up suddenly and padded out through the open bedroom door and into the bathroom. I heard the whooshing sound of the shower curtain being pulled back and then the sound of the gas boiler firing up as she ran a shower.

I felt bad for her. I had led her to believe I was ready for this, that I had wanted her as much as she had wanted me. I had let her feed me, comfort me, entertain me. I had played along with the flirting and the courting and I had even enjoyed it. After months of wishing I were dead, crying myself to sleep each night and avoiding people, the company of an attractive young woman had been welcome. The conversations had been uplifting. We had laughed and we had cried together. I had started to think of her differently. She was no longer Amber's best mate. She was becoming my best mate and perhaps more.

My new feelings towards Jade were both scary and exciting. I had begun to think of her sexually. I had found myself fantasising about her, at work, whilst driving and when I lay awake at night. But as strong as the libido is, the heart is stronger. And it was telling me loud and clear that there was no space in there for anyone new. It was still full of love for the girl of my dreams; the girl who had turned my life upside down and made me happier than I had ever thought possible. The only girl I had ever truly made love with. She might not have been my first love, but she had been my true love. The one. Amber.

I dressed quickly, grabbed my fleece jacket off the back of the settee in the living room and looked around for a pen. There was a pencil and notepad by Jade's phone on a little oak table by the window. Jade's apartment was pristine, compact, only one bedroom and an open plan lounge and kitchen, but there wasn't a thing out of place. Single people. How come my place didn't look like this? I paused a second, the pencil in my hand hovering over the pad.

I felt I had to say something. I had to explain that it wasn't her. I wrote. 'Sorry…it's too soon.'

It will be two years next month since Amber's death and I'm telling Jade that it's too soon. I'm thirty one years old; I used to enjoy making love five, seven, even ten times a week and I haven't made love once in nearly two years and I tell an attractive, naked, twenty five year old girl that it's too soon. Christ, I'm losing it.

It was cold outside. There was a dew coating the X Trail. I jumped in and pulled away keeping the revs low, like I was sneaking away. Pathetic, I know. I guess I subconsciously predicted this happening. That's why I only had the one can. I'd never drink and drive. The CD in the X Trail's stereo was halfway through J Lo's 'Waiting for tonight'. I hit the FM button. I hoped Jade hadn't been listening to J Lo too. Her wait would have been in vain. Some inane trance track vibrated the door speakers of the X Trail. I hit another button. Classic FM showed on the screen. Some fantastic pianist was playing Debussy's Claire de Lune. I turned down the volume a little and relaxed. My mind drifted back maybe twenty years. I think I was about twelve when I first heard Claire de Lune. I was sat on my board on Porthtowan beach just before sundown, my breathing just starting to slow after another wicked session body boarding. My brother, Matt was still out, catching the last few breaks. As I sat watching him flicking left and right, his body a silhouette against the blazing sky, a campervan pulled up in the car park behind me. As the noisy VW engine came to a stop, the racket was replaced with some magical piano music coming from its open windows. I didn't know it then, but it was Claire de Lune.

The scene in front of me was simply heavenly. The sun was burning almost red in an impossible pink, purple and orange stained sky. As every wave swelled and broke in front of me the sun illuminated it from behind turning the water a raft of gorgeous blues and greens. Every couple of breaths a wave would crash on the shore followed by the mesmerising whoosh of pebbles being dragged back down into the frothing sea. I don't think I had ever felt so relaxed in my life. Just thinking about it now as I listened to the tune again, driving home in the dark, was enough to calm my mind. It might have been twenty years ago, but the images in my head were as clear as yesterday. I could see Matt paddling fast on the swelling wave, then jump up fast on his board as it broke into a perfect half pipe. His silhouette danced perfectly on the rising water against the blazing sky behind. And as the wave came ever closer, the late sun illuminated the wave into a beautifully sculptured glass tube of ceruleans and azures, changing magically into lighter shades of viridian, teal, turquoise and jade.

Jade.

Wham! My mind was catapulted back to the present. Jade.

Claire de Lune was still playing, but my heartbeat had risen to about one hundred beats per minute. I sighed heavily and hit the button to drop the window on my right. Immediately the cold air hit my face and my eyes filled with water. I'm pretty sure it was the cold air that made them water. It was. Well, probably. My chest was tight. I was being force fed cold, fresh November air and yet it felt like I couldn't get enough of the stuff in my lungs. Why was it that no matter how hard I tried to think of Jade, her super wide smile, her big blue eyes, her gorgeous long dark hair, that perfect smile, those permanently tanned legs that just went on and on and...Amber's image always crept in. She permeated every thought. From day one she had planted herself in my heart and over the two amazing years we were together, her roots had anchored themselves deep. So deep, that no matter that she had been gone almost two years, her presence there had left a scar that would remain forever.

Jade lives in Durham. Physiotherapists must get paid well, because you can see the castle from her little Juliet balcony. That doesn't come cheap. I live about seven miles out. Not so expensive; up in the hills in Burnside. I was almost home when I noticed the time illuminated on the dash. Nine thirty five. Here I was, thirty one years old, single, nine thirty five on a Saturday night, (kind of) dating a sexy young brunette with killer legs, who incidentally had just told me that she loved me. I felt like I was being pulled in two different directions simultaneously. How do you let go of the past? It's been nearly two years and she still has such a hold on me.

Chapter Two

At the junction where I normally would take a right up to Burnside, I didn't. I kept my foot on the accelerator and flicked the lights onto full beam. The leaf stripped oaks that lined the road whizzed by as Debussy ended his famous movement. An annoying advertisement followed. I prodded the CD button and Lucie Silvas sang like she was singing only for me. Ironically, she sang 'Breathe in'. I did. But my chest felt tight. Constricted. I let down the window again, just a crack. Pretty soon the village of Chesters came up. I slowed to thirty as I entered the built up area. It was a Saturday night, but the only person I saw was an old man walking a little dog. Some kind of terrier, I think. I pulled off the main road and down the dimly lit drive to St. Martha's Rest Home. I parked up and walked across the block-paved drive to the main entrance. I hit the button for the door entry system. Sylvia, the manager answered.

"It's just me, Sylvia."

She let me in with the button on her desk and gave me a smile and a wave as I passed her office on the way to my mother's room. Strictly speaking, there's no visitors allowed after nine, but Sylvia knew all about my loss and she let me come visit my Mum anytime I liked.

My mum's door was ajar and she had some music on. I stood in the doorway and watched her without speaking. She was listening to the portable stereo that I'd bought her last Christmas. I forget who the singer is, but the song was familiar. 'Everyday, it's a getting faster, going faster than a roller coaster..."

Mum was clutching a diary to her chest. I knew it was a diary, because I'd seen her hold it like that a thousand times before. It was always the same one. 1966. The year she had met my Dad. I smiled at the sight of her, but it wasn't a happy smile. I felt sad for her. Dad had been gone ten years now, but the pain still showed on her face. I guess it always would.

"I love you, Mum." I told her and she turned her head my way and smiled. I walked over and sat down on the pouffe by her armchair. She reached out and held my hand with her free hand, the one that was permanently contracted since her stroke. We didn't need to say anything. We often sat like that. Our hearts had suffered the same loss. We understood each other.

"Buddy Holly." She said smiling at me.

I nodded, then got up and poured her another Martini. Her glass was empty on the table in front of her, but I could see the bottle of dark liquid on the bureau top. She smiled a thank you and held my hand again. The tape played another three short songs and then there was nothing but the sound of an old clock ticking loudly. I didn't mind it. It was comforting.

"How's Amber?"

Sometimes she remembered, sometimes she didn't. Since her stroke last year, dementia had wrecked her brain. It used to kill me when she said stuff like that. Now I just went along with it; it was easier that way.

"She was tired. She's having an early night, Mum." I lied yet again.

"What time is it, Matt?" She often called me by my brother's name.

I glanced down at my watch; the watch Amber had given me when we were first dating. It was a Seiko; plain, stainless steel and unremarkable. I loved it. "Nearly ten." I told her.

"You'd best get to bed, son. Your Dad'll be in soon…he'll go mad if you're still sitting here at this time."

I kissed her on the brow and left as quietly as I had arrived. Sylvia let me out and I drove home with the radio off. It had been seven weeks since I had last cried. I was doing well. When I got back, I went straight up the stairs without putting the lights on. There's a big round mirror at the top of the stairs and I didn't particularly want to see myself passing it. The house was cold. I'd been out since six. I kicked off my shoes, pulled back the duvet and got in fully clothed.

My mind was flashing from Amber to Jade. Amber. Jade. Amber. Jade. Mum. Amber. Jade. Mum…Amber. Amber. *Oh God, Amber!* I opened my eyes and stared at the wall illuminated pale green by the digital clock/radio on my bedside cabinet. I longed for my mother's clock. I brought my wrist up to my ear, shuffled myself into a comfortable position and listened to the quiet tick tick tick of the Seiko. I could still smell Mum's perfume on my clothes. Anais Anais. I didn't cry. Much.

The next morning I got up early, about nine. Hey, it was Sunday and that's early for a Sunday in my house. I stepped out of the front door and the cold hit me. I have a thermometer stuck on the outside wall of my cottage. It read four degrees. Four degrees! I had my cycling gear on, which consisted of a pair of cycling pants, a short sleeved tech top and a tight fitting fleece top. Call me soft, but I went back to the cupboard and got my fleece jacket and my Thinsulate gloves.

I headed out of the village along the fairly level road that heads north. There wasn't a soul on the road. After about half a mile I got off the bike, lifted it over a style and took the muddy track that led across farmland towards Quaker's Woods, a large deciduous plantation that had been planted maybe fifty years ago when the coal mine closed and they regenerated the whole area where I live.

I was beginning to warm up. My back actually felt damp with sweat, yet my hands and my face were cold. No, strike that. Bloody freezing. As I entered the wood, a young doe skipped across the path in front of me, then another, then another two. Wow! First time I've seen four together. I stopped and watched them disappear through the trunks of birch and beech. I'd woken up feeling pretty low, but now I couldn't stop myself from smiling. The sight of wild deer not a mile or so from my cottage made me feel good inside. I pedalled off again and quickly became aware of a tiny wren following me. More smiles. This might just turn out to be a good day.

About a half mile in I had to negotiate about thirty cans and bottles left strewn across the muddy path. Fosters and Lambrini, the drink of choice for today's fifteen year olds. There were the remnants of a fire just off track and I could still smell the vague aroma of wood smoke. My smile had gone.

"Friggin' little bastards!" A gruff Geordie voice called out. Some Geordie accents sound warm, friendly and likeable. Not this one. I pulled up, putting a foot down on the wet dirt and glanced around to find the source of such a delightful greeting.

"Every Saturday night they leave it like that…the little shits."

I didn't see him initially; I was too busy focusing on a huge wolf running through the dead bracken towards me. All I could see were teeth. Bloody big, sharp teeth.

"Here Tino!" He ordered the wolf and it stopped immediately, just before I was about to soil my pants.

I tried to act cool, like I wasn't fazed. I think I failed. I nodded towards the Rambo look-alike. "Morning."

He was dressed in what I could only describe as battle dress. He wore a camouflage jacket over camouflage combats, some ex army leather boots that were caked in mud and a khaki bandana wrapped around his bald head. Oh yes, and a rifle tucked under his arm. Real friendly type.

"Don't worry about Tino…he only attacks when I give him the specific command." He informed me so that I could relax. I didn't. I'm six foot and thirteen stone. This guy had four inches and three stone on me.

"What is it? Ss…some kind of wolf or ss…something?" I asked nervously. Not so cool.

"Shit! I wish." He said showing a mouthful of dirty, yellow malformed teeth. "It's a Spitz man…part of the Spitz breed…you know. Bred from bliddy wolves aren't they…that's why they look like one. Pomeranians, Chow Chows, Siberian Huskies, German Spitz…they're all wolves man!"

I nodded. This guy had a degree in wolf breeds, but he didn't impress me. I just wanted to get away from this nut and his dog as fast as I could. And preferably without the dog chasing me.

"Akita…Tino's an Akita."

I thought he was speaking a foreign language. Japanese perhaps.

"If you stick around you might see him make a kill. Better than watching a Tarantino movie, man."

"Cool." I said cool. Cool! I hate Quentin Tarantino movies. I think all of his movies are made for morons to watch. This guy was proving me right.

"That's why I called him Tino…get it?"

I chuckled. What a comedian.

"They call me AK…" He probably named himself after the gun. The AK47. Nice name. Real nice.

He held out his hand for me to shake. I shook it, watching the Akita the whole time. It looked angry or hungry maybe. Either way there was still a real danger of me making a mess in my cycling pants.

"Brendon." I said, still shaking his hand. "Brendon Hawke."

He finally let go of my hand.

"Hawke. Like the bird you mean?"

"Yeah, but with an E on the end." I informed him.

Then something caught his eye and he quickly lifted the rifle up to his shoulder. He paused absolutely still for maybe a second, looking down through the scope. Then. *Thwup.* He fired. I expected an explosion of sound. I expected to have my eardrums burst. No bang. No boom. No thundering shot. Just *Thwup.*

"Tino. Kill!" He bellowed.

I guessed that must be the specific command he was talking about earlier; some kind of special language or code that only wolves could understand, no doubt. The Akita took off, smashing heavily through the dead undergrowth. I watched it bound out of sight, or maybe it was still there. Its brindle fur blurred with the colours of autumn that filled the woods. Perfect camouflage. I saw the white of its tail flash briefly, then nothing. My new acquaintance, AK took some cigarette paper out of his jacket pocket and filled it sparingly with tobacco from a pouch. In the time it took for him to roll it, lick it and light it, the Akita was heading back, dragging something heavy through the undergrowth.

The Akita is a big dog, maybe a little over two feet at the shoulder, but I never expected to see it dragging a deer back to us. A deer! Most people throw sticks for their dogs. Hell, when I was a kid I did some beating up on the local moors. The spaniels would fetch grouse, pheasants and rabbits, but I had never seen anything like this. I was out for a bit of exercise on my bike in my local wood, not on expedition with David Attenborough following the hunting habits of a pack of wolves in Alaska.

I gasped. "Jesus!"

"Mint isn't he?' Rambo man sounded his approval.

"Yeah, mint." I said using his vernacular.

"Tino. Drop!" He gave one of his specific wolf commands again.

"It's beautiful." I said. I was talking about the deer. It was, especially when it ran in front of me not five minutes before.

"It'll be even better when I have her butchered and safe in my freezer, Hawkeye." He said, bending down, grabbing the doe's back legs.

I mounted my saddle again and took off, weaving through the empty Lambrini bottles. "Nice chatting, mate." I bid him goodbye.

He called back. "Aye, see you Hawkeye. Mind how you go." Hawkeye. Like I'd never heard that before. I glanced back and watched him with his huge dog dragging the young doe back through the trees to wherever he came from.

I like deer. I like to see them running wild around the woods and fields where I live. There's an Asda not four miles away and a Tescos maybe five. You can buy just about any type of meat you like there, all expertly butchered and wrapped in plastic and relatively inexpensive to buy. Why a man has to go out and kill a young doe like some Grizzly Adams character is beyond me. That had been the first time I had ever come across Mr. AK47 and I hoped it would be the last.

As I neared the far end of Quakers's Wood, it started to snow. It was only November and it was snowing. Great! I picked up the pace and pedalled hard through a really soft section of the track, picking up wet sludge on the knobbly tyres. I ride a hardtail, a Giant Terrago. It's not the lightest mountain bike in the world, thirty one pounds according to the scales in the shop where I'd bought it. I reckon it was closer to forty by the time I got out of the woods. As soon as I hit the main road again, I climbed off, picked up the bike and dropped it several times from about eighteen inches, bouncing the tyres on the tarmac. About half a stone worth of dirt dropped off. I jumped back on and raced down the road at probably twice the speed I had gone through the woods.

I cut my ride short and came back through Middlestead. Some kids threw snowballs at me as I raced through the village centre. Weird kids. When I was their age I was still in bed at that time of the morning.

I got back to my cottage at just after ten. A long hot shower later and I was sitting in my conservatory eating breakfast whilst watching the snow fall on the field in front of my garden. It was beautiful, very picturesque, but I was worried about the course I was due to take that week. I teach survival skills to youngsters in the dales and we usually camp out under canvas. Not so cosy when it's snowing!

I finished my bacon sandwich and sat at my desk with my mug of Rooibus tea and booted up my laptop. I wanted to know the weather forecast for Monday and the rest of the week. I really didn't want to have to cancel the course, that's how I make my living. I clicked on the Met Office website in My Favourites and put in my postcode. Not good. More snow was forecast for Monday and the temperatures were predicted to drop below freezing. I peered out the French doors and saw that there was an inch and a half of snow on top of the bird table already. Damn. I really needed to run this course; my current account was looking feeble.

I clicked into my email account. Three messages awaited me. I opened the first one and deleted it immediately. It was from a site called Ultimate Max. In the split second I gave it before pressing delete, I read that they were offering a guarantee to make my penis between one and three inches longer. After that freezing bike ride I was almost tempted to retrieve it, but I was fairly happy with what the long, hot shower had managed to recover.

The second email was from Jade. I hesitated before opening it, staring out into the garden and the field beyond. The snow was literally coating everything. Even the clothesline was an inch thick of the stuff. Bloody winter. I was going to have to make a decision about running the course; the school that had booked it would want to know so they could inform the kids and their parents.

I clicked Jade's email with trepidation. I had a feeling I had blown it. It had been sent at 9:47 last night. That was about ten minutes after I left. She was probably pretty pissed off around about then. I braced myself. It read. 'Take your time. I understand. I really do. When you're ready, give me a call. I can wait…I love you Brendon. x.'

I started to breathe again. She was really something that Jade. What did I ever do to deserve such a special girl? I was feeling humbled to say the least. I didn't reply. I couldn't think of anything appropriate. I clicked on the third and last email. I shook my head at the sender's name. 'Virgin slayer'. Some porno site, no doubt. I opened it anyway. That's when my world went to shit.
It read.

Your wife was a whore.
I know because I took your wife's virginity. She was fifteen. I had her mother countless times as part payment for what she owed me. When she couldn't pay her outstanding debt she offered me her daughter.

What ever Adele told you was a lie. I don't know how many times I used her, but she paid most of her whoring mother's debts off. 10k. She was good at it. She really got a liking for it.
Her mother still owed me 3k when she died. It's been 8 yrs since Adele took off without settling her mother's debt. That's a lot of interest. She now owes me another 10k.
I saw you on the TV. I know you can afford it.
Pay me the 10k and this all goes away.
Don't pay and I put it on the net.
I'm guessing you won't believe this.
I could tell you that her father died when she was 6 and her mother when she was 17, but that would prove nothing. You can get that stuff on the net these days.
I could tell you that she has one nipple slightly bigger than the other and her eyes are green, but amber in the centre, but there's probably a lot of girls that fit that description.
I knew you wouldn't believe any of that crap, so I've sent you some proof instead.
Click on the attachment above. When you've stopped kicking yourself for your stupidity at marrying a whore – reply to this email with one word. YES. Then I'll give you instructions on how to pay me the money.
Don't tell the police.
Don't tell anyone.
I have lots of pics like the one attached. One click and the whole world will know that your wife was a whore who shagged anybody. Think what that will do for your TV career.
I know you'll do the right thing.

Chapter Three

I stared at the screen. For how long, I don't know. Eventually, I got up and went to the toilet. I stood waiting to pee, but nothing came. I stared at the mirror over the washbasin. I had just ridden ten miles in winter conditions, but my face looked pale. I could feel my left eye was twitching, but I couldn't see it in the mirror. I walked back through into the lounge and watched the snow falling again. I shuddered like you do when you feel a chill. The heating was set to 22 degrees. I'd put it on before I left for my bike ride. I shuddered again. I sat down on the carpet with my back leaning against the radiator and stared towards my desk. The screen on my laptop had timed itself out and my screensaver was showing. It did that after two minutes of inactivity. Every five seconds a different photograph of Amber appeared. She was standing with Jade outside our local pub three summers ago. Then she was sitting in our garden with her hair down and her sunglasses on. Next she was standing with her arm around me and we were grinning from ear to ear like a couple of kids in love. We were.

This was stupid. I had no reason to fear this email. It was from some weirdo who had got me mixed up with someone else. I was never married to anyone called Adele. There was no reason for me to be upset. But I was.

I got up and sat at my desk. This was a hoax. I was sure of it. All I had to do was click on the attachment and then I would see a picture of some pornstar, no doubt. Virgin Slayer. Yeah, right. I was just about to click on the attachment when the phone rang; not the landline, my mobile. I got up, pulled it out of my sweat pants' pocket and walked through to the conservatory where I answered it.

"Yeah. What's up?"

"Megan's gone to her mother's, I was going to come across. You fancy a pint?" It was Matt, my older brother. I hadn't seen him in weeks. He hadn't even rung me in two weeks. I think he thinks I'm dating Jade. Maybe I am.

"It's not even opening time yet." I looked down at my Seiko. It read. 10:43. Hell, I'd just finished my breakfast.

"It'll be open by the time I come over."

"In this snow?" I challenged him. I wasn't really in the mood. "You've got a four wheel drive. I've got a four-wheel drive. Since when has a little snow been a problem? I'll be over in twenty little brother."

"Okay, but you're driving." I informed him. I ended the call and stared out of the window some more. The sight of a million snowflakes being blown left then right, then swirling around like in one of those snow globes kind of sucked me in. It was hypnotic and for a minute or two I let myself fall into a trance. I welcomed the escape. I needed it.

I was rudely brought out of my hypnotic state by a thump against the conservatory glass. I actually jumped back. Bloody kids! There's a public footpath runs alongside my garden fence; kids love to annoy me when I'm sitting relaxing, reading a book or taking a nap. They must have thrown a snowball. I scanned the whole length of my fence and the beech hedge that runs along the bottom stretch of fencing. Nothing. Maybe they were hiding. The snow was beginning to hypnotise me again. I diverted my eyes and immediately spotted the reason for my fright. It wasn't kids. On the patio in front of the French doors was a dead bird. Not just any bird, but a tiny wren.

In the few seconds that had passed since it had hit the glass, the snow had painted it a translucent shade of white. Every snowflake that had landed upon it appeared to dissolve on contact. The warmth of its body was soaking up each flake like a sponge. My heart felt heavy. I could actually feel my bottom lip begin to tremble like it had when I was maybe five and I knew I was in for a scolding from my Dad. I let myself drop into one of the cane chairs that faced out of the French doors. The wren was fast disappearing under the snow. I jumped up again, opened the doors and bent down and picked it up. I brushed the snow from its tiny body and sat back down in the cane chair, pushing the doors shut with my foot. I held the bird clasped between both hands like it was the most precious thing in my life. Maybe it was.

I stared out at the snow again. Boy, it should snow more often; it's amazing how quickly you can fall under its spell. Time passed. I wasn't aware of it. I was somewhere else entirely. My mind had wandered back four years when Amber and I had just started seeing each other. We were walking along the River Wear. It was winter; there was snow on the ground. On the path in front of us I thought I saw a mouse run under a holly bush. Both of us crouched down to investigate. It wasn't a mouse; it was a wren. It had broken its leg. As quick as a flash Amber reached out and caught it with one hand. She always had a thing about wrens. Being petite, she said she could relate. I told her five feet three inches of woman was a whole lot bigger than three inches of wren, but I had to concede she was just as cute as a wren.

When we got back to her place, Amber cut an ice-lolly stick down to size with a kitchen knife and taped it to its leg. Then she fed it maggots that she had bought from a fishing tackle shop on the way back.

The wren's leg healed rapidly and she released it three weeks later. She made me drive back to Weardale and let it go in the exact spot that had we found it. That was my Amber, my little wren. That's just one of a million reasons why I loved her so much.

I suddenly became aware of the door. Someone was just about breaking it down. I jumped up, put the wren down on the chair I'd just vacated and rushed to the front door. I pulled back the bolt, opened the door and felt the cold hit me like a slap.

"Christ, Brendon…it's bloody freezing out here. Let me in." It was Matt, my brother. Somehow I had forgotten about him coming over. He rushed in, trailing snow all over the oak flooring in my hall. I followed him through to the lounge where he had attached himself to my radiator.

"And you want to go for a pint?" I teased him. He looked frozen standing there with his back against the radiator, his shoulders hunched.

"Have you got a door open or something? There's one hell of a draft in here."

He wasn't wrong. I could feel the cold blowing through my lounge as I stood there. I glanced into my conservatory and noticed one of the French doors was open. No wonder there was a cold draft. As I headed for the door I remembered the wren. I quickly shut the door and turned the key, then looked down at the cane chair where I had left it. No wren. I looked at the cane settee, the other chair and the floor. I felt like I was going mad. How could I lose a dead wren?

"What's up?" Matt reluctantly left the radiator and walked through scanning the floor the same as I was. "What are we looking for?"

I stopped scanning and looked outside at my garden. The beautiful shades of autumn were all gone. Now it was just white, white and more white. Something caught my attention down near the beech hedge. A little bird darted from down low in the hedge and landed on my bird table at the bottom of the garden. It's shaped like a little house with a thatched roof on it to keep the seed dry that I put there most days in the winter. Since reaching thirty my eyes haven't been as good as they used to be. I squinted, shielding my eyes with my hand at the brightness of the snow.

I felt Matt standing next to me. He said. "Oh look! A wren. I love wrens, they're so cute."

I couldn't believe it. I had to choke back the tears. I daren't turn around and let my brother see my face. Thankfully he walked back through into the lounge.

"Are we going for this pint or what?" He shouted through impatiently. I stared out at the tiny bird on my bird table. Matt wasn't the only one who loved wrens.

The snow was worse than I realised. I offered to drive, partly because I am a bad passenger and partly because it was a good excuse for me not to drink. It's not like I never enjoyed a drink. I did. But after losing Amber I had enjoyed it rather too much. Actually, I wouldn't use the word 'enjoy'. I was off drink.

"So, you still seeing that Jade chick?" Matt asked nonchalantly. I ignored him.

I said. "You want to try The Fox?" I was heading towards Chesters anyway and The Fox was the first pub we would come to. It was just about blizzarding and I didn't see any sense in going any further.

Matt got the message straight off. He was good like that. "The Fox is good. They do good food."

I pulled into the car park behind the pub. We were the only car there. I said. "Won't Meg be making you dinner later?"

"Probably. Tell her I ate here and you're dead!"

That was my brother Matt. Thirty eight years old, seventeen stone, high blood pressure and takes his car to visit his next door neighbour. Okay, maybe that last part was an exaggeration. The thing is, he's happy, so I guess I should be glad that one of us was. We had dinner. Roast beef. Matt was right; the food was good. Matt talked a lot and I nodded a lot, hopefully at the right times. My mind was someplace else. It was after two when we left. When I got back I waved Matt off, put the X Trail in the garage, but I didn't go back in the cottage. I pulled my hat out of my coat pocket, stuck it on my head and went for a walk down the valley. It was still snowing. I didn't care. I walked.

Chapter Four

Amy sat perched on a large rock watching little black figures bobbing up and down with the waves. Some were sitting over their boards looking back towards the golden horizon. Some were submerged and constantly disappearing and reappearing like seals with the rhythm of the ocean.

"Brave or stupid?" A tall guy in a black T-shirt and baggy jeans approached from her left. He was alone, but a border collie was running up behind him. She couldn't say whether it was with him or not. Amy made like she hadn't heard him. She kept her eyes on the ocean.

"Mad aren't they?" He was close now, maybe ten feet, strolling real slowly, his feet heavy in the sand. Amy could see him quite clearly now in her peripheral vision. She kept her head facing front, but she regarded him from behind her sunglasses. He was tall, over six feet, tanned, and with muscle; large, pumped up muscle, beneath a hooded sweatshirt that was way too tight for him. His hair was a mass of blonde curls that hung down to broad, masculine shoulders. He had the whole 'surf dude' thing going on. Amy wasn't buying it. Surfers tend to have lean, hard, defined muscle. She made him for one of those guys who hang out at a gym all the time, preening themselves, painting themselves with fake tan and oil. Vain.

He stopped in front of her and looked right at her. Subtle.

"You want to move? You're blocking my view." Amy wasn't so good at playing it subtle either. He didn't move. Amy shuffled along on the rock. The vain guy sidestepped, blocking her view again.

"Look, it's like three minutes before that big red ball sinks into that big blue ocean and I watch it do that almost every night. Tonight, isn't going to be any different." Amy stared at him behind the sunglasses. He didn't move.

"Mind if I join you? Name's Darren. I love your accent by the way." He jumped up onto the rock and sat right beside her.

"Beautiful isn't it?" Darren commented as he joined Amy appreciating the sunset. Amy ignored him. She came here most nights like someone visiting their church to worship might. And like those who pray, she didn't want to be disturbed.

"You surf?" He tried to engage her, but he may as well have been addressing the rock. Amy's head was locked on the sunset.

"It's good fun. You'd love it. It's infectious. You learn really quickly." He was persistent.

"Watch those guys there…" He pointed vaguely at the ocean. "The more experienced surfers, see how they let the first swell wash over them and wait for the big one instead. Sure, they have to paddle hard to keep up with it when it comes, but watch how they position themselves, anticipating the next big one. There's a skill to it, see?"

Amy sighed heavily. She wondered if he had finished. He hadn't.

"I remember the first time I ever went out. It was Watergate…you know it?"

He was talking about Watergate Bay, one of Cornwall's most famous beaches, a favourite with surfers and home to numerous competitions over the years. Amy sighed yet again.

He continued. "Anyway, that's where I caught my first big wave. I can remember a wonderful dark, swollen bank of ocean driving towards me, building height second by second. I looked across to the other guys out there; their eyes wide in anticipation, like children on Christmas Eve. I felt their enthusiasm; that wild youthful recklessness was running through my veins also. And around me everyone paddled hard, our arms windmilling through the blue. Then it caught me. It lifted me up in the air and my whole world faded to the very corners of my mind. And right then, for just a few seconds…I was flying…skimming over the top of the ocean. It was truly magical. I didn't want it to end. I was over the blue and I never wanted to come down."

Amy broke her silence. "You finished? You sound like you just read a book about surfing."

"If you ever had a go, you'd know what I mean. The raw power of the swell beneath you as you ride high on the crest of a wave; the salt water spraying your face, stinging your eyes; it's so fresh, so invigorating, so damn good you have to do it over and over again. It affects your soul, man. It's addictive."

Amy shook her head. "Ah ha. So how come you're not out there with them now?"

"Like I said…those guys are either brave or stupid. I'm neither. That water is like maybe eleven or twelve degrees. The time to surf is in the summer when it's seventeen or eighteen."

Amy shook her head again, but kept her thoughts to herself. The guys out surfing began to hit the shore one by one as the light diminished. They clearly all knew one another. The ones who had left the water sat on their boards on the shore waiting until every last one of their buddies joined them and then they walked up the beach as one, laughing and joking.

As they came within ten yards one of them recognised Amy. "Hey Amy, you were awesome this morning. What time was that? The sun was barely up."

"About seven…best time of the day" She answered smiling at them all. Over this last eighteen months they had all grown to respect and accept Amy as one of their own. They all stopped and two of the others joined in the conversation. "How'd you get to be so damn fast? You is what I call stoked, girl!"

"Yeah, I saw you this morning too …you were working those sets like Stokes or McAvoy…I tell you Amy if you don't win the Open this year…I'll break up this board here in protest."

One of the others kicked his friend's board playfully. "I'll break it up right now, Thrash…it's a piece of shit."

The guy called Thrash kicked sand at his friend and everyone laughed.

"So anyway Amy…" Thrash leaned in to Amy's right ear and lowered his voice. "Who's the new boyfriend?"

As quick as a flash Amy jumped down from the rock and fell in line with the guys. "This here is Daryl…you should listen to him…you might learn from him." She chuckled and broke away.

"It's Darren actually…" He corrected her, but by then she was off the sand and walking up the tarmac.

"Looks like you got blown out there, bro…didn't you know she's untouchable." One of the surfers said as they started to walk away from him.

Darren called after them. "She a lesbian then?"

Thrash answered him. "She is to you mate…you got no chance…She's too cool for the likes of you." The rest of them laughed, leaving Darren alone on the beach in the growing darkness.

Amy walked with the boys passing through the carpark, along past the surf shops and cafes, which were now all closed for the winter. When they reached the Seaspray apartments Amy waved them off, hugging Thrash and two of the others then headed along the darkened path that ran along the back of the apartments. When she neared her own back door, number thirteen, she stopped dead in the path. Her PIR light normally lit up the last three yards, the sensor detecting her presence as she passed by number eleven. It hadn't and she knew it was switched on, because she had never switched it off, even during the light nights in the summer. Maybe the bulb had blown.

She took two more steps and then something hard hit her in the throat. She was lifted off her feet and thrown hard against the rough brick of number twelve's outside wall. Something clamped around her throat, squeezing it steadily harder and harder until her airway was almost closed. What air she managed to take in was no way near sufficient to sustain life. It was like sucking through a straw; a narrow straw, like one of those you get taped to a can of WD40.

Amy's survival instinct began with her left knee jerking up into the groin of her attacker. The energy was wasted as she missed her target. She tried kicking out wildly. Again she was out of range as her attacker held her at arm's length and continued to squeeze her throat. She was running out of ideas as quickly as she was running out of breath. Her adrenal glands were working overtime, pumping adrenalin around her body to feed those big muscles in her legs, her arms, her trunk.

The human body under threat is capable of superhuman acts. People have been known to lift many times there own weight, run at Olympian speeds, survive falls from great heights and endure unbelievable stresses to their bodies. They do that through ignition of the fight or flight response. When our nervous system ignites our adrenal glands, adrenalin courses through our veins like fuel, which feeds our muscles so that we can fight, run, challenge or escape. However, like petrol, or any other accelerant for that matter, adrenalin needs oxygen to give it potency. And right now Amy's oxygen supply was running out. Fast.

Amy's vision starred. Her energy and her strength were fading fast. Her world began to disappear. They say that in the seconds before we die, our lives flash before us. Amy saw nothing but darkness.

Once inside apartment thirteen, the man dragged Amy's limp body across the wooden floor and dumped her heavily on one of the settees in the lounge. He quickly found the bathroom and relieved himself. He had been waiting in the darkened recess of Amy's doorway for almost half an hour. The three pints of lager he had drank whilst he watched Amy from The Beach Bar had stretched his bladder to its limit.

He walked back through to Amy's open plan kitchen and living room. He started with the cupboard under the sink. Nothing there he wanted. He opened the next under bench cupboard. He saw a bottle of gin. It wasn't what he was looking for, but he grabbed it anyway and put it on the bench above. He opened the glass-doored cupboard above the drainer. Nope. He tried the drawers. Nothing.

He stood and thought a second, then walked back through to the bathroom, opened the airing cupboard and immediately saw was what he was looking for. A clothesline. He grabbed it and came back through to the living room and knelt down next to the settee. He took a knife out of his pocket, cut a length from the clothesline, lifted Amy's feet up off the settee and looped the line around and around her ankles and then tied a crude double knot. He used the remainder to do the same with her wrists and then he got up off his knees and looked down on Amy's limp body.

After a minute he took out a box of cigarettes and lit one with his Zippo lighter. He smoked half the cigarette watching Amy breathe and then went over to the kitchen and opened the fridge. He grabbed a plastic bottle of tonic and a hunk of cheese. Then tucking the bottle of gin under his arm and lifting a glass from the drainer he threw himself down in the settee opposite the settee Amy lay on. He poured himself a strong gin and tonic, downed it in one, then poured another and put the glass on the coffee table between the two settees. He was unwrapping the cheese when Amy opened her eyes.

The first thing Amy saw was the pattern of the brown and cream throw that covered her settee. Then she smelled the lemon disinfectant that she always cleaned her kitchen with. Good, this was familiar. She was home. Then she moved her head and saw a pair of dirty boots opposite under her coffee table. Not good.

"Don't move. You'll hurt yourself." The man warned her.

Amy tried to get up. She cried out.

"Which bit didn't you understand?"

Amy looked across at the man. He looked late fifties with close cropped, peppered, ginger hair. His face was heavily lined; his expression severe. His lips were thin and featureless except for the wetness of the gin that he brought to his mouth frequently. His eyes were small in deep dark sockets. And they were familiar. Amy had an awful feeling that she had seen those eyes before. Steely grey, blue and cold. She felt her scalp prickle and a shudder ran through her.

The man saw the recognition in her eyes. He smiled like he was drawing satisfaction from her discomfort.

"You look damn fine for a dead girl. How long has it been? Nearly two years isn't it?"

Amy said. "You must be mixing me up with someone else." Her memory had recovered. She knew precisely who he was. The man poured himself another drink and tossed the remainder of the cheese on the coffee table. "Maybe you're right. Maybe you just look a lot like a girl I once knew."

Amy looked away. She didn't like the way he looked at her. Creepy. Surfing as much as Amy did keeps a girl fit and flexible. In the space of three seconds she went from lying prone on the settee to sitting upright.

"Impressive." The man smiled at her. "But then you always were fit…in more ways than one."

Amy ignored the comment and brought her hands to her mouth. She tried to pick at the clothesline with her teeth, but it was tied too tight. She said. "Look my boyfriend is due any minute now. He's twice your size and half your age. Believe me, you don't want to be here when he walks through that door."

The man smirked and took another drink. He said. "You know Brendon is going to be really pissed off to hear that you never drowned. But when he hears you're shagging some new guy too, his heart is gonna break all over again."

Amy tried again. "Did you not hear me…he'll break your legs."

"Yeah?"

"You'd better believe it."

"Funny…I've been watching you for nearly two weeks and I haven't spotted any boyfriend…not unless you're counting that skinny kid that keeps chatting you up on the beach… What's his name again? Thrash...." He laughed. "He's a bit below your class, don't you think?"

Amy blew out a long breath. "What the hell do you want?"

"Really Adele, is that any way to talk to your first love?"

"I told you...you've mixed me up with somebody else. My name is Amy Bell...I've live here for five years and I've never seen you before in my life." Amy persisted. The man leaned forward, resting his elbows on his knees. He used his cold, steely eyes to good effect, looking straight through her, pinning her to the settee with an evil stare that made Amy feel really uncomfortable. His tone changed. No more smiling. No more relaxed manner. He was tired of pussyfooting around. Now he meant business.

"Your name is Adele...Adele Trenholm. You were born in Sunderland, Ryhope to be precise. Your Dad died when you were six. Your mother was a lush and a whore. She borrowed money she couldn't pay back and when her debt reached five grand, she offered me her daughter."

"Fuck you!" Amy spat the words out like bullets.

"Oh, you did Adele...you fucked me plenty!"

"You're delusional! I wouldn't breathe the same air as you if I had the choice." Amy looked away from him again, out of the French doors that led to her balcony. There was nothing to see but the reflected light from her kitchen hitting the glass. But it was better than looking at his face.

"You were a sweet little thing back then. Fifteen. Firm. Tight." Now he was smiling again.

Amy said. "You're sick!"

"When I told your mother I'd let the five big ones go if she left me alone with you, she didn't hesitate."

Amy bit. "You killed her...you bastard!"

"Memory starting to come back, Adele?" He was smiling again, mocking her.

Amy bit at her bottom lip. He had pressed the right buttons. She was furious at herself for reacting.

"Your mother was quite the looker once upon a time. The first time she whored herself was for a five hundred quid debt. She was worth it back then. Even better than you! I was glad to oblige."

"Like I said...wrong girl...you're wasting your time." Amy backtracked to her original answer.

"Bit late for that, don't you think? Why do you think that wimpshit you called Daddy killed himself? Your mother was borrowing so much dough off me every month, how do you think she was paying me off…and I was only too happy to clear her debts…I guess it really bothered him…sharing the same hole."

Amy jumped up lightning fast and threw herself headfirst across the coffee table. Her head struck her attacker mid-chest, knocking the wind right out of him. She lifted her head fast under his chin forcing his teeth to clash together. Her confidence grew. She brought her arms up fast and with her hands clasped together she threw all her weight into a devastating blow to his face. His nose exploded across his face, blinding him with his own blood and mucus. Amy pressed her knee into his groin, more for her own support to get back onto her feet than to injure him, but she was more than happy to hear him cry out as she increased the pressure there.

She hopped like a kangaroo across to the cutlery drawer, opened it, picked up a long, sharp meat knife, bent down and sliced through the clothesline that had kept her ankles together. She straightened her body, just as the man was raising himself from the settee.

"Get out! Get out! Get…out!" She screamed at him, holding the knife out towards him with both hands.

The man backed away from her. Amy was shaking; tears ran down her cheeks. She was as mad as hell. "I swear to God, Manning. If I ever see you again, I'll kill you."

Manning continued walking backwards towards the door. In contrast to Amy's face full of hatred, he wore a wide satisfied grin. Blood ran down over his lips and dripped from his chin, but his wide satisfied grin was unmistakable.

"You just made things a hell of a lot worse for yourself, Adele….Oh sorry, Amy isn't it? Or should I call you Amber?"

Amy rushed forward two steps like she was about to lunge at him. Manning took no chances; he turned, opened the door and fled.

Amy kicked the door shut and quickly locked it, slid the bolt along and then fell against the hall wall. She had escaped his wrath for now, but she felt no sense of relief. On the contrary, she felt an overwhelming feeling of despair. It had been almost two years since she had seen that man, but mentally, he had scarred her for life. He had taken so much from her, precious, sacred things that she could never get back. And now he had come back in her life and he wanted more.

Amy turned the knife on herself and for a moment she let herself feel the cold, sharp point prick her wrist. Evil had returned once again into her life and now she didn't know whether she had the motivation to run from it. It hadn't been long since she had stopped the Prozac. It hadn't lifted her like she had hoped, just numbed the edges of her pain. The past was never going to fade. Never. But these last months, finding a new job, winning a local surfing competition and coming second in another, it had given her hope, confidence, something to hang on to. She had even gained respect and friendship with local surfers. Now, none of it mattered.

She looked down at her wrist and saw she had drawn blood. She pulled the blade back and sliced through the clothesline.

"No! Not this time Manning!" She said to herself and then pushed the blade into the pine cladding that lined the hall. "I'm not dying for you this time…" She headed back down into her kitchen and grabbed her mobile. "This time I'm going to live!"

Chapter Five

As I trudged through the snow down the path that runs by my fence, I thought how the horses in the field below my garden looked about as pissed off as I was. But at least they would get stabled later, eat some fresh hay and nuzzle up with some other horses. I wished I were a horse. Horses don't get email.

I reached the wood at the valley floor. There wasn't much shelter; most the branches were bare. My coat was painted white; the snow was relentless. I walked on. I'd done a lot of it since losing Amber. Walking. Cycling. Driving. I fear that if I stop I might have to deal with it all. And I couldn't do that.

I came to the open barn that I can see from the end of my garden. It was full of hay. I breathed the smell in. It was kind of comforting. I stepped inside and sat on one of the square bales, patting it with my hand reassuringly. A rat darted out of the barn from a bale to my left. I watched it skim across the snow to a smaller barn maybe twenty yards away. I'd uprooted him; upset his day, no doubt. But although he had to endure the exposure to the cold and potential danger of a hungry hawk, he was soon back in a safe place.

I felt my chest tighten. My lip was quivering again. I wished I were a rat. I was sick and tired of being out in the cold, exposed. I longed to be back in a safe place.

"Bloody freezing isn't?" The weird Rambo look-a-like with the gun and the wolf dog that I'd seen earlier in Quaker's Wood came through the opening out of nowhere. I nearly had a heart attack. I nodded. I certainly wasn't going to strike up a conversation with him. I stood to leave, but the dog was blocking the opening.

"What's your rush Hawkeye? In case you hadn't noticed, it's friggin' blizzarding!" Hawkeye. Some people just rub you up the wrong way, don't they?

"Sorry mate…gotta get back. Work to do." I lied. He put his hand on my shoulder. I didn't like that. He was a big bloke and his dog was too.

"Sit down." He said with his hand still on my shoulder. I sat down. He sat down next to me and then used that special code with his dog again. "Tino. Sit!" The dog sat. He still looked angry.

"I've seen you on that bike of yours."

"I know..." I turned to him. "I just met you this morning down Quaker's...you killed the deer." Like I was ever going to forget that.

"I didn't kill the deer. Tino did." He held up the rifle, then sat beside me on the same bale. Cosy. "I can kill a hare at thirty yards with this..." He laid the rifle across his thighs. The barrel was touching my knee. "But it just stuns deer. Tino does the rest. It's powerful for an air rifle, but it won't kill deer."

What do you say to that? I said. "Right."

"What I meant was I've seen you before...on your bike...or walking...in these woods, over Quakers and sometimes up on the fell. You used to take photographs and write in your notepad. I've seen you collect berries...berries that nobody collects...Rowan, Hawes, Sloes."

He was making me feel uncomfortable. I said. "You stalking me?" Not that I was about to pick a fight. The Akita still looked angry.

"What I'm saying is you used to look happy out here. Now I see you and you look empty my friend."

My friend? This guy was really starting to creep me out. I shuffled forward on the bale. The dog stared at me. I said. "Look...AK, is it?" He nodded. "I really must get off..." Our eyes met and if I'm honest, I was close to pleading. He had hit a nerve. Bad timing. He had caught me at a vulnerable moment and it was like he could read my mind. I didn't like it. I rose to my feet.

"Tino. Fall back." He gave the dog a command. It got up and sat down behind him.

I gave him a nod and walked out into the blizzarding snow. The wind had picked up and it was driving hard. It hit my eyes and a pool of tears welled up.

I'd walked about ten yards when AK called out to my back. "I've been there Hawkeye...I know how much it hurts. Take care, my friend."

I hate that, when people think they can read you, when they think they know just how you're feeling when really they don't know shit. I was wishing I had goggles on; I couldn't stop the icy flakes from hitting me in my eyes. The snowy onslaught wet my face and ran down my cheeks. The weirdest thing is, I could taste salt on my lips.

I walked on. I walked like a man on a mission. My hair was stuck to my forehead. My face began to sting. The wind was biting cold and it wasn't even December yet! After about an hour of putting one foot in front of another I realized my back was wet. Sweat. I stopped and looked ahead of me as well as I could. Sometimes when the hills are coated white and the snow has stuck in clumps to the branches so that it resembles cotton wool, I wouldn't be the first to say it looks pretty. This didn't.

It was bleak. Like some uninhabitable planet I'd just landed on. The moon would have held more appeal. There are no people on the moon. And I think I would like that. The world seemed like a hostile place both outside and inside my head. I couldn't stand the places my mind had taken me since opening that damned email. I just wanted to go home, drink copious amounts of alcohol and bury myself deep beneath my duvet. And if I never woke up again that would be fine with me.

By the time I made it back, it was dark and I felt exhausted. I probably only walked five miles in total, but it had felt more like ten, what with the wind and the cold and the snow. My face stung like sunburn, my body ached everywhere. But worst of all, just when I thought my heart couldn't hurt anymore, I discovered it could.

When I got inside I stood in my kitchen and undressed leaving a sodden heap of clothes on the cold tiled floor. I had held all these emotions inside me all day, pushing them back, back from the forefront of my mind so that I could appear normal in front of my brother, the barmaid, the waitress, AK. Now, I could hold them back no more.

I opened the fridge and released two cans from a six-pack and walked through to the extension off my kitchen. I stopped at the door and emptied the contents of one can in about twenty seconds. I placed the empty can on the end of the bench, my eyes suddenly drawn to a dim light illuminating the far wall of my lounge. My laptop was still playing the screensaver. More emotion rose up inside of me. I flung the extension door back so hard the handle dented the plaster when it struck the kitchen wall. I strutted back to the fridge and grabbed the rest of the six-pack. I had a feeling I was going to need them all. I opened the one I still had in my hand and glugged it back as I went back through into the extension and flung back the lid on the hot tub.

There's a little green-lit display that tells you the temperature of the water. I keep it at 39 degrees all year round, but my flesh was so cold it felt like immersing myself in a giant pan of boiling water. I tapped the button that controlled the jets twice, turned up the air and the calm, warm, blue water erupted like a geyser and I shuddered as my body was forced to adapt to its new environment.

It was cool out in the extension, maybe five degrees or less. The space filled with steam quickly and I watched as condensation ran down the tiled walls, which were tinted blue by the underwater light. The bubbles reflected a dappled flow of light all around the room. We'd bought the tub two and half years ago after I'd completed my first series for TV. Amber insisted that we buy it. She said it would relax me. It had. Not now. Now I needed another can.

I emptied half of my third can and then out of nowhere came an animalistic cry from deep down inside of me. I frightened myself at the raw power of it. I was angry. Big time. How dare somebody upset me in this way. Amber was the most special, wonderful, sweet soul I had ever met. I was not going to be drawn in by this email. As soon as I had another can and soothed this aching body I would go delete it. Nobody and nothing could spoil the memories of my sweet perfect Amber.

I'd been in the tub half an hour or more and I felt hot and maybe a little woozy. I looked over the edge and saw that I'd drank five of the six cans. They say drinking never helped anyone. Well, in the short term it can be bloody marvellous. I actually laughed as I got out of the tub and dried myself off. I've no idea why. In the space of half an hour my brain chemistry had altered so dramatically that I exited the extension a different person. I was vaguely hungry, but also vaguely nauseous. I staggered through to the bedroom and threw myself on the bed. The sheets were cold against my flushed skin. I quickly wrapped the duvet around myself like insulation and let the world spin on without me.

I was walking along the top of Striding Edge in the Lakes, Dave my cameraman in tow. A Herdwick sheep was carrying my pack like that was the norm. A phone began to ring. Not a ringtone like you get from a mobile; it sounded like one of those old fashioned telephones that you hear on old British films from the fifties.

From behind the camera, Dave said. "Are you going to get that?"

The sheep stared at me like it was saying 'well…are you going to or what?' I was hundreds of feet up a mountain with a frightening void either side of me, and the scariest thing was the sound of that phone ringing.

"Brendon…you going to get that?" Dave pushed me. I didn't want to answer it. My Dad said. "Answer the damn phone, Brendon." It rang on relentlessly. I knew it would be Jade and I didn't know what to tell her. Then Dave dropped the camera from his face, but it wasn't Dave's face that I saw. It was Amber's.

Her eyes looked right through me.

She said. "Well, Brendon? Could Jade make you happy like I could?"

The ringing grew louder. It was unbearable. Amber glared at me. She looked like she was hurting. I couldn't answer the phone. How could I speak to Jade whilst Amber looked on? Then I lost my footing and I felt myself fall. I was falling…falling.

I woke up in a cold sweat. My bedroom was freezing. It was also rotating. It was making me feel sick. But more surprisingly the telephone was still ringing. Not my mobile, the landline out in the lounge. I tried to get out of bed. My legs were all tangled in the duvet. I fell on the floor and nearly vomited. I managed to crawl out of the duvet and get to my feet. Something hit me hard knocking me sideways as I negotiated through into the lounge. Pain coursed through my shoulder and I swore as I reached the phone. Vomit rose up from my stomach, the acid burning my throat. I swallowed it down and picked up the phone.

"Jesus Brendon…you had me worried there. Are you alright?" Matt.

"I was in bed. Asleep."

"Already? It's only ten past nine."

I looked at the illuminated display on the DVD player down near the floor under my TV. It read: 09:11. My brother can tell the time.

"Brendon?"

"Yeah." I was massaging my shoulder. I'd hit the doorframe on the way through.

"You never go to bed before twelve."

"What's with all the questions, Matt?" There was a pause. My eyes focused on the screen of my laptop. The screen saver was still going. Amber was standing in just about the same spot that I was standing. She was holding this very telephone, probably talking to Jade.

Jade.

Matt said. "Have you been drinking, Brendon?"

Maybe I had slurred a little. Probably.

"Brendon?"

"Can I go back to bed now, Matt?"

Another pause. Longer this time. I was just about to hang up.

"You seemed a little distracted today. Are you alright Brendon?" He seemed concerned.

I reassured him. "I'm fine. Just tired is all."

"Sure? I can come over if you like?"

I wondered if he and Megan were okay. He had been a good brother these last couple of years, but he wouldn't ordinarily offer to come across after nine at night, in the snow and when he had to go to work in the morning. I guess I should have asked; I should have been concerned for *him*. However, I didn't really feel myself right then. I don't think I would have made a very good listener.

"I'm fine Matt, really." I cut him short and ended the call. I felt like shit. I felt both sloshed and hung over simultaneously. It was cold in the cottage, but I felt clammy. And my guts were churning, big time. But I couldn't take my eyes off the laptop screen. I couldn't believe there were so many photographs of Amber and Jade together. Every other image had them together, arms around each other, on the beach, in a bar or right here in the cottage. It was a nightmare. I hit the keyboard to stop the damn thing.

Bad idea. My inbox was still open. Those words were still etched on my screen, probably burned there permanently now. Why did this stupid email bother me so much? Who the hell was this Adele and why did I care?

It was like driving by a bad road accident. You don't want to look, but you do anyway. I began to read the words again.

Your wife was a whore.

Even though I knew this could never be true, I found them offensive nevertheless. Those words were on my laptop, addressed to me and I was reading them in my home.

I know because I took your wife's virginity. She was fifteen.

Again, that was just crap. I knew it then and I know it now. I was Amber's first. She hadn't even been touched. When I met her she was twenty one. She was shy, reserved; she didn't just play hard to get, she *was* hard to get. We dated for nine months before I saw her naked and even then it was in low light. And she didn't possess any underwear that I would call even remotely sexy.

I read on.

I had her mother countless times as part payment for what she owed me. When she couldn't pay her outstanding debt she offered me her daughter.

I never met Amber's mother, but I've seen photographs. She was well dressed, smart and attractive. She didn't look like someone who needed money, someone who would sell her daughter's virginity. That was just preposterous.

She was good at it. She really got a liking for it.

I was laughing now. When I first touched Amber intimately, she stopped me. She was shy. It was so obvious I was her first. I was twenty eight at the time. When you're twenty eight and you meet a gorgeous girl who is twenty one, you don't expect her to be a virgin. However, we'd been seeing each other four or five months before we got even remotely physical. It was nearer nine before I made love to her. And as wonderful as she was, she was far from experienced.

Then he mentions her father dying when she was six and her mother when she was seventeen. I don't rightly recall when Amber said her father had died. I guess she could have been six. I know her mother died when she was seventeen, but like he said, you can get that stuff on the Internet these days.

I read on.

I could tell you that she has one nipple slightly bigger than the other and her eyes are green, but amber in the centre.

Again, bollocks. Amber had perfect breasts and perfect nipples. She didn't have one larger than the other. She didn't. I tried to remember. It had been nearly two years. A fleeting image of Jade's naked body intruded into my mind. Damn! I pushed it away.

Amber. Think Amber. I forced my memory to go back and retrieve those images. I could see small, round, pert breasts with large, dark pink, brown nipples that protruded maybe half an inch from tanned, satin skin.

Jade.

Stop that! I don't want to think of Jade. I couldn't recall Amber's nipples just then, but I know her eyes were green. Green, no other colours, just green.

I read on, shaking my head. All this was just crap. He knew about my TV series, he was threatening to ruin my career by outing my wife. But there was nothing here that proved anything. Nothing that proved he had ever met Amber. He was obviously just some nutter trying to make some quick money. I didn't need to click on his attachment. I'd read enough. He couldn't even get the name right. Adele.

I left the laptop and went over to my stove, kneeling down on the floor in front of it. I grabbed the old newspaper stored behind the log basket, crumpled a dozen pages into tight little balls and placed them on the grate. I picked a handful of dried sticks from under the stove, placed them on the paper balls and lit their edges. Once I had shut the door and opened the vents, it caught quickly. I watched the flames burn brightly in the darkness of my lounge. Dry sticks burn good and bright. I opened the door again and put a couple of big logs on. In less than a minute, the logs had caught and I could feel their heat. I closed the vents almost all the way and sat on my rug staring at the flames.

I like watching my fire. It's relaxing. There's something primeval about it, I guess. I stood up, still watching the flames licking up the sides of the logs. The sticks underneath were glowing hot like lava. My head was hurting, my guts were still churning, but the heat on my chest felt good and I couldn't take my eyes off the flames.

The phone broke the spell. I actually jumped back, nearly falling over the little oak table that my phone stands on. It sounded excessively loud. I had no intention of answering it. The DVD player was telling me it was 09:22. Maybe it was Matt again. I was in no mood to talk. It rang on another three times and then it stopped abruptly. The silence sounded louder now. I was alone in the silence. Again.

I walked into the conservatory, knocked my leg against the cane chair and stopped at the French doors. The moon was illuminating the snow and I could see right down the valley to the two barns where I had bumped into AK and his Akita earlier. My eyes weren't exactly trustworthy, but it looked like there was a flickering glow coming from the larger of the two barns where I had sat on the bales. I wondered if anyone would be stupid enough to spend the night in one of those rat-infested barns, especially with temperatures down below zero and snow on the ground. He was certainly a strange one that AK. I didn't know what to make of him.

My focus shifted and I put AK out of my mind very easily. I felt hungry. I turned on my heel and headed back to the kitchen. The light from my laptop and the stove illuminated my route enough to find my fridge. I squinted inside as the brightness of the light from the open door caused my head to throb. There was an opened packet of ham and a block of Double Gloucester on the top shelf. I grabbed them and half a carton of apple juice and went back through the lounge and sat on the rug by the stove.

I alternated between biting a chunk of cheese and a mouthful of ham, washing it down with the apple juice. It was a delicious combination. I ate with enthusiasm whilst sitting staring into my stove. I don't think it's possible to ever get tired of watching a fire burning. It's a bit like watching the ocean. It changes endlessly. It draws you in and soothes your soul. And boy did mine need soothing.

Of course, that was never going to happen as long as that email was sitting in my inbox. I had analysed that damn email to bits and proved to myself that it was nothing but somebody trying to get under my skin in order to make some quick cash. So there was no reason for this anxiety to be gnawing away at my guts, right?

Damn it! I knew I was never going to be able to get past this unless I opened that attachment. I swallowed what I was chewing and got up and sat at my desk. The screensaver was playing its sick joke again. Amber. Amber and Jade. Amber again. Amber and Jade again. How can you love two girls at the same time? It was driving me nuts, so I moved the mouse. My inbox appeared again. The words were still there and so was the attachment. I stared at the link. It read: VSPF0001; 1944KB. I tried to work it out, what it might mean. VSPF0001. Video shot photo file? Very sexy picture file? I glanced at the sender's tag again. Virgin slayer picture file 0001. That was more likely. But I didn't like that it was number 0001. That indicated that there were more.

I jumped up and walked through to the conservatory again, staring out into the darkness. Why was this so damn hard? Who gave a shit if there were more? More of what? Someone called Adele? There was still a flickering glow coming from the larger barn down in the valley. It didn't seem such a foolish thing to be there now. It seemed rather attractive.

I was stalling. I was well aware of it. I was having an argument with myself in my head. I didn't need to open the attachment. I knew the truth. I knew my Amber. No email and no attachment could ever change how I felt about her.

So why not just open it then? If there's nothing to fear, why not just click on it, see that it has nothing to do with Amber or me and then click 'Delete'. Why not indeed? I had absolute faith in Amber; faith in everything she ever told me, faith in the purity of her heart and faith in her love for me.

I walked back through to my desk, sat down, grabbed the mouse, hovered the pointer over the attachment and right clicked.

Chapter Six

Amy flicked through her contacts. She only had a handful listed, the school where she had recently got a job as a teaching assistant, the local pizza place, two taxi firms and one friend she had begun to trust enough to swap mobile numbers with. Thrash.

She knew he had a thing for her. It wasn't mutual. She didn't encourage him, but sometimes a girl living alone needs male company. This was one of those times. She called him.

"What's up, pretty girl?" Thrash answered on the second ring. He always called her that when he spoke to her alone. Never in front of the guys.

"You at work tomorrow?" Thrash gave surfing lessons in the summer season, but once it got to October he painted, decorated, did odd jobs, anything that paid the rent. Tomorrow was Saturday and Amy, being a teaching assistant, was off.

"Nothing planned. How's that?" He sounded hopeful, like maybe she was going to ask to do something together; maybe his persistence was finally going to pay off.

Amy knew she was taking advantage of him, but she had little choice, she was feeling more than a little scared. "Don't read anything into this, Thrash, but could you come over?"

Thrash didn't hesitate. "When? Now?"

"I thought I saw someone hanging around outside just after I left you and then I heard somebody messing about outside. I'm just being a pathetic girl, I know, but would you mind coming over and keeping me company for a while. I've got some Bud in the fridge."

"You don't have to tempt me with Budweiser, Amy…I'll be over in ten, okay?"

Amy was sure she could hear him smiling over the phone; he was that obvious. "Okay, but be careful Thrash, he might still be out there."

"No probs, pretty girl. See you in ten."

Amy changed into the most unattractive, unflattering clothes she could find, a baggy grey sweatshirt and jogging bottoms. She didn't want Thrash to get any ideas. She mopped up the floor where Manning had bled and threw the bottle of gin and the glass he had used in the bin. Then she poured herself a glass of gin from a fresh bottle she had bought herself for Christmas. Christmas was over a month away, but she needed it now.

The gin went down easy. Too easy. She poured herself another. Manning's face filled her mind. It had been ten years since he had first entered her life. He was there before that, of course, on the fringes, barely visible, just someone who had visited the house occasionally, she had given him no importance. He was just some boring adult who visited her Mam. She couldn't remember how far back that had been, but she would never forget when he turned his attention to her. He had stolen her youth, taken her innocence, crushed her spirit and filled her heart full of hatred.

Amy poured another drink. All the memories had resurfaced in her mind and anger had besieged her. Manning had ruined her life too many times. She wouldn't let him ruin it again. She had been free of him for nearly two tears. She had sacrificed everything, the love of her life, her friends, her home and her job, everything, to escape from the pure evil that was Isaac Manning. She had lost all reason to live. She had been to places in her mind she never thought possible. She had considered suicide. She had considered murder. In the end, she had done neither, she had merely existed, put one foot in front of another and the days had passed. And piece-by-piece she had begun to make a life for herself. She had begun working at a local school, started surfing again, made a few acquaintances, even a friend or two, entered some competitions and even won three of them just in this last six months. She was never going to get her life back; she knew that. That life was gone forever. She would never see her one true love again. That had been a hard fact to swallow. Manning had been responsible for that. So what more could he want?

There was a knock at the door. Thrash had never been inside her place, but he had knocked on her door and she recognised his knock. She stood up suddenly and then found she had to put her hand against the wall to steady herself. Her blood pressure had lowered somewhat. She regained her balance and tottered along the hall to the door.

"S'that you, Thrash?"

"Sure is, pretty girl."

Amy opened the door and let him in. She immediately started to cough as the smell of his aftershave caught her breath.

"You spill the bottle, Thrash?" She kidded with him as she went back through into the living area and fell into one of her settees.

Thrash followed her through and stood at her French doors, looking out at the stars.

"Wow…this is some place Amy. You are some lucky girl!" He turned around just as she was finishing her drink. Thrash stood with his mouth slightly open. She looked beautiful. The baggy, fleecy material swamped her body, but her face shone beautifully like one of those stars. Her hair was curling this way and that, and the light from the kitchen was highlighting tones he had never noticed before.

"You okay, pretty girl?" He said as he came over and sat beside her.

Amy shut her eyes and let her head fall back. Thrash leaned in and hovered over her face. She could feel his warm breath on her face. Still with her eyes closed, she said. "Thrash…do you know that you are probably…" She burped. "Sorry…you are probably my bestest and only friend."

Thrash kissed the tip of her nose ever so lightly. "I like that, pretty girl." He said before dropping down on to her mouth and kissing her lips. Amy let him. She had escaped into another world. A world where Isaac Manning didn't exist.

"You drunk, Amy?" Thrash said softly into her ear, before kissing it and exploring her neck with his mouth.

"I never get drunk…I'm a good girl." Amy said playfully, her words slurring slightly.

"You're not just a good girl, Amy. You're the best." He told her and kissed her mouth again. Then he ducked lower, lifted her sweatshirt and started to kiss her abdomen. Amy stayed slumped in the settee with her head back. This was the most relaxed she had felt for such a long time. The strong smell of his aftershave had mellowed now and she liked it. The sensation of moist, warm lips caressing her ribs felt good. She was in another place and another time. Her mind was drifting and she let it. She went along with it. She longed to feel loved again. And why not?

Amy woke like any other morning to the sound of seagulls. The light coming through the French doors was offensive. She shielded her eyes with her hand. Her guts churned, her head hurt and she was suddenly aware of pressure down below. She needed to pee. Now. The floor moved like the deck of a boat as Amy padded through to the bathroom ricocheting off the walls and doorjambs. She sat down and immediately jumped up again as her flesh pressed against the cold ceramic of her toilet bowl. Why would the seat be up? She lived alone. The only man that had ever been in her apartment was the plumber who had fixed her shower one time.

The memory of last night hit her suddenly like a slap. She looked down at herself. Her panties and jogging pants were around her ankles. That was a good sign. She must have slept in them. Which meant that nothing could have happened. She hoped.

"You alright in there?" Thrash called through, his voice sounding a little hoarse.

Amy heard the tap run in her kitchen. He was filling her kettle. She shouted through. "Tea, black, one sugar, please"

Thrash made tea and toast and visited the bathroom himself as soon as Amy had vacated it. Then they sat in silence eating their toast, each on their own settee opposite to each other. Amy had known Thrash for over a year. He was the first person she had felt comfortable with when she had first moved to Cornwall. Their mutual love of the beach and the ocean had cemented their friendship. And yet now, it felt awkward. Amy was pretty sure it hadn't gone too far, but she could remember bits and pieces and she couldn't look at him.

Thrash broke the silence. "This is one hell of an apartment, Amy. That view is spectacular." He was looking out of the French doors. The tide was on its way in and there were perfect straight sets coming into the bay.

"Nothing happened." He met her eyes and smiled. "You were a little drunk and maybe a little lonely, but as irresistible as you are Amy, I wouldn't have..."

Amy put her hand up to stop him. "I know you wouldn't, Thrash. And I wasn't drunk." She jumped up, put her mug and plate in the sink and went over to the French doors.

"What time is it?"

Thrash read his watch. "Eight ten. Why?"

"Solid sets coming in. I'm going out...you up to it?"

"Hell yes. I'm stoked. I'm always stoked!"

Ten minutes later, Amy was making her way down the beach, her board under her arm and an offshore breeze blowing her hair in front of her face. She passed the lifeguard station on the way down. It had been closed since September, it only opened for the summer season, but the big digital thermometer was on show in the window all year round. It read four degrees.

When Amy neared the shore, she bent down and attached the leash to her ankle, tied her hair up and put her neoprene gloves on. She'd cleaned and waxed her board ready after yesterday's session. The breeze was wintry. Very. She didn't hesitate; she waded in fast, skipping over the small, foamy waves that washed pebbles painfully over her feet with the backwash. She'd greased her ankles and feet against the cold, but some of those pebbles were stones and some of those stones were the size of coconuts. They hurt. At waist level she mounted her board, lying belly down and paddling hard through the breaking waves, the icy water washing over her head. About thirty yards in she was rising and falling with the swell. She sat up on her board and surveyed the beach. No sign of Thrash. He had needed to go back to his place and get his wetsuit and board, but he was as keen a surfer as she was, he wouldn't be long.

Amy was five feet three and eight stone. Her board was six feet seven and fast. Within a minute she had caught her first wave. It was a little messy, but the offshore wind was lifting the waves four to five feet and Amy rode that first one for maybe a hundred yards. She dropped back in the water and paddled back out, starting to warm up. There were few lulls; the waves were coming on fast and strong. There was going to be no time for resting today. Amy was glad; it was far too cold to sit around. Within a minute she was paddling hard to catch another wave. As quick as a flash she snapped up on her feet again, riding up to the crest, dropping off the tip and back down the face of the wave again. The action was peachy, just the way Amy liked it, she was shredding it down through the hollow, trimming along her board to maintain her speed. The waves were working her hard now, some were close to six feet and she performed cutback after cutback giving herself a real workout.

Thrash spotted her from the beach. He had watched Amy surf many times, but she never failed to impress. She was a natural. He ran into the breakwater and dived on his board almost immediately, paddling like crazy to reach her. He knew she hadn't spotted him and he wanted to surprise her with some cool moves. He had waited so long to be this close to Amy and last night had spurned him on even more. If he could just keep up the momentum, he might just get the girl of his dreams.

Amy spotted Thrash just as he was paddling in. She dropped off her wave and submerged herself next to her board. Thrash was confused. One minute she was up there, riding like a pro and then she was gone. He paddled hard. He didn't like this feeling he had. Maybe she had fallen, suffered a total wipe-out. Even the Amy's of this world get pummelled now and then. The ocean doesn't discriminate. Thrash powered on, his arms windmilling through the oncoming waves. He hadn't seen her for maybe a minute. He was starting to panic.

"Duh dum. Duh dum. Duh dum." Amy mimicked the Jaws theme tune and Thrash spun around quickly in the water.

"You punked me…you little snake" Trash joked and hit the surface of the water with his hand sending a wide spray over Amy's head. "You got me there…I thought that wave must have hammered you."

"Ah ha…and what if I bought it…would you save me?" Amy teased as another wave lifted them both together, their boards colliding nose to nose.

Thrash angled his board out of her way. "Maybe. You seem a lot brighter …you got the buzz back, Amy?"

"I'm what you'd call amped, Thrash…I always feel this good out here." Then she mounted her board again, belly down, paddling just enough to catch the next wave. Thrash watched her shape as she snapped up on her feet, her wetsuit accentuating her curves, her form a perfect silhouette against the cool blue winter sky. Thrash caught the next wave and watched her in front of him the whole time. She was awesome. Simply awesome. Her figure was a perfect hourglass. She looked amazing and she moved like no girl he had ever seen. She would have given Alan Stokes or Gabe Davies a run for their money. She owned the waves. She was quite simply Thrash's idea of perfect.

Chapter Seven

They left the water when Amy could no longer touch her thumb and smallest finger together. That was her test so that she never stayed in too long when it was this cold. "I'm going straight back, Thrash." She told him as she walked ahead of him.

"Give me a shout if you like later." Thrash told her.

Thrash waved her off and headed up the village shivering with his board under his arm. Amy ran with her board buffeting against her hip. When she got in her apartment she stood under the shower for five minutes solid before she even unzipped her wetsuit. Finally, when she had thawed out she changed into her sweatshirt and joggies and made breakfast. She sat on her settee eating her porridge and watching the ocean. The sky was heavy and grey and there wasn't a soul on the beach. Amy put her bowl down on the floor and held her mug of tea with both hands. The sea was choppier now: spray blowing off the tip of each swell before it even broke. Something caught her eye. It was a lone figure walking slowly down past the lifeguard station toward the beach. The walk looked familiar, but not in a good way. Whoever it was stopped and turned. If she wasn't mistaken, they were looking up towards her. She blinked her eyes and focused as best she could. No, she wasn't mistaken. And yes, he was familiar. It was Manning and he was staring right at her.

Amy shuddered involuntarily. Her whole body was covered in goosebumps and her heart had begun to race. She was just about to jump up and move away from the French doors when he raised his arm in the air, spreading his fingers out. Not like a wave, more like he was gesturing. Five. Then he turned away from her and walked back up the track. She didn't know what to make of it, but she didn't like it. She jumped up and grabbed her coat. There was no way she was going to wait and see if he would come to see her again. She grabbed her car keys off the wall hook and put her coat on. As she walked to her back door, she spotted an envelope on the carpet. She froze. It was Sunday. No post on a Sunday. Which meant only one thing – it had been hand delivered.

Amy picked the envelope up. There was no name, no address, nothing. She shoved it in her coat pocket and continued out the door.

She had her own parking space at the other side of the public car park. She ran to her car, got in and drove. There were a lot of parked cars around the village, but she didn't see any people. No sign of Manning. She climbed the coast road out of Porthtowan and headed over to St. Agnes, the next village up the coast. There's a layby up on the top road with a commanding view of the Atlantic. Amy pulled in and pulled the handbrake on. She kept the engine running for warmth. She stared at the white envelope sitting on the passenger seat. It stared back. She stared at it some more. It was maybe six by eight inches, not particularly thick, sealed and white. Totally unremarkable.

Amy picked up the envelope and slid her middle finger under one corner and ripped it back fast.

"What the?" Amy stared at the contents of the envelope. The torn envelope revealed an eight by five print of two people in the throes of lovemaking. Amy recognized those two people instantly. It was her and Thrash. The photograph had been taken with a zoom lens, but not a particularly powerful one. It didn't need to be. Whoever took it had probably stood on the beach and pointed their camera straight up at her French doors. The result was dark, grainy and revealed very little. It looked like a couple canoodling on a settee. Big deal. You couldn't make out Amy's face and Thrash had his back to the camera.

Amy lifted the print out of the envelope, revealing another. This time she saw her own face quite clearly. Her eyes were closed, her head thrown back and her mouth open. Thrash was kissing her ribs. Half her right breast was visible. It looked very racy. It looked like he was making love to her and she was enjoying it. It wasn't how she remembered it at all.

She lifted that one out and it got worse. The next one showed Amy with her sweatshirt pulled right up revealing both breasts. Her head was still thrown back, her eyes still shut and her mouth still open. Amy cringed. It looked vulgar. It looked like Thrash was eating her. Maybe she had been more drunk than she had first thought. And maybe Thrash had taken advantage of her after all. Amy was mad, mainly at herself, but she was mad just the same. She pulled the photograph out and there was one more still in the envelope. It was facing the other way so she had to pull it out to see it. That's when her heart stopped.

It was another picture of a couple in the throes of lovemaking. But it wasn't Amy and Thrash. It was much worse. It was Amy's husband and her best friend. There was no mistake. They were naked and in bed together. It was horrible. Amy filled up immediately. Then her mobile rang. Amy nearly jumped out of her seat.

Thrash's number showed on the display. She answered with a less than friendly tone. "Yes?"

"Five pictures Adele. And all I want is fifty grand…in five days." Not Thrash. Manning.

"Wrong number. No Adele here." Amy ended the call. How the hell did Manning have her number? Shit! How the hell did Manning have Thrash's mobile?

Her mobile rang again. She answered it. "Put Thrash on."

"You're in no position to demand anything Adele."

"You said there were five pictures…there were only four. And where the hell do you think I'm gonna get fifty grand? You've had everything you're ever gonna get off me. I'm dead to Brendon now. It's over. He obviously has someone new…so just leave me alone, Manning!"

"Adele…" He began menacingly. "You hang up again and it'll be the last time you see your little friend." Manning warned her.

Amy didn't like the tone of his voice. "Where's Thrash?"

Manning ignored her question. "Fifty grand or I send those lovely pictures of you and your current shag to Brendon."

Amy hated the hold Manning still had on her. She looked at the photographs again. The worst one showed Thrash kissing her torso, his left hand was holding her left hip, his right hand cupping her right breast. She was drunk, semi-conscious, out of control. But she didn't look drunk and she didn't look out of control. She looked like she was mid-orgasm, what with her eyes closed and her mouth open. It was a false account. That wasn't how it had been at all. Seconds later she had stopped him. Nothing had happened. Nothing.

"Fifty grand in five days or he sees those pictures and a few more from your early days…think what it would do to him Adele. I'll be in touch." He hung up.

Amy sat with her mobile to her ear long after he had ended the call. Still. Her eyes staring out at the ocean. Unblinking. She was in shock. She dropped the picture of Thrash and her on the floor and picked up the one of Brendon. A pressure built in her chest. His body was lean and hard; his muscles well toned and defined like she remembered them. Only the right side of his face was visible, because he was facing Jade, but he looked as beautiful as he ever had. Jade was lying opposite. Close. Naked. Intimate. Even in the poor light, Jade's face looked flushed. Her body looked tanned. Her body language was confident. She looked in control, like she was seducing him, about to make love to him. Brendon. Amy's man.

Amy crumpled the photograph in her hand, her fingers making a tight fist. Tears flooded her face now and she broke down, sobbing into her hands. She didn't have a clue what to do. She needed help with this. But the only person in her life that could possibly help her was Thrash. And Manning had him.

Amy wiped her face and drove back down into Porthtowan. She parked up, grabbed her coat and walked down to the beach. She had to think clearly now or Thrash might end up hurt. The tide was well out so she headed to the right side of the bay. When the tide's out at Porthtowan a person can walk a good mile along the beach to the next bay at Chapel Porth. Amy walked. The wind was bitter and the sand soft and still full of water from the outgoing tide, but she walked on, her head down against the wind and her mind racing.

Trying to raise fifty thousand wasn't an option. She barely made enough in her new job at the school to pay her rent and get by. Her savings amounted to less than five hundred pounds tucked away in an envelope under her bedside cabinet. Going to the police was not an option. They would find out her true identity and she could be charged with fraud. After all, she had faked her own death. And then Brendon would probably find out and he would find out about her past too. She couldn't do that to him. She loved him too much.

As she reached a headland, she had to deviate further out to the shore where the waves were sweeping up the beach. It was difficult to judge when the next one was going to come or how high up the beach it would reach. Amy just ran for it and hoped for the best. She managed to get around to the other side of the headland without getting too wet, but she didn't like what she saw when she got around the other side.

"Well, hello…if it isn't the little surf girl."

It was Darren, the good-looking guy she had dismissed the day before.

"What's up cutiepie? Where's your surf buddies?"

Darren looked right into Amy's eyes. She felt vulnerable, teary. She looked away, her hair blew across her face and she was glad of it. It hid her expression.

"Hey, you alright?" He leaned in and put his hand on her shoulder. It was a step too far, Amy started off again. Darren stood and watched her walk away, not sure what to do. He wouldn't normally follow a girl after she'd given him the brush off, but there was something about the look on her face that concerned him. He ran after her.

"Look, maybe I can help." He said as he ran up beside her.

Amy didn't break her stride. "No. You can't!" She said off hand.

He grabbed her arm again, stopping her. "Let me help you."

Amy met his eyes. He looked genuinely concerned. She had no one else to turn to. Maybe there was something he could do.

"You can't help with my kind of trouble." Amy said with her eyes welling up. "I don't even know you."

"So get to know me…come on…I don't know many people myself. I could do with making some new friends. I'm not hitting on you. I'm not trying to go out with you. I just want to help."

Amy nodded and started walking again. Darren walked by her side. Chapel Porth was just around the next headland. The beach café that stands in the carpark was open. Amy hadn't expected that; after all it was out of season. They went in and sat down at a table near a window. A young Asian girl came over with a pencil and pad in her hands. Darren ordered two mugs of milky coffee. They were the only two customers in the place. Amy relaxed a little and told him the basics. She didn't mention her past and she made a point of saying there was nothing romantic between Thrash and herself. She spoke quickly and she spoke quietly. She didn't want the young girl at the counter hearing any of it.

"This Manning, he's sounds like a real nasty piece of work. How do you know him?" He quizzed her.

"What does that matter?" Amy looked at him perturbed.

"Sorry" Darren looked down into his mug.

"Look…it's a long story. He used to be a loan shark. He owned girls and ran a strip club…" Amy stopped herself. The waitress arrived and placed two mugs of milky coffee on their table. Darren paid her and she went back to the counter.

Darren brought his coffee to his lips and met her eyes. "Look, I don't judge people Amy."

"I wasn't a stripper if that's what you're thinking." Amy said, her volume just raised enough for the girl behind the counter to look up from her magazine.

He took a slurp of coffee, but kept the mug in his hands. "I wasn't thinking anything. I'm here to help and if you want to get your boyfriend back unhurt then I suggest you let me."

Amy said. "He's a friend, not a boyfriend."

"Whatever…I think you should let me help." Darren finished off his coffee and pushed his seat back, the metal legs scraping the tiled floor. The girl at the counter looked up from her magazine again.

Amy looked up, confused. She said. "You going already?"

Darren stood up. "Yeah, come on, drink up." He signalled with his eyes toward the girl who had served them. Amy pulled a puzzled face. She didn't understand his meaning.

"I haven't finished my coffee." She informed him.

Darren zipped up his anorak and made for the door. Amy had no choice; she quickly finished off her coffee and followed him. The girl at the counter gave her a sisterly shrug of her shoulders as if to say 'Men!' Amy raised her eyebrows in reply and left the café.

"What was that about?" Amy shouted across the carpark to Darren who was a dozen paces ahead of her. He slowed for her to catch up.

"In a crowded café, people talk and nobody listens. In an empty café a bored waitress has nothing better to do *but* listen."

Amy nodded in agreement. "What do you think I should I do then?"

Darren walked on back down to the beach; his blonde curls blowing across his face. Amy waited patiently for his reply.

"When he rings next, arrange a meet."

"And?"

"And I'll follow you."

"And?"

"And then I'll deal with the bastard!"

Amy didn't know what to say to that. But she wasn't in a position to question his decision.

When they got back to Porthtowan Amy paused at the path leading to her row of apartments. She felt uncomfortable about inviting Darren into her apartment.

"What's up?" Darren gave her a bewildered look.

Amy fidgeted with her keys, not meeting his eyes. "So you think we should just wait for him to ring?"

"How else are we going to make contact?" Darren asked.

Amy shrugged. "Okay…so you wanna come in for a cuppa maybe?" Amy invited him in, but her tone sounded like she was unsure.

"Hey, if you don't want my help…" He said starting to turn away.

Amy grabbed his arm to stop him. "No, I do…come on, I'll make us a cuppa." She walked him along the path to her apartment. They had tea this time and sat looking out at the ocean talking about the best bays for surfing in the area. Darren said he had lived in Cornwall all his life. However, Amy's knowledge of the area was a lot greater. She found that a bit odd, but then maybe he was more of a surfer wannabe than a bona fide surfer. The conversation was just about drying up when Amy's mobile rang.

"You gonna get that?" Darren pressed. Amy sat staring at her phone on the coffee table between them. It had rang three times already.

"What if he won't meet?"

"We're never gonna know unless you answer it Amy." Darren said and then blew out a long sigh. Amy sensed a tension in his voice. She picked up her phone. Thrash's number was displayed. Manning.

"Yes?"

"What, no niceties? You see Adele, that's what's all wrong with your generation. No fucking manners." Manning said sounding sanctimonious.

"What have you done with Thrash?" Amy demanded.

"What did I tell you Adele? Fifty thousand and all this goes away."

Amy had her mobile on speaker so that Darren could hear everything. She looked across at him now. He nodded and mouthed the word 'meet'.

"Okay, Manning…where can we meet?" Amy tried to sound assertive which wasn't easy, she was sitting there nervously pulling at her ear lobe with her free hand.

"You got the money already Adele?" He sounded surprised.

"I want to meet. I want to see Thrash is unharmed, then we'll talk about the money." She sounded more confident the more she talked.

"Okay, Adele…I never tire at looking at your pretty face." He told her, sounding smug again.

"Where?"

"You know that lay-by you parked up in this morning?"

Amy glanced over at Darren, her face showing her indignation at been followed

"I don't miss a trick, Adele. I'll see you, same place, thirty minutes."

"Bring Thrash…Manning?" Amy raised her voice. The line had gone quiet. "Manning?"

"He's gone. Come on…I suggest we leave separately." Darren stood up and walked over to the French doors where he could scan the beach.

"What's up?"

"Nothing…just looking to see if anyone's got any binoculars pointing this way. Know what I mean?" He stepped away from the doors again.

"Well?"

"Nobody out there. Can't blame them can we? It's bloody freezing!" He walked around the back of the settee Amy was sat on and was heading for the door. "So anyway, I'll leave first. Wait ten minutes, then pick me up on the top road."

Amy stood up. "Where on the top road?"

"Just start to slow down after the sign for Porthtowan and I'll run out of the bushes and jump in. Nobody will spot me up there."

"Yeah, but what about a plan. How are we going to play this?" Amy said getting more anxious.

"Don't worry 'bout a thing. I'll handle him. We'll get your buddy back no probs. See you up there in ten. Take your time, I've got to run up through the houses to get there before you."

Darren left, slamming the door behind him. Amy's heart was racing. She felt ill.

"Oh, shit! Oh, shit!" Amy walked back through to the French doors and stared at the ocean. Then she went back upstairs to her bedroom.

"Oh, shit! Oh, shit!"

She paced at the bottom of her bed a while, then finally she got her brain into gear and started doing something constructive. She pulled off her shoes and socks and got fresh socks out of her bottom drawer. Two pairs. It was cold out there. She picked up her wet socks, put them in the laundry basket in the bathroom and put her shoes next to the radiator to dry. She went back into her bedroom, changed her damp jeans for clean, dry combats and got a pair of well-worn walking boots out the bottom of her wardrobe. She stuck another sweatshirt on top of what she had on and then her fleece jacket on top of that. She felt warm. But then anxiety does that to a girl too.

She was ready to leave, but her mind was in turmoil. She stood at the kitchen sink looking at the block of knives next to the drainer. Should she bring a weapon? Could she use a knife on a fellow human being? Then again this was Manning she was dealing with.

"Wait a minute..." She said out loud. She picked the block up. It holds six knives of assorted sizes and blades, straight and serrated. Her seven-inch straight edge blade was missing. It was the one she used for meat, because it was the sharpest. She sharpened it often with a sharpening stone. If she was going to take any of them for a weapon, that would have been the one.

She hadn't used it since Thursday and it was Sunday. Three places it could be. In her hand, in use. On the drainer after being washed. In the block with the rest of the set. It could not be anywhere else. Amy didn't like things out of place. She didn't keep her apartment clean and tidy. Shipshape. She kept it like a show-apartment, like one of those apartments you get shown around when they've just built a new development. Her carpet was almost two years old. It looked new. Her cooker gleamed. The glass in the French doors was spotless. She cleaned her home meticulously, bordering on being OCD.

"So where the...?" Amy didn't like it. She hated anything being out of place, but a knife, her sharpest knife, that was alarming. What if Manning had taken it? What if he's used it on Thrash?

Amy glanced at her watch. It had been more than ten minutes since Darren had left. Time to go.

Chapter Eight

I clicked over the attachment and it started to load. One line at a time the photograph began to emerge from the top of my screen. About an inch down it became obvious the photo had been taken indoors. Another inch and I began to see the top of someone's head. A man. It was the back of a man's head; a man with shoulder length, ginger hair. His shoulders were uncovered. I could see more of the room now. I didn't recognize it, but it was clear it was a bedroom. There were posters on the wall, NSYNC and Enrique Iglesias. I guessed it was a teenage girl's bedroom. Judging by the posters, the photo was probably taken about ten years ago. The ginger man's back appeared, it was bony and freckled. He was bent over with his arms out for support. He looked about thirty five, maybe forty, it was difficult to say, I could only see the right side of his face. I didn't like how this photograph was beginning to look.

It was opening up faster now. There was someone under the ginger man, a girl. She had blonde, curly hair and she looked…she looked like…

The photograph had downloaded. All of it. I couldn't take my eyes off it. The girl was naked. The sight of her sickened me to my very core. Not because she was naked, but because the girl I was looking at was my Amber. She was younger, much younger, maybe fifteen or sixteen. Her face was pale, thinner, her expression blank, oblivious, but her eyes were the same beautiful eyes that I had fallen in love with. She looked trusting, naïve, innocent. I've seen pornographic photos before. Not like this. I've never seen child porn, but to me, that's what this was. I've felt anger before, many times. But words like anger and hatred don't come within a thousand miles of describing my feelings right then. I felt repugnance. I felt revulsion. My blood was boiling. I felt like my heart had been ripped out and now someone was tearing it apart, not with hands, but with teeth. Sharp, barbed and jaggered teeth.

I didn't just hate this man. I wanted him dead. I wanted to rip his head off and stamp on it. I wanted to pull him off my Amber and kick his bony body until it was skinless. And then I wanted to piss all over his wounds and finally pour buckets of bleach over his evil face and cleanse the world of his presence. Would that do it? No. After all that, I'd have to push him in a vat of petrol and burn the bastard to hell. Then I might be done. Only then.

I was seething. I was enraged. I picked up the laptop and hurled it across the room. It clashed against the low wall in the conservatory and broke into several pieces. I stamped across to it and jumped on the screen. I dug my heels in hard, smashing the plastic, pummelling it into the cold tile floor. I could hear myself screaming, swearing, crying. I wanted that bastard dead.

The screen was no more. It was smashed into smithereens. But I could still see that sickening image in my head. It had burned into the plasma of my brain. A lump the size of my fist was pushing up from my solar plexus and pressing into my heart. I couldn't breathe. Something was making my feet slide on the tiles, something viscous. I looked down and saw that I was sliding on my own blood. I had cut my feet on the sharp plastic of the laptop. I fell to my knees. The lump in my chest was choking me now. Then my guts contracted and I vomited violently, retching repeatedly until all that came up was a yellow bile that stung my throat. And even then my guts contracted some more, just to make sure I was totally empty. And that's just how I felt. Empty. I slumped onto the hard floor and curled up like a child and cried.

The darkest, most painful thoughts that could infest a man's mind filtered through now, unchecked. They weren't just thoughts, they were images, crude, crass and callous. Wasn't it enough for a man to lose the love of his life? Did I have to have all my wonderful memories pissed on too?

The phone made me jump. I lay there listening to it for a while. The distraction was most welcome. I focused on the simple, high pitched, repetitive sound. Prrurt prrurt; prrurt prrurt. It filled my empty house. It filled my empty head. Then it stopped abruptly and my head was no longer empty. The cruel images intruded again, spreading through my mind like a cancer. I was ready to explode once more.

The phone started again. Prrurt prrurt. This time I jumped up and grabbed the phone off the little oak coffee table. I dropped it on the floorboards, my hands were wet and sticky with the blood I'd gotten off the conservatory floor from my feet. I grabbed it again, like it was a lifeline, somebody to take me away from all this insanity.

"I know I said I would give you time Brendon. I can't help it. I can't wait…I love you." It was Jade. My lifeline?

Not a second passed and I said. "Can I come over?"

"God, I wish you would Brendon." It had only been a day. She sounded like it had been a month.

It was late when I got to Durham. Jade's window was the only one lit up in her row of apartments. I didn't knock; her door was open. Her apartment smelled of citrus fruit. I walked through her kitchen, switching the light off as I entered her lounge. The only light illuminating her lounge came from a lone candle flickering down on the thresh of the Juliet balcony that overlooked the river. It was a big, square, yellow, orange and red striped candle; hence the citrus aroma. Music was playing low, so low I couldn't make out the words, but it was the kind of music that went with candles and the lateness of the hour. My eyes adjusted themselves to the low light and were drawn to the sensual shape of a semi naked Jade draped across the oversized, brown suede settee that sat left of the glass doors that opened to the balcony. The flickering light of the candle kept changing the shadows on the sheer white silk of the chemise Jade wore, but it didn't hide the fact that it was just that, sheer. She wasn't naked. She was better than naked. She was self-assured, sanguine, cool and unabashed. She looked like a woman who needed a man. And right then I was happy to be that man.

I woke in a really light and airy bedroom with fresh air washing across my face. The air was coming from the open glass doors that opened onto a second Juliet balcony. I could hear birds and traffic and water. They were nice sounds to wake up to. Jade walked in with two mugs of tea. She was naked. I felt kind of embarrassed, uncomfortable. I took a mug from her and sipped at it, averting my eyes from her flesh. It was hard. She looked amazing.

"You were fantastic last night." She informed me and then kissed my brow and joined me back in bed. She was wrong, by the way. I wasn't.

"I've waited all my life for you Brendon…" She said kissing my bare shoulder. I was still feeling uncomfortable.

"Here, let me take that a second." She took the mug from me and put it next to hers on the bedside cabinet. Then she kissed me some more. Her hand wandered under the duvet.

"Woah! I…Em, I need to pee." I said sliding out the other side of the bed and padding out of the room. The lounge was in front of me and I could see shoppers on the other side of the river through the double glass doors. I ducked down, holding my crotch.

"Where the hell is your loo?"

"Back through here…it's an ensuite, silly." She called through to me, giggling like a teenager.

I walked back into the bedroom, still holding myself.

Jade giggled some more. "Are we feeling shy? We weren't feeling so shy last night gorgeous."

I ducked behind the sliding mirrored door that concealed her bathroom and stood at the toilet unable to pee.

"Hurry up, gorgeous. I need you."

That didn't help.

"I'm sorry…I feel a bit unwell." I lied. Well, maybe I didn't actually. It would be wrong to say I felt well.

"Oh, babe…what's up?" She sounded genuinely concerned.

"I dunno…I just feel really sick…must be the crap I ate last night." I tried to think what I ate.

"What did you have?" I just knew she was going to ask that.

"Cheese…I seem to remember a lot of cheese." Well, I wasn't lying. I came out the bathroom and sat on the side of the bed pulling my shorts and socks on.

"You rushing off?" She said sounding more than a little miffed.

I stood up to pull on my jeans, my back to her the whole time. "It's nearly eight and I've got a course to organize and I feel like crap, Jade…It's best if I just get off."

"Well…if you feel you must." Oh yes, she was definitely miffed.

"It's nearly eight on a Monday morning…you telling me you haven't got work to go to?" I had my T-shirt on now and I was reaching for my jacket.

"Well, yes, of course…I just thought…"

I leaned over the bed and kissed her on her brow, stopping her mid-sentence and then realized how inadequate that gesture was considering we had just spent the night together. I dropped my mouth down onto hers and kissed her soft and slow. That seemed to put a smile back on her face.

"I've really got to go, Jade…" I said standing to leave. "As soon as I find out what's happening with this course, I'll give you a call, okay?"

"Okay, Brendon. Love you." She said in the sweetest voice, looking up at me with puppy dog eyes, her breasts all bare and round and pert. I felt like an absolute bastard.

When I got home I was met with the bloody mess I'd left the night before. I brushed up the remnants of my laptop and binned the whole lot, then washed the tiles and the oak flooring with something that smelled like Jade's candle had. Then I rang the school that had booked my course. There was still a covering of snow on the ground, but the sky was blue and it was three or four degrees outside. I didn't see a reason to cancel, other than the fact that my heart had been ripped out and my head was all over the place.

The Head of Year Eight tried to put me off, mouthing on about health and safety of the children and risk assessments and other such shit. I told her that the BBC wouldn't have just commissioned me to do another new series if it didn't think I were qualified to teach survival skills. I told her the weather would add a new dimension to the course. I was talking total bullshit, of course. I had made one, six part series, which I had sold to Channel Four over two years ago; they had repeated it twice on More Four since and I had done nothing but watch my life fall apart ever since. But she didn't know that and my website still made me sound current and good value for money.

"Okay, I'll call all the parents." She'd bought it. "If at least eight of the twelve parents are okay with it we'll go ahead. I'll email you before the end of today."

"Oh, could you call me instead." I gave her my mobile number. "I won't be near my PC all day." Well, not unless I stood next to my bin. She agreed to ring before four that afternoon. I thanked her and hung up. Then I stood in my conservatory and stared down the valley where the horses stood nibbling each other's necks and a mist shrouded the trees below the two barns where I'd bumped into AK.

There was nothing to organize in preparation of the course. I own a field in Weardale with five small log cabins. If a course gets the go ahead, all I have to do is switch the water on, buy some food in and get the minibus out of my garage and fill it with diesel. The rest of it, the knowledge, the lesson plans, the aims and objectives; that was all in my head. My watch read ten past nine. I had potentially seven hours before I knew, for sure, if I was running the course or not. Images were filtering through now; nasty, filthy, cruel ones. I knew I had to stop them or they would destroy me. I put my cycling gear on, filled a flask and grabbed some food and got my bike out of the garage. I slipped my mobile in my pocket and plugged my earphones in. I've got about two hundred tunes on the inbuilt mp3 player and I figured if I played the music loud enough and rode hard enough I might just keep the hellish thoughts at bay. Not a good long-term solution, I know, but I was just trying to hang on to my sanity for now.

I headed straight down the track to the woods, the ground was hard and the front forks were using most of the four inches of their travel as I bounced down the rutted track into the impending mist. Some cute young black girl called Alexis Jordan was singing about 'Happiness' in my earphones loud enough that I couldn't hear myself panting. It was a good tune with a thumping beat, but the words were a bit insensitive to say the least. As the track levelled out I started pedalling hard, standing up out of the saddle, my arms swinging the bars left and right in a solid rhythm. I could feel sweat beginning to wet my back under my daypack, but the air was cold as I sucked in lungful after lungful and I could feel my chest tighten. I kept my brain focused on the tune the cute young black girl was singing and my eyes on the track ahead of me. I hadn't eaten yet, but I felt like my legs could have pumped those pedals like that all day long.

The path broke off in a Y up ahead, right across the fields to Burnside or left through the greyness of the woods. I headed into the greyness, keeping the same pace. Another song filled my head now. The Wanted started singing, 'All time low'. Jesus, the music was supposed to distract me not send me suicidal. I flicked the button on the headphone lead to forward to another tune. Not a good idea to take my hand off the bars at that speed on a rutted path. I managed to stay on, but the next song hit me even harder. Rhianna was singing, 'Only girl in the world.' It was like a bloody conspiracy. I reached down for the button again, just as the front wheel hit a root protruding out of the earth. My left wrist folded as the bars were pushed into my left side and I careered over the top at break-neck speed. A young silver birch slowed me down from about twenty miles per hour to zero as my right shoulder crashed into it. I rolled over the hard, snowy earth; my head ricocheting off more exposed roots and I finally lay still on my back in a great degree of pain.

Rhianna was still telling me I should make her feel like she was the only girl in the world. I ripped the earphones from my ears and pulled the lead from the phone in my pants, except it didn't pull free and my phone got pulled out too. It catapulted out somewhere into the trees. I lay looking up at the sky as it started to snow again. I guess I should have been glad I was wearing my helmet when I fell or I might have been lying there dead, but frankly, right then, I couldn't have cared less.

Then the images came again and some bastard was fucking my Amber. That's when I began to come apart. I don't remember exactly what I did, but I know I cried an awful lot and I screamed a hell of a lot too, mostly at God. I wasn't too happy with the big guy. He'd allowed some bad things to happen to my girl and I couldn't understand why he would do that. And then he had given her to me for little over two years only to take her from me. I hit the earth with both fists by my side; still lying on my back, snow falling on my face. More perverse images filled my head and no matter how hard I tried to run from them, more and more came flooding in. I cried like a baby. Pain like nothing I had ever experienced gripped my heart. Give me toothache, sciatica or second degree burns any day. Hell, I know women around the world will argue that nothing compares to childbirth. Sorry, girls, I must insist. Nothing equals the pain of a broken heart.

Sometime later, I realized I was still lying there. Cold. Broken.

"Come on mate, you've had enough…Get up."

I turned my head and AK was knelt down next to me. His Akita was a few yards behind him, just standing there, panting. I felt embarrassed, but not enough to stand up. I sat up and blew out a long sigh.

"Come on mate, you'll freeze here." He said holding his hand out for me. After a few seconds I took it and he hauled me up onto my feet. I wiped my hands across my face; tears and snow were stinging my skin. I don't remember saying anything to him. All I recall is walking with my bike with AK and his dog by my side along the track with a light fall of snow dropping before me.

We got to a clearing where a large wooden shed stood. There were a handful of hens scratching under the piles that it stood on. The dog ran ahead and crawled into a triangular shaped kennel. I could see hay in the bottom of it. It made itself at home. AK led me around the side where he opened a padlock with a four digit combination and opened a thick panelled door into a dark interior. He went in first and beckoned me in. I hesitated and looked about me.

"I don't get many visitors. You'll have to take me how you find me." He said from inside. I looked about me again, unsure. I don't know what I was looking for, maybe some characters from that movie, 'Deliverance'. I stepped up into the doorway. There was a window at the back that actually gave quite a lot of light. The shed was more of a cabin actually. It was about the size of a large garage, maybe eighteen by twelve. A stove was lit on one side; AK was kneeling down to feed it with some logs out of a basket. There was a futon type bed on the opposite side of the stove and to my right was a kitchen of sorts. There was a ceramic sink, a bench and a larder.

AK got up off the floor and grabbed something out of the larder. As he passed me I saw it was a large bone. He stood at the door and threw it out to the dog, then shut the door and sat down on his futon.

As I stood there in AK's humble abode waiting for him to say something, I shuddered involuntarily. I began to feel again and I felt cold. Very. The only sound was the crackling of the fire. I took a couple of steps forward and sat in front of the stove. After a while I took my helmet off and unzipped my jacket. I began to thaw out.

AK went over to his kitchen and within a couple of minutes I could smell the aroma of fried bacon. A few more minutes and a kettle was whistling. I never took my eyes from the flames the whole time. It was hypnotic.

"Hawkeye." AK said standing over me. I hadn't noticed him standing there. I looked up and he had a mug and a plate in his hands.

"You gonna take these from me or what?"

I reached up and took the mug and the plate. The mug was black tea. I've no idea which variety, but it tasted good and sweet. The plate had a large stottie on it. I lifted the lid to inspect it. There was a chicken breast covered in two rashers of bacon, melted cheese and a large slice of mushroom. I hadn't eaten since the block of cheese the night before and boy did that stottie taste good! I was halfway through it when AK spoke.

"Good?"

"Very. Is there some kind of sauce on it?"

"A splash of Worcester on the cheese and some mayo on the bottom of the chicken. Good?"

I said. "Mm, very."

We finished our breakfasts and AK refreshed our teas and threw me a Mars bar. It was cold and firm and tasted a lot better than I remembered a Mars bar ever tasting. I guess I was hungry.

"So…you wanna talk about it?" AK said out of the blue.

"No." I didn't.

"Hurts doesn't it?"

I stared at the flames. He was scratching at a scab I didn't want scratching.

"You think I always lived here, in this shed, in this wood?"

I glanced up at him. "Seems pretty cosy to me."

"Not the same as living in a nice home with a good woman though is it?"

I couldn't tell if he was talking about him or me.

"I didn't always live like this. I had a good job in Newcastle…a lovely home not three miles from here…a car, money in the bank…and…the sweetest girl that ever walked this earth."

I didn't know what I was supposed to say to that, so I said nothing.

"I see you my friend and I see myself a couple of years back. It's a killer. It hurts like hell doesn't it?"

I kept my eyes on the fire. I didn't trust myself to look his way.

"You have to let go my friend…at some point, you have to let her go."

Now I bit. "S'that what you're doing then? Letting go?" Bit of a low blow, I know. I tried to take it back.

"Sorry…it's just that this…" I glanced around the shed. "This doesn't seem like moving on."

"You never saw me three years ago when I first lost my Claire. This…" He did the same glancing around thing that I had done. "This is like a hundred per cent better than where I was then."

"My situation is different." I informed him.

"Your wife died…you hurt like hell…and now you're alone and you're finding it a bastard to deal with. Sound about right?"

"Not quite…it's a bit more complicated than that."

AK said no more.

The silence filled the room.

I hardly knew this man. I undoubtedly thought him a little strange. And yet sitting there in his cosy cabin, in front of his roaring woodstove, and full of his food, I felt undeniably comfortable. I'm not normally a man that opens up easily. There's no way I would share my recent discovery about Amber with my brother. But maybe I needed the relief of telling someone. Maybe I needed to offload. I don't know why, but once I started telling him I didn't stop until I had told him everything.

He got up and walked over to the window at the back of the cabin. I thought I would feel better, lighter, relieved or something. A problem shared is a problem halved and all that. It isn't. His silence made me feel uneasy. I was beginning to regret telling my secrets. I felt like I had betrayed Amber in some way. I got up off the floor, put my mug and plate on his drainer and zipped my jacket up like I was making to leave. AK turned around when he heard the noise I made.

"Sit down."

I didn't want to sit down. I opened the door.

"Hawkeye, please sit down a minute. I might be able to help you."

I couldn't think how he could help me. I couldn't think how anyone could. I stood where I was.

"Have you still got the jpeg, the photo?"

"No." I didn't need to tell him how I had smashed my laptop into a thousand pieces.

"Maybe it can be recovered?"

I told him it couldn't.

"I used to work in IT. You'd be surprised." He was persistent.

"No. Believe me, you can't recover it. The laptop's in the bin."

AK nodded like he understood. "Still, it might not have been real. It could have been faked."

"Didn't look faked to me."

"No…I can tell it cut you deep."

That was the understatement of the century.

"How much did you say they want?" He asked. He knew, he just wanted to hear it again I guess. I told him again.

"So he wants to ruin your career…expose your wife…sell the pictures to the papers or put them on the Internet?"

"There was only one picture." I corrected him.

"There's a good chance there's more though, isn't there"

"Thanks, mate." That's all I needed, someone to wind me up even more.

"Look, mate…your Amber was a good girl…she loved you…she devoted her life to you…she married you. Everybody has a past…I bet Amber wasn't your first. A lot of people keep sexy pictures of each other. So what! It means nothing. She finished with this bastard long before she met you, so he couldn't have meant that much to her. Focus on what you had with her…on how she was with you…what she meant to you and what you meant to her."

I knew he just meant well, but he didn't seem to get it at all.

"Did you ever see a man having sex with your Claire, AK? A man twice her age? An ugly man? And not just that…who else was in that room to take that photo? There must have been two of them. Two of them! Imagine it, man. It's fucked up all my memories of that sweet girl I married. Don't you see it…I married a bloody slut!"

I walked out. The snow had stopped, but it was biting cold. I couldn't remember which way I had arrived at the cabin so I just walked anywhere, so long as I got away from there, quick. Soon enough I recognized a stream we had crossed on the way there. I was home in less than half an hour. I was angry again. In fact, now I was angry with myself too. I shouldn't have told AK. What was I thinking? Bad enough that I had found out all this ugly stuff about my wife, but now someone else knew. I couldn't bare it. Talking hadn't helped. It had just made me feel worse. I felt about as low as a person could feel. I didn't know how else to deal with it, so I opened a can. Then another. And then another.

Chapter Nine

Amy left without a weapon. She decided that she wouldn't have the bottle to use a knife anyway. And not just that, Manning could take it from her and use it against her. She locked her apartment and walked quickly to her where her car was parked. Just as she was approaching it she noticed someone had a skip parked outside of their house. It was full of old plaster and joisting, like maybe someone had pulled an internal wall down. There was a piece of two by two sparring sticking out the top. She walked over and pulled it out. Three feet long. No nails to stick in her hands. Perfect!

She stuck the spar behind the front seats and drove off out of Porthtowan. As she approached the signpost up the hill out of the village she eased off the accelerator and scanned the bushes on the right for any sign of Darren. She was nearly at the top of the hill and beginning to panic, when he bolted out of some laurel bushes just in front of her. She'd barely come to a stop and he had pulled the back door open and dived in the back seat.

"Speed up! Speed up!" He ordered.

Amy changed down and accelerated up to forty as the road began to level out.

"Darren…I'm a bit concerned. One of my best knives is missing. I think Manning might have pinched it." She said changing up into top gear.

"I've got it. He's bound to be armed. I needed something to even the odds, know what I mean?"

"Jesus, Darren?" Amy said sounding more and more nervous.

"Just drive, Amy. When you see him, park alongside him, but maybe six feet apart and a little ways back, so you're a bit behind. That way he won't spot me when I slip out. Leave the rest to me."
Darren sounded confident, like he'd done this before. Amy didn't think this was the right time to ask, but his self-assured manner was helping her to relax a little.

Another half mile and she could see a black van parked in the lay-by where she had arranged to meet Manning.

"There's someone there. A black VW Transporter." Amy informed Darren who was crouched down in the back.

"Okay…like I said, park alongside, a couple of yards apart and a little behind. I'll jump out as soon as you stop. Don't look behind…you'll give me away."

Amy indicated left and slowed down. Her heart was beating out of her chest now. She thought she might pass out. She pulled in and positioned the car as Darren had instructed. Darren slipped out the back as he said he would. He managed to close the back door almost silently. Amy applied the handbrake, but left the motor running. There was room for the van to open the driver's door in front of Amy's car. She waited.

Nothing happened. No sign of Manning. She didn't like it. She was getting ready to bail. What felt like a month later the driver's door on the van opened and out stepped Manning. He looked flustered. He signalled with his head for Amy to get out. She got out, but stayed behind her open door.

"Where's Thrash?"

"In the back. You got the money?" He asked nonchalantly.

"I want to see Thrash." She demanded. But her voice had a tremor to it. She was tense. On edge.

"Okay…anything for a pretty girl." He said walking between his van and Amy's car. Amy stayed where she was, beside her open door. Manning got to the back of his van and opened the door.

"Well…you want to see him or what?"

Amy didn't want to leave the safety of her car. She was torn, whether to stay where she was or go to the back of Manning's van. *Where was Darren? When was he going to make his move?*

"Bring him out, so I can see him." Amy stood her ground.

Manning coughed up a ball of phlegm and spat on the frozen earth next to him. "You want to see him, you come see him."

Impasse.

Where the hell was Darren?

Amy reluctantly walked to the back of her car, leaving her door open and the motor running. Manning had the right hand door open at the back of his van. She couldn't see inside. She was going to have to walk over to him. She wished she had brought a knife now. She could hardly go back in the car and grab the piece of sparring she had taken from the skip. That might not look too friendly.

"Thrash!" Amy called out to her friend.

"Wasting your time...he's tied and gagged. Think I'm just gonna have him sitting here all comfortable and able to tell the world he's been abducted?" Manning said, shaking his head and chuckling to himself.

Amy had no choice but to go look for herself. She decided to be bold and just go for it. Six quick steps and she was standing not a yard from Manning. When she peered into the dim interior of the van, shock sent her reeling off balance and Manning had to grab her to stop her from falling back over.

"Darren!" She cried, sticking her fist in her mouth.

Darren was sat on the floor of the van with his hands behind his back and duct tape wrapped around his head covering his mouth. His eyes were wide and red rimmed. He looked scared.

"Nice meat knife this." Manning raised his arm towards Amy and in his hand was the meat knife Darren had taken from her kitchen. He waved the blade provocatively inches from Amy's face, then tossed it back behind him. Amy watched it spin in the air before it disappeared over the cliff.

"Where's Thrash?" Amy said with anger in her voice. She had stepped back a couple of steps when Manning had waved the knife at her, but now she stepped back again, closer to her car.

"Oh yes, Thrash..." Manning smiled to himself. "He's okay ...for now. He sent you this." He pulled a small plastic container out of his coat pocket and threw it at Amy. She caught it in her right hand and looked down at it. The writing on the container said it contained multi-vitamins. She pulled the lid off.

"You..." Amy threw the container up in the air in alarm. She screamed something animalistic, then retched and threw up her coffee. The container bounced off the hard earth and a severed finger rolled under the boot of her car.

"You're fucking crazy, Manning. You'll never get away with this." Amy said through gritted teeth. She wasn't angry. She was incensed. "Why? Why would you do that?"

Manning slammed the van's door shut and started to walk back around to the driver's door. He stopped and looked at her, his smile gone. "I knew you wouldn't bring the money, Adele. And I knew there was a chance you would recruit this arsehole who tried to knife me."

Now it was Manning who was angry. "I told you that I never miss a thing. It's fifty grand by Wednesday, six pm, or you never see either of these two clowns again. You understand?"

Amy was visibly trembling now. Her resolve had just been decimated. Tears ran down her face. "I haven't got fifty grand...I can't give you what I haven't got."

Manning climbed into his van and started the motor. The diesel ticked noisily. Manning shouted above it. "No, but you know a man that has." He pulled his door shut and let the window down. "Wednesday, six pm...or your two buddies will have nasty surfing accidents. I'll be in touch."

Manning's wheels spun on the dirt as he pulled away from the lay-by. Amy stood by her car and watched the van get smaller as it sped along the road north to St Agnes, or Newquay, or Devon or anywhere for all she knew.

She bent down and looked under her car. The sight of Thrash's finger appalled her. It looked like it had just been severed. There was still wetness in the tissue where it had been cut, although it appeared to be devoid of blood. She reached under and picked it up. It felt cold, gruesome and alien. Quickly, she stood and dropped it back in the plastic container and pushed the lid back on. Her brain was operating her body automatically now. The hundreds of crazy thoughts that had been racing around in her head a moment ago had all but disappeared. It was like someone had just turned the volume down on their blasting music system. No more noise. No more mayhem. Her mind hadn't crashed, it had just found another way of coping. A person can only take so much stress before their systems become overloaded. Some people cope and some people crash. Amy was coping by going into autopilot.

The car drove itself back down into Porthtowan. Amy was at the wheel, but not consciously. The first thing she did when she got home was stick the plastic container containing Thrash's finger in her freezer. Later, she wouldn't remember doing this. Then she put the kettle on and made herself a mug of tea. She drank her tea staring out of her French doors. Sleet was falling on her balcony, running down the glass doors in little streams. Amy stared, blinking rarely.

Somehow, half an hour later, Amy was sitting at a PC in an Internet café in Redruth.

"Do you need help, Miss?" A young oriental woman quizzed. She was standing right next to Amy's workstation. Amy wasn't ignoring her. The woman's voice just hadn't registered in her brain.

"Miss?" The woman repeated a little more firmly. Amy sat motionless, staring at the monitor.

The woman put her hand on Amy's right shoulder. "Excu…"

Amy jumped like she had been prodded with an electric cattle prod.

"Sorry, Miss. I thought you might like some help. You've been sat here a while and you've only paid for thirty minutes. Do you know how to use a computer?" The oriental woman couldn't have been more helpful.

"Yes. I'm fine." Amy said in a monotone voice. The woman shrugged and walked away.

"Thanks." Amy called back to her, but the woman was already attending to another user.

Amy finally clicked on Windows Explorer and almost immediately the Google homepage popped up. She found Yahoo and opened her account. Since starting her new life almost two years ago, she had closed her old account and opened another in her new name, Amy Bell. She had used it at the school she was working at to communicate with other teachers and teaching assistants. Nobody else. She didn't know anybody else. There was a message waiting for her from a colleague. She ignored it. It wouldn't be important.

Then suddenly, sitting alone at the PC, she emerged from autopilot. The gravity of what she was about to do hit her like a wave. A tsunami. But she had no choice. It was time to contact Brendon.

Two years ago, a man from Amy's past sent her an email asking for ten grand. That man was a man Amy had naively trusted as a fifteen year old. At a time in her life when she had nobody to love her or take care of her, she had accepted his version of love. She had done as he had asked and gone along with what he had wanted, like the lost little puppy she was. Then he had arranged for her to work in one of his clubs. At first it seemed like an exciting way to make a living. Glamorous even. Within a few short weeks she found out that it was far from glamorous. The man she had thought she loved and trusted had led her into a life of exotic dancing that would soon become a life of prostitution.

At sixteen years old, being a 'high class escort', as he had put it, and making a grand a week, seemed like an exciting, glamorous and easy way to earn a living. Then she discovered what 'high class escorts' actually did. And she saw the men who she was expected to do it with. She could not understand why the man she had trusted would want her to do such things with perfect strangers. Very quickly she realized that he wasn't the man she had thought he was. The man was a manipulative, greedy, evil man who preyed on young, vulnerable girls like Amy. The man used girls like slaves to make money for him. The man had no limits to what he would do to make money. The man had no morals and no heart. The man was Isaac Manning.

One night after working in his 'gentleman's club', Amy ran away. She had escaped Manning's clutches. She moved to a new area, changed her name from Adele Trenholm to Amber Lavene. She went to college and trained to be a learning support assistant. She got a good job that she enjoyed, working with five year olds in a lovely little village primary school. A few years later she met the man of her dreams. Brendon Hawke.

At first she was wary of him. She was twenty years old and hadn't kissed anyone since Manning. She hadn't liked what that had led to, so she was suspicious of all men. But Brendon was different. He was honest, romantic, genuine, attractive and funny. And he had a heart of gold. He treated her like a lady. Like his princess. Within a short time, Amber knew that he was 'the one'.

Two years ago, Manning found her. He threatened to tell Brendon about her past. Brendon had always believed that he had been her first. That she was a sweet girl who worked in a school and had never had a boyfriend in her life. Finding out that she had lost her virginity to a man like Manning, worked in his strip club and had almost become one of his 'high class escorts' would have destroyed their marriage, for sure. But that wasn't all. Hawke had just made a new series for TV, 'The Survivor'. He had been on TV for six weeks in a row. He had given interviews on 'This Morning' and had appeared on 'The One Show'. He had written articles for magazines and he even had a book out to go along with his TV series. It was his big break. He was fast becoming a household name.

When Manning discovered that Amber was married to such a prominent figure he was rubbing his hands together. He soon found out where she was living and threatened to go to the press. He said he would get a lot of money for such a good story. *Up and coming TV presenter Brendon Hawke is married to a former stripper and prostitute.* He reckoned he could get twenty grand from The News of the World.

But Manning offered an alternative. If Amber gave him ten grand then he would go away. Amber paid him the ten grand. Brendon had just made a bundle on his TV series and she was able to take it out of one of their long-term investment accounts without his knowledge. However, a month later Manning sent her another email asking for more. This time he had wanted twenty grand. That had been a lot harder to get, but Amber couldn't risk Brendon finding out about her past. She had found her true love and she wasn't about to lose him. So she paid. A month later, Manning had demanded another twenty. Amber had been suicidal. She knew she couldn't get more money without Brendon finding out. She knew Manning would never stop blackmailing her.

Amber had found a wonderful man to love her and she didn't wanted to lose him. But she was sure that she would if Manning got to him. And she was sure it would destroy Brendon's career too. Amber would do anything to ensure Brendon's happiness. She decided to let him believe her dead rather than have him find out about her past. She knew it would break his heart. But hearts heal. And after seeing those pictures Manning had recently sent her of Brendon in bed with Jade, it appeared that she had been right. His heart had healed.

In the empty Internet café and with tears rolling down her cheeks, Amy started typing.

Chapter Ten

I was outside in my garden with a hammer in my hand. I think I was making a shed. There was timber, lots of it. The wood was really tough. No matter how hard I hit the nails with my hammer, the nails wouldn't go in. The noise I was making was hurting my head really bad. I put down the hammer, but the banging continued. The noise hadn't been coming from the hammer hitting the nails. The banging was in my head. And it was getting louder. Louder. Louder…

I woke up on my living room floor. Cold. The banging hadn't stopped. My dream had somehow emerged into reality. I rolled over and got up off the floor, holding onto various bits of furniture. I had no idea what time it was, but it was dark. I flicked a light on and glanced at my watch. 4:12pm. Shit! What happened? I must have slept through half the day. The banging continued.

I made it to my front door and opened it before someone knocked it in.

"Phone." AK held my mobile out in front of him.

"Bike." He pointed to his left. I peered out and saw my bike parked up against the front of the cottage.

"Laptop." He lifted his other arm and held up a laptop bag that looked heavy enough to have a laptop in it.

It was like talking to Tarzan. Me Tarzan. You Jane.

"I thought you could use my laptop and I could have a look and see if that photo was a fake. There's a good chance it is, you know."

He was stringing words together now. But they still sounded like shit to me.

"It wasn't a fake, AK."

"Look, take this bloody phone off me…I glued it by the way. Put your super posh bike away before it gets knicked…Oh! And before you do any of that…put the kettle on."

I guess I was beginning to warm to this guy. He was straight-talking and I like that. I put the bike in my garage and put the kettle on like he said. The banging was still going on in my head.

"You've got three missed calls, by the way."

"You've been reading my phone?" It came out wrong. I knew it came out wrong.

"Hey, Hawkeye…I can leave right now if you like. I didn't read your damn phone. After I glued the thing back together, it rang on three occasions. I was going to answer it in case it was important, but it's not my phone, so I didn't." He stood in my kitchen with his face all pulled. I think I might have upset him.

"Sorry, I didn't mean…" I started to apologize. He jumped in.

"I only came up here with your damn bike and your damn phone and my damn laptop so you could use it. But if you think I'm some kind of …" Yep. I definitely upset him.

"Shh... Head." I pointed to my head. "Sorry. Here…tea." Now I was talking like Tarzan. Must be catching.

He shut up and so did I. He took his mug from me and we sat in my conservatory and drank tea. My head still hurt.

"Gonna check your phone then. It might be important." AK said without looking up from the floor.

I checked my phone. It had been the teacher from the school who wanted me to run one of my courses. She must have rang three times. There was a message. She had decided the weather was too bad. I didn't care one way or another.

I looked up and AK had his laptop open and I could hear it humming away.

"Here." He held it out to me.

"What?" I knew what he meant. But right then, I didn't have a great inclination to look at a photograph of my dead wife having sex with some ugly bastard again.

"Look…just get me into your email account and I'll soon tell if it's a fake or not. You needn't look again."

Call me funny, but I didn't have a great inclination for AK to look at the photo either.

I ignored him a while and drank my tea. The banging in my head had reduced to maybe a mallet hitting a dowel now. Still painful, but I could focus on other stuff.

Reluctantly, I took the laptop from him and entered my email account. There were three new emails waiting. My heart began to beat harder in my chest.

"What?" AK had read my face.

"Three new ones."

"Here…" AK pulled his laptop away from me and sat back in his seat with the laptop on his lap.

Tap. Tap, tap, tap. He thumped the keyboard. "Who's Amy Bell?"

I shook my head. I had no idea. "Maybe somebody from the school I've been arranging a course with."

AK had his head down. Reading. Hours passed. Probably a couple of minutes, but it felt like hours.

"Long email is it?" I was growing impatient and the mallet was still banging in my head. Bad combination. "AK!" I snapped at him.

He looked at me and sighed. His expression was one I didn't care for. Sympathy.

"What?"

"I think you do know who Amy Bell is…I think you know her very well, actually." AK's face was pissing me off big time. I hate that look. He passed his laptop over and I took it from him and sat back in my chair as he had. Then I started reading and my world changed yet again.

Brendon, how do I begin? Two years ago I did a terrible, unforgivable thing to you. I left you. Not only that, I let you believe that I was dead. I know you will never forgive me for that. It is unforgivable. But I had good reasons to do what I did. A man I knew before I met you was blackmailing me. He would have destroyed our marriage and your career and I couldn't allow that. I gave him thirty thousand of our money. I am so sorry, but he would have sold a story about me to the newspapers that would have humiliated you and finished your TV career. Of course, once I had paid him he wanted more and more. I was distraught and suicidal. I never wanted to hurt you.

I realize that you have moved on with your life and I wish only for you to be happy. I would never have contacted you, but this man has found me again and now he wants fifty grand or he will kill two innocent young men that he has kidnapped. These men are not important to me. Only one man was ever important to me. One is a friend and the other I hardly know. But I would not want anyone to die because I didn't pay. Will you please help? I know how hard it must be to hear from me. I know you will be angry and hurt. I only ever wanted for you to be happy and if I hadn't paid this man two years ago, then you would not have been happy, because you would have found out about my past and it would have destroyed us and your career. Please, if you can put aside your feelings for me and think only of saving the lives of these two innocent men. I will explain everything later.

The man who is blackmailing me is called Isaac Manning. He is a very nasty, violent man. He has cut a finger from one of the young men already. He says he will kill them both if I don't pay by Wednesday six pm.

Please, please, please help me Brendon.

Amber.

PS. I am using an internet café to send this, but will be able to access my email from work tomorrow. Please contact me soon. Lives depend on it.

My mind was reeling. I read the email and reread it three times. I could feel myself trembling internally, like my blood was rushing too fast. I must have been chewing the loose skin on the pads of my hands where I get blisters from cycling, because the sensation of pain was beginning to seep through the soup in my mind. When I looked at my hand it was bloody.

"Is it possible?"

I'd heard a noise. AK's voice. But my mind was still trying to cope with the biggest kick in the balls I'd ever felt.

"Is it possible?" AK again. I was ignoring him. Too busy reading the email again. I finished reading it and looked across at AK. My eyes were full, but they weren't leaking. Yet.

"Well? Is it her? Is it your Amber?"

The words sounded stupid. Silly. *Is it your Amber?* How the hell could it be Amber. She drowned almost two years ago. We had a memorial service and everything.

"Of course it's not my Amber. It's this fucking crazy nut playing games with my head again, isn't it?" I got up and stood at my window. It was dark outside. I stared out anyway.

"What did I tell you he asked for last time....fifty grand or he was going to give that sick photo to the newspapers."

"It couldn't be her, then?" AK said with a face straighter than a 12'' ruler.

"I ignored the bastard didn't I? So he's thought of a new angle. He must think I'm simple!" The mallet in my head had been exchanged for a hammer again. A six pound engineers hammer. I walked though to my kitchen and got some paracetamol from my medicine cupboard. The water from my tap made my teeth hurt. It was so cold. Bloody winter!

When I walked back through into the conservatory, AK was reading from his laptop again. "The words seem very sincere."

I sat down again. My heart was banging in my chest nearly as loud as the hammer in my head.

AK started reading bits from the email. "*I had good reasons to do what I did. A man I knew before I met you was blackmailing me...*She was being blackmailed, just like this guy is trying to do to you now."

"Nobody is blackmailing me, AK. Cos it's all a croc of shit!"

"Listen here...*I gave him thirty grand of our money...* Have you checked? Did thirty grand go missing before she died?" AK had sunk his teeth into this email and he wasn't about to let go.

"I dunno, for Christ's sake...it's two years ago!"

"Well, I think *I* would notice if thirty grand went missing from my account. But then *I'm* not some rich TV celebrity, am I?"

Sarcasm. I can't say that I ever appreciate it.

"Neither am I, you might have noticed. I haven't done any steady work since I lost her. I've been living on my savings this past two years."

"You still didn't answer my question. Is there thirty grand missing?" AK was still biting on to this bloody email.

"No." I wasn't lying. I couldn't see how I would miss thirty grand going out of any of our accounts.

AK met my eyes for a long time without blinking and then he started reading the email again. I was grateful to him for bringing my phone back and my bike, but now I just wanted him to go.

He started reading out loud from the damn email again. "*...once I had paid him he wanted more and more. I was distraught and suicidal. I never wanted to hurt you.* That's makes perfect sense to me. If she was being blackmailed like she says and she couldn't tell you then maybe she *was* suicidal."

I stopped him. He was really irritating me now. "AK…she drowned…a surfing accident. If she had been suicidal she would have committed suicide…there would have been a note explaining all this back then. And before you ask…No, there wasn't a note."

He ignored me and continued. "She talks about you moving on with your life and wishing only for you to be happy. Then she says, *I would never have contacted you, but this man has found me again and now he wants fifty grand or he will kill two innocent young men that he has kidnapped.*"

"So…" I really wanted him to leave now.

"So? Can't you see it? If this were the guy who sent you that photograph, then why would he pretend to be Amber and say that two men are going to be killed if you don't pay the money? Why pretend she's still alive and has two friends that might get killed if you don't pay up. It doesn't make sense. He could have just sent you another picture and threatened to give it to the press again."

"Cos I ignored his last email, like I said. He realizes he can't get to me with pictures so he makes this dumb story up that she's still alive and her friends have been kidnapped." I was standing over AK now, arguing.

He stood up suddenly. We were face to face. "Dumb story eh?"

"Yeah…the guy obviously hasn't got the brains to think this thing through. He thinks he can just make a quick kill and get fifty grand out of me. Arsehole!"

I was shouting. Also, I think I might have spat on his face when I spoke. He pushed me back gently, but firmly. Then he wiped his face with his sleeve. *I had* spat on his face. Oops!

"So tell me this Hawkeye…why would she explain that these two men are not important to her. A scam artist would surely want you to believe that they were very important to her. She says that only one man was ever important to her. Why say that? Eh? Why would some arsehole who wants to blackmail you say that?"

I'm sure I felt some spittle hit me on the chin. He was right in my face. I guess he owed me.

"Come on, Hawkeye…explain that."

I couldn't. AK was starting to make sense and I didn't like it. I stepped back and sat down in my seat again. AK did the same. The mist of testosterone in the air began to clear.

AK picked up his laptop again. “She says this man is called Isaac Manning. Is that the same guy that emailed you that photo?”

“Dunno. He called himself ‘The virgin slayer’. Pathetic piece of shit that he is.”

“So if this email was from the same guy, then why give you his name now when he didn’t before?”

I sighed. In fact, I had sighed a lot since he had opened that bloody email. My chest felt tight.

“She’s alive mate...she’s bloody alive!” AK had made a strong case, but I was a one-man jury and I wasn’t buying it.

“What’s wrong with you, man? What would you rather believe? That she drowned? That she committed suicide? Or that she was being blackmailed by this bastard and she faked her own death to save your career?”

AK was standing now. Looking down at me.

I argued. “What could she have done that would be so bad she needed to fake her own death?”

AK said. “I dunno mate. But I think your girl is still with us. I think that this Amy Bell is your Amber and she needs your help.”

He walked away from me, back through my lounge. I guessed he was thirsty or needed the toilet. I was wrong. I heard my front door open and then slam shut again.

“What the...?” I got up and rushed through to my back door. I could just make out AK walking down my drive. “Hey...AK! Where’re you going?”

He shouted back. “I’ve got a dog to feed, my friend. And you have a lot of thinking to do. If you need me... you know where I live.”

I stood at my front door listening to AK’s footsteps on the gravel. The crunch, crunch, crunch got less and less and then it was gone. I’d been on my own for nigh on two years, but I suddenly felt very alone.

I walked back through my lounge and realized that AK had left his laptop in the conservatory. I picked it up and sat back down in my wicker chair. I read the email yet again. This time the words sounded different. I could hear Amber saying them. I could also feel something growing inside my chest.

“Listen to yourself, Brendon. Stop it! Stop it, right now!” I had let myself fall for it. Two years of trying to accept that she had gone and here I was grabbing at a chance she might be still alive. It was crazy. Amber died. I mourned her. I was still mourning her. She was dead and she was never coming back and this email was just a sick, cruel trick played by some sick bastard trying to get easy money. Well, good luck, you sick bastard. If he only knew how little I had.

I read the last sentence again.

He says he will kill them both if I don't pay by Wednesday six pm.

My brain was processing the words. Analysing them. *Wednesday six pm.* A deadline. If I ignored the email and nothing happened at six pm on Wednesday then he would lose all credibility. That would be a really stupid bluff. All I had to do was ignore him again and when nothing happened on Wednesday at six, then I would know for sure that he was just some stupid wannabe blackmailer.

Unless something did happen.

God, this was killing me. It was torture. One second I was thinking rationally, remembering the facts and only the facts. And the next second I was hearing Amber say those words in that email. It was no good; I needed to end this now. I shut the damn laptop and walked through to my bedroom. There's a hatch in my room that I can access my loft through. I reached up, opened it and pulled the ladder down.

I hadn't been in my loft since putting Amber's stuff up there almost two years ago. When I switched the light on the first thing I saw were the handful of boxes stacked around the hatch. That weird sensation was growing in my chest again. Being a man, I'm not the most organized person in the world, so I hadn't labelled any of the boxes before I'd put them up there. I was wishing I had now. The first box I opened had shoes in. There were maybe a dozen pairs. You wouldn't think you could get upset looking at shoes. Let me tell you, you can. Two pairs in particular really shook me up. A pair of tan leather sandals adorned with little wooden beads brought back a multitude of memories.

I remembered her riding horseback in Minorca along a gorgeous beach in St. Tomas. She had a balconette bikini top on, indecent, denim shorts and those sandals. She looked stunning. Another time, I remembered her in our garden mowing the grass. I played hell with her, because I'd read about a man losing his big toe wearing sandals when he was strimming. She had been wearing those sandals pushing the Flymo around our lawn.

I put my hand in the box and with my little finger I lifted a pair of high heels. Not just any high heels. These were patent black leather. They had straps that went half way up the calf. The heels were maybe five inches and there was something about the whole shape of the shoes that was just bloody amazing. They brought a whole different set of memories back. I dropped them back in the box and closed it up again. My eyes were a little blurry. Must have been the dust up there.

I'd learned my lesson, so the next two boxes got a mere glance. I couldn't stand looking through more boxes of her clothes and her make up and her handbags and stuff. Of course, sod's law, the box I wanted was last one I looked in. I pulled it under my arm and half stepped, half fell down my ladders. Try holding onto ladders and a cardboard box full of bankbooks without falling when you've got an injured shoulder and a hangover. Not good.

I laid the books out on my bed. There were a lot of them. Amber had kept all the accounts. She took care of our finances. I used to be useless with keeping balances and paying bills and the like. After she died I was forced to learn a whole new set of skills.

I went back to the month before she died and compared Amber's accounting with the corresponding bank statement for that month. She had checked all the statements herself at the time. There were ticks against each amount. I did the same thing myself now. I went back a whole year. Nothing out of place. No suspicious cheques. No dodgy withdrawals. I started on our ISAs and NS&I accounts. There wasn't much left of them. Since losing Amber, nothing had gone in, but a whole load of cash had gone out. There was a pound in two of the Building Society accounts; just enough to keep them open. There was five grand still left in a Cash ISA and seven left in a Maxi. I really needed to find some work; funds were getting low. But that was by the by, I hadn't found what I was looking for.

I put the files and the books and the statements all back in the box and shoved the box under my bed. I wasn't going to risk those ladders again. So that was that. AK was wrong. Amber hadn't paid anybody thirty grand, not unless she'd robbed a bank anyway. That feeling in my chest began to fade now. I'd gotten all worked up for nothing.

I took a shower and had a shave and tried my best to lift my mood. I even whistled to myself as I got dressed. I tried to put the stupid email out of my head and instead thought of something that was real. Jade. I'd been feeling really guilty about sleeping with her. I guess I felt like I had cheated on Amber in some way. But now, I knew different. Well, I'm not sure what I knew actually. If that email was total crap then maybe that photo had been too. Maybe Amber had a secret, dubious past before I met her or maybe she didn't. Maybe I'd never know. Maybe that was for the best. But I was sure that email was a scam and Amber was sadly still dead. On the other hand, Jade was alive and she had told me that she loved me. Maybe I should just hang on to that. She was a nice girl and I was a lucky man. I tried to focus on that.

I padded through into my kitchen with just my socks on and stared at the contents of my fridge. Hangovers tend to make me one of two things, hungry or nauseous. And I was bloody starving. I grabbed some ham and some cheese and made an omelette with three eggs that had been there since I don't know when. It tasted bloody fabulous. I was washing it down with some apple juice when the phone started ringing. I looked at my watch. 5:57pm. I thought about ignoring it. I had other plans for my evening, like seeing Jade, and I didn't want to put off seeing her. I'd upset her this morning, leaving so soon. I needed to show her that I was genuinely interested.

The phone stopped and I breathed a sigh of relief. I sat down in the chair next to the phone with my apple juice, just about to pick it up to ring Jade when it rang again. My brain couldn't deal with the sudden change of plan from picking it up to call Jade, then having to ignore it because it had started to ring again. I ended up picking the receiver up by mistake.

I held it to my ear, but said nothing. I didn't know why I did that. Who did I think would be calling?

"Hello? Brendon?" It was Jade after all.

"Wow! You must be telepathic. I was just gonna ring you. I was sitting right by the phone."

She seemed to like that. "Oh yes? And what were you going to say?" She was talking really soft and sexy. I liked it.

"Well, I was going to ask if I could come over…if you'd like me to, that is." God! I sounded like a teenager.

"Well, isn't that funny. I was just ringing to see if you were going to come over."

I hadn't heard her do that sexy thing with her voice before, but I really liked it. A lot. "Half an hour?"

"I'm just about to have a bath. I might be dressed by the time you get here…I might not." That Jade. What a tease!

"In that case, I'll be there in twenty."

"Come right in…I'll be the naked one smelling of soap."

"Don't use too much…I like a girl when she's still just a little bit dirty." I couldn't believe I just said that. There must have still been some alcohol in my bloodstream.

I walked back into my bathroom, applied some aftershave and had a spray of deodorant, checked my hair and brushed my teeth. I was like a kid going on his first date. I checked the cooker was off in the kitchen, checked the bedroom light was off and walked through to check the backdoor was locked. All of these checks were totally unnecessary of course, but I always get a touch of OCD when I'm nervous. And boy, was I nervous? I was acting like a kid!

As I walked through the conservatory I realized AK's laptop was still humming away. I picked it up off the chair and put it on the coffee table, so I could log off and close it down. I should have just closed it, the damn thing would have switched off just the same. But I didn't. I looked at the screen and saw the two unopened emails that were still highlighted bold in my inbox. I wondered why AK had left them. Maybe we got so engrossed in that fake email that we forgot. I don't know, but there they were.

One I didn't recognize. Spam maybe. The other was the arsehole that called himself The Virgin Slayer. I had no reason to open it. I'd just proved that all this shit was just a scam to get some money out of me. The best thing would be just to delete it without opening it. Why waste my time, right?

I opened it. There was a short message and an attachment. Another photograph. I didn't read it. I backed away from the screen and kept on backing away until my back hit a wall. I stood there shaking my head. There was no way I was going to fall into this guy's trap. I was *not* going to be suckered in. AK would have opened it. I know he would, but then it's easy when it's someone else's life. I didn't need to. I had all my wonderful memories of Amber in my head and that's all I needed. I didn't need anyone to provoke me, to sow any seeds of doubt. I knew everything I needed to know about my wife and I believed everything she ever told me. Yes, that's right Brendon, keep that line of thought going.

I turned my back on the conservatory and grabbed my coat from the hanger in the hall. I patted my pockets to make sure I had my wallet, my phone and my car keys and I left.

There was quite a heavy frost and the key wouldn't turn in the lock of the garage door. When that happens I usually go back in for some hot water to pour on the lock. Not today. No way was I going back inside. I took the key out and cupped it in my hands and blew warm air into the space I'd created between my palms. Ten seconds later I wiggled the key in the lock and it opened. A minute after that and I was on my way to Durham.

Chapter Eleven

Jade. Think Jade, Brendon. Focus on nothing, but Jade. The X Trail warmed up pretty quickly, but the gauge that reads the outside temperature read minus one Celsius. I could see frost on the paths and even on the grass verges. Winter had definitely arrived. The snow had thawed on most places except the hills, but the frost had replaced it. And more snow was forecast for tomorrow. Great!

Jade. Think of Jade, Brendon. I was on my way to see a beautiful girl who was in love with me and I had no doubt she was going to be waiting for me either in the bath, on the bed or draped across that big suede settee she had. Probably, she would be naked. Or maybe she would be treating me to some really hot lingerie. I bet she looks damn sexy in black. Brunettes always look good in black. Or white. Or red. That's good, Brendon. Keep your mind on Jade. Think about nobody and nothing, but Jade.

I hit the brakes. The X Trail stopped quickly despite the conditions. A car whizzed past me with its horn sounding. He shouldn't have been following so close. I checked my mirror just in case there was somebody else back there, then did a three-point turn and headed back. I looked at the clock on my dash. 6:33. Just over half an hour since Jade rang. Okay, so I was going to be late, but not a lot.

I knew there would just be more threatening words and another fake photo, but when something gets under your skin, you just have to scratch it, right? I was nearly home. I pulled off the main road and sped down my drive. The car was sliding on the gravel. I pulled up and marched across to my front door. This guy wasn't winning. I wasn't being suckered in. This would just take a minute. I'd be back on my way to Jade's just as soon as I'd shook my head at whatever pathetic story he had concocted this time and laughed at his photo-shopped picture.

I was inside. I sat down and lifted the laptop onto my lap. I read the email. Same sort of shit as the first time. It simply demanded fifty grand by six pm, Wednesday or he was sending the photo to the press. Like I said I would, I was shaking my head at how pathetic this guy was. I clicked on the photo.

I sat back in the wicker chair and checked my watch again. 6:39pm. I blew out a long sigh. Here I was again waiting for an image to download at about half the speed a snail might slither down my screen. I was tutting now and checking my watch again. 6:40. Jade would be expecting me any minute. Come on. Come on. It was like waiting for a guy who stammers to finish a story you weren't even interested in hearing.

I could see about a quarter of the image now. The ceiling of somebody's lounge maybe. It was a dim image, taken in poor light and very grainy. A guy's head appeared next. Light hair. Blonde, with some highlights, maybe from the sun. No wait, it was a girl. Right, here we go. It was Amber's face. Her eyes were closed, but it was definitely Amber. Her hair was different, shorter and a bit lighter and she looked different in some way. Not quite how I remembered her. Her mouth was open and she looked like she was very relaxed. Contented. A little more of the image appeared. She had something wrapped around her neck and shoulders, a sweatshirt maybe. Then I saw flesh. Her breasts appeared. They were as round and as beautiful as I remembered. My mouth went dry and that sensation was back in my chest again. Within seconds I saw more hair, just under Amber's breasts. Straw-like fair hair. A man. Another man, not the same one as in the other photo when she looked about fifteen. His face was pressed against her torso, like he was kissing it. He looked naked. Apart from the sweatshirt pushed up above her breasts, so did Amber. I couldn't see if either of them wore any pants or underwear. The image stopped at roughly their waists. The photo had downloaded. All of it. I stared at it without blinking. I think I might have stopped breathing too. I was absolutely certain now. It was no fake. It was Amber.

After I had stared at it until I was beginning to feel physically sick, I found the first email he had sent and opened that picture file. My guts churned even more at seeing that one again. I didn't need to stare for long to convince myself that that one was real too. They both were. I closed that email and opened the one from Amy Bell. For what was probably the fifth or sixth time, I read it again. Slowly. After I was done reading I shut the laptop down and put it back on the coffee table. Then I sat back in the wicker chair and cried. A lot.

While I was crying my heart out I'm pretty sure I heard the phones ring; the landline and my mobile. Jade, no doubt. When I'd finally ran out of tears I went back in my bedroom and got the bank statements out and began checking again. There was one sentence in that email from Amy Bell that rang true. It wasn't the parts where it said that she was sorry, or where it said that she hadn't wanted to humiliate me or hurt my career. Anybody posing as Amber could write that shit. The one sentence that really stood out was when she said that once she had paid him, he wanted more and more. I thought about those words a lot. If the blackmailer had written the email, then he wouldn't want to inform his victim (ie, me) that once he got paid, he was just going to continue asking for more like he had with Amber. No blackmailer would divulge that. The whole point of paying the person who's blackmailing you is to stop the threat of them leaking the information that is going to harm you. So now I was convinced that it wasn't the blackmailer who wrote that email, or anyone called Amy Bell for that matter. AK had been right. The email was genuine. It was Amber. All I had to do now was find the missing thirty grand and I would be convinced, one hundred per cent.

As I was flicking through each statement again, I heard the landline ring. Seconds later and my mobile started again. I stopped what I was doing and ran back into the conservatory where I'd put down my mobile and answered it.

"Thank God for that! Where are you? You've had me bloody worried."

She sounded relieved, like a mother would when their kid finally arrived back late from school, or maybe a wife when their husband didn't turn up for dinner. I didn't know how I felt about that.

"I'm sorry, Jade. Something came up and…" I hesitated. I hadn't really thought about what I should say to her.

"And what?" She sounded miffed.

"Look, I feel really bad about this, but can we do this another night, something's come up." Well, I wasn't lying to her. Something had definitely come up.

Silence. But I could hear in the pattern of her breathing that she was pissed off.

"I'll come across tomorrow…okay?" I sounded pathetic. I know I did. But my mind was like a train on a rail track and there was no way I could turn off.

"Please tell me your not breaking up with me, Brendon?" Jade said with a voice full of dread. I hadn't realized we'd become something of a unit that could be broken.

"No…don't take it that way." I reassured her. At least that's what I was aiming for.

Obviously I hadn't. Her tone got more anxious. "So how should I take it?"

"Like I said, something's come up. I'll see you tomorrow, Jade. I'm really sorry. I'll see you tomorrow. Okay?"

"Okay. Love you, Brendon." She sounded a little better. I think.

"Goodnight."

I felt rotten about not telling her that I loved her too. But I wasn't sure that I was comfortable saying it yet. I would say it when I was certain I meant it. I hung up and got back to my bedroom and continued where I'd left off.

When I'd finished checking every book, every bank and building society statement, every NS&I account and every ISA account again and came up with nothing again, I began to question myself. But not for long. I was sure that email was genuine. And the photographs too. She must have got the money from somewhere else. But where? I had an idea. I punched the freephone number from my NS&I statement into my phone and within half a minute someone answered. A real person. I was impressed.

"Hi, my name's Brendon Hawke and I hold two accounts that I know of with yourselves, an ISA and some index-linked certificates. Could you tell me if I have any other accounts?" I know that sounded crazy, but I thought it was possible that I might have forgotten about some account with NS&I. Like I said, Amber looked after our finances.

"Is that Brendon Hawke from The Survivor?" She said in a broad Lancashire accent. I guess I should have been flattered.

"It is. Can you let me know?"

"Oh, I think you're great…" She giggled. Then. "I'm sorry Mr Hawke. Yes, I can, but I'll have to ask you a few questions first for security reasons. Is that okay?"

I told her it was okay and answered a bunch of silly security questions. She was satisfied, so then she asked me to hold. I held. I was treated to the tinniest rendition of Vivaldi's Four Seasons I'd ever heard while I waited. I was starting to lose my patience when she finally got back to me.

"Hello, Mr Hawke?"

"Still here."

"You have no other accounts with us, sir."

That *wasn't* what I wanted to hear.

"However…a little over two years ago you cashed in your Premium Bonds."

"I did?"

"Yes, you held thirty thousands pounds with us for just over a year, but withdrew ten thousand in September 2008 and then closed that account when you withdrew the remaining twenty thousand on 8th November 2008."

That was what I wanted to hear.

"Can I be of further assistance, Mr Hawke?"

"No…you've been just great, thank you." She had. She'd told me just what I wanted to hear.

I ended the call and blew out a long sigh. It was official. Amber had been blackmailed. Not only that. She was very much alive.

Chapter Twelve

My mind was awash with emotions, from one end of the spectrum to the other. The thought of someone you've loved and lost coming back to life is one of those irrational thoughts that anyone will have when they lose someone special. But here I was with that dream coming true. Amber was alive. At the same time my dream was fast becoming a cruel, cruel nightmare. Because no wife pays a blackmailer thirty grand to keep something from her husband, unless that something is something she thought he would never accept. And after seeing those photographs I was beginning to wish she'd just stayed dead.

It was nearly nine and snow was falling lightly on my windscreen as I drove back to Durham. This time there would be no turning around. I was going to see Jade, but not for the same reasons I had originally being going for. I needed to ask her a few questions.

When I got there I didn't just walk right in. I stood at the door and knocked. After all, she wasn't expecting me this time. She came to the door in a crimson, satin robe. She looked stunning.

"Change your mind?" She said in a low sultry tone, leaning sexily against her door.

I hesitated a second. I think she could detect my mood, because she wrapped her robe around herself a bit tighter and straightened up. I said. "I need to have a chat about something."

She stood back and opened the door to let me in. I followed her through into her living room and we sat on her big suede settee. She still had the blinds open at her French doors and I could see people walking along the waterside under the glow of the neon lights from the bars down there.

When she sat down she did that thing that some girls do where they tuck one leg under the other. Because she was wearing a short nightgown it rode up on both her thighs. I tried to keep my gaze at eye level.

"So you want to break up?"

Boy, was this girl ahead of herself. I put my hand on her hand to reassure her. "Jade…I don't think we've come quite that far that we have anything to break up. But just for the record…I'm not breaking up with you."

"You don't think we've come quite that far? Jesus! Thank you for making me feel so special…I mean, did making love with me not mean anything to you?'

Her whole body language changed as she said it. She moved along the settee away from me and untucked her leg from beneath the other, pulling her nightgown down at the same time.

"Jade…" I reached out and tried to grab her hand, but she pulled it away before I could touch her. "Listen, I'm very confused at the moment. Something's come up."

"Yes…you said already."

"I need to ask you about Amber."

She blew out a heavy, harsh sigh. "Jesus, Brendon! It's been two years. You need to let her go and start living your life again. As much as I loved Amber, she's gone." She shuffled a little closer now. The crimson satin slid up her thigh again, but she didn't appear to mind. I kept my eyes on her face.

"When did you two meet?"

"Jesus, Brendon! What's this about?" She pulled her head back and looked at me with a puzzled face.

"Just tell me when you met."

"Why?"

"I just want to know about her past…before she met me. Who did she go out with? What kind of people did she socialise with?" I tried to sound cool, like it wasn't a big deal.

"What is this, Brendon? Why the third degree? Don't you think you should have asked her those questions when you first met?"

I rubbed my hand across my face. The events of the day were beginning to make me feel weary. I tried again. "How old was she when you met her?"

She did the heavy sigh thing again. "I dunno…maybe sixteen."

"Did she have many boyfriends?"

"Brendon…she's gone. She's been gone almost two years. What does this matter now?"

I didn't have time for this. "Look Jade… just tell me for Christ's sake. Was she seeing a man called Manning?"

That changed the look on her face. It was like I'd just slapped her. Hard.

"Who?" She asked me who, trying to act like she didn't have a clue who this guy was, but I wasn't buying it.

"Scrawny. Ugly. Ginger. Not what you'd call a very nice bloke. You know him don't you, Jade?"

"Never heard of him." The lips said one thing, but the eyes said something entirely different. She was lying.

"Okay, that's how you want to play it." I jumped up quickly and looked down at her. "You don't want to tell me that's fine. If we can't be honest with each other, Jade, then I don't see the point." I told her and started to walk away. I'd barely reached the door into her kitchen when she called after me.

"Brendon…don't be like that."

I stopped and turned to face her. "Well? You either know him or you know of him."

"Kind of."

"What does 'kind of' mean?"

"Okay, yes. Manning got his hands on her for a little while."

I could feel that sensation in my chest again. I swallowed it down.

"She loved him?"

"No. I wouldn't have called it that. Manning preyed on girls. He used them. Manipulated them. I think he liked Amber's innocence, her vulnerability."

That hurt. The images were creeping in now. I could see that photo of that bastard on top of her. My mind was producing more nasty images to go with it. My chest was threatening to cave in now. "He was her first?"

"Brendon…why are you doing this? She loved you. You were her first. Her true love. Manning doesn't count." She got up and walked over to me, putting her hands on my chest, sliding her fingers under my shirt and touching my skin.

"The past is the past. History. Don't look back. Now is what counts. Us." She was looking up at me with eyes that would melt any man's heart. But I'm not so sure they were melting mine.

"I just need to know the truth, Jade. Tell me."

"Why? Why now?" She pleaded.

"Cos I think she's alive." There. I'd said it. I'd been thinking it all night, but I have to admit saying it out loud sounded absurd.

She looked at me with eyes that bore into my soul. Words weren't necessary; her look said it all.

"I've had an email from someone called Isaac Manning. He's trying to blackmail me. He says he'll tell the world about Amber's past unless I pay him fifty grand."

"So…you're going to pay him are you?" She gripped my arms and squeezed as she said it.

"I couldn't pay him even if I wanted to. I haven't got the money. But he's sent me photos…" I stopped mid-sentence. The emotion that those photos evoked in me was enough to choke me.

"Photos?" Jade quizzed.

I told her. "One from way back when she was just a girl…maybe fifteen or sixteen and another that looked recent. The first one showed her naked with Manning. In the second one, she was with some other younger guy."

"Shit!" Jade summed up her feelings in one word.

"So it's true? She was a whore like her mother… like he said?"

Jade pulled away from me and walked over to her French doors. With her back to me she said. "You shouldn't ask questions if you can't handle the answers, Brendon. I told you…don't look back. Never look back."

I crossed the floor and stood right behind her. "Just tell me who the girl I married was, Jade?"

"You don't want to know, Brendon." She said, turning around to face me.

I put my hands on her shoulders and shook her. "Just fucking tell me, Jade. I've got to know if I married a lie."

"You want to hear that she was a pro… a girl who made her money in a strip club, doing lap dances for a fiver a time…handjobs for a tenner behind closed doors…and a hell of lot more for not a lot more money. Is that what you want to hear? That Manning used her as his plaything, taught her everything she knows, groomed her to be one of his so-called escorts? Is that what you want to hear, Brendon? That your Amber was everybody's Amber well before you laid a finger on her."

I pulled back from her. Her words were like knives that cut through my flesh and pierced my soul. All the fears I had held were now been confirmed. And it hurt. It hurt like hell.

I stood there silent. Sweat ran down my brow and stung my eyes. Every muscle in my body was tensed so tight there was a real risk of me exploding. My chest was doing weird things. Palpitations. My lungs were been squeezed and I felt like I might pass out.

"If that's true…how do you know this?" I stared across at her and she walked across to me again.

"She told me one night when we both got pissed. I guess she just wanted to offload. She just wanted to tell someone. She was ashamed. I didn't judge her, Brendon. Nor should you."

"Did you know she was being blackmailed?"

"No." She answered me immediately. No hesitation. I couldn't figure out if that was sign she was lying or a sign she was telling the truth.

"You didn't know she was being blackmailed?" I repeated the question anyway.

"You heard me…No!" She sounded annoyed.

"So how long was she doing that stuff…stripping? Working as an escort?"

"Brendon…why does any of this matter now." She walked over and put her arms around my neck.

"She's alive, Jade. And she needs my help."

"She left us two years ago Brendon. If Manning sent you an email, then it's bullshit. Nobody wishes she was alive more than me…" She gave me an embarrassed look. "Except you, of course. But we found her board remember. It was her favourite surfboard. It cost five hundred quid or something. Her car was left with all her clothes in. There was nothing missing from her home. Her handbag, her money, her passport and her credit cards…everything was still there. If she had planned some kind of Reggie Perrin faked death, she would have left some sort of clue. She wouldn't have done that to you, Brendon. Believe me, she wouldn't." Jade said it more for her own benefit than mine. It sounded like she was trying to convince herself.

"But she did, Jade. This Manning wanted thirty thousand or he was going to tell me about her past and then tell the media. She paid him. In her email to me she says that she paid him thirty grand, because she knew it would have humiliated me and hurt my career. I've got the proof. There's thirty thousand missing from an account that I'd forgotten about." I'd said enough. I turned and made to leave.

Jade grabbed my arm to stop me. "If she's alive…does that mean you'd want her back…even now that you know everything about her?"

"That's just it. I don't know everything about her."

"Do you want to know all of it? Can you handle that, Brendon? The fact that your wife slept with strangers…How many? You'll never know…" She pulled me to her and held me tight. I let her. I didn't know what I wanted anymore.

"Jade, I…"

She stopped me. "Don't look back, Brendon. I love you. I would never deceive you…or lie to you…or be unfaithful to you. You know I can make you happy…so please, Brendon…just let me."

She kissed me firmly on the mouth. She tasted like wine, red I think. I began to notice other things. Her perfume had a citrus aroma, like oranges and limes. Her shiny, silky, long dark hair bordered her radiant face. Her eyes looked a little puffy, now that I was close up. She'd been crying before I got there. I guess it must have hurt when I rang to cancel. She kept on kissing me and I let her. It felt good and warm and sensual.

She pulled back from me a couple of inches and spoke soft and sexy, like she had on the phone. "I'm real. I'm here. Now. And I love you so much that it hurts. Please stay here, Brendon…with me."

I wanted to. Her eyes, her lips, her scent, her body; it all lured me in. And part of me wanted to be lured in. I was being seduced and it felt good to be seduced. But I was holding back. I couldn't help it. It was a force I couldn't resist. I got hold of Jade's hands and lowered them down to waist level between us.

"I think we have something here…I think you're a beautiful, sweet girl and I'm a very lucky guy to have you. I love being with you…Really, I do…"

"But?" Jade said it for me. She was right, there was a but.

"But, if Amber is alive and needs my help…then I could never live with myself if she or someone she knows got hurt or worse because I didn't help."

She pulled her face again. "So you're just gonna pay this guy, just like that?"

"I told you I couldn't if I wanted to…I haven't got that kind of money anymore."

"So what are you gonna do then?" She said with her eyes brimming with tears.

"I don't know yet, but I want you to know…" I'd started to tell her how I felt about her, but once I'd started I wished I hadn't, because the truth is I wasn't sure about how I felt.

"You want me to know what?" She asked with a tear escaping down one cheek.

I wanted to be honest with her. But I wasn't even being honest with myself. I eluded the question by pulling her to me and kissing her full on the lips. We stayed like that until I needed air and even then she pulled me close and kissed me again. Finally, I broke away and she let me.

"I'll call you…promise…just be patient with me, Jade." And with that I walked out of her door without looking back. Maybe if I'd looked back I might have changed my mind and stayed with her. Maybe. But if Amber was alive, then I there was no way I could abandon her.

When I got home, I packed some essentials and threw them in the back of the X-Trail. Food, clothes, water, some camping gear. Enough to last me a few days. That's all I would need. After all, this Manning character had given me a deadline of Wednesday at six. It was late Tuesday night now, less than twenty four hours. I wasn't going to need much.

When I had everything I needed, I locked up and left. I had a plan. Not much of one, but it would do for now. I sped down the road about two miles and then pulled over on the verge where I thought I needed to be. I left the car, crossed the road and climbed over a dilapidated fence into a field. The ground was hard and frosted and there was still snow in places. I could smell wood smoke now. I cut across the field diagonally to follow the scent. After maybe a hundred yards I saw the large dark shape at the bottom of the field close to the woods. I'd guessed its location from the road pretty well. Not bad, since it was dark. A few seconds later, I heard the low growl of a big dog. I hoped it was tied up. When I got to AK's cabin I hit the door hard with my fist and shouted his name so he would know it was me.

He came to the door in less than three seconds. He had his gun in his hands, but put it down when he saw it was me.

"Tino…good boy. Rest." He called to his dog, then ushered me in. The heat hit me. It was wonderful.

"I'm going to face off this guy, Manning. I was wondering if I could borrow your rifle."

"You shoot?" He said with just a hint of sarcasm, like the idea of me being able to shoot was ludicrous.

"Can I borrow it and some ammunition? I'll settle with you when I get back."

He grabbed a rucksack from a hook on the wall and started to fill it with a few things. "Where?"

"Where what?" I asked as I watched him pull on his boots and his jacket.

"Where are we heading?"

He stood in front of me now, camouflage jacket on, black beanie hat, green combats, rucksack, also green, and his rifle by his side.

I said "You going hunting?"

"That's right."

"Not with me you aren't." I stood firm.

"So let's see. You go to have it out with this thug, Manning, and he has a friend. A big friend. Maybe five big friends. Cos you just know he will. You that hard, Hawkeye?"

Okay, he had a point.

"You don't know me that well, AK. And you sure don't owe me anything."

"Bye then." He started to usher me back out of his cabin.

I stopped him. "Woah! Hold on a sec…can I have the rifle or what?"

"You can have the rifle. But it comes with a dangerous dog and a dangerous man. That's the deal. That's the only deal."

I blew out a heavy sigh. Why did I like this guy? I forget.

"Alright…I guess the more the merrier."

We left his cabin and he locked up and then untied the Akita and we walked back across the hard earth to my car. I made some room in the back and with one word from AK the dog jumped up and settled down on the floor next to AK's pack.

I turned the car around and headed for the hills.

"So where is he?" AK finally asked about ten minutes into our journey.

"Where's who?"

"The pope."

I glanced sideways at him.

"Manning…who do you think?"

I switched the radio on; it was going to be a long drive. "How the hell should I know? I'm going to get Amber."

He shut up, raked his seat back and reclined it. When I looked across at him he had his eyes closed. Yes, it was going to be a very long drive.

About midnight I pulled into a petrol station just before I joined the M6. AK still had his eyes shut. I filled up the tank and bought some chicken and stuffing sandwiches and two Styrofoam cups of tea. AK was outside the car when I got back, the Akita was offloading its bowels on the grass. Nice.

"I'll take over if you like." AK offered and I was only too glad to let him. We ate our supper on the go.

"So…I see we've done almost a hundred miles. How many more to go?"

I gave him a puzzled look. He pointed to the dash. He'd obviously taken a note of the reading on the speedo before we set off. Observant guy that AK.

"About another four." I informed him.

"Miles?" He asked. But I could tell he knew he was wrong just by his expression.

"Four hundred miles…Wales? Devon?"

"Cornwall." I told him.

"Why Cornwall?"

"Cos that's where she is."

"And you know this how?"

I told him about the other email, the one with the picture of some guy all over Amber. How I had stared at that photo maybe twenty times after he'd left and all I'd felt was rage, because all I could see was some shit having sex with my girl. However, the last time I looked at it I saw a whole lot more. The exposed brick wall behind triggered something in my mind. Then when I looked closer I noticed the pine banister of an open staircase that ran up that exposed brick wall. That definitely looked familiar. A closer inspection revealed the edge of a microwave under the stairs. That's when I'd realized I'd seen that set up before. Not that specific room, but one almost identical. The kitchen-come-living room with the open staircase to the mezzanine bedroom was common to all the apartments in that row. It had to be the place I was thinking of.

When I married Amber I took her to Cornwall for a holiday. Not a honeymoon. We went to the south of Spain for that. This was a few months later. I'd just finished filming in Scotland and we hadn't seen each other much, so I arranged a fortnight in Porthtowan, on the northern coast of Cornwall. Amber loved surfing our coast. South Shields and Tynemouth were her favourite places for catching the waves. But there's no place better in Britain than down that northwest coast of Cornwall. I know this, because as a kid I used to holiday there. I just knew she'd love it.

We rented an apartment over the beach. It was one of twenty that ran along the back of the beach with shops and cafes and bars running beneath them. She loved it there. We talked about moving there the way people talk when they go somewhere nice for their holidays. I hadn't noticed the apartment when I first saw that photograph. Who would? The sight of some guy clambering over Amber's exposed body kind of grabbed my attention more than the décor. But once I'd recognized a few things, it all made sense. She couldn't have picked a better place to escape too.

With his mouthful of chicken and stuffing, AK said. "You do know that whoever designed those apartments probably used that design in apartments all over the UK."

"Probably. But I also lived in Cornwall when I was kid. I'm sure that's where she is."

"You lived in Falmouth, didn't you?"

"Your point?"

He gave me a sideways glance. "So that's on the southern coast of Cornwall, isn't it?"

"She's there, AK. I just know it."

"So we're driving the best part of five hundred miles on a hunch?" He was staring at me, but the car was still travelling along at eighty.

"Keep your bloody eyes forward, will you…I want to arrive there in one piece." He looked ahead again. I told him how I knew we were going to the right place. "I googled the name…Amy Bell with Cornwall and surfing."

"Ah ha?"

"Amber didn't just surf a little, AK. She owned those waves. She won competitions and stuff."

"Ah ha?"

"It was there in black and white. Some local newspaper had written a piece on the 2010 Gul British Championship. It had been held at Watergate Bay…Guess who came first in her class?"

"Let me see…" He held his chin between his finger and thumb like he was thinking about it. "It wouldn't be a certain Amy Bell, would it?"

I took a gulp of my tea and washed the last of my sandwich down. "Okay. Okay! You were right and I was wrong. Amy Bell is my Amber." I admitted.

"And the thirty grand?" He glanced at me with his eyebrows raised.

"She'd emptied a NS&I account and closed it. I rang up National Savings…they confirmed it."

AK finished his tea, passed me the empty cup and accelerated up to ninety. "How long did it take you last time you went to this Porth town?"

"Porthtowan…" I corrected him. "Nine hours, but we stopped to go to the loo a couple of times and it was through the day."

He read the clock on my dash. "Twelve thirty three. Should be there about fivish."

The way he was driving, I believed him.

Chapter Thirteen

Katerina came in from work about six. It was cold in her flat and the electric fire that stood against one wall in her lounge took forever to heat the place. To keep warm she went into her kitchen to start on her dinner. She'd been single more than a year, but she still made enough dinner for two. However, after months of scraping leftovers into the bin, she had started to freeze half of what she made. Now she cooked one week and ate frozen meals the next. She was standing looking in her fridge when she remembered that it was her 'frozen' week. She shut the fridge door and opened her freezer door instead and stared at the small plastic boxes she had prepared the week before. She picked out her favourite English meal. Mince and onion with mashed potatoes. She had been trying to cook traditional English meals ever since she had decided she was going to travel there. She took the lid off the box and put some cling film over it and then bunged it in her microwave on full power. She had just turned the timer dial to six minutes when her mobile rang.

"Dobryy vecher, Kat. Kak dila?"

"Good evening to you too, Anya. Have you forgotten?" Katerina said in her polished English.

"Prastite?" Anya continued in Russian.

"You know if we are ever going to get any good at English we have to speak it all the time. It's the only way." Katerina reminded her friend.

Anya sighed down the phone. "Da…yes, I know. So…" She sighed again. "How are you, Kat? Have you heard from Dan this week?"

Dan was the English guy Katerina had met through the Internet.

"You sound good Anya…you must be practising. Yes, I was just speaking to him last night online. On krasiv! He's beautiful!"

"Da?"

"He wants me to visit him." Katerina could hardly keep her excitement in as she said it.

"Ya dumayu, chto Vy l'ubite yego!" Anya teased.

"English, Anya. English!"

Anya hesitated while she thought of the right pronunciation. "I think that you love him. When will you come…I mean go?"

"Soon. He is going to meet me in France."

"France?" Anya quizzed.

Katerina explained. "Da. I can get a lift with Tatiana's father to the west coast of France."

"Tatiana from the office?"

"Da. He drives a lorry full of rapeseed to a processing plant in Montoir every two weeks. Then all I have to do is get a bus to Saint-Nazaire where I will meet him. We will travel on his boat to Cornwall. It sounds romantic, no?"

"A boat. He's rich, then?" Anya probed.

"I think so. Da."

Katerina's microwave pinged. Her meal was ready.

"Why don't you come over Anya? We could have a drink and chat."

Anya paused. She was trying to think of a clever way of answering in English. "Okay. Why the hell not?"

Katerina laughed and repeated what her friend had said. "Why the hell not?"

"Why the hell not?" Anya said again, laughing. "Okay Kat. I will be over soon. O poluchase. Goodbye." Anya said sounding ever so formal.

"Net Anya…say Bye." Katerina corrected her.

"Okay Kat. Why the hell not?" Anya laughed again. "O poluchase…about half an hour. Bye."

Katerina had lived in Nikolaev for less than a year. Before that she had lived with her fiancé in Odessa for six years. Her work had been there. Her mother. Her friends. Her life. Her fiancé Dmitry worked down the docks in Odessa. He was a hard working man with old fashioned values. He did not like it that his fiancé worked for the Tourist Information Service. As part of her job, she often talked to foreign tourists, many of whom were single men coming to the area to search for Russian brides. Dmitry could not tolerate her working there and once he had even beaten her during one of his jealous rages. She had worked for the Tourist Information Service for almost two years and was looking forward to a potential promotion to Office Manager of the Odessa office when Dmitry went too far.

After finishing work early one day, he spotted Katerina showing a group of American men around the town. She looked stunning in her navy blue uniform with the pencil skirt just above her knees and the short tailored jacket that was cut in such a way that it highlighted her small waist and the perfect roundness of her bottom. He saw how the men flirted with her and looked her up and down as she spoke. He wanted to kill them all right then. Instead, he waited for one of them to go off alone and then he attacked him. Katerina had no proof of this, of course. She didn't witness it. But a colleague was sure she saw Dmitry kicking the man on the ground later that evening. She later discovered that the American needed twelve stitches to his head and he also lost his front teeth.

When Katerina confronted Dmitry about the attack, he thought that she was siding with the American and could not understand her lack of gratitude at defending her honour. That night Katerina had to pay a visit to the hospital in Odessa herself. She needed several stitches to her mouth and because her face was so badly bruised, the emergency doctor thought it wise to X ray her skull. Fortunately, her injuries had been only superficial. However, the bruises were still visible three weeks later.

She had loved Dmitry. He had been her only boyfriend. She had agreed to marry him and wore his ring to prove it. But although they had been engaged for four years and shared an apartment in town, they had never planned a wedding. Dmitry always had some excuse that they must save more money so they could do it right. In the meantime, he drank, he smoked and he bought overpriced clothes from the west. He might have hated the Americans and the British, but he loved their shirts and their jeans. Now Katerina was glad she never married him. He was the greatest mistake of her life.

One day, in the spring of 2010, she pretended to go to work. As soon as Dmitry left for the docks, she doubled back, packed her bags and left. She left a simple note saying that she had moved to St. Petersburg where her grandparents lived and that she no longer loved him. In reality, she had confided in her manager at the Tourist Information Office and being a bitter divorcee herself, her manager had agreed to give her a transfer to the office in Nikolaev. It had turned out to be a good move. Nikolaev is a beautiful town, with almost no crime. Although it's only about eighty miles east of Odessa, it feels like a different country almost. The people there are so friendly and trusting. Her neighbours don't even bother to lock their doors.

But the men there were no better than in Odessa. They all seemed to have hard shells and no sensitivity or understanding of what a woman needs. She wanted to be treated with respect and admiration. She wanted romance and real love. She did not want to go to bed with a man to have sex. She wanted to be made love to like she was the only girl in the world. She wanted someone to think she was special. Treat her like a princess. She wanted to find her true love and she knew she would never find it in her home country.

Her job had given her the opportunity to meet men from all around the world. However, it was the English men who she found the most attractive. Most of them that came to visit Odessa or Nikolaev were older than she preferred and very few were physically attractive, but still, she like their manners, their warmth and their ways. She was twenty seven now and was full of regret at wasting six years of her life with Dmitry. But instead of wasting more of her life waiting for Mr Right, she had decided to take control of her own destiny. Joining an online dating service was her first step.

"Zdravstvujte, Kat. Vy tam?" Anya called out as she came through Katerina's door.

"I'm in here, Anya."

"There you are." Anya changed to English as she walked into Katerina's lounge and sat down next to her.

"Ah ha. That's better. You really sound good, you know."

"Ya znayu. I know. I'm good, am I not?" Anya said sounding pleased with herself. "So this Englishman. Are you…em." Anya hesitated while she thought of the right word. "Are you serious on him?"

"Am I serious about him?" Katerina corrected her friend.

"Da. Are you serious about him?"

Katerina stood and walked through to her kitchen. "Vodka?"

"Da."

She came back with a half bottle of vodka and a bottle of sparkling apple juice nestled under her arm and a tumbler in each hand.

"Kat?" Anya pushed her friend.

"Here…" She passed a glass to Anya and poured her a drink. "Serious is not the word I would say."

Anya gave her a puzzled look.

"I need to leave this place, Anya. I need to do something with my life. I am twenty seven. Time is passing too fast."

"Musor!" Anya exclaimed.

"It's not rubbish. It's true. There is nothing here for me now."

Anya put her arm around her friend. "I am here, Katerina. Ya l'ubl'u Vas!"

"And I love you also, Anya. But I need a man's love. I need my life to change. There are too many bad memories here."

Anya finished her drink. She poured herself another and topped up Katerina's glass too. "Odessa may have many bad memories. But not here in Nikolaev. Here you have a good job and a nice apartment. People eat healthy here. They live to over one hundred years. In England people eat rubbish food. They are fat and die young."

"They don't all eat junk food. That's Americans you are thinking of, Anya."

"I know a woman in one of the villages in the hills. She is one hundred and thirty years old…no, I think one hundred and forty. Da. One hundred and forty years old. And she still picks food from her garden." Anya argued as she finished her drink again.

Katerina filled her friend's glass again. "Anya…it is not how many breaths we take, but how many times our breath is taken."

Anya pulled a puzzled face again.

Katerina tried to explain again. "It is not how long we live. It is how well we live that is important. Net?"

Anya laid her head on her friend's shoulder. "Da. You are right, Katerina. You are always right."

"So, when will you go to see your Englishman.?"

"I have taken a holiday from the office for two weeks. I go tomorrow."

"Net!" Anya raised her head in surprise and met Katerina's eyes.

"Da Anya. It is time to start living my new life."

Anya dropped her head back on her Katerina's shoulder again and closed her eyes. The vodka had made her sleepy. "Voz' mite men a s Vami, Kat."

Katerina stroked her friend's hair as she lay against her. "English Anya…English."

"Take me with you. You are my best friend. I might love an Englishman also."

Katerina didn't answer. Vodka often made Anya say things she would regret later. Instead she continued to stroke Anya's hair and quietly hummed an old Russian song her grandmother used to sing when she used to stay with her in St. Petersburg. "Vdol po Piterskoi…mm mm, ma mm ma mm ma hmm." She hesitated while she thought of the English words. "Along the Petersburg Road…along the road a girl went…mm mm, ma mm ma mm ma…"

Chapter Fourteen

Manning drank the last of his Jack Daniels. He banged the glass down heavily on the table and stood to go to the bar. "Same again, Danker?"

"Make it a double, Isaac. I think I deserve it, don't you?"

Manning came back with their drinks and they clinked their glasses together in celebration.

"Six you say?"

"Six absolute beauties. Youngest is nineteen. Oldest is twenty seven. All dark. All fit. And all with bodies like friggin' pornstars. A couple are a bit skinny, but hey…some guys like that, right? Friggin' gorgeous they are." Danker bragged to Isaac and sipped his Jack Daniels.

"So what time they due?" Manning said as he swung his left leg up onto an adjacent chair.

"Probably about dawn…Don't worry, I'll get down there about four to be sure."

"I think I'll give you a hand…check the goods, if you know what I mean." Manning said with a sickly grin on his face.

"Yeah…why not? But I'll warn you, they're always a bit groggy and pale when they arrive. Don't judge them when they land. A fake tan, a few good meals and some slap on their faces and they'll look a like the hottest girls you ever saw." Danker sounded like he was making excuses in anticipation.

"You trying to tell this old man how to suck eggs?" Manning gave Danker a look that would strike the fear of God in a lesser man. Danker brushed it off.

"Yeah. Yeah. You're the man!"

A young girl was hovering around the tables next to the two men. She was leaning over a table collecting glasses. She already had maybe a dozen stacked under one arm and now she was stacking up six more for her spare arm.

"Hey, sweet thing?" Danker called to her as he swung back on his chair, balancing on the back legs. He reached out with his hand and flicked the girl's short flared skirt playfully, exposing her thigh.

She gave him a sideways glance with a face that said she was not impressed. However, her expression softened quickly once she caught his smile. She gave him a smile in return that sent an altogether different message.

"Do me a favour…pop those two glasses on top of here." She said with eyes that could seduce a monk. Danker was only too happy to help. Now she had both arms full of glasses almost up to her chin. Danker looked her up and down. She was only maybe nineteen.

"I'm loving that skirt." He reached out and flicked the hem again. And again he and Manning got a glimpse of bare, tanned inner thigh.

"I got it in Newquay if you want one…what's your size?" She smiled mischievously.

Danker liked that. She was cheeky as well as sexy. "Well…I know a way you could measure me up, if you like?" He grabbed the hem of her skirt and pulled her close. She didn't stop him.

"Sure of yourself…aren't you?" She looked down at him; her tongue just peeking between her full wetted lips. Danker let go of her skirt and slipped his right hand up the inside, tracing a finger lightly up her thigh. Manning watched, then shook his head and turned the other way. The girl looked over both their heads and checked she didn't have an audience.

"You like?" Danker asked in almost a whisper.

"I don't know…you're not quite there yet."

Danker reached the spot he'd being heading for and stroked her through her panties. "What time you get off?"

The girl glanced at the clock behind the bar. "Twenty. You got a car?"

"I'll wait outside for you." He said as he pulled his hand back and made a show of putting his middle finger in his mouth. She gave him a wicked smile to show her approval at his behaviour. Then without another word, the girl walked away, taking the empties to the bar.

"You finished?" Manning said, still with his back to Danker.

"Just getting started actually." Danker said into his glass as he emptied it.

Manning stood and turned to look down at his friend. "I hate good looking bastards like you…I hope you catch something!"

Danker laughed. "I'll give her one for you, Isaac. Not the first one. That'll be good and hard. Maybe the third time when I'm feeling a bit knackered and past my best, you know…like an old man. "

Manning pulled his coat on and emptied his own glass. He banged it down on the table in front of Danker and leaned in close. With his face inches from Danker's, he said. "Don't bother…I've already been there."

Danker watched him leave the pub, pulling his collar up as he opened the door in anticipation of the cold. The last thing he did before he stepped outside was look back at the girl behind the bar. No words were spoken. But the look on her face was enough to let Danker know that maybe Manning hadn't been jesting.

Manning jumped in his van and drove back to Porthtowan. He had Amy under surveillance twenty-four-seven, but even predators like Manning need a break sometime. As he approached the carpark he flashed his headlights at a VW campervan parked close to the row of apartments that Amy lived in. The campervan flashed back and pulled out from its spot. Manning met the van halfway across the carpark and dropped his window.

"Anything Clive?"

Clive filled the cabin of the campervan. He wasn't just big. He was huge. He was chewing something when he also dropped his window. He finished up chewing whatever it was, swallowed it and then wiped his mouth on his sleeve. Manning couldn't fail to notice that whatever it was had garlic in it.

"She went to Tesco in Redruth, bought a pizza, some frozen fries, big two litre bottle of Diet Pepsi and some women's things. She got petrol on the way back and she's been home ever since. That was just after six, boss. Since then, nobody's come and nobody's gone."

"You sure you didn't rob her of her pizza? You stink of garlic?"

"Nah…could be the kebab I just had. Or maybe that Indian from earlier on, boss." Clive said as he checked his mouth in the rear view mirror, wetting his thumb and wiping it over his lips.

"Women's things?" Manning threw Clive a puzzled look.

"Eh?"

"You said she bought a whole lot of stuff to eat and some women's things?"

Clive pulled his face in embarrassment. "You know…what you call'em things? Sanction pads. That's it."

Manning shook his head in disbelief. "How old are you now, Clive?"

"What? Me? Em, fifty three next birthday. How's that?"

"Do you know what sanction means?" Manning asked, but he wasn't expecting a sensible answer. Clive just shrugged.

"It's like an agreement. An allowance…" Clive's face still looked blank. "Like a go ahead, Clive. A green light, you know. In other words you couldn't be more wrong. You couldn't get a light more red that a friggin' *sanitary* pad."

"Hmm. Good one, boss." Clive did a little chuckle, but Manning still wasn't convinced that Clive understood the meaning. "Can I get off now boss? My Mum will have my dinner in the oven."

Manning scratched his head. "Dinner? You know what time it is, Clive?"

"Oh, I know boss. But my Mum always leaves my dinner in the oven for when I get in. I wouldn't dare leave it. She'd be upset." Clive's face was deadly serious.

"I'll call you in a few hours, Clive. You go home and enjoy your dinner. And have a nap." Manning said as he pushed the button to raise his window.

Clive drove off and Manning parked up in the same space that Clive had just vacated. He checked his watch. 11:17pm. It was going to be a long night. He raked his seat back and reclined it as far as it would go. With his feet up on the dash and a blanket pulled over him he settled in for the night.

Amy was in bed, but she wasn't asleep. She hadn't slept well since she first set eyes on Manning. Now her friend, maybe her only friend Thrash had been kidnapped as well as that other young guy that had tried to help her, Darren. In her mind, pandemonium reigned. She was in big trouble and she knew she wasn't going to fake her way out of it this time.

She got up and pulled her jeans on. It was so cold in her apartment that they felt damp. It was a rented apartment and the heating consisted of one two kilowatt fan heater. She stuck her feet into her slippers and went down the stairs to her sit on one of her settees, the one that faced the open staircase. She pulled the heater close and switched it on. Her chest felt constricted. Tight. The cold just made her worse as she huddled in front of the inadequate heater.

It was Tuesday night. Almost Wednesday. In approximately eighteen hours Manning would be knocking on her door, or ringing her phone or texting. Two men's lives hung in the balance and her only hope of raising the fifty grand had not returned her email. She'd stayed late at school and checked her emails every break-time. The last time she checked was just before five. She had no reason to stay late, so when the head teacher had walked in and asked what she was doing, she had told her some story about research into dyslexia. She could tell her head teacher didn't buy it, especially since she had her email account up on the screen when she had walked in. Tomorrow, she knew she would be watched. But then she had no other option. She couldn't go back to the Internet café in town, because she was certain that Manning was watching her. The first time she noticed was at school on Monday. When she first saw the big guy in the campervan outside the school, she suspected he was a paedophile. When she saw the same man parked outside her apartment block, she knew that he worked for Manning. The same campervan with the same sumo size stalker inside it had been there tonight. She was trapped.

Amy opened her back door and slipped out onto the path, making sure she stayed behind the recess. One peek was all she needed to confirm that she was still being watched. As soon as the PIR light popped on she rushed back in, locked her door and returned to the settee. The fat guy in the campervan had gone, but Manning was back. Even if she had the guts to jump from her balcony at the front and escape that way, she had no idea where she would go. There was no one to run to for help. Time was running out.

Manning was beginning to drift into a dream state. A light came on in front of him. One of the PIR lights along the back of the apartments had sensed something. Or someone. He sat up and stared along the path that led to each of the apartments, waiting for a figure to appear. For a full sixty seconds Manning stared unblinking. The light went off. Manning started the van quickly and flashed the lights on full beam. Still nothing.

"Damn whore!" He cursed. Maybe she had slipped out before he noticed the light come on. Or maybe she was hiding in the recess of her doorway waiting for him to get tired of watching and switch his lights off again. He wasn't going to take the chance. He got out into the cold, stood still and listened. Nothing to hear, but the wind whistling through the telephone wires above him.

"Jesus!" He cursed again under his breath. As quietly as he could he walked slowly along the path towards Amy's back door. His headlights sent his shadow thirty feet ahead of him. If she was hiding in the recess, she certainly wasn't going to be unprepared. Manning pulled his knife out of his inside pocket and opened the blade. He held it at his side out of view, but at the ready. When he got to the door before Amy's, he deviated right off the path and up onto the hillside so he would be out of striking distance if she was hiding. She wasn't. There wasn't a single light on in her apartment. She was probably in bed, fast asleep. Paranoia; the curse of the stalker.

When Manning got back in his van, it was like entering a mini-oven. In the five minutes he'd been out, the van's heater had been running on max. He appreciated it now. He switched the lights off again, but left the heater and engine running. With his feet planted on top of the dash again, he settled in once more for the long haul.

At three in the morning, Manning decided he'd had enough. He was tired. He was hungry. And he was cold. He pulled out his mobile and rang Clive. Clive answered on the fifth ring.

"Yeah, boss?" He sounded groggy.

"Get back here would you, Clive? I need to go meet Danker. The boat's due in another hour or so and I need something to eat before I go down there."

"Okay, boss. You want me to bring some of Mum's pie? She just baked it today."

Manning had eaten Clive's Mum's pie before. It was good. "I'd like that, Clive. Don't be long."

Clive was parked up next to Manning ten minutes later. He only lived four miles away. He dropped his passenger window and passed two pieces of his Mum's pie wrapped in tin foil over to Manning.

"Thank your Mum for me, Clive. What kind?"

"Steak and onion, boss." He said sleepily.

Manning nodded his approval. "Either me or Danker will be back about six or seven. Ring me if she moves one inch."

"Yes boss. See you later, boss."

Manning left Clive in the carpark and followed the coastal road up to St. Agnes. There was nothing on the roads at that time of the morning and he didn't spot a single light in any houses on the way. About five miles up the Newquay road he took a left and let the van coast down towards St. Agnes. Bypassing the village centre, he turned off right down to the waterfront and switched the engine off. No sign of Danker. He checked his watch. 3:32. More waiting.

Just before four am, as Manning was finishing his pie, Danker pulled up beside him in the small carpark that overlooks the sea. Manning hadn't even heard the van pull up. Danker had switched his engine off before he entered the residential area. Most of the owners of the homes on the seafront would be in their main residences in Bristol or London or wherever. Not many used their holiday homes in the winter, but there were a few local people who still lived close to the seafront and most of them were elderly. Danker was well aware that older people tended to sleep lighter, get up earlier and look out of their windows more than younger people who worked and needed their sleep more.

"Got any of Clive's pie left?" Danker asked as he climbed in next to Manning, closing the door as quietly as he could.

"I don't remember you offering to share that little tart from The Ship earlier tonight." Manning snapped back.

Danker was quick to rise. "Jesus, Isaac! She was eighteen years old…how old are you now? Sixty? Get over it, you jealous old git!"

"I'm only forty nine, you cheeky bastard!" Manning raised his voice and then glanced out of the van's windows as though he might see someone who had been alerted by his raised voice.

Danker sniggered to himself. "I love winding you up, Isaac."

The men waited together in Manning's van. The only words spoken were occasional moans about how cold it was and how hungry Danker was. The only other sound was the constant wash of the waves on the small pebble beach in front of them.

At 4:27am by Manning's watch, they spotted the small flashing red light that they had been waiting for. It was about a quarter mile out and just visible in the early morning mist.

"How long does it normally take to get to the jetty?" Manning asked Danker. He was talking about the boat he was yet to see.

"Depends on the conditions, but I'd say no more than ten…fifteen minutes." Danker had been smuggling people in for three years now, but he'd only been using St Agnes the last three times. It was always a good, safe policy to keep changing the location so that nobody got suspicious.

"How long will they have been at sea?"

Danker did a little shrug and pulled his face. "Fuck do I know, Isaac. I see their photos on the Internet. Pick the ones I want and pay the man the money. How they get here…I couldn't give a shit…as long as they don't die on route and they look more or less how they looked in their photos."

"Well, excuse me for being a bit nervous…you little shit! I know we've done business before, Danker. But I've always used British girls."

Danker opened the van's door. "Come on Isaac, let's get down there…and you'll soon see why you'll never use an English lass again."

Chapter Fifteen

Katerina woke early. Her one large suitcase had been packed for three days, ever since she had accepted Dan's offer to visit him in England. She wished she could take more clothes, but there was a limit to what a girl of her small stature could carry. She washed and dressed quickly, then checked herself in the mirror. She'd had her hair trimmed earlier that week, but it was still halfway down her back and the light above her mirror picked out the autumnal tones in her thick brown mane. Without make up she could see dark circles under her eyes, but she would fix that after breakfast and add her favourite green eye shadow to bring out the green in her eyes.

She padded through barefooted to her kitchen and switched on the kettle, filled a bowl half full of milk and bunged it in the microwave for two minutes. Then she jumped about three miles up in the air as she felt someone touch her shoulder from behind.

"Eto – tol'ko ya!" Anya said, jumping back herself. "It's just me!"

"I forgot you stayed Anya. You scared me."

"I noticed."

The girls ate a breakfast of kasha, a type of porridge, and pancakes washed down with hot tea.

"So you go today?" Anya said, but it was rhetorical and she didn't sound happy about it.

Katerina nodded and continued eating her pancakes.

"And what of your friends. Natasha from Odessa. Svetlana and her sister you have known since school. And Tatiana and Mariana from the office in Nikolaev."

Katerina didn't look up from her bowl.

"You have not see Alina from Odessa in six months. Have you told her you are going? You used to be best friends."

"Net" Katerina looked up and met Anya's eyes. "She was never my best friend. You were always my best friend, Anya."

"Yes Katerina. But you are leaving me."

"Net. No. It is just a vacation."

Anya corrected her. "The Americans say vacation. Come on, Kat. Get it right. The word is holiday. You are going on holiday."

Katerina grabbed her friend's hand and squeezed it. "You see, Anya. You are getting better than me. Maybe you should come?"

"You forget, Kat. My life is here. My boyfriend, Ivan. My mother who relies on me to get her shopping. My uncle at the shop could not manage without me."

"It's just a holiday, Anya. I will be back in two short weeks." Katerina tried to reassure her.

"Maybe…Or maybe you will fall in love and forget to come home."

Katerina dared her. "So come!"

Anya wolfed her breakfast down, dashed back to her apartment and was back at Katerina's within twenty five minutes. She had changed. She had a rucksack on her back and a hold all in her hand. She was grinning from ear to ear.

"Have you told your mother?" Katerina quizzed.

"I ring my sister…she can run errands for a change."

"And what about Ivan?" Katerina was glad her friend was coming, but surprised that she would leave Ivan alone for two weeks. He had been known to have a wandering eye in the past.

Anya pulled her face. "Ivan? What about him?"

The girls heaved their luggage to the end of her road where Katerina's friend's father picked them up in his lorry. Pavel was a small, round man with a shining bald head and a grey moustache that covered the whole of his top lip. He'd lived just outside Odessa all of his life, but he spoke very good English and his French was just as impressive. His job driving an HGV, delivering grain and rapeseed to all over Europe meant that he had to communicate with other drivers, customs officials, freight handlers and the like. French and English were the most commonly spoken languages, so he had learned them well. The girls practised their English on him. They enjoyed his company as they travelled mile upon mile through the Ukraine, Poland, the Czech Republic, Germany and finally France.

When they eventually pulled up in the small port of Montoir, they were sad to leave him. They had shared many stories in their epic thirty eight hour journey together. But they had his mobile number and they would ring him in two weeks when they would travel back home together. Now, it was time for Katerina to meet Dan at La Plage de Port Meleu, a few miles down the coast where she would begin her romantic ocean journey to Cornwall, England, even if now she would have Anya by her side as chaperone.

A taxi dropped them in Prefailles, a small village close to the coast a few miles south of Saint-Nazaire. Dan had said to walk down to the beach, the one called La Plage de Port Meleu, where he would meet Katerina about seven in the evening. In her head, she had imagined meeting him on the sand; his beautiful yacht anchored a little way offshore with a gorgeous sunset beyond. But now she was here, the reality couldn't be more different.

It was black dark and the wind coming off the Atlantic was blowing bitterly cold. Not that the girls could see the ocean. There were very few streetlights near the beach. There were no houses, no buildings, no cars and no people. They felt vulnerable. They decided they wouldn't go any further than the last streetlight. Katerina stood her suitcase up on its end and sat on it. She was hungry and she was cold and she was beginning to worry that maybe Dan wasn't going to turn up. Maybe this had been a bad idea. Maybe she should have gotten to know him more before travelling nearly two thousand miles across Europe to meet him in the dark on a deserted beach.

"Katerina." A voice called out from the beach. Katerina stood and stared into the darkness. Anya stood by her side, anxious.

"Quick. We have to go before the tide goes out." The voice called out again. It was an English voice, young, manly and friendly. Katerina grabbed the handle on top of her suitcase and pulled it down the path until the tarmac turned to sand. Anya followed reluctantly.

"Dan? Is that you? Where are you?"

Chapter Sixteen

We were heading along the A30, the main road through Devon. It was just after five according to the clock on the dash of the X Trail and by my reckoning we were going to be there before six. I slowed to seventy just in case there were any police tucked away in a lay-by or an opening to a field.

"Wadebridge." AK broke the silence. He was referring to sign for the next turn off. It was the first thing he'd said in two hours.

"Yeah. Padstow's that way too. Lovely little harbour town with over priced restaurants."

AK nodded and shut his eyes again. About twenty minutes later I saw the sign for St. Agnes. Porthtowan is just a few miles further down the coast. I turned off.

"We there yet?" AK opened his eyes again.

"Not far now."

"Breakfast time, I reckon." AK announced and then reached back behind him and pulled something from his pack. Tino got up and put its paws on the back of my seat. I could feel its breath on my neck.

"You might want to feed Tino first, before he takes a fancy to my head." I wasn't joking. I was pretty sure my head would fit in the dog's mouth.

AK chuckled, but ignored what I'd said.

"Banana?" AK pointed a banana at my face like it was a weapon. I shook my head and focused on the road ahead. In a little while we were entering the village of St. Agnes. I made a right turn and headed down a hill. I wasn't sure about where I was heading, but it felt right. Except it wasn't.

"That sign back there said *No through road.*"

"What sign?"

"Never mind. Just turn back around when we get to the bottom of this hill."

I followed the road down and we came to more houses. There were several wooden houses, detached, painted in seaside colours no doubt, except it was almost five in the morning and the sun wouldn't rise for another two and half hours, so any appreciation of colour was lost. The road ended with a low wall that might have stopped me driving into the ocean had my brakes failed. There was a small pay and display carpark on my left with two vans parked side by side and I could see several bungalows beyond. I stopped the X-Trail and turned the engine off. I was tired and my back ached. And my neck. And my head. My heart wasn't fairing so well either.

"Is this it?" AK sat up in his seat.

I breathed in deep, filling my lungs to capacity, then letting the air out slow between pursed lips.

"What the hell am I doing?" I wasn't asking AK. I was just venting my feelings.

AK got out and walked to the wall in front of us. I watched him as his image moved in and out before me. My eyes were playing tricks. Driving four hundred and eighty miles in little over seven hours, in the dark, when you're tired before you even begin and when you're stressed and scared of what you might find will do that to you. I was still moving. I was sat absolutely still, slumped in my seat and yet I could feel my body moving through space. I needed to lie down. I needed sleep.

Suddenly, I jumped out of my trance. AK was rapping his knuckles on my window. I dropped it quickly.

"What's the matter?"

AK looked behind him and then back at me. "Is this the place? Is this where she's living?"

I shook my head. "No…we're not there yet. It's a dead end like you said. Porthtowan's about another four miles away."

He looked back again. I tried to focus my eyes in the darkness, but I had no idea what he was looking at.

He turned back to me again. "Do you think fishermen land their catch in the dark?"

I was too tired to answer trivial questions about the practises of Cornish fishermen. "Get in."

"How many women do you think go fishing at night?" He was asking silly questions again and I wasn't in the mood. I blew out a heavy breath. "AK, get in."

He ignored me and walked through the gap in the wall and I watched as he disappeared into the darkness. I thought maybe he was going for a pee. I sat for a few minutes and let myself drift. I wanted sleep. I needed sleep.

"Hawkeye!" AK's voice brought me back from my coma like state. He'd jumped in the back and was closing his door quietly behind him.

"What the..."

AK jumped over his dog and put his hand over my mouth.

"Shh...climb over quickly and lock the doors."

The look on his face told me he was serious. I jumped between the front seats and got in the back with him. The Akita was breathing on my face. Foul.

"You need to teach Tino to clean his teeth...he's got dog's breath!"

AK gave me that look that just said *shut up*. Some people just don't share my sense of humour.

"What's going on?" I whispered.

AK said. "You can't see through these back windows in the dark, can you?"

"You can't see through them in daylight. Not from the outside. Privacy glass. How's that?"

"Keep down and keep quiet. I don't like what I saw down there."

I got as comfortable as a person could kneeling on the floor of a four wheeled drive with a vicious dog breathing in his face. I was staring outside for something to happen, but nothing did. I looked at my watch. Five minutes had passed.

"How long's it been, AK?" I said quietly.

"I dunno...five minutes."

"No...I mean since Claire passed."

AK shuffled off his knees and sat on his bottom instead. I did the same and tried to put some distance between me and the Akita. Maybe two minutes passed and I'd almost given up on him answering.

"It feels like yesterday."

I don't know what I expected him to say, but his words kind of surprised me. "That raw?"

"That raw."

"You think you could ever love another...I mean what are you now? Forty?"

He blew an exasperated breath. "What's this about, Hawkeye?"

"I'm confused. I have the love of a gorgeous girl who is mad about me…"

"Jade?"

"Yeah, Jade."

"Then you're a lucky man. Hold on to her."

That wasn't what I expected him to say either.

"So why have I come here? "

"Because two young guys might die otherwise?"

I knew that, of course. But that wasn't what I meant.

Suddenly, AK tapped my shoulder and pointed through the tinted glass. I don't know what I expected to see, but it sure wasn't anything close to the sight in front of me. There were three, four, five gorgeous looking girls walking towards us. No, there were six. I hadn't seen the blonde one at the back. A tall, wiry man, maybe late fifties was walking to their right and a good looking, blonde guy in his late twenties to their left. Some of the girls were staggering like they'd been drinking. The older, wiry guy stopped and looked at the X-Trail. Instinctively, we both ducked to the floor even though I knew he couldn't see us.

"Danker…where'd this come from?" He said to the younger guy, pointing at my car. The other guy opened the backdoors of one of the van's parked next to us and ushered the girls in. I could see their faces clearly. Pretty. Very pretty. But they looked tired and somewhat dejected. It made me feel uneasy.

"Fuck do I know, Isaac. Just get in here quick, before someone comes."

The older man was just about to put his head to the glass of my front windows when one of the girls made a break for it. The sudden commotion alerted the dog and it jumped up at the window, knocking me sideways.

AK said. "Tino. Down." The dog dropped down to the floor again.

We watched as the petite, young woman ran from the van back down towards the ocean, her long dark hair blowing wildly in the wind. The wiry guy next to the car ran after her, but the other one shut the doors at the back of the van and got in the driver's seat. I could see him tapping his fingers on the steering wheel impatiently.

"You thinking what I'm thinking, AK?"

AK said. "Any of those girls look like your Amber?"

Amber was blonde. Her curls danced as she walked. She was unmistakable. No girl looked like my Amber. I shook my head.

I said. "These guys aren't fishermen are they?"

AK said. "If that's what fishermen catch these days, then I need to change career."

I said. "We should do something." I meant it. Adrenalin was flooding my body now and I couldn't sit still. AK put his hand on my shoulder.

"Not now....Wait!"

We waited, but I wasn't happy. I needed to do something. "AK?"

"Shh! Wait."

I looked at the guy in the van. He was still tapping his fingers on the steering wheel. Who were those girls in the back? Why had one of them run away?

"We could take that van now. He's alone."

AK said. "This is nothing to do with us. For all we know those girls could be pros that were hired to service a ship full of sailors."

I shuffled around and looked at him. "You think?"

Just then the wiry, older guy came back. He was breathing hard. He spat as he passed us. He was alone. He flung open the driver's door of the van his mate was sitting in. There were words spoken, but I couldn't make them out. I tapped AK on the shoulder. He looked at me and shrugged his shoulders. Neither of us had heard a word they'd spoken. The younger guy got out and they both went back down the path into the darkness.

I asked AK. "What's down there?"

"A small jetty. There was a boat...looked like a fishing boat to me."

I got up off my behind and opened the back door.

AK called. "Where do think you're going?"

I ignored him. I got out and rushed around to the back of the van closest to us. The lock had been replaced with a hasp, the type you would use on a shed. There was a padlock stuck through it, but it wasn't pushed closed. I opened it and opened the hasp. Then I opened the doors.

"You've done it now, Brendon." AK said as he stood behind me. All five girls stared out at us, their faces full of terror. I turned around and realized why. AK had Tino by his side. That dog had a permanent angry expression on it's face. I held my hand out towards the girls.

"Are you here by your own choice?"

No answer, just blank stares.

"Where are you from?"

AK grabbed my shoulder and pulled me back. "Brendon…we haven't got time for this. If those guys come back they might be armed."

"Last chance girls…do you want to come with us and go wherever you like. Or do you want to stay in this van?" Still nothing.

I turned to AK and shrugged.

"Come on Brendon…let's go find your girl."

I was just about to close the van's doors again when one of the girls jumped up towards me. "Wait!"

She climbed out of the van and stood in front of me. She was tall with almost black hair and her eyes were amazing, even in the dim glow of the street light.

"Where're you from?"

"My name is Anya. I am from the Ukraine."

I looked past her into the van. "Anyone else not happy with their situation?"

Anya turned around and said something in Russian to the other girls in the van. Almost immediately they all got up off the floor and joined us outside.

"Good one, Hawkeye. Now what's your plan? You came here looking for one girl and you leave with five." AK said sounding amused with the situation. I turned around, opened the back of the X-Trail and ushered them all in. They didn't hesitate, which surprised me actually. For all they knew, AK and I could have been worse than the other two guys.

I jumped back in the driver's seat and AK got in the front again, but this time he raked his seat all the way back to squeeze the Akita in the footwell. I looked at him with the dog's big head between his legs and then looked in the back at the five girls sitting all over our gear. I had to shake my head.

I looked at AK. "Tell me what I'm doing here, will you?"

"I'm pretty sure we're doing the right thing."

I nodded.

"You might wanna leave now though." AK inclined his head forward with his eyes wide in surprise. I looked out of the windscreen and the young, blonde guy was running towards us with the older guy bringing up the rear.

"Shit!" I started the motor and in reverse gear, letting the clutch immediately, we darted back out into the centre of the road. The blonde guy ran at my bonnet just as I sped forward again. Either my left wing hit his left hip or his left hip hit my left wing. Hard to say really, we were both moving forward at the same time. But I've no doubt his left hip suffered more than my left wing.

"Oops!"

AK turned to me as I gunned the X-Trail back up the lane the way we came. "Oops. That all you can say? Oops?"

"Maybe I should go back see how he is…eh?"

AK chuckled. So did I. None of the girls chuckled, but then nobody seemed upset either.

"Are you police?" The girl calling herself Anya asked from behind me.

"No. We're just a couple of guys that happened across the van you were in. Do you work for those two?"

"Work? Net. I don't know these girls here, but the one who ran is my friend Katerina. I came with her for a holiday. She came to meeting her boyfriend from the Internet. I don't think this was meant to be."

I turned to AK just as he turned to me and he gave me a look that told me he was thinking the same as I.

"What was the Internet site called?"

The girl said something in Russian to the other girls then answered me in English. "I did not see it. I don't own a computer. But they say it is called Club Nadia."

"You heard of that?" I asked AK.

"Club Nadia, Club Natasha, Single Baltic Bride, Russian Brides 2B…There must be at least a dozen of those sites."

I wondered if he'd been looking at those sites for himself. I didn't think it was a good time to ask.

"I'm going to look for someone we came here to seek. I can drop you girls anywhere you like." Regular taxi driver that I was.

Anya spoke up again. I loved her accent. "We have to go back for Katerina."

I was halfway to Porthtowan. I didn't like the thought of facing those two guys after we had taken something they had just imported. "We will…but it's not safe now. Later."

I caught a glance from AK again. He had his eyebrows raised and a cynical grin on his face. I ignored him and focused on the road. There were no streetlights. It was narrow, twisty and I was totally unfamiliar with this route. Something flashed in my rear view mirror. AK saw it too. He turned around and signalled for the girls to duck down.

"We've got company."

"Hmm."

I tried to speed up, but the road was twisting without warning and the girls in the back were making the type of noises that made me think that maybe they were starting to doubt my ability to keep us on the road. And maybe they were right to.

Chapter Seventeen

Amy couldn't settle. She was pacing the floor all the way through from her back door to the French doors that opened onto the balcony. Back and forth. Back and forth. Her mind was analysing everything that had happened. Manning turning up - in Porthtowan of all places. His threats to expose her past to Brendon and ruin his career. Thrash being taken. This guy Darren offering to help her out and then being taken himself. The photographs of Brendon in bed with Jade, her best friend. Manning guarding her house and that fat guy following her into town. The email she had sent to Brendon begging him to help. The thoughts had been racing around in her head without any purpose, just winding her nerves up tighter and tighter. She was marching now, faster and faster, lap after lap of her apartment, back and forth and back and forth. Her mind was all over the place. She was heading for the French doors again, walking at a hell of a pace. If she didn't slow down, she was in real danger of ploughing straight through the glass.

She stopped dead at the doors. She opened them and stepped out on to her balcony. Her brain stopped its chaotic ride through the events of the last few days and one thought remained in her current consciousness. It just hung there on its own. Her email to Brendon.

She had had to use email, because there was no other way of contacting him. She knew he had changed his phone numbers, because she had tried to ring him a year earlier just to hear his voice and both numbers were no longer in use. She read on his Internet blog at the time that he had been hounded by the press so was forced to change his telephone numbers. Shortly after that his blog also ceased. It was like he had severed all contact with the outside world. She had emailed Brendon, begging him to help her, but who was to say he had even read the email. Who was to say that he wasn't off somewhere working abroad, filming some new adventure? Who was to say he still used the email account she had sent her message to? It was likely he had changed that too. It had been two years. Maybe she was waiting in vain.

Before she had a chance to change her mind, she climbed over the rail and let herself drop into the darkness below. The ground pushed her knees up hard and she folded as she hit the dirt. Ten feet doesn't sound like a long way to fall, but when you're only five feet three and weigh no more than eight stone, it hurts. Amy lay stunned for a few seconds and then she brushed herself off and made her way along past the shops that were situated under each apartment's balcony. There were no lights to illuminate the path, but then she didn't need them. She knew exactly where she was going. When she got to the end of the block, she stopped and glimpsed around the corner. The van was still parked in its spot, but Manning was gone and the fat guy was back. He looked like he was messing with his phone, either texting or playing a game. Either way he wasn't doing his job properly. Amy skirted wide around the dunes to the far side of the carpark and jumped in her car. The little Clio burst into life on the first turn of the key. She floored it out of the village and headed north. She had thought long and hard about this and even though she wasn't sure she was doing the right thing and she felt horribly guilty for leaving Thrash in the hands of Manning, she was fleeing.

Tears were running down her cheeks. Snot was running over her top lip. "Oh God!....Oh God! I'm so sorry Brendon...I'm so sorry..." If Brendon wasn't coming to her, then she was going to have to go to him. It was five in the morning. She knew she could make it back up north to Durham by noon. That would give her six hours before Manning's deadline. She didn't know whether she was doing the right thing or not, but she couldn't stand sitting in that apartment a moment longer. She had to take action.

"Floor it you useless fucker! This is your doing." Manning thumped the dash as Danker sped up the hill away from the seafront.

"Isaac...*you* could have stopped the little whore if you'd been a bit quicker on your feet."

"You were supposed to drug them...so they couldn't run away. You were supposed to put them in the van and lock it....You were supposed..."

"Ah, go fuck yourself, Isaac! Derek told me they'd all had a dose of sleeping pills when he got them aboard in Saint-Nazaire. That's what happens every time we do this and we've never had any runaways before. Anyway, you heard the splash. The little whore more than likely has her lungs full of water now …Fish food she is…I guarantee it."

Manning took out a cigarette and lit it. He blew out a heavy breath of smoke that filled the van's cab. "One whore lost I can live with…but if we don't get those other five back …I swear to God, Danker, you'll pay me back twice what I paid you…Got it?"

Danker chewed on his bottom lip and kept his foot on the accelerator. He didn't like been talked to like that and he didn't like losing business either.

We were less than a mile from Porthtowan now, bombing down a little lane at silly speeds with a car full of foreign ladies. It was surreal. Crazy. How the hell did I end up here? We were just about to meet the main road. The headlights from the van behind us were filling my rear view mirror. I raised my left hand to flip the mirror, dipped the clutch and handbraked it around the junction into the main road. I changed down into second as we were sliding sideways. Then just as I floored it on the smooth tarmac of the main road, my whole vision starred with blindingly bright light. There was a car coming straight at us.

The next few seconds are something I'll never recall. They're lost forever. Whatever was heading for us went around us by going up on the verge, virtually on two wheels. I remember closing my eyes and then opening them when the anticipated crash didn't happen, breathing out a heavy sigh of relief. Only that feeling of relief was the most short-lived feeling of relief ever. The anticipated crash was replaced with a bigger, louder, more violent, unanticipated crash about two seconds later when I lost all control and we veered violently left through a five bar gate. Pieces of four by two splintered everywhere as we slid sideways across a field full of sheep.

The Akita was first out of the car. The crash had spooked it. Then AK. I saw two of him pulling two of the girls out of the back. Twins. No matter how much I blinked and tried to clear the double vision I was still seeing twin AKs. And twin Russian ladies. Then I saw more sets of twins, running. Lots of Russian ladies running into the darkness. Where were they running? Then I heard a loud crash behind me on the road. I couldn't see what had happened. Too dark. When I turned to look at the girls running again, they'd disappeared and I was left staring into blackness.

Danker was right on the X-Trail's tail. He could actually see the girls' heads bobbing about in the back of the car as it bounced along the country lane at speeds approaching sixty miles an hour. Suddenly, he realized they were hitting the main road as the car in front slid sideways out at the junction.

"Watch out!" Manning screamed.

"Fuck! Isaac…you wanna drive this piece of shit?" Danker said as he managed to avoid hitting the back of the car in front.

"Jesus!" Manning grabbed the wheel as a small car scraped past the car in front, climbing up the verge and spreading a whole load of dirt onto the van's windscreen. "Who the fu…"

Just as Manning and Danker were reeling from one near miss, another set of headlights filled their vision. How it missed the X-Trail in front was nothing short of miraculous. Danker was wide eyed at the scene in front of him, slamming his foot on the brake and swerving the van to the right. Unfortunately, the driver heading for them swerved in the exact same direction and hit them virtually head on.

Manning screamed like a girl as a plank of wood crashed through the windscreen, piercing Danker's left shoulder. As the sharp, splintered piece of the five bar gate cut through his brachial artery, a wide plume of liquid filled the void between the two men and then Manning felt the warm wetness hit his face and he tasted the hot metallic flavour of Danker's lifeblood. As the van came to a halt, he looked down at what resembled a thousand diamonds set in wet gloss paint all down his torso. He wiped the sticky liquid from his eyes and tried to comprehend what had just happened, but although he could hear himself breathing and therefore believe that he had survived, he couldn't put it together why more and more waves of gloss paint were washing the diamonds down his belly, puddling in his crotch.

"Danker? Danker?" Manning cried out, but Danker's face was blank, pale and growing paler as his body leaked more and more blood. Manning realized the diamonds set in the gloss paint were pieces of his van's windscreen swimming in Danker's blood.

"You useless shit…Don't die on me now!" He snapped at Danker as he shook his limp body.

Suddenly a flash of movement caught Manning's eye and when he turned he saw two girls run out of the field in front of him. They looked scared and confused. Lost. Manning unbuckled his seatbelt to get out of the van.

"I don't feel so good." Danker uttered the understatement of the century. Manning had his door open, ready to leave. He didn't want to lose the girls. Danker grabbed his arm and pulled him back.

"Help me Isaac…I'm bleeding…I feel…"

Manning undid the leather belt from his trousers, pulled it free and looped it under Danker's armpit, over his shoulder, through the buckle and then pulled it tight. Danker made some girly noises. Manning pulled a bit more and the bleeding subsided. Maybe it even stopped; Danker didn't comment. People generally don't after they've passed out.

Manning got out of the wrecked van and went to investigate where the girls had gone. He had seen them cross the road, jump the low fence at the other side and now there wasn't a sign of them. His knee hurt. It must have hit the dash in the collision. There was no way he was going to run across fields in the dark looking for a bunch of Russian girls in the state he was feeling. He blew out a long, heavy sigh and shook his head and then turned his attention back to his vehicle. The nearside headlamp was broken and so was the indicator. The bonnet was bent up a little and the bumper was hanging loose and the windscreen was smashed on the passenger side where the post had smashed through and injured Danker. But overall, Manning was surprised there wasn't more damage.

He pulled the front bumper free and threw it on the verge and then walked over to see what had happened to the vehicle that had collided with them. To say he was upset when he discovered it was Clive driving the other van wouldn't quite cut it. The van was lying on its side in the dyke. Every window had imploded and the back doors had broken loose so that one of the doors lay flat against the earth. Clive was lying limp with his head down towards the ground where the passenger side door was. Manning dipped his head and entered the van from the back doors. When he saw Clive he raised his foot and kicked him so hard, there was a good chance he broke a rib or two. Clive didn't say a word. Dead men don't feel pain.

"You useless lump of lard! I oughta resuscitate your fuckin' fat arse just so I can kill you again " Manning wasted insults on Clive.

"Friggin' fantastic! I don't need this shit!"

Manning dropped Clive's seat back as far as it would drop and then with a torrent of expletives and some serious sweating, he managed to haul Clive's huge carcass into the back. Clive slid easily along the metal side panel that was flat against the earth, but he was not so easy to slide along the grass and the tarmac. By the time Manning had dragged Clive's body to his own wrecked van Danker was conscious.

"You gonna help me or what?" Manning said to Danker, but Danker sat motionless. His breathing sounding laboured. Manning managed to pull Clive's body into the back of the van and then he went to investigate the vehicle they'd been chasing.

"Hold tight while I go see if we've got any merchandise left. This is the last time I'm bringing in whores through Cornwall!"

I was still sitting in the X Trail. It was too dark to see anything; just a weak beam was shining from a stationary vehicle's headlights on the road. I turned around to see how the girls in the back were doing and realized I was sitting in the car alone. I got out and as my eyes adjusted to the dark I spotted AK sitting on the grass with the girl called Anya.

"You alright?" AK looked up at me with a bent cigarette in his mouth.

"Never better. Where have all the girls gone?"

"I think they changed their mind about us. They've run off."

He didn't sound particularly worried about that, but I noticed he was wrapping some material around Anya's shin. Closer inspection revealed a piece of his shirt was missing from his sleeve. What a hero!

I said. "Shouldn't we go find them? They might be hurt."

Anya looked up at me. Her eyes drew me in. They were amazing. I looked at AK again and noticed him noticing me noticing Anya. If I wasn't mistaken there was just the tiniest hint of possessiveness in his eyes. I suppose if you're going to save someone, it's always a good idea to make it the pretty one.

She said. "I don't think anyone was hurt. They think you are friends of the one calling himself Dan. They not trust you."

"So why did they get in the car with us?"

She shrugged her shoulders.

I was just about to ask her why she hadn't run off too, when I heard movement behind me. Someone was moving around back on the road. I thought I should go investigate.

"I think we better go see how those guys are."

AK finished dressing Anya's rather shapely leg and stood up in front of me.

"Ah ha…Why?" He said with a cloud of smoke escaping from his mouth as he spoke.

He had a point, I suppose. But I don't think I'm quite as cold as AK. I couldn't think of an answer that would make any difference to AK, so I walked back to the road alone. Why I didn't just get us all back in the car and drive away, I'll never know. I walked across the hard ground back towards the headlights. There were ruts in the earth where we'd skidded across the grass.

"I don't fucking believe it!" A tall, wiry guy with a gun in his hand said as I almost stumbled into him in the dark. Lights from the crashed cars on the road were throwing a weak beam across the field and I could just make out the lined and pockmarked face in front of me. His hair was short, ginger and peppered grey. There was something familiar about him, but I couldn't place where I knew him from. Yet.

I spoke directly to him, but my eyes never left the pistol he was holding in his right hand. "Do I know you?"

He stepped forward and stuck the barrel of the pistol in my chest, hard against my sternum. "Let's just say we have a common interest."

Maybe I had banged my head when we crashed through the gate into that field, but I hadn't worked it out yet. "Come again."

"Adele…Amber…Amy. Call her what you like…we've both been there!"

Cogs turned in my head. Two and two got added together. It probably didn't take more than about one full second, but when the penny dropped something ignited inside me that had never been ignited before. It rushed up from the pit of my stomach and flooded every fibre of my being and in an instant I exploded like a stick of dynamite.

Amy had her foot to the floor. The Clio revved high in third gear as she hit sixty and changed into fourth and then dropped it into top. Just as the road ahead levelled out, she spotted a flood of light coming from a car on the left up ahead. Maybe it would pull out. Maybe not. Amy dropped down in to third gear again, keeping her foot firm on the accelerator. She glanced at the speedo. It was in the seventies and climbing. The lights from the left reached the junction, but they didn't stop. Suddenly, they were in her face.

"Shi…….te!" Amy screamed as she veered right and drove up onto the verge. She missed the other vehicle by a few inches and very nearly lost control, but miraculously she kept on the road. It was a good ten miles later before her heartbeat returned to it's normal rate. But she hadn't slowed down any. By the time she reached the M5 the sun was beginning to light up the sky in front of her. She was glad to be finally heading north with the sun on her right rather than in her face.

By eleven o'clock on Wednesday morning she was heading east again on the A66. She still had more than fifty miles to cover, but already the adrenalin was kicking in. It had been very nearly two years since she had seen Brendon and she was beginning to feel anxious. All of her fears were crowding her head now. How would he react when he saw her? What if he's with Jade? How would she react? Hell! How would she herself react?

Chapter Eighteen

Jade got up Wednesday morning and rang in sick. She wasn't ill, but she was in no fit state for work. The man she had patiently waited for, for two years was finally hers. Or so she had thought. Now everything hung in the balance. She was a mess. She was sat on her bed flicking through an old photograph album when she came across a photo of herself with Brendon and Amber. It had been taken about three years ago on a bright, sunny day. They were standing beside the river below Jade's apartment, all of them smiling from ear to ear. Brendon had a tan. He looked healthy, radiant, gorgeous. Jade touched the photograph, caressing his face with her fingers as though he were here with her.

Then her attention turned to Amber, who was standing with her arm around him. Her hair was golden in the sun. Her eyes were big, bright and beautiful. There was no denying her beauty. Jade had always envied her for her looks. Jade was happy with the way she looked, but although she was fit and slim, her body didn't curve so dramatically the way that Amber's did. Amber had an hour-glass figure and even in this photograph, wearing a faded loose fitting summer dress, Amber still managed to ooze sex appeal. She had been dead two years, but Jade still felt a twinge of jealousy when she looked at the photograph.

She threw the album face down on the bed and stripped out of her pyjamas and got in the shower. She stood directly under the blast of hot water, letting it sting her face as she fought to control her emotions and hold back the tears.

"Bloody Amber…you'd better not come back to haunt me. Brendon's mine now. Mine! All mine!" She said to herself as anxiety spread through her body like a fire spreads through a barn full of hay.

She got out, towelled herself dry and slipped into her sexiest lingerie. Whatever she slipped on over her Victoria's Secret white lace bra and knicker set would only add to the confidence that wearing her favourite lingerie brought. Next she stood in front of her mirror and brushed a coat of foundation over her face. Over and over she dipped her brush into the Arabian Glow bronzing pearls and slowly built up a beautiful glowing tan over her entire face. Then she added subtle browns and autumn shades around her eyes, applied a deep brown liquid eye-liner and plumped out her eyelashes with the darkest mascara in her make up collection. She smiled at the image in front of her.

"Try resisting me now, Brendon." She said to her reflection in the mirror. Finally she painted her lips with a glossy coat of something called smooth mocha and blew herself a kiss in the mirror. Jade was not a natural beauty. She had to work at it. But when she did work at it, she could be stunning. Standing there in her bedroom in the white lace bra and knickers with her body all toned and lightly tanned from her weekly visit to a tanning salon and her face looking fit for a magazine shoot, she looked exactly that. Stunning.

It was cold outside. After all, it was winter. However, Jade decided on a deep, crimson red halter neck dress that cut low at the back, revealed a fair amount of cleavage up front, helped generously by her push-up lace bra, courtesy of her friend 'Victoria" and ended about four inches above her knees. She hadn't knick-named it her 'killer' dress for nothing. She looked a knockout!

Ten minutes later she was speeding along in her MX5 on her way to Burnside. She had a smile on her face, forced of course, but she was keeping it there nonetheless. Her heart was banging in her chest and her emotions were in turmoil, but she was not going to let go of that smile. Was Brendon going to be home? She had no idea. She had rang his mobile maybe thirty times and his land line a dozen times or so too. Straight to voicemail every time. Maybe he was out somewhere paying this Manning off. Maybe he was meeting with the reincarnation of Amber. Or maybe he had come to his senses and accepted that she was never coming back. Jade dared to hope. She had wanted Brendon for a long time and now that she finally had him, she was going to do everything in her power to hold onto him.

As Amy turned right into the small village of Burnside her heart felt like it might jump out of her chest. Breathing was difficult. Her vision blurred. She wanted to turn around and drive away. Fast. And yet part of her also felt some kind of relief. She had been living a lie for almost two years and now she was coming home to face the truth. She pulled over and parked, turned the radio off and sat staring across the fields that surrounded Burnside. Two years had past. Four gigantic new wind turbines stood on the opposite side of the valley towards Durham. Two others were on the eastern horizon. She remembered those. They had been erected when she moved there with Brendon five years earlier. The winter wind turned their blades effortlessly and Amy could hear their rhythmic whoosh, whoosh above the sound of the Clio's idling engine.

The sound took her back a few years. She recalled hearing them as she lay in bed next to Brendon, his breathing keeping pace with their constant whoosh, whoosh after he had just made love to her. Then finally his breathing would lessen and quieten and she would drift off to sleep with the sound of the wind turbines still chopping the air gently, sounding like a mother's heartbeat might to an unborn child. Bliss.

She started the Clio and pulled away from the verge. The road took her through the village centre, but she saw no one. A dog wandered close to the road, some kind of terrier. It stopped and sniffed at a lamppost. Amy coasted past it, down through the village and soon she saw the rooftop of her old home. Her heart banged against her ribs now. She had never felt more nervous in her life. She indicated right and turned in on the gravel drive. The cottage looked the same as she remembered it. The garage doors were closed and there was no car in the drive. Amy parked and got out. Her chest felt so tight she feared she might stop breathing.

"Amber!"

She turned around and caught Brendon's brother ducking between the laurels that bordered the drive. "Matt…I…"

Matt stopped dead in his tracks, his mouth agape. "It is you isn't it?"

Amber took a couple of steps towards him. Her face flushed. She couldn't think what to say. "How are you?"

Matt said. "Like I just saw a ghost."

Amber didn't even try to reply to that. She said. "I'm looking for Brendon?"

Matt stared at her some more, then walked past her and up to the front door of Brendon's cottage. He reached up to a hanging basket and fished a key out of the dried up sphagnum moss that lined the basket. He opened the door and turned to Amber who was still standing in the same spot on the drive.

"He isn't home, but you should come in…after all, it was…em, *is* your home."

Amber walked up to the door and stepped back in time. Matt followed her in and ushered through the hall into the lounge.

"You look amazing." Matt said standing not three feet from her.

Amber stepped back, then turned around and walked through to the conservatory. She looked down the garden and the valley beyond. The view in front of her was the reason why Brendon had decided on that house. Her eyes welled up and the view in front of her blurred.

"Can I ask why you've come back?" Matt said to her back.

Amy didn't turn around. She wiped her eyes and sighed heavily. "It's complicated."

She felt his hand on her shoulder, quickly followed by another on her waist. Then she turned around. "Matt..."

Matt pulled Amber to him and kissed her full on the mouth. He was holding her tight, pulling her to him. She was caught off guard. She stumbled back and fell on the settee.

"Matt! No!..." Amber started to say, her arms outstretched pushing Matt back. But he used his weight to his advantage and fell on top of her, his body pressed firmly to her and again he kissed her passionately.

Jade had never seen a Renault Clio parked at Brendon's place before. It surprised her, but not in a good way. She parked beside it and got out, peering inside it for clues as she walked up to the front door. Just before she got there she stopped and walked back towards the Clio. There was a make up bag on the passenger floor and a pair of sunglasses on the dash top. Ladies' sunglasses. Jade sighed heavily. She didn't like what she was seeing. She didn't like it at all.

She stood at the front door, her finger hovering over the doorbell. A voice in her head stopped her from pressing it. She moved away from the door and walked around the side of the bungalow to the rear. Once she turned the corner she saw a couple embracing in the conservatory. Relief. It wasn't Brendon. It was Matt. Jade looked away a moment. Then it struck her that Matt's wife was a brunette, not a blonde. She took a peek again. They'd disappeared from view. Intrigued, Jade stepped forward keeping low until she was just below the conservatory window.

"Matt! Oh!..." A woman's voice called out. At least it sounded like oh. It might have been no. Jade peeked again. Whoever the blonde was, was now under Matt on the large settee and it all looked very passionate. Jade strained to see the blonde girl's face, but Matt's head was obscuring her view as they rolled around playfully on the settee.

Jade retreated back around the side of the house and headed for her car. She concluded that Matt was having some sort of affair and using Brendon's place for a rendezvous. Jade made no judgments. That was Matt's business, but did he have to use Brendon's place? She walked back around to her car; got in and flipped open her phone. Just as she pressed 'B' for Brendon a loud slam made her look up from her phone. It was Matt. He had slammed the front door shut as he left and was striding fast towards the garden at the side of Brendon's garage. Jade closed her phone and waited to see if the blonde girl followed. She didn't. Then she heard the low, deep rumble of a four stroke engine and moments later Matt came thundering through the trees on Brendon's old quad bike. He blasted past Jade's car without even so much as a sideways glance. Jade grimaced as she heard gravel hitting her paintwork like shrapnel as he revved the engine high. Seconds later he was gone and she was left puzzling about the blonde.

Amber dried her eyes and wandered through to the kitchen. It looked just as she had left it. She opened the fridge door. Beer. Beer, beer and more beer. Not good. She shut it again and made her way through to their bedroom or his bedroom as it was now. She recognized the duvet cover immediately. She had bought it herself from Fenwicks in Newcastle. She sat on the bed on the side Brendon had always slept and stroked his pillow. There was still the indentation from where his head had been. She drew comfort from the fact that the other pillow was fluffed up, untouched. No one had slept there. At least not last night.

The silence was broken by the sound of the front door slamming. Someone had entered. The door had been shut. Amber had definitely heard it shut when Matt had left. So someone had come in, for sure. The silence returned, but this time it weighed heavily on Amber's chest.

Jade stood motionless. The only sound she could hear was the rush of her own blood thundering in her ears. As the adrenalin made its way around her body, she felt the brachial muscles in her arm contract and her fingers tightened their grip around the cold steel of the tyre iron she had taken from beneath her car seat. This was Brendon's home. She wasn't happy about Matt just waltzing in like he owned the place, bringing some mistress here to shag behind his wife's back, no doubt. And then leaving the bitch to wander freely around Brendon's belongings; some strange blonde poking around what potentially could be Jade's home. One day. She moved forward towards the lounge, the tyre iron raised high above her head.

Amber braced herself. She hadn't seen Brendon for almost two years and here she was sitting on his bed, second's away from seeing the love of her life walk through the door. Or maybe it was Matt again. Maybe he'd come back for another bite at the cookie. Maybe this time he wouldn't take no for an answer. Maybe this time she wouldn't be able to fight him off. Amber looked around the room like there might be some escape. Or something she could use to defend herself. She spotted a tall crystal, heavy bottomed vase that stood on the windowsill and reached across the bed to grab it. It had been a wedding present from some TV producer Brendon had worked with. It was maybe a foot tall. The ballooned base had been drawn up to a fluted cylindrical neck that opened out again like a daffodil in spring. She held the neck in her grasp with the heavy base raised ready to strike. It was heavy. Good and heavy, like it could inflict a lot of damage with just one blow.

Jade stopped dead. There was somebody moving in the bedroom. Brendon's bedroom. Why was some blonde bitch in Brendon's bedroom? Forget about moving quietly and sneaking up on this bitch. Who did she think she was snooping around in Brendon's bedroom?

Jade raised her leg and kicked the bedroom door back. It smacked against the pine drawers on the inside wall. Amber screamed with the shock of it. Jade barged in with her tyre iron at the ready. When she spotted the blonde, she saw that she also had a weapon in her hand. No time to think, Jade lashed out with the tyre iron and struck the other woman hard. There was a crack of steel on bone and the blonde dropped like a puppet with its strings cut. She crumpled and hit the floor with a thud. Jade stood over the folded body with the tyre iron still raised. She was trembling. Surplus adrenalin made her limbs buzz and her vision blur. Slowly, she knelt down next to the motionless body, placing her weapon on the floor, releasing it like it had suddenly burned her. As Jade leaned over to see the woman's face her heart stopped beating. Blood rushed to her brain too quickly. Or maybe it drained away. Either way her brain couldn't cope with what her eyes were seeing. Blood had already spilled from the gash to the right of the blonde's head, down her forehead, over her right eye and was dripping from her cheekbone onto the thick rug that covered the bedroom floorboards. But even with blood half covering the woman's face Jade was in no doubt as to who she was. Her best friend. Her lover's wife. Her rival. Amber Hawke.

Chapter Nineteen

My head didn't hurt. Instead, it felt detached. I could hear the familiar thrum of a diesel engine and I could feel it resonating through my whole body. I opened my eyes, but it made no difference. The darkness persisted; at least initially. I rotated the cannonball that was my head and found a glimmer of light. I was having trouble processing the information filtering through my eyes and ears, but gradually I became aware that I was in the back of a van. I started to get my bearings as I realized that the light was obviously coming from the cabin up front. My brain cranked up again and with the pain in my skull came the realization that this wasn't just any van. It was Manning's van. I could remember running at him in the field. He had a gun in his hand. He must have hit me with it I guess.

"What the fuck we gonna do now, Manning?"

Yep. There was the confirmation. And now I knew there were two of them.

"Grab Hawke's bitch, then bury these two in the back."

Two in the back? So I wasn't alone then. AK?

"Grab the bitch and do what?"

"The chance of any money's screwed now. We better finish this and get back up north."

So Amber was right. This was all about money. If they only knew how little I had.

"So we kill Amy too?"

Whoever this other guy was, he wasn't doing anything to win my affections. I waited, but Manning didn't answer. Funny, but that didn't make me relax any about Amber's welfare. I needed to think. And think fast, which isn't easy when you've just regained consciousness from being pistol whipped.

The note from the van's diesel engine changed. Higher. Harsher. Manning's foot had suddenly grown heavier. I reached forward to feel around me. He'd said 'we need to bury these *two* in the back', so clearly I had a companion back here. And I had a horrible feeling it was going to be AK.

The van made a tight turn and I rolled across the floor. Boney knees and steel floors aren't a good combination. I swallowed the pain and rolled with it, expecting to hit the other side. I didn't. I hit something soft instead, like a huge beanbag.

Hell! Slow down Manning…or Clive will end up tipping us over."

Not a beanbag then. I think I just found Clive. I reached out in the gloom and found flesh. Cool flesh. Whoever Clive was, he was a big man. A very big man. And now he was a very big dead man. At least it wasn't AK. That gave me hope. I eased myself back off Clive and shuffled across the floor towards the back of the van and located the doors. The van was tossing me about a fair bit. Either we were on a rough road or Manning's foot was getting heavier. Or both. I initially fancied my chances at opening the back doors, but the thought of hitting tarmac at speed made me think again.

My head started to clear a bit more, like coming out of a thick fog. I needed to think of a plan. And fast. If we were heading to wherever Amber was, then maybe I should wait until they grab her. That way we could tackle them together. Two on two. Better odds.

Then again, if I waited until then it might be too late. They might kill me before they grab Amber. Not so good. Then again, didn't I just hear Manning say something about *burying* those two in the back, as in me and the big guy, Clive? Well, maybe I had it wrong, but people normally don't get buried until *after* they're dead. Well, there was little doubt about the state of my travelling companion. Nobody's flesh feels the way Clive's did when there's warm blood still pumping around inside it. So, I guess they thought they'd killed me too. If the pain in my head was anything to go by, then I couldn't blame them for thinking that way. But they'd be wrong. And that gave me an advantage. My odds were starting to look healthier.

"For fuck's sake Manning, slow down…" I heard the other guy moan. He didn't sound so good. The engine seemed to roar even more. Manning was either deaf or he didn't like being told what to do.

"Manning! I'm fuckin' bleeding out here…you need to stop and see to me."

"Suck it up, Danker…you're young…you'll live!" Manning assured the other guy. I had no idea why the other guy was bleeding or where he was bleeding from, but I'm not ashamed to say that I was sure glad to hear about it.

"Manning?" He sounded pitiful, like he was in pain. A lot of it. Funny, but the more I heard about it the less I thought about my own.

The bleeding guy moaned some more, but it sounded like his batteries were fading. More good news. I'd decided if I was going to make a move then the sooner the better. I had no idea how long we had before we would reach Amber, but I knew we were only maybe four or five miles from Porthtowan when we came off the road, so we had to be close. Of course, I was assuming she was still in Porthtowan. None of this had been confirmed. I'd only guessed that she was staying in that apartment by the beach, the one we had holidayed in with the open stairs and the balcony, because it had looked kind of like that in that gross photo Manning had kindly emailed me. I could have been wrong. And although the guy up front sounded pretty unwell, like he was going to bleed to death, maybe he had nothing worse than a little scratch and he was just the type of person who liked to whinge a lot. And although my head pain had subsided some and I could think straight and I was breathing and all, I hadn't stood up yet. Maybe I wouldn't be able to. Maybe I had some other injury I wasn't aware of yet. Hell, it was so dark in the back of that van I could have lost one of my legs and not known about it. I patted myself down just in case. Okay, so both legs were present and I could feel them. And as I'd used both hands to pat myself down, then ditto for my hands and arms too, but still, there were a lot of unknowns here.

"Danker? Danker?" Manning shouted above the engine. He wasn't doing anything to reduce its volume any.

"Danker, you little shit…Wake up!"

I felt the van swerve. Manning sounded desperate. I guess he had taken his eye off the road a moment.

"Danker?" I rolled towards Clive again.

"Danker?" Every time I had heard Manning's voice, it was always so monotone. Flat. I would never have guessed his range could go up that high.

Finally. "Fuck!"

I'm not a fan of bad language. Rarely use it myself. And when I hear someone shout out the 'F' word the way I had just heard Manning shout it out, I often get the urge to walk over and punch them hard in the face. It offends me. There's so many other ways of releasing the disappointment someone obviously feels when they feel the need to say it. Damn! Hell! Bugger! Shit! They all do the same job, but don't upset my ambience anywhere near as much. In fact, I know a bloke who says 'bugger', or 'bugger me', or 'bugger it' all day long. And I smile every time I hear it. It's part of his charm. But the 'F' word never added anything to anybody's charm. And it certainly never made me smile. That is, until now.

Who would have though that one word, and such an ugly word at that, could be so informative. The guy Manning had been calling Danker hadn't been the type of guy who whinged about a little scratch after all. He'd obviously had good reason to sound the way he did. Wherever this Danker had been bleeding from I had no idea. Didn't particularly care either. The only thing that had me interested was that it wasn't bleeding anymore. And how did I know this? Because of one little word. Not just the word, but the way in which it had been delivered. The rising desperation beforehand. The tension in the voice. The frustration. The anger. The fear. The denial and the disbelief. And then finally, one word said it all. The confirmation. Danker was dead.

The van speeded up again. We hit a pothole and my bum lifted in the air. When I landed again there was a collection of sounds that you might expect when hitting a pothole at speed in a van. The clunk of the shocks bottoming out. The boom of the steel panelled sides buckling with the stress. The juddering of mechanical parts moving around on their mountings somewhere beneath the floor. And the unmistakable clang of a tyre iron bouncing up off the floor and back down again. I reached out and felt around the floor in the darkness. I accidentally brushed over Clive's cold flesh and my skin crawled, but it was no time to be squeamish. I continued to palm the steel floor left and right, back and forth until I had covered every inch it. Nothing. I had distinctly heard the empty clang of steel on steel. I was sure of it. Maybe, Clive had a prosthesis, one of those super hi-tech titanium legs that you sometimes see athletes running on in the Para Olympics and that only Para Olympians could afford, courtesy of super generous sponsorship deals. Again, I could have been wrong, but Clive didn't strike me as an athlete, so I was guessing there was no sponsorship deal and most likely he had all four of his limbs. So where was that bloody tyre iron then?

The van's engine dipped. Manning was changing down. It revved a little, then dipped again. I pawed at the floor again frantically. Where the hell?

The van swung this way and that and then it revved hard, maybe in second gear. And then we stopped. Shit! Now I was swearing. Now I was feeling those emotions. Fear. Denial. Disbelief. This time *I* was getting the confirmation. We were here. Wherever Amber was, we had arrived.

The driver's door opened. The courtesy light came on up front and then the door slammed shut. My heart stopped. I stopped breathing. Adrenalin flooded by body and then my heart started up again, bang, bang banging in my chest. I got up off my arse and onto my knees and pawed the floor again frantically like I'd just lost a contact lens. The rear doors were going to open any second. I had the element of surprise. I could take him. But I could take him a lot easier with a tyre iron in my hand. The floor was rusty. I was sanding it with my palms like a carpenter might sand a tabletop. My thumb caught something sharp. I felt it sting. I was bleeding. If Manning didn't kill me, I was going to die of blood poisoning. I could see it now, front page in all the tabloids: BRENDON HAWKE, SURVIVAL EXPERT DIES FROM RUST IN CUT THUMB.

I've scaled frightening cliffs on treacherous mountains, spent many a sleepless night under the stars in bear country and eaten snakes and rats and even grubs I've dug out of rotten trees. In 2006, I spent three weeks with the marine corps in Helmand with the Taliban taking pot shots at us. My last book sold over two hundred thousand copies and the DVD from my series on Channel Four outsold Bear Grylls' DVD on the run up to Christmas. I'm no big head, but if there's one thing I know plenty about, it's how to survive in just about any situation. Yet here I was facing certain death in the back of an old rusty van. Great! Just bloody great!

I felt something hard stuck to the floor. It was cold, metallic and cylindrical. Had to be a tyre iron. I tried to lift it, but it was glued. Okay, it probably wasn't glued, but it wasn't moving either. I fingered my way along its length and surprise, surprise, it was stuck under my travelling buddy, Clive.

I managed to pry my fingers under the iron and then I pulled with all my might. When I finally managed to release it I fell backwards and crashed against the side of the van. If Manning was standing outside the van, then my element of surprise had just been shattered. I got up off my knees and crouched, tyre iron gripped tight in my hand, ready to strike.

Maybe it was the way I was standing, knees bent and head ducked because of the low roof, or maybe it was the adrenalin overdose flooding my system. Either way, I could feel my hamstrings trembling big time. I waited. Seconds passed. The tremble was making its way up to my buttocks. If I had to run now, I had no chance. What was he waiting for?

My ears strained to hear footsteps, the scrape of a boot on tarmac, the click of a hammer being pulled back on a pistol, breathing, anything. But all I could hear was the whisper of the wind blowing along the gutters on the van roof. If I didn't move soon my left leg was going to give way. It was shaking like Elvis's midway through Blue Suede Shoes. I tried to straighten up, but my head ended up jammed against the roof. I'd been waiting ten seconds or more and my nerves couldn't take it any longer. I've never been a patient man. I couldn't wait a second longer. I was just about to burst out the back doors when I stopped myself.

The brain is not just like a computer. It is the original computer. It can gather information through all five senses, analyse it, make a thousand yes/no decisions, then send just the right amount of nutrients, adrenalin, oxygen and ultimately energy to the appropriate muscles to initiate action. Even when the vessel that holds that brain is beaten with something hard, it still manages to complete this process in record time.

My brain was working just fine. And it was telling me not to go out of the rear doors. I turned and faced the front of the van. The light up there was brighter. Street lighting was illuminating the cab. I took two steps forward and peered over the front seats. I recognised where I was immediately. Porthtowan. So I had been right about that photograph. I could just about make out the row of apartments where Amber and I had holidayed a few years earlier. I could see the silhouette of the fell behind against the night sky. I could see an old VW Beetle parked to my right and I could see raindrops just starting to spit on the windscreen. I could see the back of Danker's head, which was resting against the door pillar. And I could also see keys were still dangling from the ignition.

I rolled over the top of the seats and landed in front of the steering wheel. I glanced left and made sure Danker was dead. I lifted his wrist and felt for a pulse, but judging by the amount of blood on his shirt there was little point. He was dead alright. Movement up ahead caught my attention. Light flooded out onto the path from one of the apartments. A figure darted out and was walking fast towards me. Manning. No Amber. As he got closer I saw that he had the pistol in his hand. I still had the tyre iron, but guns hurt more than tyre irons, so I turned the ignition instead. That surprised Manning. So much so, that he stopped and pointed the gun right at me. I don't think I've ever travelled in reverse gear as fast in my life. I floored the van until Manning looked about six inches tall and then without even touching the brake pedal I stopped abruptly. I'd backed into another vehicle. Hard.

Manning might have looked about sixty, but he moved like someone thirty years younger. The van had stalled. I turned the ignition and the starter turned. It kept on turning. After the longest five seconds in the history of time the engine finally fired up, just as Manning reached the bonnet. He had the gun held in both hands, pointing right at me. My brain did that quick compute thing again, even faster than last time. I bunged the gear stick into first, floored the accelerator and let the clutch out all in less than a second. Manning dived left and I heard him hit the wing, but I was stopping for nobody. The wheels were spinning wildly on the wet carpark. I changed up and the van darted forward. The diesel engine faulted as I revved it hard, swerving through the gateway out onto the sandy road that ran alongside the dunes. I didn't stop until I was way out of the village, up on the top road that headed north towards St. Agnes. There was a lay-by that over looked the village. I pulled over and got out.

My whole body was buzzing. I felt breathless. As I stared down at Porthtowan the streetlights starred and felt like I was going to pass out. I leaned against the side of the van for support.

Come on, Brendon. Snap out of it!

I blinked like crazy, trying to focus my vision on the streets below, looking for movement. Any movement. Nothing. Should I go back to the X Trail and see if I can find AK? Should I go back down in the village and knock on every apartment door until I find Amber? They say that just the right amount of adrenalin can help you focus, sharpen your senses and help you make those critical decisions when you're in a fix. What they don't say is that you have no control of the tap on your adrenal glands. Mine were pumping the stuff out like a burst pipe and I couldn't find the stopcock. My whole body was tensed up like the spring on a rattrap.

Calm down, Brendon. Calm down.

There was no time to go back for AK. If Amber was still alive then her only chance was if I went back down there now. It was decided. I got back in the van, turned it around and headed back down the hill towards the village. As I hit the beach road I killed the motor and the lights and coasted across the carpark towards the apartments. I grabbed the tyre iron again and got ready to jump out. Last second, I thought to check the glove compartment just in case Manning kept a second weapon in there. He did.

I've used rifles plenty times; twelve bores and .22s mostly. But pistols are alien to me. It felt weighty and sturdy in my hand and I immediately felt more confident. I hoped it was loaded. When I got to where Manning had parked I jumped out and ran along the path, gun in hand, to where the light was still burning. I slowed as I neared the door, holding the gun out in front of me like I remembered Bodie and Doyle used to in The Professionals. Of course, they had a 2.8 litre Ford Capri as their get away car, not a beat up VW van. And Gordon Jackson was always holding up the rear. My Elvis leg thing returned.

The door was open wide. Number thirteen. I'm not in the least bit superstitious, but still. I glanced back along the path towards the van. Nothing. Nobody. Where was the skinny bastard? I made my way into number thirteen. It was just like I remembered. Three steps in, a door was ajar to my right. A bedroom. No light on. No sound. I opened the door slow. Real slow. Glancing forward along the hall first, then into the bedroom, then back to the hall. The bedroom was empty. And I mean empty. No furniture, no carpet, nothing. I took three steps back to the path and peered out towards the van again. Still nothing. I had no idea where Manning was, but I had to search this apartment to see if Amber was still here, so I stepped back in again.

I walked past the bedroom door and looked into the bathroom. The door was open wide against the tiled wall. No Amber. No Manning. Nothing, but a flannel hanging over the side of the bath. I continued straight along the hall to the lounge/diner. There was a lamp on in one corner near a TV so I could see the whole room. I couldn't say if this had been the actual apartment that we stayed at three years earlier, but it was laid out much the same. A cane floral three piece faced the patio doors onto the balcony; a pine open staircase ran up the right adjoining wall leading to a mezzanine above me and over the L shaped kitchen. There were mugs hanging from hooks under one unit. A bottle of gin stood on the drainer and a pizza box peeped out of the pedal bin that stood next to an empty plastic, vegetable rack. There were no pictures on the walls. No personal items left around. No Amber and no clues that she had ever been there. I couldn't decide if that was good news or bad, but I could feel myself deflate a little.

I kept glancing back along the hall in case Manning decided to pay me a visit. I knew there was only one way in and one way out of these apartments and I didn't fancy the idea of being trapped. I quickly ran up the open stairs to the mezzanine and could see right away there was nobody there. It was just as I remembered: a simple pine bed with bedside cabinet to the left side and a pine wardrobe at the top of the stairs. The same generic seaside scenes adorned the bare brick walls. I climbed the last few stairs anyway, just to see if there were any clues of Amber's presence. Maybe, she'd left some clothes, a book, a lipstick or something. I searched the wardrobe, the bedside cabinet and under the bed. She hadn't.

I treaded lightly down the pine stairs again, my pistol trained on the hall the whole time. I was so wound up that if Manning stepped inside just then there was every chance I'd blow his head off. I don't know if you can do that with a pistol. I didn't even know if the damn thing had any bullets in it, but that's just how I felt. I got to the bottom of the stairs and looked around the living room again. It looked tidy. Too tidy. Amber always was super tidy verging on OCD, but that didn't mean she had been living there. If the place had just been professionally cleaned by an agency that came in between lets, it would look just the same. Then I remembered the bin.

I pulled the top off the pedal bin with the pizza box still stuck in it. It was a four cheese pizza, thin crust; Asda's own brand. No clue there. Amber liked pizza, but so did half the population. I pulled the whole bin bag out and emptied it on the floor and then knelt down to sift through the contents. An empty gin bottle spun around on the wooden floor. Again Asda's own brand. I guessed there must have been an Asda store nearby. Did Amber drink gin? Maybe. I couldn't remember. She wasn't a big drinker. When we went out she'd have half a cider, a glass of wine or maybe a fresh orange juice depending on who was driving. I couldn't recall her ever drinking gin, but maybe she did now. There was a few used teabags, two squashed bottles – one lemonade and the other Pepsi Max. There were crumpled tissues or kitchen roll, hard to say, but I wasn't going to look through them to find out whether it was kitchen matter they were full of or human matter. I fingered through some other empty packets, crisps and sweet wrappers, nothing that meant anything. I was just about done when something caught my eye. One of the crumpled balls of tissue had dark print on it, black lettering, not printed like Bounty or Charmin or Kleenex, but hand written.

Unfolding it, I realized it was heavy tissue, kitchen roll. It was unstained apart from the writing. I lay it out on the floor and flattened it with my palms. And then something rose up inside me and constricted my chest. I felt like I was going to choke. I recognised the handwriting immediately. Small letters, neat and tidy script. The words were simple, straight to the point. It said. 'Where we first became one – I'll see you there. Same day. Same time. YAMOAOL'.

And there it was in black and white. Only one person would know I would search through this bin. Only one person I ever knew wrote in that style. Only one person ever finished her birthday cards, letters or emails with YAMOAOL. Amber. I remember the first time she wrote it on the back of a photograph of herself. I was going on a film trip up in the Highlands for a week. We had only been seeing each other for four weeks and she gave me a photograph of herself so I wouldn't forget her. As if I would after one week. The first night of the trip I was camping halfway up a mountain, just crawling into my sleeping bag when I pulled her photo out of my notebook. Staring at the image of her in the flickering candlelight, I guess that's when I realized I was in love. When I was putting the photo back between the pages of my notebook I saw that she written YAMOAOL on the back. It puzzled me all week. I didn't have a clue what it meant. As soon as I got back I asked her. She looked at me with those big sexy green eyes of hers and said. "You are my one and only love."

I folded the tissue, stood up and put it in my back pocket. My heart was jumping up into my throat. I now knew without a shadow of a doubt that my Amber had never drowned. That she had been alive these last two years. That she had lived there in that apartment. I also knew that Manning didn't have her. If she'd been there when Manning got there, I would have seen him bringing her out, else she would still be there, in all probability, dead.

I took one last look around the room then headed out. I got to the bathroom door when I heard a noise outside. I stopped dead with the pistol pointed at the doorway. I looked at the pistol in my hand a second; saw there was a little lever at the back. The safety was on. I flicked it off. Finger on trigger I started retracing my steps, back to the safety of the living room. I heard the floor creak. Shit!

I've shot rabbits before. Pigeons, pheasant and deer I've shot them all. They were game. I shot them in a field or a wood. For food. None of them were likely to fire back at me. I guess if a pheasant flew low at me it might put my eye out, but other than that I was pretty safe. Now my quarry was a human being. Well, maybe. I hated this bastard like hell, but could I kill him? Maybe. Maybe not. But then, he sure as hell wasn't going to stop and think about shooting me. I kept moving backwards until I kicked the patio doors with my left heel. I had nowhere else to go. This was it. It was him or me.

The next few seconds were a blur. I saw Manning, just a flash of his ugly face in the hallway. Since I had found the pistol in his van I'd been asking myself a question. When push came to shove would I shoot him? Now I knew the answer. When faced with my greatest enemy pointing a gun directly at me I didn't think twice. In fact, I don't think I thought at all. I shot at the bastard, simple as that. I only heard one shot. We must have fired together. Anyway, that wasn't the most frightening thing. The glass shattering behind me was what scared the hell out of me. Obviously, he missed me; otherwise the glass wouldn't have shattered. But, as I was up against the doors at the time, I fell backwards onto the balcony. As I was falling my finger stayed on the trigger. The gun kept on firing repeatedly. It was like world war three; I've never heard so much noise. I found out later that the gun was a Glock. Apparently they do that, keep firing until all seventeen rounds are spent. Most people don't do that. They fire once or twice or maybe three times. That usually gets the job done. I hadn't used a Glock before. I think I might have overdone it.

When I hit the concrete floor of the balcony I became acutely aware of two very important facts. The first fact was that despite firing seventeen shots at Manning, none of them had actually done any damage. The bastard was still very much alive. I couldn't see him, because the vertical blinds were still hanging over the space where the glass doors had been. But I knew he'd survived my onslaught, because he shouted at me.

"If you ain't dead Hawke...ye gonna be...you and that fuckin' whore of yours!"

Shit!

The fight or flight response is a primeval response that all humans experience in times of acute stress. It ensures our survival. All that adrenalin and massive oxygen intake triggers the heart to pump more and more blood to those big muscles in our legs so we can stand and fight, or run like hell. This is where I became aware of the second very important fact. If I didn't get up off my arse and get out of there – I was dead man.

I heard Manning fire again. I heard him crunch on the broken glass and I heard him call out to me. I didn't understand a word of what he was shouting, because at that point I was scampering over the dunes as fast as my legs would carry me. I noticed that at least half of the apartments and bungalows near the beach had their lights on now. Two guys firing guns at each other in the middle of the night tends to get people out of their beds, especially when one them fires seventeen rounds off the belt.

Once I cleared the dunes, I was on the beach. The tide was out. I could just sea the shore in the moonlight. Theoretically when the tide is out I could walk along the beach for almost a mile to Chapel Porth. There would be lots of nooks and crannies and caves and such like to take cover in en route. In the dark of the night Manning would never find me. However, I had no intention of running that far or hiding from him either. I needed to find Amber. And as she wasn't at the apartment, then the only chance I had of finding her was to follow Manning. He obviously didn't have her or he wouldn't have gone to her apartment. But he wanted her dead, so my best chance of finding her was to follow him. Without a gun and without AK I knew that that might just be a little bit tricky. But then I wasn't known as Brendon Hawke 'The Survivor' without taking on a few challenges in my life.

Chapter Twenty

AK let go of Anya and stood. He heard a motor fire up. It sounded like someone was leaving. He held out his hand for Anya and as she rose she pulled him to her and put her head on his chest.

"Please…don't let me go." She sobbed into his shirt. When she spoke she sounded like a child, a child pleading as if her life depended on him. Maybe it did.

AK held her for a moment longer than he needed to. It was good to feel a woman in his arms again. It was good to feel needed.

"Look. We'll go get young Hawkeye and go find your friend…what was her name?"

Anya looked up at him with her big, watery eyes. "Katerina. Can we go now? I am afraid for her."

AK grabbed her hand and walked towards the road. There was the sound of a diesel engine accelerating hard. Then light lit the field green and AK and Anya watched as a van took off down the road.

"Tino!" AK called out as he walked towards the road. "Tino! Come on boy,"

"Your dog?" Anya guessed.

AK looked about him as he walked. "Yeah…I think he must have been traumatised by the crash. Dogs can suffer from shock too, you know."

"We look for him now?" Anya asked, still holding onto AK's arm as they walked across the field.

"No. We'll see what Brendon's up to first. Tino won't be far."

When they got to the road there was only one van lying flat on its side. AK knelt down to see inside the cab and then he stood up again scratching his chin.

"Something isn't right."

Anya walked around to the back of the van and pulled a door open. The sound of it crashing against the tarmac made AK jump.

"Anybody in there?"

Anya had her head inside. She said. "Net…No one."

AK looked up the road like he was expecting somebody.

"I don't like this. I don't like this at all. Come on."

Anya ran after him as he strode back into the field towards the X Trail. " What? What is it, AK?"

AK didn't answer. His got to the X Trail, opened the door and pulled out a long green padded bag. He unzipped the bag and pulled out his rifle, throwing the bag in the back of the car.

Anya stood back. "No AK. I not like…" She searched for the word, but gave up. AK ignored her and jumped in the driver's seat. He looked back at Anya expectantly and she jumped in beside him. That's when he noticed the blood on the dashboard in front of her knees. He reached across and touched it as though it might give him some clue. He pulled his hand back smearing blood across the grey plastic fascia.

Anya looked at him puzzled. AK turned the X Trail's motor. As it turned without firing, he said. "It's Tino's. He must be hurt."

Anya said. "We must go. We must find Tino."

AK was still turning the motor. "Come on you piece of Japanese shit!"

Finally, the motor fired up and he turned the X Trail around in the field and they left the way they came in, except this time the gate was in pieces all over the grass and the road instead of hanging on the old stone post where it had probably been standing for the past forty years.

"What about Tino?" Anya persisted.

AK had stopped when they reached the road. He was looking left and right like he was at a tennis match

"AK?" Anya put her hand on his left knee and shook it to get his attention. He stopped with the head shaking and sat staring at the overturned van.

"AK?"

AK ignored Anya. He dropped his window and called out into the night. "Tino!" He looked up and down the road and then louder, he shouted. "Brendon?"

Anya said. "What will we do, AK?"

AK sat motionless, staring at the van again. Maybe he was deep in thought. Or maybe he was out of ideas. Either way, he didn't answer.

Suddenly, AK let the clutch out and headed left down the way they had been going before they took the detour to St. Agnes. He hadn't gone fifty yards when a big, light coloured shape jumped out from the verge. AK swerved, missed it and stopped as quickly as the ABS brakes would let him. He opened the door and Tino jumped up into the cab before he even had the chance to get his legs out.

"Hey, how you doing boy? Eh? How you doing?" AK fussed over his dog and the dog settled on the floor between Anya's legs. It had a bloody lip, which looked like it had split up towards its nose, but the blood had clotted and it didn't look serious. Anya put her hand on AK's thigh again and gave him a reassuring smile.

"He'll be okay. We just have to find Brendon now." AK told Anya and then drove on again. The road twisted along past field after field and after a minute or so rain spat on the windscreen and AK could feel the wind catch the sides of the X Trail. There had obviously been two vans involved in the crash. One of them had driven off. There was only one explanation that AK could think of to explain Brendon's disappearance. He must have been taken by force. Whoever had smuggled Anya and her friend into St Agnes had also chased them up that lane. The car that had blinded Brendon and forced them to crash through the gate into the field must have also caused the van behind them to swerve into another vehicle coming in the opposite direction. There were no survivors left at the scene and no bodies. AK thought about that, scratching his chin with one hand and steering the X Trail with the other.

"Where are we going?" Anya said, sounding concerned. The Akita had its head on her thigh and was licking her hand affectionately.

AK didn't appear to have heard. His eyes were focused on the road ahead.

"AK?" Anya called out above the din of the motor.

AK took his eyes off the road and looked at her. "What?"

"Where are we going?"

AK looked ahead again and sighed heavily. The road narrowed and twisted and AK slowed as a right turn came up ahead. After he made the turn he shot her a glance and said. "We're there already. Porthtowan. This is it. If Amber is here, then maybe Brendon is too...." Then under his breath he said. "At least I hope he is."

AK slowed down to less than twenty, driving past the Porthtowan Hotel, the surf shop and the post office. The village was well lit, but the main street was deserted, save for a parked up beach buggy and a transit van. No signs of life.

When they hit the sandy beach road that led to a large empty car park, things looked a little livelier; maybe a little too lively for five thirty in the morning. At the far end of the carpark there was a row of low-rise apartments overlooking the beach. Every other window was lit up. Some of the dwellings on the hillside had lights on too. Maybe folk got up early around here. Maybe there were a lot of fishermen in the village. AK pulled up, killed the motor and the lights and dropped the window.

"What? What is it, AK?" Anya whispered loudly.

"Shh!"

Over the other side of the carpark AK spotted a figure walking fast towards the dunes. Whoever it was, they were tall and thin and they walked with a slight limp. Judging by their gate, they were male. But it didn't look like Brendon.

"Shift boy." AK moved his dog's head back from the dash and opened the glove compartment. He pulled out a small pair of binoculars and held them to his face.

"What, AK? What is this man?" Anya said, sounding increasingly anxious.

AK watched as the man reached the edge of the carpark and stood on a low wall looking out towards the dunes and the beach. He was mostly in silhouette, but AK recognised him in an instant.

"Get back Anya!" AK pushed Anya's legs back as he reached over her and opened her door.

"Tino. Kill!" AK commanded his dog and the Akita squeezed past Anya and jumped out. As the dog hit the tarmac, AK hit the headlights and Manning was lit up like an actor on a stage. Even with its paws losing grip on the wet surface, the Akita covered the distance of the carpark in less than three seconds; fast enough to surprise any man. However, Manning was not any man.

Chapter Twenty One

I lay flat on the damp sand, waiting. I knew I could only afford to wait for so long. With all those shots going off, it would only be a matter of time before the police arrived. As I lay there in the dark I saw light after light coming on across the whole bay. It might have been out of season, but obviously Porthtowan had more permanent residents than I had realized.

Just as I was beginning to shiver I heard the unmistakable noise of a diesel engine. I dared to raise myself up on my elbows to see if I could spot it. No lights. Nothing moving on the road. But I could definitely hear a diesel. But then the motor died. I strained my eyes in the dim light, but nothing. Then I saw Manning. I hit the sand again. He was looking my way, scanning the beach, but I was sure he couldn't see me. Pretty sure. Well, at first I was sure, but the longer he stood there staring in my direction the more my confidence dwindled. I was beginning to feel rather nervous. Okay, very nervous.

Then someone put a spotlight on Manning. Man was he ugly! He also had the gun in his hand. Ugly and dangerous, not a good combination. Then a miracle happened. Tino! I couldn't believe it. Out of nowhere I spotted AK's dog sprinting across the carpark. He was a vision of perfection. It was like watching a nature programme. *The Siberian Husky chases its prey.* Picture it: Sir David Attenbourgh narrates with that unmistakable resonance that only he can articulate. 'The wild, ruthless, killer has stalked his prey patiently. And now he takes full flight and goes in for the kill. His quarry might call him intimidating, ruthless, violent or merciless. But as we watch him spring into action, his hind legs powering him at an incredible, no, frightening velocity; his jaws open, in anticipation; his eyes fixed on his target like the hunter taking aim through his scope, we see that he is an animal at his very peak. Magnificent. Mesmerising. Majestic.'

Manning lifted his gun from his side and fired. Sir David shut up. The cameras went into slow motion. Tino dropped like a lead weight, sliding along the tarmac like it was the ocean floor. I stopped breathing. My heart had hit the pause button. The miracle was over.

Manning glanced in my direction one more time and then he raised his gun again and fired. Not at me, across the carpark to the source of the light that had lit up his stage. I heard the diesel start up again. This time I could see it. It was the X Trail. My X Trail. AK. Man, I was really starting to warm to that guy.

Manning fired again and then he ran towards his van. He might look like a wizened old man, but Jesus could that bastard move!

I got up off the sand and ran as fast as anyone can run in damp sand. By the time I reached the tarmac, Manning was halfway across the carpark in his van. AK had the X Trail sideways across the exit blocking Manning's escape, but Manning was flooring it big time with no sign of avoiding AK's roadblock. There was no way he was getting out of that carpark without righting off the X Trail. Shit! I loved that car. Okay, I was beginning to like AK too, but metallic forest green X Trails are like hen's teeth. I'd have a hard job replacing it.

At the last second the van swerved. Manning drove straight at the low brick wall that bordered the carpark. It was thirty inches high, maybe a little more; single brick. There was a hedge of berberis running along the outer edge. No sane person would point their van at such an obstacle and drive at it at speed. But then, whoever said Manning was sane? He hit it head on, doing maybe thirty miles an hour. The van leapt up in the air, landed heavily, continued along on two wheels and then it was free. He kept his foot to the boards all the way out of the village, dragging a trail of berberis after him.

Then silence.

I must have been in some sort of trance, because I hadn't even seen AK walk up to me and yet there he was with the Russian girl, not six feet away.

"You alright?"

I blinked a lot and rubbed my eyes. I guess I was tired. I'd been awake now for more than twenty two hours.

"Hawkeye, are you alright or what?" AK asked again, putting his hands on my shoulders like he was checking me out.

I walked past him nodding my head. "Yeah…He shot Tino." I walked on over to where the Akita lay on his side and knelt down on the wet tarmac. AK got down next to me and examined the wound.

"I don't think I could have survived these last few years without this lad here." He stroked the dog's head and then slid both hands under his flanks and lifted him up, all one hundred and ten pounds of him. AK carried his dog over to the X Trail and Anya ran ahead and opened the tailgate for him. Once he had placed his dog in the back he came back over to me and put his hands on my shoulders again.

"You sure you're alright, Brendon?"

I nodded. "Yeah…Come on, let's get out of here." I could see people in their gardens now and out on their balconies; men with long dressing gowns and women in even longer dressing gowns, clutching their husbands for warmth. The sound of gunfire and vans roaring across carparks, smashing down walls will wake most folk up I guess. And it had.

We all got in the X Trail and I drove out of Porthtowan with the lights off. Maybe someone had already taken my registration number. I was hoping not. Keeping the lights off would lessen the chances.

Once we hit the main road I switched the headlights on, or rather headlight; crashing through that farm gate must have broken the nearside light. After maybe quarter of a mile we spotted a flashing blue light up ahead. Nobody said a word. It passed us and kept on going. My foot pushed down on the accelerator instinctively. I wanted to put as much distance as possible between that flashing blue light and us.

AK said. "Aren't we going back?"

I said. "You wanna explain to the police what all that shooting was about?"

He said. "But what about Amber?"

I told him about the apartment, how tidy it had been. I told him about the gin bottle, the pedal bin and the note.

He said. "You know when you first read that email from Manning…what'd he call himself? The Virgin Slayer? How sure were you she was alive?"

I answered him. "Not at all…not really. "

"And when you got the email from Amber?"

I was tired. I couldn't really remember what'd I'd thought. "I dunno…maybe fifty or sixty per cent sure."

"And when you came for me to drive down here with you?"

I said. "I didn't come for you…you invited yourself!"

AK punched my thigh lightly. "Are you complaining?"

"No…"

"Well?"

I thought about it a second. "A bit more…maybe eighty percent…maybe more."

"And now…after reading that note?"

I didn't need to think about that one. I turned and met his eyes. "A hundred and ten percent!"

About half a mile later we came to the point where we had left the road earlier. The other van was still overturned in the dyke and there was still debris across the road. I wondered why the police car that had just passed us hadn't stopped. Or maybe it had. Maybe the police had taken a look, found no bodies and continued on to Porthtowan to investigate what all the shooting was about. I didn't worry about the police for too long. I had something else on my mind.

I made a left down the narrow lane, back down to St. Agnes.

"Thank you, Mr Hawkeye." Anya said from the back seat.

I said. "We'll have to be quick. If we don't find your friend in five minutes, then we leave."

"We'll find her." AK said with absolute conviction.

When we got to the little car parking area near the seafront we all got out and headed for the shore where Anya and the other girls had landed. There was no sign of the boat they had arrived in. And there was no sign of Katerina. I had a horrible feeling she was never going to be found. Or maybe she would, one day, cold and bloated on one of Cornwall's pretty beaches.

"Kat!" Anya called out above the whoosh and roar of the waves hitting the shore and washing the pebbles back and forth. I worried about the residents of the village hearing her. I wanted her to be alive; I wanted us to find her. But I wanted it to be now, so we could get out of there before someone came.

"Katerina!" Anya called out again. We all did. Anya shouted something in Russian. She sounded desperate. There was very little shore and it banked away steeply with wave upon wave beating endlessly upon it. I couldn't see anywhere to hide. There was nowhere to hide. If Anya's friend had ran down here and Manning and his sidekick had followed, then I couldn't see anyway she could have escaped them. Anya was still walking back and forth along the natural rock jetty looking about her as though her friend might just appear out of nowhere. AK was standing still and looking out at the black ocean. I knew he was thinking the same thing I was.

"Anya." I called to her. She didn't hear me. I called her name again, but she still didn't hear me. Or maybe she didn't want to hear me. I guess the tone of my voice said it all.

"Anya…Come on, we have to be going."

I caught AK's eye. He was giving me a headshake, saying *leave it.* As I walked back up toward the X Trail I glanced back and saw that he had his arm around her. She was going to need it. I hadn't known her friend, Katerina, but the thought of her floating somewhere out there in those icy waters made me shiver involuntarily.

I got back in the car and started the motor, turning the heat up high. There were a few lights on around the village. I guessed most the residents would be retired. People like to retire to the seaside. And old people get up early. I hoped there were no dog walkers out yet. Old people tend to walk their dogs slowly, taking in their surroundings. They notice things. Like cars parked in their village that aren't normally parked in their village. I revved the engine impatiently, hoping AK would get the hint.

About a minute later AK came back up from the shore. Anya had a hold of his hand and was leaning in to his shoulder as they walked. They looked like a couple in love. As they got closer I could see Anya's eyes were streaming. She wasn't in love. She was in grief. I knew how that felt. I knew she had to be hurting bad. But I also knew that nothing anybody said would make her feel any better. They got in the car and nobody spoke. I reversed out of my spot and drove off. I was tired. I was feeling bad for Anya. But I was also having a whole load of other feelings. The note from Amber confirmed she was alive. I had no doubt now. But I just didn't know how I was supposed to feel about it. The thought of her having sex with that monster made me sick. The thought of that young, blonde guy kissing her breasts, kissing her body, kissing her anywhere – made me sick. And angry. God, was I angry!

Stop that shit! I shouted to myself inside my head. I couldn't be dealing with these thoughts right now. A man could go mad thinking such thoughts. I fixed my eyes on the road again. Dawn was just starting to illuminate the eastern skies. I said. "I'm sorry about your dog."

AK didn't acknowledge what I'd just said. Instead he asked me about the note. "What does yamoul mean?"

I was just about to tell him when someone ran out in front of us.

"Jesus!" AK cried out as I swerved violently. I was only doing maybe thirty miles an hour, but the sudden change of direction had us up on two wheels and then within seconds I was off the road and scraping us along a dry stonewall. I tried to veer away from it, but my nearside wheel was stuck in some rut or dyke and I had to battle with the wheel. Finally, we stopped and the horrible screech of metal on rock stopped too.

"Kat! Kat!" Anya was screaming in my ear and then she was out and running back down the road. I looked at AK and he was smiling.

I said. "No way."

AK said. "Way."

We both got out of the X Trail and watched the two girls embracing each other in the middle of the road. It was a beautiful sight, but it was getting light and I suddenly felt vulnerable.

AK walked down to the girls and I heard Anya speaking in her native language again. And then I heard the one called Katerina and I could understand every word she said. She spoke perfect English. I waited by my open door as the three of them walked back up and then I saw Anya's friend. I didn't recognise her. She had fled almost as soon as I had opened the door of that van. She looked unscathed. She was bone dry. She had never been in the sea. She also looked incredible. Her eyes were mesmerising.

"Hello Hawkeye." She spoke with a slight accent, but it was a cool accent. I liked it. It made her sound mysterious and sexy. She *was* mysterious and she *was* sexy. I realized I was staring, so I glanced away a second. I looked at AK and he was giving me a funny look, like he knew what I was thinking.

I caught Katerina's eye again. "Call me Brendon." I held out my hand and she took it and clasped it between both of hers. They felt small and soft and very cold.

She said. "Thank you for what you have done for us, Brendon."

Wow.

I was staring again and I think my mouth might have fallen open. Forget what I said about her looking incredible. Incredible was a vast understatement. She looked stunning. No, amazing. No, actually there wasn't a word that could do her justice. She looked like you might imagine Miss World's better-looking sister to look like, if she had one. Only better.

I said. "Right, okay, we'd better go." And then I jumped in the X Trail and started the motor. AK put two seats upright so the girls could sit properly and he arranged all the clobber back there so they wouldn't have to look at his dead dog. The girls climbed in the back and AK jumped back in the front and we got on our way.

I adjusted my rear view mirror so that I could see through the gap between the girls' heads, but I found I wasn't seeing much of the road back there. Katerina was proving to be rather distracting. I drove back up the narrow lane to the main road where the van still lay on its side and as I turned left to go north I narrowly missed a road sign.

AK said. "I think I should drive…you looked whacked!"

I didn't argue, he was right. We swapped over and I reclined the passenger seat back a little way and put my feet up on the dash top. I couldn't see the Russian girl in any mirror anymore and I was glad of it; I didn't want to look at beautiful women and I didn't want to think about any. I just wanted to sleep and then maybe I could wake up and all this might just have been a bad dream. The girls were talking quietly in the back. They were speaking in Russian so I couldn't understand a word, but their voices were sweet and combined with the hum of the X Trail's motor they helped me to relax. My mind was floating aimlessly as it does just before we drift off, but I was aware of those bad thoughts lurking just beneath the surface. If I could just keep them at bay a few minutes longer then maybe I could fall into a nice deep sleep.

"So anyway…you were going to tell me…what does yamoaol mean?" AK caught me just as I was falling. I ignored him and tried to recapture that lovely warm, fuzzy feeling he'd just pulled me from.

"Sorry. I'll let you sleep." He said, like that was going to happen.

"YAMOAOL…you are my one and only love." I told him and as I said it I felt my tear ducts fill. The power of a few little words never fails to surprise me.

"You are one lucky man, Hawkeye. Not many people get a second chance like this…she sounds like one hell of a girl."

"She was…I mean she is…" My heart was pushing up towards my throat. I didn't know what I felt or how I was supposed to feel.

"Go to sleep Hawkeye…we'll swap back over when we get passed Birmingham."

I shut my eyes, but my mind, tired as it was, fell into a deep melancholic river that flowed down deep into the darkest recesses of my brain. What's a man supposed to feel when he discovers his wife never really died; that she has been living here on this earth for the past two years; eating, drinking, working maybe. How is he supposed to understand why she would do that to him? That she had found another man and lain with him; loved him and enjoyed him. She had promised herself to me and only me. Forever. How was it that I felt so happy and yet so sad at the same time? So elated and yet so low.

I felt angry. And I felt cheated. I had so many images, so many memories floating around in my head. The way that she would smile as she walked into a room. The way that her hair bounced as she walked. The sound of her voice laughing; so carefree, so happy, so young. The sound of her giggling was always such a turn on. It was so girly and sexy. The curve of her hips as they danced as she walked. The roundness of her bottom in her cut-off denim shorts. The taste of her mouth and the aroma of her body. The way that I could still taste her on my lips hours after we had made love.

Then the dark thoughts came again. The lies and the deceit. The fact that she had been somebody else's before she had been mine. And not just anybody else's. A vile and ugly man had stained her with his filth. She had been his, to use as he desired, to fuck like a whore, to desecrate, to ruin. She had never been mine. She had never been that truly wonderful, pure and perfect girl I had fallen in love with. It had all been a lie. A cruel and unforgivable lie. What had she ever seen in such a foul and ugly bastard? Why had she stooped so low?

"You alright, mate?' AK said quietly above the engine noise. I glanced in the door mirror, which had been knocked inwards, probably when we smashed through the farm gate. It was pebbled with raindrops, but I could see Anya and Katerina were asleep in the back. Katerina had her head resting on Anya's shoulder and Anya's head was resting on Katerina's. I daren't look at AK by my side. I could feel the bottom lashes of each of my eyes were heavy with tears. I tried not to blink lest I spill them. Real men don't cry. Brendon Hawke, 'The Survivor' doesn't cry. My chest grew tighter and I sighed the heaviest sigh and I focused on nothing else but the road ahead of me. But I could not stop my eyes from blinking and the tears from falling.

About ten miles out of Lauceston I picked out some lights ahead of me. It was after six in the morning now, but dawn wasn't making much impact on the heavy, grey clouds above us. The X Trail had its one headlight on and I could see just fine, but I was worried it might be a police vehicle up ahead. I was just about to tell AK to hold back when I felt him ease off the accelerator. He must have read my mind. It was going to be a long drive home.

Chapter Twenty Two

Jade ran into the kitchen to get some ice. She couldn't believe what she had just done. She couldn't believe who she had just seen. In Brendon's house for Christ's sake! She grabbed a tea towel and soaked it under the cold tap, wringing it out like her life depended on it. Her mind was in turmoil. She hadn't meant to hit Amber so hard. She hadn't known it was Amber. Christ! She might have killed her. She looked up from the sink and caught her own reflection in the glass of the microwave door. Was she as pretty as Amber? Was she as sexy? Who would Brendon want now that Amber was back? She had flirted with Brendon so many times when Amber had been alive and Brendon hadn't even sparred with her. Not once.

Her instinct had caused her to come into the kitchen and soak the towel and it was still controlling her behaviour as she opened the freezer, lifted the ice tray out and hit it on the bench. But as she emptied the ice cubes into the damp towel and bundled it up into a pouch, her movements started to slow. Her mind had taken on another persona. And the same question kept turning over and over again in her head. Who would Brendon choose?

She walked back through the hall to the bedroom, her legs moving like she was wearing diving boots. She got to the door and paused before entering. Her ears were switched on to hypersensitive. She could hear a low hush. Breathing? No, it was the sound of the fridge freezer starting up again after she'd had the door open. Or was it? She took a step forward and then another. Amber was lying in the exact same position that Jade had left her in. The blood pool had grown. It looked huge, like a big crimson halo around her head. Jade backtracked out of the bedroom again.

The towelling pouch full of ice cubes was freezing her hand. She took it into the kitchen and dropped it into the sink. Then she grabbed a bottle of wine from Brendon's wine rack and walked through to the lounge. She forgot to get a glass out of the kitchen, so rather than go back, she just drank straight from the bottle. As she sipped from the bottle she walked through to the conservatory and looked down the garden to the valley beyond.

Jade was not a bad person. She had never committed a crime in her life. Maybe she drove a little too fast now and then, but who didn't? Amber had been her best friend. But things had changed. Jade's life was finally starting to go somewhere and she didn't want it to end. If Amber would just stay dead everything would be just fine.

Jade took another drink from the bottle. She thought about what had just happened. Why had Amber being getting it on with Matt? Had she faked her own death to be with Matt all along? Why would she do that? Brendon was so much hotter than his brother; better looking; more successful; a better lover. And Jade would know; she had slept with Matt one Christmas when her innocent flirting had gone too far. She hadn't anticipated that Matt would go all the way. She had teased him knowing he was married to Meg; knowing it was safe; he wouldn't go too far. Jade had often flirted with married men; it was fun; she enjoyed teasing men. But Matt hadn't walked away like the others. Matt had taken the bait and Jade had landed her fish. Pity it hadn't been the big fish. His brother, Brendon. She had thrown Matt back and gone fishing several times since then. But nobody special had swam her way. And then Amber had drowned. And suddenly the pond had grown a lot smaller and her big fish had swum a lot closer to her line. She had no intention of letting him go.

Jade was just slipping into a deep daydream, fantasizing about her man when someone rang the doorbell. She jumped up a little too quickly. Her eyes took a little longer to catch up to where her head was and she had to grab the back of the cane settee for support. She walked through the lounge passing the bedroom where Amber lay. She pulled the door closed, checked herself in the pine framed mirror that hung in the hall and stood looking at the back of the door. The doorbell rang again and Jade jumped with the shock.

"Who is it?" She tried to sound upbeat, friendly.

"Em, hello…It's Lenny…Is he in?"

Jade recognised the voice. And his name was kind of familiar. Why did she recognise that voice?

"He's away for a few days, Lenny." Jade told him in the same friendly, upbeat tone. "I'm sorry, I was just getting showered. Have you tried calling him?"

"He's not answering…it's going straight to answer machine. Where is he?"

Jade was frantically racking her brains, but it wasn't coming to her. Who the hell was this Lenny? "Oh, you know how he is…was there something you needed to see him about, Lenny? I'm dripping wet here. I'm sure he'll return your call."

Lenny hesitated a few seconds; Jade wondered if he was still there. Then when he spoke, he sounded a little off, a little perturbed maybe. "Just some work…I guess I'll catch him sometime this week."

"Okay, then…Bye." Jade called through the door. Bright. Cheerful. Buoyant.

"Bye." Lenny said, sounding just the opposite.

It came to Jade then. She remembered who he was. Lenny was Brendon's agent. Shit! Jade let herself fall against the wall, then slid all the way down it until her bottom hit the wooden floor. She sat staring at the bottle in her hand. How had she landed herself in this mess? Brendon hadn't earned a penny in ages and here was Lenny with the promise of some work. And what does Jade do?

"But I had no choice!" Jade said to herself. She brought the bottle to her lips and swallowed back another mouthful. She held the wine bottle in front of her, clasping it with both hands and looking at it like it was a dear friend. "What was I supposed to do?" She shook the bottle in her hands as though that might evoke some sort of answer from it. It didn't. Merlot doesn't generally talk back. She brought it to her lips again and drank freely like it was a bottle of pop.

"Hey, Amber?" She'd put the bottle between her knees now. Bottles don't give answers, so maybe Amber would.

"You listening in there?" She called over her shoulder. Nobody answered. "What was I supposed to do? This is all your fault anyway…if you wanted to play dead so you could go off shagging Matt, why couldn't you just stay dead? Why'd ya have to come back and spoil everything? Why couldn't ya just stay dead, Amber? Ey? Why?"

Jade lifted the bottle to her mouth again, a little too quickly. Her coordination was a little off. The bottle top hit her top lip, just under her nose and the cold liquid spilled freely over her mouth, rather than in it. She corrected the move and took the whole top in her mouth and let it flow, swallowing eagerly as the spilled mixture dripped from her chin, down onto her chest, ran between her breasts and soaked her bra and top. When the bottle was empty she sucked the end like a lamb at its mother teat and then finally pulled the bottle away from her lips with a loud sucking, kiss-like noise.

"You always thought you were better than me, didn't you?" She was talking over her shoulder again, talking to Amber. "Just cos Manning made such a fool of himself over you. Just cos he made you his little princess. Well, you weren't the first, you know." Tears were hanging from the bottom of each eye now. "He wanted me before he ever wanted you…in fact, he loved me. He made me his number one girl on stage…number one dancer…number one escort…number one princess." Her words were starting to slur and the tears were falling down each cheek like condensation dripping down a cold, tiled wall in a steamy bathroom.

Jade lifted the empty wine bottle up above her head with her right hand and hit it hard against the wall behind her. "Hey! Are you listening or what? You hear what I said? I'm number one princess…not you. Isaac fucked me first, not you! And Matt…Matt fucked me first, not you! And Brendon…" She fell apart a little now. "Brendon…" Sobbing now, she stumbled with her words. "Brendon…Brendon loves me…he loves me…he…"

Jade let her arm drop and the bottle fell from her hand and spun across the floorboards. Her head flopped forward onto her chest and her back slid a little more down the wall. She lifted her feet from the wooden floor and let herself slide all the way down until she was flat on her back staring up at the ceiling.

"I love you, Bren…"

The white, random patterned, artexed ceiling swirled around above her like big cumulus clouds on a hazy day and then the walls came in and the light faded. And Jade just let herself fall, welcoming the safety of sleep.

Chapter Twenty Three

Lenny Jackson had been agent to Brendon Hawke for more than a decade. He wasn't just an agent; he was a friend. After Brendon's father had passed, his mother had dealt with her grief through writing. Lenny had been an old school friend of Brendon's father. Keen to help in any way he could, he had suggested writing as a way of escapism, relaxation and dealing with her grief. Initially, she had gone through every family photograph and put them in a whole series of albums making corresponding notes under each one.

This is Matt's first holiday in Cayton Bay when he was two. Note the missing right sandal, lost to the sea on his first day on the beach.

Here we see Brendon munching on a Farley's Rusk, stolen from his brother's plate, even though his brother was too big for them now and shouldn't have had any of Brendon's rusk's anyway. Just shows that he had the survivor instinct even then!

And here are the boys fun fighting on the lawn. Seconds after this was taken Matt came running with a bleeding bottom lip after his younger brother got the better of him.

When she had filled seventeen albums she turned to writing poems. The first ones were very dark and melancholic, reflecting her mood at that time. But as the months passed, her writing turned to new ideas. She focused on more positive things: springtime, laughter, children, nature and love. Back then Lenny worked for a small publishing firm in Newcastle. He asked Brendon's mother if he could submit some of her poems. His bosses liked what he showed them and Brendon's mother ended up having her poems published in a small hardback book that went on to sell more than fifteen thousand copies. They were all very proud of the fact. But Mrs Hawke stopped writing poetry right after the book was published.

"It's served its purpose." She told him. Lenny encouraged her constantly to the verge of badgering, but she never wrote another word.

"I've said all that needed to be said." She told him. But Lenny would still come around the house once in a while and pester her. As Brendon grew older he realized that it wasn't just his mother's poetry that Lenny came for. For as long as Brendon could remember Lenny lived alone. He'd looked after his sick mother until she had passed when he was forty three. There had been talk that he had once a wife and a daughter and that she had left him when the child was very young, but Brendon had never known Lenny even ever have a girlfriend or a date. However, he was always dressed smart when he came to see Brendon's mother. He always brought sweets for Brendon and Matt, or collecting cards when they were older. And he always brought a small bunch of flowers for the boys' mother. Lenny Jackson never acted untoward in anyway. He was the perfect gentleman. He always kissed Mrs Hawke's cheek when he arrived and he always kissed the back of her hand when he left.

When Brendon wrote his first book about survival techniques, it was Lenny who got him his first publishing deal. By then, Lenny had left the small company he worked for in Newcastle and had set up as an agent. Brendon was one of the first writers he had represented and although he only visited three or four times a year now, since moving his office to Carlisle, he still popped in to see him if travelling in County Durham. And whenever he could, he would pop in to see old Mrs Hawke at the nursing home.

"Lenny!"

Lenny heard a girl's voice, but he could see no-one. He stood with his car keys in his hand ready to leave, but the voice had stopped him.

"Lenny! Over here."

Lenny followed the direction of the voice and when he saw whom it belonged to he almost had a heart attack. Amber was sitting on the grass beside the garage. Her hair was matted with blood and her face was white as a sheet.

"Amber? Is that you?" He could see her clearly, she wasn't ten yards off, but he had to check. People don't normally come back from the dead two years after they've drowned.

Amber had her head in her hands. They were drenched in blood, and she looked like something from a horror film. Lenny dashed across to her as well as a sixty seven year old man in need of knee replacements can dash, that is.

"It is *you*, isn't it?" He bent over and held her in his arms.

"Get me out of here, Lenny." Amber pleaded.

"Yes, of course. What happened to you? Who did this?"

Amber was in no fit state to explain. She wanted to get out of there as fast as she could. Lenny had never been a big man; five eight and ten stones maybe. He struggled to lift her to her feet, but once she was up, Amber managed to walk with him to his car.

"We need to get you to A & E right away." He told her as he ducked her head, easing her into the passenger seat. Blood dripped from Amber's fingers onto the beige carpet and the cream leather bolstered seat. Lenny had always driven Jaguars. They were his only indulgence. This latest model was his favourite, the X type. 2.5 litre diesel, metallic British racing green, cream leather seats with green piping and beige, deep pile, wool carpeting. Beautiful. Amber's blood looked almost too red against the beige and the cream.

"No!" Amber said in no uncertain terms. "We can't."

"But Amber…"

"No, Lenny. Promise me you won't. Just take me somewhere I can clean myself up…I'll be alright, really."

Lenny had known Amber since Brendon had first met her. He remembered how she could be stubborn and headstrong. He didn't argue. But he did take her to the local A&E department. Amber had her head back against the headrest the whole time, her eyes half closed. Lenny drove as fast as he could without alarming her. As he pulled into the City Hospital carpark, Amber opened her eyes and almost threw a fit.

"Lenny! What'ya doing? I can't go in there. Get me out of here!"

Lenny pulled into the first available spot and switched off the motor. He turned in his seat and put his hand on her knee. "Amber…" He blew out a long, heavy sigh. "We lost you once…we're not going to lose you again…"

"But Lenny…" Amber had her hand gripped so tight on the door handle her knuckles stretched her skin taut and white. Her whole body was tensed ready to escape. Lenny tightened his grip on her knee instinctively.

"We'll give them a false name and address…they'll never know. But you need that head looking at, Amber and I'm not gonna rest until you do, okay?" He spoke in a calm, rational manner. Non-threatening. But he never let go of her knee.

"You just can't make up a name Lenny. They have records on computers…they'll suss it and…"

Lenny loosened his grip on her knee and patted it reassuringly instead. "You've been living somewhere, somehow without any of us knowing for the past two years...Somehow I find it hard to believe you didn't change your name."

Amber turned away from him and looked out of the window. The sky was dark, brooding, and full. The wind buffeted the side of the car and Amber shuddered involuntarily. Without changing her gaze, she said. "I never needed to go to a hospital or a doctors or anything."

Lenny opened his door and patted her knee one last time. "Come on. You need to see a doctor now."

He got out and walked around the front of the car to Amber's side. Amber had opened the door, but she was still seated. "What should I say, Lenny? I don't know what to say."

Amber sounded close to tears. She couldn't meet his eyes. She looked down at her knees instead. "I'm tired of this life, Lenny. I'm..."

Lenny leaned in and grabbed her hand. "Come on, sweetheart. It's all going to work out. I know it will."

He helped her to her feet, shut the door and they walked slowly across to the double doors that went into A&E. As they approached the doors and they opened automatically Lenny, put his arm around Amber's shoulders and said. "Just leave it to me. I'll do the talking and when they ask you your name...tell them it's April. April Jackson, born May 13th, 1981."

"But that would mean I was nearly thirty, Lenny. Have I aged that much?" Amber said as they walked through the open doors and walked along the short corridor.

"We all have, Amber. In these past two years, we've all aged. Now just remember...name's April Jackson, born 13th May, 1981 and you're living with me temporarily. Oh, and by the way...anybody asks, I'm your Dad."

Chapter Twenty Four

When I woke it was full light. The sky was as grey as elephant hide, but it was definitely daytime. I rubbed the sleep from my eyes and saw from the digital readout on the dash that it was nearly eleven. I also saw that we were doing sixty miles an hour. I looked out of my window and saw that we were no longer on the motorway. The land around us was gently sloping with field after field full of sheep and cattle and the farm buildings were built of red stone. I recognised the landscape. Cumbria.

I sat up in my seat and combed my fingers through my hair. "Where are we?"

AK whispered. "Just approaching Melmerby...not far now."

Melmerby is about ten miles east of Penrith. That's only maybe fifty miles from my cottage. I whispered back. "Why are we whispering?"

AK kept his eyes on the road, but raised his left arm and pointed behind him with his thumb. I looked over my shoulder and saw the two Russian girls. Oh yes, now I remembered. Anya and Katerina. I eyed Katerina for a long moment, watching her sleep. Her face was nothing short of perfect, like a piece of art. I forced myself to look forward again.

"What are we going to do with those two when we get back?" I whispered.

AK said. "Well, let's see...I live in a wooden shed in a field with one homemade bed and a bathroom that consists of a tin bath and a bucket, although I guess you could say it was en-suite. And you live in a large, three bedroomed, bespoke built bungalow with a full bathroom, en-suite and Jacuzzi."

Sarky sod! I rephrased. "I meant, what are we going to do? They know nobody. They're in a strange country and most probably they'll have no money to get back home."

AK slowed us down as we approached the little village of Melmerby. As he brought us to a stop on the side of the road he said. "They *do* know somebody. They know *us*. *We* can take care of them and show them a nice time...kinda like a holiday. And when they're ready to go home, you can buy them a couple of tickets."

He seemed to have it all worked out. I said. "Have you seen my bank balance?"

AK said. "At least you've got a bank balance. I don't even have a bank account, never mind a balance."

I'm pretty sure he meant it too. I said. "In case you'd forgotten, AK…I'm kind of in the middle of something here. I can't have two beautiful Russian ladies sleeping at my place right now. What's Amber going to think when I see her?"

"So you noticed then?" AK said as he stopped the X Trail and got out. I got out myself and we passed each other at the front of the car.

"Noticed what?"

"That they're kinda beautiful?"

I rolled my eyes at him as I settled myself in the driver's seat.

AK continued. "It's funny you saying what will Amber think…How about your other bird, what's-her-name?"

Jesus! I hadn't even thought of Jade.

"Jade." I reminded him and pulled away from the verge.

"Yeah, Jade. You've got beautiful girls coming out of your ears, mate. Could be a bit of a problem!"

I adjusted the rear view mirror, AK had obviously moved it, as well as the seat. I reached under the seat and pulled the lever to ease myself forward. In the rear view I eyed Katerina, just opening her eyes and pulling a yawn. It was like watching sleeping beauty just waking from her slumber. My insides fluttered at the sight of her. Her face was like a magnet to my eyes. Here I was driving home to meet up with the reincarnation of the love of my life; the girl I had wept for this past two years, who had left such a painfully empty space in my life and a devastating void in my heart and what am I doing? Ogling another beautiful woman. And that's not all. If I didn't feel confused enough, then ask yourself this, Brendon. Was I coming home to Amber or was I coming home to Jade, my new best friend; my new lover, my saviour and confidante. The girl who had watched and waited while I worked my way through my grief. The girl who had listened and counselled and lifted me countless times from the depths of despair; the girl who had told me that she loved me and had shared her body with me. And not just any body, but the body of an Olympic gymnast. The girl who had started to fill that empty space in my life and fill that void in my heart with the seeds of new love and the signs of fresh hope. Boy, was I in a stew!

"Yes, me boy. You sure got yourself a problem here. Mind you, Hawkeye..." AK punched my thigh playfully. "What a wonderful problem to have!"

I ignored him and flicked the rear view mirror up against the roof lining. If I needed to look behind me I could always use the wings mirrors. The road climbed up over Hartside and through the small market town of Alston. AK gave the girls the coach tour treatment, pointing out places of interest like they were on their holidays and had never been abducted by sex traffickers. Or involved in a high-speed chase that had resulted in some fat guy called Clive dying. Or us crashing through a five bar gate into a farmer's field. Or AK's dog been shot dead. Or me getting taken at gunpoint and shot at repeatedly as I escaped. AK. What a guy!

We drove through Weardale with its lush green fields full of sheep grazing lazily on the lower slopes, their lambs hardly distinguishable now that they'd been fattened up over the summer. The girls were talking quietly in the back, but AK hadn't spoken for nearly half an hour. I thought maybe he had nodded off. He hadn't.

"Lunch." He said as he stared out of his window. It was more of a statement than a question.

"Ey?"

He pointed up on the craggy hillside to the north of us. "Lunch. I can count six full size rabbits up there. Easy pickings up this dale...I'll have to come back with Ti...unhh!"

For a minute he'd forgotten about his dog. I could hear the pain in his voice when he realized what he was about to say. He was quiet for a minute and then he turned around in his seat and started up a conversation with the girls. I guess they were a good distraction.

Within half an hour I was driving through my village. It was Twelve thirty on a cold and dreary Wednesday. The village shop was closed as it always was on a Wednesday afternoon, which was partly why I couldn't see a single person on the main street. But even so, the village looked even deader than normal; like a ghost town. As that thought entered my head another one joined it. Was Amber here already? Waiting for me? My very own ghost.

As I indicated right and pulled into my drive, my heart rate doubled and I suddenly found it difficult to fully exhale.

Katerina said. "What is this place?"

I struggled to control my breathing. I couldn't answer her. Not just because I was choking with anxiety, but I honestly didn't know what the cottage in front of me represented anymore. Was it home? Or was it just a shell of distant memories of a perfect life I once had. A perfect life that had turned out to be nothing but a cruel lie.

AK spoke for me. "We are at Brendon's home, Kat. You will be safe here. You can stay with us for a while...can't they, Brendon?"

Us? For a while? That AK! At any other time I would have been mad at him for putting me in such a position. But, not now. Now, I was struggling to stop my heart from bursting. Now my mind was a million miles away from beautiful Russian damsels in distress. Katerina could have been spread-eagled naked on the back seat and I wouldn't have even glanced back. No, really. Not then.

I put the X Trail alongside Jade's little MX5 and switched off the motor. Why was Jade here? And who did the little Clio belong to?

"You've got company."

Clever guy that AK. I got out and walked over to the Clio, peering through the glass. No clues.

"You know who it is?" AK stepped out onto the gravel.

"Nope."

"This here Jade's car?"

I nodded.

"You want me to leave now?"

"Thanks a lot, you sod!"

I walked on up to my front door. I didn't have a clue how I was going to handle this. Was Amber in there with Jade? Had Jade told her we'd been seeing each other? Who would I go to first? Shit! This was a mess. I turned around to AK who was standing in front of Jade's car.

"Just stay with the girls, will you AK?"

AK gave me a nod and got back in the X Trail. Part of me wanted to join him. Maybe I could just drive away and never come back. Maybe the beautiful Katerina would fall in love with me and she wouldn't drown on me, or fake her own death, or have me trail a thousand miles in two days only to get shot at and still never find her. Nice idea, Brendon. I opened my front door.

Chapter Twenty Five

When Amber woke the first thing she noticed was the scent of lavender. She could see the stain on her pillow like someone had poured drops from a bottle. She raised herself up on her elbows and looked around the room. The walls were white, but just about everything else was shades of lilacs and purples. The curtains, the duvet, the carpet, all lilacs. The wardrobe and the tallboy chest of drawers were purple; light purple, but purple none the less. Someone liked purple. That was plain to see. The curtains were drawn, but they were thin and they were lilac so they wouldn't do a good job at keeping light out. And yet there was no light coming through.

Amber looked at her watch. It was half past five. She must have slept all afternoon. She got out of bed and padded across to the window. When she pulled a curtain back there was nothing to see, but darkness, not even a street light. Her bladder told her it was full and she went in search of a bathroom. The door opened onto a small landing and it was well lit. There were two doors, both closed and then there were stairs going down which Amber could see were open with pine spindles and beautiful carved posts.

She tried the door on the left and immediately realized it was a bedroom. She shut the door and tried the other. Another bedroom. The pressure suddenly increased in her bladder. She tried downstairs.

"Oh, you're up…How you feeling?" Lenny was sat on a large, brown leather settee with a laptop on his knees. He jumped up when he saw Amber.

Amber had never been to Lenny's house. In fact, she didn't really know him that well. Usually, she would pass the phone straight over to Brendon when he rang. Two or three times he came over and once she cooked a meal for him. She felt self- conscious.

"Er…okay, I guess. Can I use your bathroom? There doesn't seem to be one upstairs."

Lenny put his laptop down on a low table in front of him. He held his back with both hands as he straightened his back up. "Sorry…I did tell you, but you were pretty dazed when we left the hospital. There's an ensuite in your room. It looks like a wardrobe, I know, but it's there."

Amber turned back up the stairs.

"There's also a loo under the stairs. Take your pick."

Amber didn't like the idea of using the one under the stairs, which was less than ten feet from where Lenny was sitting. She thanked him and started back up the stairs. After she relieved her bladder, she stared for a long time in the mirror, leaning on the hand basin. Her face looked pale and drawn. She'd been through a lot these last few days. Her hair was matted with dried blood, but it was evident someone had washed her face and her neck, although she couldn't remember it. There was a shower on her left and a thick lilac towel hung on the back of the door. Amber brought it to her face and sniffed it. It was super soft, super thick and it smelled of, yes, you guessed it, lavender.

She showered, but didn't dare wash her hair properly. With her fingers she could feel the long line of little bumps that ran from her hairline back towards her crown. There must have been a dozen stitches. She gingerly dried her hair and put the same clothes back on and sprayed herself with some deodorant she found in the little bathroom cabinet. Her top was bloodstained quite badly around the neck and shoulders, but it was dry and she felt cleaner and fresher after her shower.

When she went downstairs for the second time, Lenny wasn't there, but he must have heard her on the stairs.

"Through here." He called out.

Amber walked through barefooted into a large kitchen diner. The kitchen cabinets were gloss white; the high walls tiled randomly in shades of blue. There was one of those huge American style fridges on one wall and a small glass table ran along the opposite wall with two chrome and leather padded chairs at each end.

"Sit down. I hope you like meatballs and pasta, cos this is my best dish." Lenny told her as he scooped the steaming contents of a saucepan onto two plates of cooked pasta shells. Amber took a seat.

"Where are my shoes?"

Lenny looked over the top of his glasses, which were steamed up from the food. "Oh! I put them under your bed. If your feet are cold on the tiles I'll get you a pair of my socks."

"I'm alright."

Lenny brought the food to the table and went back to the fridge and opened the door, which stood taller than he did. "We got wine, apple juice, cola, lemonade…what you feel like?"

"Lemonade's fine, thanks." Amber watched him as he poured out two tumblers full of lemonade. "Where am I?"

He brought over the drinks and sat at the table with her. "Eat up. You're safe now."

Amber tucked in and was surprised at her own appetite. "Mm, good."

"I mince my own venison, mix it with a little black pepper and chopped onion, roll them into balls and fry them in some olive oil. The pasta is Tesco's cheapest and the sauce I make with two tins of chopped tomatoes, a good dollop of ketchup and a smidge of Tabasco. Well, maybe a few smidges…" He sounded nervous. He was talking too fast. "I'm afraid I was right out of mushrooms…had to use tinned. But the onions are fresh and…"

Amber stopped him. "It's good, Lenny. Really."

Lenny nodded.

No-one spoke for maybe a minute, but the silence was too much to bare for Lenny. He started off again. "I've lived here for, ooh, what will it be now? Six, seven years now. We're a little ways out of Carlisle. Nearest village is two miles away. What a wreck this place was when I first got it. Took me almost two years to get it like this. Put the en-suites in myself. And the kitchen. I had to get just about every wall plastered. What a mess! I paid someone to do that, of course. I'm no plasterer. But the décor and the tiling – that's all me. First go. Never tiled in my life. But hey, I had some time back then. Work was a bit slow, you know. Thought I might as well get on with this place…"

Amber smiled at him. It stopped his flow. "What?"

"It's nice, Lenny. Really nice. I thought you must live with someone, you know. My bedroom is very feminine. I thought that maybe…"

Lenny got up and took their empty plates to the sink. He stood there with his back to her. A tap was running, but Amber could see his arms were gripping the sink, not washing the plates.

"I'm sorry. I didn't mean to pry or anything."

He turned around to face her. With a big smile he said. "Tea, coffee, wine?"

"Have you any red?"

Lenny went through what looked like an extension and came back through with a dusty bottle of red. He held it up and ogled the label with his arm at full stretch. "Vintage of 2010. Vin de table. Produced in France for Monsiour Tesco." He said monsieur in a bad French accent, but it did what it was supposed to do and made Amber smile.

"I shouldn't really. Not on a school night, but hey…when the boss is me, then I can bloody well please myself."

He hadn't opened the bottle yet, but Amber could see he was tense and she thought that maybe the wine would relax him a little. He was acting a little uptight, like he'd had too much coffee or something. Maybe the pasta sauce had more than just Tabasco in it. They sat at the table and drank their wines and Lenny continued to ramble on about nothing in particular. Amber got treated to his story about the saga of his boiler packing up last winter. Then there was his last visit to the dentist. She heard how his cholesterol was on the increase and what he was doing about it. He told her about his latest signing and almost gave her the entire story, chapter by chapter.

They were on their third glass of Vin de Table, courtesy of Monsieur Tesco when Amber said. "Does he hate me?" Just like that. No warning. No build-up.

Lenny looked at her, his mouth still agape, mid sentence. He closed his mouth and looked down into his glass for what seemed like a very long time. Finally, without looking up, he said. "I don't think Brendon is capable of hate. I don't think there's a man on this earth ever loved a woman the way he loved you."

Now it was Amber's turn to stare into her glass. "Sorry, I didn't mean to…" She blew out a sharp, but heavy sigh. "We've both been avoiding the obvious all night, Lenny. I just need to know he's alright."

Lenny lifted his head and the expression on his face set the tone even before he spoke a word. Amber saw his pupils dilate, the lines on his brow deepen and his face flush. She averted her eyes, first to the cooker, then to the door and finally back down into her glass.

"Alright? Alright? Alright?" Each time he said it he cranked up the volume and went up a semitone. Once he reached that 'mad as hell' pitch he stayed there. "The day you disappeared, he had to go down that beach and identify your broken surfboard. Not alone mind you. Oh, no…he had maybe fifty people from the press and the TV there to gawk at him and stick microphones in his face and ask stupid bloody questions like… 'Was she depressed? Was she a good swimmer? Have you being having relationship problems?' It wasn't just devastating to think that your wife had drowned and was out there somewhere on the bottom of the ocean. It was humiliating too. For months he was under the microscope. The police came back to him again and again, asking the same ridiculous questions. The press hounded him. He couldn't cope with any of it. His heart broke that day and I don't think he will ever fully recover."

Lenny grabbed his glass, emptied it in one gulp, then got up and walked back through the door to wherever he got the wine from. He came back through with another bottle and opened it at the sink. Then he filled his glass again and walked over and topped Amber's up. Standing over her, he started off again, spitting the words out like bullets.

"Alright? You don't have a clue. He had a breakdown. Nobody could help him. I tried…I rang…I came over…He lay in bed for days! He lost weight. It was noticeable. He wasn't eating. I feared for him!"

Amber kept her head down. She held her glass with both hands and watched the image of her wine blur through the tears.

Lenny took a step back and then sat at the other end of the table again. For a while his breathing was still laboured, but it settled after he blew out a long heavy sigh. Then when he spoke again his tone was quieter. Any anger had evaporated. "When all hope has gone and you know you've lost someone you've loved...you can deal with it…in time. You can move on. People do. When you don't know, for sure, that they've gone…" He swallowed and rubbed his hand across his face. "…you can never move on. Because there is still hope. And hope is crippling. It stops you moving on."

Amber's tears dripped onto the table. She sniffed noisily and breathed heavily. Lenny wasn't finished. "Brendon hasn't been living these two years…he's been merely existing. He couldn't move on, because he couldn't bury you. He hasn't worked for two years. I'll bet he's skint by now."

He fell silent for a minute, caressing his glass, rubbing the rim with his thumb. He coughed and cleared this throat. Then he continued in a lower tone. He was almost whispering. "In these past few months I think he seemed brighter. I've haven't seen him since September, but I think he was starting to go out a little. I think he may even be seeing someone and I hope he is…he deserves some happiness in his life."

Amber looked up. Her face was a mess. Her eyeliner was smeared; her eyes were all red and puffy. Lenny got up and grabbed a sheet of kitchen roll from the workbench.

"I've just got one question, Amber…Why?"

"I can't tell you…it's complicated. And it's personal, Lenny."

"Will you tell Brendon?" He asked, standing over her again. He realized how threatening he appeared and sat back down.

Amber sniffed "He knows."

"He knows?"

"That's why I came back. The past came back to haunt me and…" Amber got up and tossed the tissue in a chrome pedal bin next to the sink. "It's between me and Brendon, Lenny. I'd like to keep it that way."

She got her glass from the table and put it on the bench near the sink. "Dinner was lovely…I appreciate what you've done for me, Lenny."

Lenny didn't look up. He was busy examining the back of his hand.

Amber stopped and paused by the door that led back through to the lounge. "Who's April Jackson, date of birth thirteenth of May, 1981?"

Without looking up Lenny said. "It was just a made up name. She's nobody."

"But the nurse entered the details into the computer and I saw her write down a long number on that card. It was the NHS number. It can't have been made up…it must have brought up a record. April Jackson exists. She…"

Lenny met her eyes now. He cut her off mid-sentence and snapped. "She doesn't exist! I made it up I tell you…people do that. In fact, people like you. Amber Hawke…We all believed that *you* no longer existed."

They held each other's gaze for maybe five seconds until Amber felt the tears well up again in her eyes. Then she turned and went back up to her room. She felt exhausted. Her head ached and her heart was weary. She wanted to sleep for a very long time and then wake up ten years earlier so she could change her past. But even with the heavy scent of lavender in the room, falling asleep was as impossible as changing the past. Instead, she lay awake in the darkness with her thoughts torturing her mind and shame eating away at what was left of her strength.

Chapter Twenty Six

When I saw Jade on the floor I thought she'd been attacked. She looked awful. Then I noticed the empty bottle across the floor.

She looked up at me, surprised. "Brendon!"

Immediately, she began to cry and started to crawl up my leg. I grabbed her arms and helped her to her feet. "Christ! What happened to you?"

"I…I…I love you, Brendon." She sobbed into my chest. She seemed hysterical. I feared the worst. Had Manning got here first? Had he hurt her? Had he…

"What's happened, Jade? Tell me…did someone attack you?" I tried to hold her at arms length, to see her face and get a good look at her. Maybe she was injured. But she held onto me, pulling me close, sobbing the whole time. In the end I just held her tight, running my fingers through her hair and caressing her scalp. I tried to see through into the lounge, but the light was off. Then I noticed something on the floor.

I peeled Jade's fingers from my shirt. She tried to hang on, but I forced her back.

"Brendon…Brendon…" She didn't sound like the Jade I knew. The strong, confident 'can do' woman I knew had all but disappeared. She sounded feeble. Pathetic. Someone had knocked the stuffing out of her and I had a good idea who.

When I finally shook her off I crouched down and examined the marks on the floor. It was blood. Crimson little drops formed a pattern from my bedroom door. They were smeared into the grain of the floorboards near the front door, like someone had walked through them. Maybe it had been Jade's attacker. Or maybe it had just been me.

"Come here." I pulled Jade toward me and had a look at her. I held her hands up, looked at her arms, looked at her neck and looked at her torso. No blood. No apparent injury. I dropped her hands and she let them flop like a rag doll. What the hell?

"Brendon…"

I walked on past her and into my bedroom. Jesus! I never saw so much blood. Someone had died here, I was sure of it. I stood there stunned. Jade was standing out there in the hall very much alive, so who did all this blood belong to?

"Jade?" I called out to her. I heard the front door hinge squeak. It always did that after it had rained. "Jade, what the hell happened here?" I stepped back out into my hall and Jade had gone. What the…

I ran outside and AK looked at me with his hands up, as if to say 'what's going on?' I wish I knew. I ran down my drive, cursing the gravel as it hampered my chase. When I got to the main road there was no sign of her.

"She went around the back, Brendon." AK was out of the X Trail and running around the side of my bungalow. I about turned and followed him. The Russian girls were getting out of car as I passed.

"Where'd she go?" I said when I got around to my back garden. AK was shaking his head, pointing down the valley toward the woods.

"What's up with her?"

"Stay here and watch the girls…I'll go get her…I think she's in some sort of shock." I ran down my garden and leapt over the fence at the side and followed the public footpath that runs down the side of my garden to the woods at the bottom of the valley. I was tired. I was confused. I didn't have a clue what was going on. I hadn't eaten since yesterday. I was running on pure adrenalin, but by the time I got to the edge of the woods my legs were beginning to feel heavy.

I got to the stream at the bottom of the hill where the woods begin and that's where I saw her. She was on her knees, her head in her hands. I slowed up and got my breath back. She turned around and when she saw me she shut her eyes and dropped her head.

"It's okay, Jade. I'm here now. You're safe." I fell to my knees beside her and held her in my arms. She was shivering. Her brow felt cold against my cheek.

"It was Ma…Ma…" She blubbered. I held her closer.

"I know. I know. We're going to get him. Whose is the blood, Jade?"

She was sobbing uncontrollably now. Her whole body convulsed. I'd never seen her like this. Or anyone, for that matter. "Is it Amber's? Did he hurt her? Did you see what happened, Jade?"

"He…He…hit her...her head." She managed to tell me.

"You saw her?"

She was convulsing again. I tried rubbing my hands vigorously up and down her back to warm her and comfort her. "She was alive…she was beautiful, but…"

"Come on." I pulled her to her feet, wrapped my arm around her and led her back up the path.

"Was Manning alone or were there others?"

She staggered beside me. I could smell the stench of wine on her. She looked up at me, her eyes unable to maintain eye contact. "Manning?"

"Yes…was he alone? Did he have a van?"

"You mean Matt?" She slurred.

I wondered if she'd been hit on the head. "Matt?"

"She's been…she's been with him…all this time, Brendon."

"Who? Manning?" She wasn't making any sense.

"Not Manning…Matt! That fuck betrayed you, Brendon!" She was slurring her words quite a bit, but I heard her clearly. Trouble was, her words weren't making any sense.

"You're getting confused, Jade. You mean Manning, right?"

We were back up beside my cottage now. I had no intention of climbing the fence, so we continued up the path to the main road. We could come back around and down my drive.

"I mean Matt…your brother, Matt! She's been fucking him these past two years…I would never do that to you, Brendon…I love you."

I heard her words loud and clear. But I didn't understand. She wasn't making any sense. I said. "You're pissed. You don't know what you're saying."

"She never drowned, Brendon…She…she just wanted to be with your shit of a brother…can you believe it?"

She was pissed, that was for sure. But she was speaking with such conviction; I just didn't know what to think. AK was standing at the back of the X Trail when we came down the drive. The look on his face informed me that he had just heard what Jade had said. He looked as bemused as I was.

I let go of Jade and went back inside. "Come in." I shouted back, but I didn't wait by the door to welcome anybody in. I located AK's laptop and took it through to the conservatory and plugged it in. AK showed the Russian girls in, they were walking through the lounge towards me. I waved them back. "Just make yourself comfortable in there…AK make them something to eat and drink. See what's in my fridge. I need some time to myself, okay?" AK gave me a nod and I turned my back on them all and focused on what I needed to do.

"You fancy a curry, Hawkeye?" AK shouted through.

"Anything."

While the laptop was firing up I dialled my brother's number. It rang and rang and rang. Nobody home. I felt my pockets for my mobile. I didn't have it. I must have left it in the car or dropped it or whatever. Shit!

"Catch." AK had been watching me. He threw me his phone from where he was standing.

"Thanks."

I had to dig deep to remember Matt's mobile number, but I could remember it was all five's and two's. I think I had it right. I punched it in.

"Matt Hawke. Who is this?"

I nearly said, who'd you think it is, stupid? Then I remembered I was using AK's phone.

"Matt, it's me, Brendon."

Silence.

"Matt?"

"Hi Brendon, I didn't recognise the number." He sounded funny, like he was nervous or something.

"I've been away a couple of days. Have you been over?" I tried to sound light. This was just silly ringing him anyway. Right?

More silence.

"Matt?"

"What?"

"Did you happen to come over today for any reason?" Why did I feel like some detective in some TV crime series?

More silence. Again. I didn't like the silences. This was creeping me out.

"Why? Why would I?" He didn't just sound funny. He sounded defensive.

"Have you seen Jade, today?"

"What the fuck is this, Brendon? What's she saying?"

Why would he think Jade was saying something?

"So you saw Jade then?

Silence. I was getting really pissed off with this. "Matt, just tell me for Christ's sake!"

"I don't know what you're talking about Brendon. Look, Megan's calling me for my tea. I'll see ya."

"Matt? Matt?" He had hung up.

Jade couldn't have been speaking the truth. No way. Matt and Amber. Not a chance.

I hit Internet Explorer on the laptop. The Google homepage popped up. I punched in 'Isaac Manning'. There were seventeen entries. Seventeen Isaac Mannings. Imagine if they were all clones. What a nightmare!

The first site I clicked on was Linked In. It was a kind of business contact network. There were eight of them. I went through the lot. None of them had any photographs. None of them were based even remotely in the North East. One was based in Cornwall. I tried him, but the site wanted me to buy credits to see more information about him. What a con! Then I spotted his profile, which said he was in the twenty five to thirty four age range. Not him. Not in a million years.

I tried the next results. Amazon had Isaac Manning's 'wish list'. I opened it up. DVDs, slushy rom com titles that I couldn't see Manning buying, but you never know. Maybe he was one of these guys with a hard shell and a centre like goo. There was some X Box games on there and some children's toys; lego, duplo, Fisher Price stuff. Imagine Manning poring over that stuff on the net with a toddler on his knee. Nah!

I clicked on Facebook. All eight Isaac Mannings popped up. Five had photographs and all five looked nothing like the bastard I knew. Lucky them! I tried the other three. One had filled in about one percent of his profile. Some help. The next one had some sort of anime character where the photograph might have been. On his 'wall' was a whole load of teenage speak. Words like 'mint' and 'sick' jumped out at me. I didn't realise there were kids still been named names like Isaac. *Hey, Isaac. That's sick, man!* Just doesn't work, does it? I clicked on the last Isaac Manning.

This Isaac had a Golden Retriever where his photograph might have been. His interests were listed as 'carpet bowls, dominoes, Wilbur Smith novels, family history research, his allotment.' Need I go on?

So Isaac Manning wasn't on the net. No surprise, I guess. It was long shot. I looked through into the lounge. Anya was just going into my kitchen. Maybe she was going to give AK a hand with the food. I hoped so; I was getting kind of starving. I couldn't see Katerina or Jade. Then a light flicked on and I eyed Katerina returning from the bathroom. That feeling ignited inside me again, like electricity. She walked like she was dancing. Maybe she'd spent some time on a catwalk. She had pendulum hips that hypnotised me. I don't think I blinked once until she settled back into the settee. When she landed she threw her arms up above her head in a long, drawn out stretch. Her back arched and her breasts pushed the fabric of the top taut, pulling it so tight she may as well being naked. In amongst all of this turmoil, heartache, anger and depression, I felt myself become aroused. Crazy, eh?

She turned and caught my eye. I feigned an itch to my ear, covering my face with my arm and then looked back down at the screen in front of me. Funny, I didn't feel guilty. Embarrassed, for staring too much maybe. But not guilty. I found that curious in itself. All the time that I'd been getting closer to Jade I felt guilty because I felt like I was betraying Amber in some way. When I went to bed with Jade, I couldn't even go through with it the first time. Such were my feelings for Amber.

I had kept my hand over the side of my face, holding my head up with my left elbow planted on my knee. I opened my fingers and peered between them to sneak a view of Katerina. She was just sitting there, looking around my lounge. Her face was not human. It was a piece of art. A sculptured piece of art. There weren't even statues of Greek goddesses that looked that good. Think Kate Beckinsale's face, blend in some Natalie Imbruglia to enlarge those gorgeous eyes, slice in Nicole Scherzinger's hair and skin tone, put all that on Flavia Cacacia's body and if you can stand it, photo-shop the whole lot together. Are you there? Can you see her? Too good, right?

"Dinner's up." AK came bounding through my lounge with a tray and a can. I put the laptop on the settee beside me and started to get up to get my food.

"Sit. Eat." AK was in front of me, shoving the tray in my face. I fell back in my seat and took the tray and the beer from him. AK went back through and he and Anya brought Katerina's out with their own. Everyone found a place to sit and everyone ate like they hadn't eaten for a week. I devoured my plateful. It was the best food I'd ever tasted. Big chunks of white meat, mushrooms, onion, sliced peppers and some uncooked green leaves that were kind of bitter - sweet, lemon – tasting. All of that was swimming in some sort of spiced, curried sauce, over a bed of egg noodles. Bloody amazing!

"I think I might have to marry you." I said as I laid my clean plate down on the floor and brought the cold beer to my lips.

AK said. "I'll let you know when I ever get that desperate."

Katerina said. "It's good. Is it chicken?"

AK told her. "I got three rabbits at the weekend. They've been hanging four days so they're good'n'tender."

I said. "You went back to your place to get'em?"

AK nodded. I knew that that couldn't have been easy with no Tino there.

Anya said. "That was the better stew I have ever eaten."

I caught AK's eye. "Yes…you can make that stew anytime you like, mate."

He scowled at me like a cat. But he couldn't stop his mouth from bending into a smile. "Stew!" He said under his breath.

I'd been too busy ringing and surfing the net and eating that I hadn't even noticed that Jade wasn't here. "Where's Jade?"

AK looked around him like she might have been hiding behind the furniture or something. "I've been in the kitchen. I thought she was with you."

Shit!

I jumped up, checked the bathroom and the bedrooms, saw the blood again. Not good. She wasn't here. She must have left. I opened the front door and looked outside. It had got dark since we were last out. I couldn't see a damn thing, but I couldn't see her car. I shut the cold out and marched back through to the cloakroom beside the kitchen. I grabbed my coat, the one with the fleece liner and poked my arms through.

"I see you found the bastard!"

AK was at the other end of the cottage. I'd been looking for Jade. Why was he calling her that? I walked through the lounge, past the girls, pulling up my zip. "What did you just say?"

"Manning…I see you found the bastard." AK had his laptop on his knees. He had a puzzled look on his face. Maybe, because I had a mad look on mine.

"Manning? He's not on there."

"He is." AK swivelled the screen around. I fell into the space beside him and stared at the screen.

"Well?" It was one of the Facebook entries. The one with no photograph and one percent of the profile filled in.

AK clicked a few times and it led to a link. In my haste, I hadn't seen the link. He clicked on the link.

'Manning's Mansion' filled the screen. Huge gold letters in a brushed script were laid on top of a montage of photographs. Each photograph showed pretty, scantily clad girls draped in a variety of positions on sumptuous beds in amazing bedrooms, all with different themes. Some of the girls were brunettes in black lingerie on red satin sheets. Some of them were blonde with white lingerie on black satin sheets. There must have been a dozen girls, all in different themed bedrooms. Every girl looked like she had just stepped off the Miss World stage and not one looked older than twenty.

"You think this is where Anya and Katerina were destined?"

I instinctively turned around and looked at the girls who were sitting together in my lounge. They were chatting away quietly in their native tongue. I looked back at the screen. "So he's still in the same game, then."

"Hmm."

I said. "Scroll down. I want to know where this place is."

AK scrolled down. There was a section dedicated to each girl. They all had names like Devon, Brandy, Candy and Cindy. Further down was a section describing each bedroom. There was the Victorian suite, the Honeymoon suite, the Group room, Devon's Dungeon, Cindy's Bedroom of Sin. You get the idea.

AK said. "They never had places like this when I was kid."

I said. "I don't think these places are aimed at kids, AK. I think you're just about the age range their trying to target…you know middle aged, single…"

He stopped me with a hard punch to my arm. "There…click on there."

I clicked where it said 'Enter', which was made to look like it was embroidered on a girl's panties. When I clicked it, the girl opened her legs. Really classy.

There was an email address and two telephone numbers, both mobile, of course. And probably untraceable. I said. "Give me your phone."

AK passed me his phone and then snatched it back again. "Hold on a minute. Why use mine?"

I explained. "Cos I'm Brendon Hawke, TV presenter, author and course coordinator and if word got out I was patronising seedy escort agencies, I'd be ruined."

AK's eye brows threatened to join his hairline, which is some feat, since he hasn't got one. "And what about my reputation?"

I said. "AK…at the moment you're homeless, jobless and live in a shed in a field. If you get exposed, it can only improve your standing in the community. It'll give you street cred."

AK fired back. "I read once in some Sunday supplement that you were 'a thoroughly nice chap'. Just goes to show you, you can't believe everything you read in the papers."

I chuckled. We stopped sparring and AK punched in one of the mobile numbers. He passed the phone to me and I passed it right back. "You'd better do it. I can't see Manning manning the phones, but you never know. I'd hate for him to recognise my voice."

AK shot me a 'whatever!' look and held his phone to his ear. I could see by his focused face that someone had answered, but maybe it was a machine, because he wasn't speaking yet. He took the phone from his ear, punched in another digit and then stuck it back against his ear again.

"Machine." He whispered. Then. "Hi. Yes. Thank you, Chantelle, I'd like to book someone tonight actually, but I haven't made up my mind yet. Can I just come along for drinks maybe? Okay…Okay…Cash is fine. Doors open at eleven…great. I'll see you there. Bye."

I said. "Sounds like you got yourself a date."

AK reached over me, grabbed my beer and emptied the can. Then he said. "I need a suit, a shirt, a tie and money in…" He glanced at his watch. "…less than five hours. Oh, and some sleep would kinda help too."

"You can borrow a suit, a shirt, a tie…they'll all be a bit tight on you. How much cash you need?"

"Entry is free. To spend time with one of 'their ladies'." He mocked. "It's three fifty."

I said. "For the night?"

AK laughed at me. "For an hour."

I said. "Jesus! That's why guys like us get married. I couldn't afford those rates."

AK said. "I hope you can, cos I haven't got that kind of money handy."

I showed him my bathroom and the second bedroom and told him I'd wake him at about nine when he could shower and change. In the meantime I got five hundred cash out of my floor safe. When I shut the door on AK I saw that Anya and Katerina were still sitting on the settee, but they weren't chatting anymore. They looked tired. Or maybe bored. I walked through, put the TV on and threw the remote in Anya's lap. She thanked me. I told her I had to make some calls and that they should make themselves comfortable, help themselves to drinks and that sort of thing. The whole time I kept eye contact with Anya and as hard as it was, I didn't glance at Katerina once. I daren't. My mind was all over the place as it was without falling into the eyes of the beautiful Katerina.

I left them to it, then went into my room and lay on my bed and rang Jade's number. Her car was gone, so she had most likely gone home to Durham. I was worried about her. It's only five miles, but she'd been drinking. Her phone went straight to voicemail. I tried her landline. I was ready to give some sort of apology. There was no way I could believe Amber would have left me for my brother, but the way that Matt had acted on the phone had made me think that maybe, just maybe, something had happened between them. Maybe he had helped her in some way and Jade had misinterpreted it. Maybe there had been some truth in what Jade had told me. The phone continued to ring. My mind was imagining all sorts of things. Was she passed out on her bed? Was she in a cell after been picked up by the police? Was her car in a dyke, her face all mashed up and covered in blood? For Christ's sake, Jade, just answer the bloody phone!

Chapter Twenty Seven

Jade wasn't upset. She was heartbroken. This had to be the worst day of her life. Amber had come home and no matter what Jade told Brendon, he didn't want to hear it. He was ready to welcome Amber back with open arms. And Jade would lose her man. If not to Amber, to some Russian whores. The one called Katerina had caught Brendon's eye, Jade had noticed. And she had also noticed Katerina's eyes on Brendon. Jade not only had competition from the past, she also had younger, more beautiful, more mysterious Russian competition to contend with. Life could be so unfair sometimes.

When AK and the Russian girls followed Brendon inside, Jade stood and watched them. And when the door shut she stood there for maybe five minutes waiting. Brendon didn't come out to see where she was. He obviously hadn't missed her. He didn't care. Nobody came out. Nobody cared. So Jade got in her car and left.

Jade had never driven under the influence of alcohol before and now she knew why. It was scary. The kerb leapt out at her. The markings in the centre of the road wandered the whole time and it was damn near impossible to stay in between the two. The streetlights starred like a firework display and when they ended the view ahead was black. Too black. Of course, it didn't help that Jade had only put her sidelights on.

She had only travelled maybe two miles when the whole interior of her little MX5 was lit up with a flashing blue light shining in from behind. When she eventually managed to come to a stop, she left the road and parked at an angle on the verge.

Sergeant Michael McArdle had worked for Durham Constabulary for eighteen years. He was never going to rise above the rank of sergeant, but then he had no intention of trying. He didn't need to. He had a new townhouse on the outskirts of Durham, a two-year old Porsche Boxster in his garage and the pick of several gorgeous young girls to sleep with every week. He also had two failed marriages behind him, but he could care less. Life was good. And it was just about to get a whole lot better.

"If you could get out of the car for me Miss." The rather portly, middle-aged sergeant asked her in a condescending tone. Jade got out unaided and stood pretty well at first. But when McArdle asked her to accompany him to his car, she tripped and fell, twice. First it was the long, uncut grass that caused her to lose her footing and secondly it was for no other reason than she was just about paralytic.

Sergeant McArdle got no sense out of Jade. The only way he could identify her was by calling in the number of her car. When the girl at the station read out Jade's name and date of birth, something registered in McArdle's memory. It was a long shot, but it was worth checking out.

He got Jade into the back of his panda car and then pulled out his personal mobile and hit number one in his contacts. All of his contacts were listed with a number rather than a name. He knew who they all were and if anyone ever found his phone the contacts would just read like a list of numbers.

"Well, hello Isaac. I have someone here that I think you'd like to see."

"I don't have time for this shit, McArdle!" Manning said. There was music in the background, loud music with big beats. He sounded like he was in his club.

"Oh, I think you will, Isaac…I think you will."

"I'm hanging up in five, four, three…"

McArdle let him get to one and then he let it drop. "Jade Morgan. I have her here in my car. You want to trade?"

Manning didn't hang up. The sounds of Nelly boomed through McArdle's mobile. After maybe a full ten seconds Manning said. "How d'you know it's her?"

McArdle shifted in his seat so he could get a good look behind him. He started with Jade's face and worked down. "Long, shiny, brown hair. Nose pinched just a little, but cute as a button. Eyes brown and sexy as fuck. Square athletic shoulders. She's toned and tanned like a fuckin' model. Very nice. Breasts small, but pert…I'd say 34B. Her belly's flat, ripped. Hips are boyish, but her legs are all woman. She's five seven, maybe five eight and not an ounce over eight and half stone I'd say. Oh, and according to the police computer her date of birth is thirteenth of May, nineteen eighty one.

Manning said. "Bring her to me. Now."

McArdle answered him sounding about as cool as Harry Connick Junior after three shots of valium laced bourbon. "But I've just picked her up for drink driving, Isaac..." He paused for effect. "Give me a reason why I shouldn't take her in."

Manning tutted. "Okay. What do want this time, McArdle?"

Chapter Twenty Eight

"I'll drive myself." AK said as he pulled on my too tight jacket.

"No way. I'm taking you. That way we can get away fast if we need to."

AK insisted. "I can get away fast myself. You need to stay here and take care of the girls."

I glanced at the girls sitting on my settee in the lounge. Anya was flicking through one of my survival books and Katerina was looking right at me. Her hair was swept back off her face and she had her legs tucked under herself. The creased cotton of the old T shirt I'd leant her to use as a night shirt barely covered her thighs. I smiled and her face lit up. I looked back at AK feeling light-headed.

"No. I'm coming with you. No arguments." The expression on his face told me I'd said it a bit too firmly, but I didn't want to be left with Katerina. She was a distraction, for sure. But not one I could cope with right then.

We got to Sunderland in half an hour. It was dry, but the pavements were damp and I could see AK's breath as he got out of the X Trail. I dropped the window. "The first sign of trouble you ring me, right?"

"Yes, Daddy." Sarcasm. Never clever.

I gestured with my head. "I'll park over there, in front of that skip."

"See ye in about an hour. Less hopefully."

I said. "Don't spend all my money."

AK took off across the road. He called back jokingly. "Hey, I might need to leave a tip." I think he was joking.

I locked the doors, racked my seat back and reclined it some. Procrastination is a dangerous game. But I had nothing else to do. I tried to ring Jade three times, but it went through to voicemail every time. And so my mind was pulled magnetically back to Amber. I tried to remember the good stuff. Amber and me. But Manning had spoilt everything for me now. I couldn't get the two of them out of my mind.

The solid oak door opened as AK approached. A man three inches taller and thirty pounds more than AK held the door open for him and nodded a welcome. AK stepped inside. The reception area wasn't grand. It was plain. The walls were freshly painted in magenta with dado rails and cornicing painted ice white. The ceiling was high. Twelve feet. A fantastic chandelier hung down and lit it all up. AK's eyes flitted between the three doors that led off, left, right and straight ahead.

"Good evening, Mr Kennedy. I am Chantelle." A beautiful, tall girl in her twenties came striding out from the door on the left. Her face, her hair, her dress: immaculate.

AK smiled. "Evening."

"Welcome to the Mansion. If you would follow me this way." She turned her back to him and walked back through the same door. AK followed maybe four or five steps behind. Her accent was eastern European. Romanian, Hungarian or Ukrainian maybe. The way she walked, her deportment, shoulders back, hips dancing, feet pointing to the centre as though she were walking a beam. It was enough to entertain any man even if that was the whole show.

AK caught up to Chantelle just as they reached the end of the hall they were walking along. At the end, she stopped, opened an ornate wooden door and stood aside. "Come in and make yourself at home, Mr Kennedy."

AK smiled and walked on ahead of her, not knowing what to expect. As he stood perusing the huge lounge in front of him, Chantelle grabbed his left hand and led him over to a large oak desk positioned facing in over in a large bay window. There was an A4 sized book with lined pages laid out on the desk and a silver, expensive looking pen resting across one page.

"If you could just sign the register Mr Kennedy and I'll take your payment. Then you can enjoy the company of our ladies." Chantelle stood him in front of the desk with her hand placed in the hollow of his back.

AK smiled at Chantelle as he bent over the desk and signed the book. Then he took his wallet out and made a show of leafing through the folds all the time surveying the room as discreetly as he could. The ceiling was high again, but this time the lighting was courtesy of maybe twenty low voltage spots. The walls were still magenta, but the flooring was deep pile and the darkest crimson. The dado rails were chrome and the far wall was mirrored behind the long bar that ran along it. There were maybe eight stools in front of it. Four blondes occupied four of them. Three had short black dresses on and one had a shimmering red number that went all the way down to her ankles, but was split almost to her knicker line. Between the bar and where AK stood with Chantelle were four large, dark red, leather settees. Two brunettes sat crossed legged on one, a glass in their hands. A redhead was chatting to a man with a grey suit and grey hair on another. The settee opposite was empty and the one nearest to the desk had an Asian looking man in it with a blonde at one side of him and a girl with really short cropped black hair on the other.

AK emptied his wallet, holding the three fifty in his right hand, but keeping it firmly between fingers and thumb. He smiled at Chantelle. "What if I decide I don't like any of the girls?"

Like a heron pulling a minnow from a stream, Chantelle snapped the notes from his fingers and folded them down her smooth, tanned cleavage in one fluid movement. "I assure you, Mr Kennedy. You will."

AK closed his wallet and put it back in his inside pocket. Chantelle gave him her best smile and led him to the empty settee in the middle of the lounge. "A beer perhaps or a glass of wine?"

"I assume I've just paid plenty to cover it?" AK said as quietly as he could, but the Asian man across from him still gave him a look that made him feel six inches smaller.

Chantelle bent over and leaned in to his ear. She whispered. "You have merely paid for the time you spend here, nothing else." Then straightening up again she said. "But the first drink is on the house."

AK straightened his trouser leg with the flat of his hand and then ran his fingers over his head as though he might if he still had hair there. "Lager will be fine."

Chantelle walked only the way that Chantelle could walk across to the bar. AK caught the eyes of some of the girls sitting around him. He smiled nervously, fingering his ear lobe between thumb and forefinger and averted his eyes to the next girl, who also smiled and so he repeated the move again and again. Wow, so many beautiful women in one room and they all appeared to be smiling at him. Even the Asian man smiled and the older guy in the grey suit.

AK didn't know where to look. Everyone was smiling at him. He started to wonder if he had left his fly down or had a smear of toothpaste across one cheek.

Chantelle walked back from the bar. Smiling. He was beginning to think he'd just paid three hundred and fifty pounds for a bunch of folk just to smile at him. But then Chantelle sat down next to him and shuffled close, knee to knee.

Like the beautiful Russian spy might say in a Bond movie, Chantelle said. "What kind of man is our Mr Kennedy?"

AK looked at her, puzzled. He tried to keep his eyes on hers, but they were magnetised south towards the satin brown skin of her breasts and the endless dark cleft that parted them. Maybe, like most men he was captivated by the firm flesh that gave shape to her silk dress or maybe he was wondering how difficult it would be to pluck his money back and run out of there.

"Let me put it another way. Are you a breast man, a bum man, a legs man? Do you prefer blondes, brunettes…? I've just heard we have a new girl starting tonight. Tall, athletic, tanned, long shiny dark hair all the way down to her…" She put her hand on his thigh. High on his thigh. "Well…" She giggled. "You get the idea."

AK looked directly at her and smiled with his eyes. "And how about you, Chantelle. Where are you from? I love your accent."

Chantelle pulled back a little, but kept the smile. "I am only the host here. I chat to our guests until they choose a girl to spend time with."

She hadn't told him where she was from. Had she not heard him right? Or was she hiding her country of origin for other reasons? AK tried again. "I see. But that accent…Russian? Polish? Czech perhaps?"

Chantelle rose from her seat like a time-lapse film of a grass shoot unfolding in the sun. "To be a mystery is to be more desirable, don't you think, Mr Kennedy?"

AK watched her walk back through the door that led back to reception. She never glanced back, but he noticed her nod to the two brunettes on the settee across from him. Immediately, they crossed the floor and sat either side of him, their arms draping around his shoulders and their faces coming in close less than a foot from his own.

"So girls…you from around these parts?" AK, so smooth he could dance in a puddle without making a splash.

"You very handsome man." The one on his left said. Her impossibly long eyelashes swept down over huge, sparkling, childish eyes on every word as though she had spoken with her eyes rather than her mouth. AK smiled and felt his face blush. He turned his head to the other girl.

"Very handsome." She echoed the same words. AK averted his eyes from hers in case he fell into them. His gaze instead, was drawn about eighteen inches further south. The girl had perfectly round breasts that floated, buoyantly from her chest. Her dress was loose, red and silky, which added to the illusion. Her skin creamy and unblemished appeared luminous.

AK cleared his throat and turned his head back to the other girl. Her dress was a cream, figure hugging lycra number. Her breasts were smaller, but equally as firm with a language all of their own, saying *here I am, come get me!*

"So what do they call you, sweetheart?" AK, again with the smooth lines.

Cream dress leaned in to his ear, kissed his lobe softly and whispered. "My name is Brandy. I am warm and…" She bit her bottom lip and moaned or it could have been a purr. "And oh. So. Wet."

AK was not here for this. But the lower part of his body had other ideas. Red dress sensed his arousal and put her hand on his thigh, then started to walk two fingers north very, very slowly. He slowly rotated his head around the other way and found her nose maybe three inches from his own. Her breath smelled of something citrus. Her scent was subtle, but nonetheless intoxicating. And those breasts…

"I…am Candy." Her tongue flitted between her plump pink lips teasing him further. "Sometimes I am soft and juicy and you can nibble me like candy." She lifted her eyebrows and held them there a second just in case he didn't get the message. "And sometimes I am the type of candy you can lick and suck…" Her fingers stopped walking when they found something firm below his belt. "And I can promise you…" She stopped to bite her bottom lip, crushing it with her top front teeth and then letting it fill with blood again until it appeared even redder and fuller than before. "…I promise you I taste better than any candy you ever tasted."

Her accent and the way she articulated her words was enough to turn a gay man straight. AK turned from Candy to Brandy and then back to Candy again. "So girls…do you come as a pair or do I have to choose?"

Candy giggled and said. "You have to choose, silly."

AK studied the girl's face. No signs of abuse. No scarring. She wore a lot of make up, but as far as he could see there was no signs of bruising anywhere. She didn't appear to be drugged or under the influence of alcohol. He turned and smiled at Brandy. Her face also looked perfect. His eyes dropped down to her arms. He could see the inside of her left forearm. No needle marks. He glanced back at Candy, smiled and dropped his gaze to her right forearm. Nothing.

"Well, girls…I think you're both gorgeous and I could never choose between you."

AK was stalling. If Anya, Katerina and the other girls he and Brendon rescued from Manning's van were all destined for some place like this, then AK couldn't believe they would be the first, but these girls certainly didn't appear to mind their jobs. He wriggled out between Candy and Brandy and stood up in front of them. "Fancy showing me the rooms here. I hear you cater for every taste."

The girls looked at each other and said something in a language AK had never heard in his life. Then Brandy gave him one of her sexy smiles and said. "Wait here."

Candy leaned into him and curled one of her feet around his calf. AK had had worse experiences. He watched Brandy's hips swing over to the bar. She picked up a phone and after hitting only one number was speaking to someone. A few seconds later AK watched Brandy's hips dance on back.

"Isaac says for you to stay here." Brandy informed Candy. "You…" Brandy licked a finger and placed it on AK's chest. "Follow me." She grabbed AK's hand and led him back out the door they first came in through. Back in reception Chantelle was applying more lipstick. She stopped and told AK to enjoy himself as they walked passed her. AK said he most definitely would and then Brandy led him through a door on the right and up some stairs. Halfway up, Brandy turned, lifted her dress and showed AK her most private parts. A lot of girls shave these days, but AK wondered whether Brandy had ever even been through puberty. Then she lifted her dress all the way to her neck. AK was pretty sure she had.

"I know you didn't say you choose me, but what you say now?"

AK tried to act as cool as a man who hadn't had sex for more than three years could with a beautiful, naked twenty year old girl standing in front of him. "The sooner you show me the rooms the sooner you'll know."

Brandy let the silk pour down over her naked body, made an exaggerated crestfallen face and continued up the stairs. AK followed watching the silk polish her peachy behind. He tried to remind himself why he was there.

When they got to the top it opened up onto a large landing, maybe eight feet by twenty. AK counted twelve doors, all black with large chrome knobs halfway up. He also counted eight had large red heart shapes hanging from them. Brandy led him to the first door that didn't have a heart hanging from its knob.

"We have the choice of four. This one..." She opened the door and stepped inside.

AK's mouth made a noise before his brain told it too. "Shit!"

"This one is Devon's Dungeon. We all have our own rooms, but it's okay to use any if they're free."

Initially, AK thought he had entered some kind of weird gym for disabled people. There was a bed that looked like one of those profiling beds you see in hospitals, except the sheets were black. Black PVC. There were a number of leather straps hanging down from the ceiling with metal rings on the end. Maybe they were used to help people elevate their broken legs. Maybe not.

AK said. "What's that?"

There was something resembling a recumbent cycle next to the weird hospital bed. It had a black leather seat, almost Recaro style, no pedals, but there were two padded footplates at the bottom end and instead of handlebars or maybe a steering wheel coming up the middle, there was just a long hydraulic shaft that would probably make your eyes water if you braked suddenly. That's if it had brakes, of course.

Brandy bent over a black wooden trunk just inside the door, lifted its lid and fished out a huge dildo. She lifted it up to AK's face. "This end here..." She showed him a screw thread at the base of the dildo. "We screw on the end of the long bit and then you sit in the seat and switch it on." She started towards the machine. "You want me to show you?"

AK almost said yes, just out of curiosity. "No…this is not really my thing."

Brandy brought the dildo to her lips, kissed the tip playfully and then dropped it back in the trunk. She said. "Spoilsport!"

The next room was set out beautifully with mock electric candles flickering on a mock electric fireplace, illuminating the whole room. There was a mock beamed ceiling, wooden floorboards, a king-sized four poster bed with cream silk sheets and voiles hanging from the turned, dark oak posts. A single red rose lay on each pillow and double sheepskins lay on the floor at either side.

"This is our honeymoon suite. Cute, no?"

AK got a flashback to the cheap hotel room in Scarborough where he and his wife shared their first night together as a married couple. He remembered feeling the pain of the springs digging in his knees on the old, worn mattress. He remembered the damp patch on the wall behind the crooked headboard. He remembered spraying the bed with aftershave to hide the mustiness of the room. How he wished he could have spent their first night in a room such as the one he looked on now.

He said. "Next."

Brandy went to the door at the far end of the landing. It had several hearts hanging from the knob. "I have the feeling that this is the room you will like most."

As Brandy twisted the doorknob AK said. "But isn't it busy?"

"Oh yes." Brandy said grabbing his hand again as she pushed the door slowly open. "Very."

About three feet in was another door. Glass. AK stood next to Brandy and looked through the glass door. Brandy whispered. "One way glass. We can watch them, but they can't see us. Wanna join them?"

It was poorly lit inside. A few spots shone down from a dark ceiling, but AK didn't need to be told that this was the group room. He could see maybe a dozen people in there in four separate groups. Closest to the door, on a huge leather beanbag was a couple going at it like there was no tomorrow. Behind them on the floor was a blonde girl on her knees with two guys in front of her. Thankfully, the nearest guy's hip obscured her head, but both their faces were showing all the usual signs of contentment. In the far corner, at first glance, two girls and three guys looked like they were playing naked twister. After a few seconds AK realized they were playing an altogether different game.

AK said. "I don't think I would fit in." He glanced back at the last group and shook his head. "Literally."

Brandy squeezed his hand. "Oh, you would be surprised. I've taken four in one go. One in my…"

AK walked back out onto the landing. "I get the idea. What's in this room." He took three steps over to the only other door without a heart hanging from its knob.

"Oh, that's Candy's room. You want me to go get her?"

"I'll just take a peek first, if that's okay?"

AK opened the door and found the room wasn't empty at all.

Brandy said. "Oh, wow…Jade! I didn't know you were back. What's he got you doing this time? This the new rape room?"

AK had turned to leave when he first saw the naked girl tied to the bed, but when he heard Brandy say the name 'Jade' he looked again. Initially, it was difficult to look at the girl's face. She was spread-eagled across the bed. The bottoms of her feet were yellowed, unclean. Red ribbons tied her by her ankles to the turned wooden posts at the foot of the bed. The same red ribbon kept her arms back behind her head, tied in the same fashion to the wooden headboard. The sheet she lay on was whitest white and a stark contrast to her tanned skin. Her sex was on full show. No underwear or pubic hair to hide her most intimate parts. AK tried to blot out her body and focus on her face. Had he seen this girl before? Was it the same Jade who had left Brendon's home just a few hours earlier? Was it the same girl who Brendon had been seeing?

"This your sort of thing, then?" Brandy tugged his arm. AK ignored her and walked to the side of the bed. The girl had eyeliner so thick she might have used a whole stick. Her lips were painted the reddest cherry red and glistened in the light from the overhead spots. Her hair was a mass of long, black swirling curls. She looked beautiful. But false.

Brandy took a step forward. "Jade'll take care of you, won't you honey?"

The girl on the bed moaned something inaudible and then said. "I love him."

Brandy said. "Me too...he's cute, no? You still look like a knockout, Jade. I wish I could ravish you myself."

AK had seen all he needed to see. He looked up at Brandy. "Sorry, Brandy. This is the one for me."

Brandy walked over to him, grabbed his hand and lifting her dress with her other hand pressed it between her legs. "That's what you missing mister." Then she bent over the girl on the bed, kissed her passionately on the mouth and then she ducked down and kissed her right nipple. As she walked back to the door she lifted the back of her dress to flash her bare buttocks. Just before she swung the door shut she flicked her head around and said. "Enjoy!"

As soon the door clicked shut AK paced over to the window, lifted an ottoman seat, brought it back over to the door and angled it against the doorknob. With the door secure he went back to Jade, took out a knife from his shoe, opened the blade and cut all four ribbons.

"Hurry, get up and get dressed." He told her as he walked back towards the window allowing her some privacy to get dressed.

"I love him." She repeated. This time she slurred a little more than last.

AK turned around and she was still in the exact same position on the bed. "Jesus!"

"I will always...love my Bren...jon." She slurred again and then she lifted herself up on one elbow and looked right at AK. "Hey! Don't I know you?"

AK didn't know where to look. Here he was standing not six feet from Brendon's girlfriend lying naked on a bed, breasts nosing out pertly from her chest, one leg outstretched, the other propped up at an angle exposing the folds of her sex, chatting to him freely, totally disinhibited. In a brothel.

He addressed the ceiling and said. "Put some clothes on for Christ's sake and let's get out of here."

Jade said. "Where are we? Is Brendon here? Are we having some...some sort of ménage a trois?"

"Ah Shit!" AK started looking about the room for any trace of her clothes. He opened a mirrored wardrobe door and found three lots of clothing on hangers. He flicked the hangers left and right to see what they were.

"Costumes…bloody costumes!" He closed the wardrobe door again and tried the two drawers at its base. Nothing. One held a selection of sex toys and the other was full of condoms.

"Where're your bloody clothes?"

Jade reached over and grabbed AK's arm, pulling him to the bed. "You think I'm attractive, AK?"

AK tried to step back, but she pulled him closer. "You're pissed Jade. Maybe you've been drugged too. I don't know, but we've got to get your clothes on and get you out of here, alright?"

Jade made her way up onto her knees, leaning into AK for support. She let go of his shirt with her left hand and grabbed his hand instead. Then she placed it over her breast. "For Christ's sake, girl. Stop this shit. What the hell are you on?"

Jade let go of him and slumped back on the bed, her face all sullen. "He doesn't want me, you know. He still loves fuckin' Amber?"

AK opened the wardrobe again and fingered the hangers, sighing heavily. Under his breath he said. "With a mouth like that, I wonder why?"

Jade raised her voice again. "Hey! You. You gay or what? You could have me now. Anyway you like you could." AK pulled one of the costumes off its hangers and flung it at her.

AK leaned over to her and whispering, he said. "Shut up. And put that on."

Jade gave him slits for eyes and started putting arms through the costume. "What the? I can't…"

AK watched her struggle with thc costume, putting her left arm through the neck and her right through the left arm. "Christ!" He pulled it back over her head again, grabbed her hand and fed it through the right hole. He did the same with the other and then pulled the material over her head. "Pull it down for Christ's sake! Have some bloody respect!"

"Fuck you!" Jade said, pulling the costume down as far as it would go, which wasn't very far at all.

'What the hell did they do to you? How did that girl know you? Are you friends with these people?" AK fired at her. Jade got up off the bed, sighed a sigh big enough to collapse a lung and then flopped back down on the bed again.

AK launched into her. "You know…I was thinking. Maybe you're pissed. Maybe you're even drugged. Maybe Manning grabbed you and tied you up here as some sick joke on Brendon. But you know what?"

Jade did a major eye role then stared at the back of the door. AK continued. "I think maybe you look like you belong here."

Jade didn't bite. The expression on her face didn't alter.

AK let out a long breath and let the tension out of his body. In a calmer tone, he said. "How do we get outa here?"

Jade had left the planet.

"Jade?"

Nothing

AK pulled out his phone.

Chapter Twenty Nine

Sitting outside in the X Trail I was wondering how my life got to here. A couple of years ago I was looking at a celebrity lifestyle. I had a one-hour prime time slot on Channel Four. My DVD was outselling Bear Gryll's. My book was placed centre shop in WHSmith's and selling well. I had a beautiful, loving wife and we were even starting to talk about children. Our bank account was constantly five figures and our savings were growing into the six-figure region. We had just acquired the X Trail and I remember Amber's face when she first saw it at the garage. Dark metallic forest green, big chunky tyres, a rack up top for her surf boards and tan heated leather seats. I always loved to see tan leather and dark green together.

"That car is so you, Brendon."

Amber was right. I bought it the moment I saw it. Now, two years later I was sat here in the same car with probably about three thousand pounds worth of damage to the front and the side. I wondered what Amber would say now. I wondered where she was. I wondered where Jade was. I wondered what AK was doing. Then the phone rang.

"Hawkeye. Got some good news and some bad news."

I said. "Just tell me, AK."

"Good news is I found Jade."

I shrieked. "In Manning's Mansion?"

AK said. "That's the bad news."

I said. "Is she okay?"

AK informed me that she would be if she wasn't so pissed and he could get her out without anyone seeing. I told him to ring me back in three minutes. I needed time to think of something.

I got out of the car, opened the back door, got my fleece and pulled it on. It was four degrees with a stiff breeze blowing. I blipped the X Trail's doors and walked along the street in front of Manning's place. The whole building might have been a hotel in a former life. There were six big bay windows to the front and four steps up to the huge wooden door. The building next door was identical, but empty. The next one was a nursing home. I could see light coming from every window and one still had its curtains open. There was a carer pulling a hoist past the window. I watched her a moment and thought of my mother. Then the curtains were drawn and I carried on walking. The only light I could see from Manning's place was from the little window above the front door and two of the upstairs windows gave off a very faint glow.

I got to the end of the road and headed around the back. There were no streetlights. It was a narrow back lane and every back yard had high walls and high gates. I felt a bit vulnerable. Sunderland is not a town I'm familiar with. As I counted the buildings down and worked out which part was the back of Mannings, my phone rang again.

"Brendon. You got any ideas yet?"

AK sounded edgy. AK never sounded edgy.

I said. "You at the back of the house or the front?"

AK said. "Shit do I know!"

I said. "Well, which floor you on?"

"Second. There's only two floors."

From where I was standing there were three. I only saw an upstairs and downstairs from the front, but the land must have sloped away at the back, so they had a lower floor too.

I said. "Hold on." Then I used my phone to illuminate the lane in front of me and make my way to the gate. It was locked. I shone the phone up to the top of the wall. It was maybe seven feet or so and someone had kindly cemented shards of glass along the top.

I spoke into my phone a second. "Hold on while I figure this out."

I shone the phone along the back lane again and took a look at the adjacent houses. The windows were set out all the same. The roofline was similar. And there were fire escapes to every house. The first house had one coming from the second first floor window. The second had one coming from the second first floor window. The third house was harder to make out. Too dark. And then there was Manning's.

I lifted the phone to my ear again. "There should be a fire escape second room from the left on the floor your on. There's three floors at the back, so you'll have three floors to climb down."

"Your left or mine?"

"Yours, if you're looking to the rear of the house."

AK said. "What's at the bottom of the fire escape?"

I said. "A yard. I can't see inside, because there's a high gate and an even higher wall. The wall's got some nice decorative glass running along the top."

AK said. "Nice."

I said. "Nice area."

The phone went dead. I said. "AK? You still there?"

He said. "Can you see a light on in the room where this fire escape comes from?"

I said. "Can't see a damn thing round the back of here."

AK said. "Good. That might mean that room's empty. Might be possible." Then. "If you can't see anything, then how comes you know where the fire escape comes from?"

I said. "I said 'there *should be* a fire escape second room from the left'.

"You're not inspiring confidence here." AK. What a moaner!

I said. "Look, it's your only way out unless you gonna get her out the front door without anyone seeing?"

AK said. "Okay. Watch out for us. And be ready to kick that gate in, if I can't unlock it from the back."

I said. "See you soon."

About half a minute later I heard a window open. No lights. I whistled softly like they used to in the old war movies. John Mills would give a call like a nightjar and then Richard Attenborough would make like an owl. AK whistled back. Like AK, not like Richard Attenborough and nothing like an owl. I was waiting staring over the top of the wall, but I couldn't see a damn thing. I pressed a button on my phone to light the screen and waved it about frantically above my head so he would know where the hell I was. Then I heard a voice. Not AK.

"Hey arsehole!"

It was a low, deep voice. Sounded like it belonged to someone big. I pocketed my phone and ran.

Then I heard someone messing with a gate. AK. I stopped and flattened my body against the wall. I figured since I couldn't see anyone then they couldn't see me either. I figured wrong. Someone hit me. Hard. I fell to the ground. My shoulder felt like it had been hit with a sledgehammer. Maybe it had. I scampered away along the lane on my knees in the dark.

"Brendon?" I could hear AK from over the wall.

"Brendon?" AK repeated a semi-tone higher. I heard feet in the dirt. Big feet. Whoever hit me turned and headed towards AK's voice. I contemplated shining my phone on my attacker so I could have an even chance at a fair fight, but then that would give my position away and I wouldn't have an even chance. First rule of survival, if you can't see your enemy and they can't see you, keep it that way.

"Where the hell…" AK sounded frustrated and then I heard the gate hit the wall like it had been pushed inward very fast, say by a kick from a big foot. A big foot belonging to a big guy. A big guy who hits bloody hard. If he hit AK as hard as he hit me, then we were screwed, because I couldn't even get up off the ground yet.

I heard someone make a noise like they had been inflicted with a sudden and severe pain. Then nothing. My ears were straining for more information. What was going on? I was beginning to hear the blood rushing in my ears. Louder like a Boeing crossing the sky coming in to land. I opened my mouth and stretched my jaws to pop my ears, so I could hear more clearly. I wanted to shout out to AK. I daren't. I tried to get up. My arm felt like lead. It was just a heavy chunk of meat hanging from my torso. My shoulder hurt like hell.

Then there was light showing me the wall I was leaning against. The bricks were blackened red and heavily pitted with half the pointing missing. Then I saw the dirt of the lane and then I was blinded as the light filled my vision.

"Get up quick! We need to get out of here. I think I just killed that guy."

It was AK. The throb of my heartbeat left my throat and went back down to where it was supposed to be. Relief.

"Come on, quick!" He grabbed my arm and dragged me up on my feet. He switched off his phone and we walked. Fast. We got to the end of the street. There was light and now I could see him. I saw a girl the other side of him. Jade.

"Jesus!" I paused and gawked at her. She was dressed like a French maid. It was one of those short and skimpy numbers you can buy from Ann Summers designed to tantalise your lover. It didn't.

AK pulled my arm and said. "No time mate. Gotta get outa here. Now!"

We jogged like war wounded around to the front, heading for the X Trail. I'd parked it further away than I remembered. We were on the other side of the street from Manning's Mansion when the front door burst open and two guys stepped out with guns in their hands. I hadn't noticed it before, but there was a garage opposite. We were just passing it. The wooden doors were ajar. One was hanging off and there was graffiti everywhere. AK pushed Jade inside and pulled me in after him. Again into the black. I was tripping over stuff. Cans, rubbish and God knows what! The stench was overpowering. It was like a thousand people had urinated in there. Maybe they had. We heard a shot. Jade screamed. I think I did.

Suddenly we were out in the open again. I could see shop fronts. A group of people were across the street. They were all walking with newspaper packets full of fish and chips in their hands. A couple were staggering in the other direction hand in hand. Three young lads were heading towards us shouting abuse as soon as we hit the street.

"Wey hey! Dirty bastards bin shagging 'ave we?"

They looked pissed and were obviously itching for a fight. AK headed us right at them. "There's two homos in there." He pointed back at the hole in the wall we'd just climbed out of. "Filthy pervs need a good kickin' you ask me."

"Fuckas! Let's get'em!" The biggest one yelled and ran straight passed us. Then we were running. I noticed Jade was bare footed and I was getting flashes of her buttocks as the wind lifted her outfit as she ran. But she was running just as fast I was. AK was a few yards ahead. We heard shots. Three? Four? Hard to say, it all kind of merged. AK glanced behind and swore. I glanced behind and swore. The two guys with the guns were running after us. Adrenalin kicked in and we were running for our lives.

"This way!" AK threw himself into a pizza shop. The little guy behind the counter flung his arms up in the air shouting. "No! Please…Don't!"

I didn't understand his reaction. Then AK got behind the counter, pushed by the little guy and I understood. AK still had his knife in his hand. It had a five-inch blade and it was still smeared in blood. Even I was shocked.

I pushed Jade ahead of me and we ran after AK through a kitchen into a back yard full of crates and empty boxes. AK tried a gate. There was a padlock holding a bar in place across the gate.

"Jesus!" AK turned and stared at me. I didn't want to get shot any more than he did. I pulled two crates full of pop bottles over to a stack of empty crates next to the wall and clambered up on to the top of the wall. Glass grew from the top of the wall like stalagmites. I pulled off my fleece, doubled it over and lay it over the top. I got one leg over and sat on my fleece and then held my hands out for Jade. She clambered up the same way with AK right behind. We all managed to slip over the other side unscathed. AK had toppled the crates as he came over last and then we were running again.

We got maybe twenty yards and we heard more gunfire. We were running down a street in a well-lit area, semi detached houses blurring by each side of us and none of us had a clue where the hell we were going.

AK gasped. "Where is this?"

Jade shouted. "Hendon…we're heading for the docks."

Another shot rung out and the car I was passing lost its windscreen. More adrenalin powered me on.

"This way…" AK ran down someone's garden path. Jade was by his side now. I was maybe three paces behind. We came out the other side onto another street, ran up that street maybe ten yards and did the same again, zig zagging our way through a housing estate.

"Shit!" AK stopped ahead of me. Jade almost fell over him. They stepped back into the garden we were almost through and I joined them hiding behind a dilapidated garden shed.

Panting, I whispered. "Whatsermatter?"

AK said. "Police. Three of them. Armed."

I said. "Good!" I looked back half expecting the two guys with the guns to come running behind any second."

AK held up his knife. "I just killed a guy, Brendon. How do I explain that?"

I looked at AK. Street lighting made his eyes look wide, scared. Maybe it wasn't the lighting. Maybe he was scared. I looked at Jade in her French maid's outfit. She looked away. Shame?

Then there was a horrendous crash in the shed we were hiding behind. Like something had exploded inside. Splinters of wood struck my face. Jade screamed. I heard the scrape of feet running fast behind me. It was the guys with the guns again. They'd just shot at us.

"Aarrgh!" AK screamed and ran out into the street.

"Aarrgh!" I followed him. We ran like escaped convicts right in front of the cops. Jade was sprinting ahead of me. More shots. I never looked back. AK was slowing. I was by his side now. Jade was ahead of us, running like a young Steve Cram in drag. It was surreal. We were leaving the well-lit area of the housing estate now and heading back into blackness. There were high fences either side of us. We were running down the centre of a wide road to God knows where. I could feel a growing pain in my chest. I started to think I was going to have a heart attack.

"Where're we going?"

AK shouted back. "Just keep running. Don't stop!"

I didn't stop. My chest got tighter. My throat burned. But I didn't stop. Jade was well ahead of both of us now; maybe ten yards. It wasn't the same girl I saw earlier covered in Amber's blood. It wasn't the girl I'd been seeing these last few months. It wasn't the girl I thought I loved. Her legs looked implausibly long. Her skirt kicked up on every stride revealing tight, muscular buttocks. She wasn't just fit or muscular. She looked like Kristanna Loken from Terminator 3. She had buns of steel. Even dressed in a French maid's costume she looked masculine.

More shots cut through the sound of my gasping lungs. They were further away, but just as alarming. My legs kept moving and my feet kept pounding. The road ahead seemed never ending.

"Helicopter!" AK yelled beside me. Then I heard it. The sound of the rotors chopping the air hundreds of feet above us. Shit! I 'd had enough. My legs were slowing. AK was ahead of me now.

"Come on…"

I felt my resolve diminish. I had nothing left. My tank was empty and I had nothing left in reserve.

"Brendon! You're a survivor….Survive this!"

My feet were slapping the tarmac now. The engine had stalled and I was just freewheeling to a stop. Jade was a hundred feet away easy. As I came to a stop I noticed she was stopped also. Looking back. AK was between us.

Jade screamed. "In here. They'll never find us!"

AK ran on. He shouted back. "Come on Hawkeye. Come on survivor!"

He sounded part encouraging, part sarcastic. I wasn't even sure if I wanted to survive anymore. I didn't know if I even had a reason to survive anymore.

I looked behind and saw flashing blue lights way off in the distance. The sky was dark and heavy above me. There was a bright white lightsaber stabbing at the earth and coming towards me. The bap bap bap of the helicopter filled my ears. I caught my breath and looked ahead again. AK was standing near a gap in the fence. Only now did I notice it was sheet metal. Corrugated sheet metal fencing. I walked along next to it letting my fingers rub against its profile the way kids do nonchalantly.

"Come on…For Christ's sake, Brendon!" AK screamed at me. I got up to him and he grabbed my shirt and pushed me through the gap in the fence.

I said. "Where the hell are we?" I could see more fencing. Wooden boards and pen wire hemmed us in on the right. There was some sort of shed on my left.

I couldn't see her, but I heard Jade say. "Allotments. Get in here now and cover yourself in this shit. They'll never find you."

I looked down where I thought her voice came from and could just about see her face near the ground. "Jesus!" I could smell it. Horse manure. She was neck deep in the stuff.

AK said. "Clever girl." And then I watched him wade in and do the same. The helicopter grew louder above. A beam of light illuminated the fence not thirty feet away. My survival instinct ignited once more and I dived into the heap and burrowed into it like a rabbit with a ferret on its tail. I hadn't realised how cold I had been until I felt the warmth inside that shit heap. I didn't stop burrowing until I was sure I was completely hidden and prayed AK and Jade had done the same. The noise from the helicopter was deafening now. So close I feared it might land upon us. There were flashes of light cutting through the manure and I could see the yellow of the straw and the green caramel of the shit close to my eyes, so close that the warm, wet straw scratched my eyelids. I pushed my head back deeper into the warmth and hoped my face wasn't visible.

The smell wasn't too bad actually. Not as bad as that abandoned garage we trudged through. And it was very warm. There could have been worse places to hide out. The helicopter hovered above for maybe five minutes. It would have heat signature technology. We've all seen how that works on Crimewatch on TV. I could picture them now in the cab of the helicopter looking down at a great big blob of white. I smiled to myself. Clever Jade. Maybe they would search through the heap with pitchforks. My smile disappeared. But then, we weren't the ones shooting people. Surely, they would be focusing on the gunmen. Yeah, we weren't the bad guys here. The police would soon give up on us once they had the gunmen, wouldn't they? Then I remembered AK's knife. It was covered in blood. Whose blood? Maybe the guy had survived. What if AK had killed him? Shit! I remembered that little dark skinned guy in the pizza shop. He was bound to give the police a description of all of us. Shit again! AK had the bloody knife in his hand. The pizza guy would probably say we had threatened him. Double shit! Maybe the little guy was foreign. He looked Iranian or Turkish or middle eastern. He sounded foreign too. Yes, I liked this train of thought. Maybe he was working here in the UK illegally. Maybe he would keep his mouth shut. Maybe.

My mind went round and round like that for what seemed like hours. I heard the sound of feet running around and the static of the police radios. I heard them searching and shouting and then I heard nothing. In time, the noise of the helicopter faded and so did the sound of distant sirens. After a while, the only noise I could hear was the sound of the wind above me and my own heartbeat in my ears. It was kind of cosy actually. I was all warm and moist and I could have quite easily nodded off. I wondered if this is how it felt like in the womb.

"I haven't heard a damn thing in over an hour." It was Jade.

"What time is it now?" AK.

"Two fifteen."

"Brendon?"

I was so comfortable I could have just ignored AK and gone to sleep.

"Brendon?

I said. "We really are in the shit aren't we?"

AK said. "I'd really like to go home now. I don't like Sunderland."

I poked my head through to the fresh air. It was freezing. I could see the outline of AK's head and Jade was standing up, brushing herself down. I said. "Why were you in there, Jade?"

Jade continued with the brushing down, picking bits of straw off her costume and out of her hair. I said. "Jade?"

AK stumbled out of the heap and stood brushing himself off. He said. "You gonna answer him or should I?"

Jade said. "Fuck you, old man."

I was confused. What the hell was going on? I left the warmth of the shit heap and stood out of it onto terra firma. I said. "Will someone tell me what the hell is going on?"

AK, totally matter of fact, said. "Your little French maid here. She used to work for Manning. As one of his escorts."

Jade again. "Fuck you!"

I said. "Jade?"

She stepped over to me. I could just about see her face. She looked like she had two black eyes. "Don't listen to him, Brendon. Come on, take me home."

I said. "Why are dressed like a tart?"

Jade explained. "Ask him. He made me put this on."

AK. "Because she was starkers on a bed and it was either that, a schoolgirl uniform or some PVC bondage gear."

I said. "Why were you naked in Manning's place?"

Jade grabbed my shirt and pulled herself close to me. "The bastard kidnapped me, that's why!"

"What does AK mean…you used to work for Manning?"

"He's talking shit!"

"AK?"

AK pushed past me to the gap in the fencing. He said. "You've been had, Brendon."

I said. "Jade?"

"He's just jealous of you and I, Brendon."

AK pulled my shoulder. "Come on, let's get outa here."

I rubbed my shoulder, it didn't hurt too much now, but it felt kind of crunchy. I stepped out onto the street and looked left and right. Nothing.

AK held out his hand. "Give me the keys."

"Why?"

AK said. "No reason for us all to take a chance. I'll go see if its still there and if everything's okay I'll come round and pick you up, okay?"

I gave him the keys and he took off. I got back inside the fence and picked more straw and stuff off myself. Jade was standing a few feet from me. Without looking up, I said. "Just tell me the truth, Jade."

Jade wrapped her arms around herself against the cold and leaned against the shed behind her. She said. "You don't want the truth, Brendon."

I looked up, but her face was lost in the blackness. I said. "Try me."

She said. "Do you still love Amber?"

It threw me. I didn't know how to answer her. "We're talking about you here, Jade. How well do you know this arsehole, Manning?"

She said. "About as well as Amber."

I was thinking AK had been right. I had been conned. "You working for him now?"

She got up off the shed and tucked herself against me. "God no! I haven't seen him in years. I got pulled by the police when I left yours. Next thing I know I'm in that place and they're stripping me naked."

"Why?"

"I don't know do I…I was pissed outa my head."

"Why did AK think you worked there before then?"

Silence. She started to play with the gold chain around my neck. It was the first thing Amber had ever bought me. I pulled her fingers from it.

She said. "Why do you think Amber faked her death?"

I said. "I know why. We're talking about you. Not Amber."

She fell back on the shed again. "*I* didn't leave you. *I* didn't lie to you. I got *you* through all that pain. I was there for you, remember?"

"Did you know she was alive all this time?"

"No. That was just as much a shock to me."

I went back to my original question. "So again. Did you work there? For him? Manning?"

She made a noise. It sounded like she chuckled. "You're so naïve, Brendon. That's where we met, me and Amber. I was dancing in one of his clubs. Not that one. It was in town. It's closed now."

"Go on."

I couldn't see her face, but I saw her shaking her head. "He brought her along one night. She looked about twelve. She was a real greenhorn. I don't think she'd ever set foot out of Ryhope."

I said. "So you showed her the ropes."

She said. "Kind of…we became friends. Manning wanted her…I guess he thought she would make him a pile."

"And did she?"

Jade did the chuckle thing again. "That's why I said 'why do you think she faked her own death?' She knew she was screwed once Manning found her again. She knew you wouldn't want her just like you don't want me now. Isn't that right?"

I didn't even bother to answer that. I heard the sound of a diesel way off. AK.

Chapter Thirty

The one working headlight belonging to my X Trail came down the road towards me. Jade stepped out from the gap and said. "You think you could take me home to Durham? I'm really not in the mood to meet those girls I saw at your place."

I just looked at her. AK pulled up at the side of the road and I opened the passenger door and got in. Jade jumped in the back.

"Hi gorgeous. Fancy seeing you with these two arseholes."

I swung round in my seat and was confronted with Manning pointing a pistol at my face. "Shit!"

AK said. "Sorry."

Manning said. "You know, that's not very friendly."

I said. "Neither is abducting young girls from Russia and forcing them to work as sex slaves."

Manning said. "So that's why your crony here was in my establishment. Drive."

AK said. "Where?"

"Turnaround and head out of Hendon. South towards Seaham."

AK said. "I'm not from around these parts."

Manning poked his gun in AK's shoulder. "Just drive…I'll keep you right."

I don't mind admitting I was feeling more than a little nervous. I hated this man with a vengeance and he knew it. He'd already tried to shoot me once, so I knew he was serious. I had to think of a way to survive this and think quickly.

"The police are all over the place. Best AK drops you at your club. If we get stopped you'll be…"

Smack! The bastard whacked the side of my head with his gun. "Shut the fuck up, Mister Survival. We're not gonna get stopped by no cops. You think you know it all, don't you? Lemme tell you…you know sweet FA!"

My head was stinging. If he thought a blow to my head would shut me up, he was wrong. It just made me madder. I said. "So

Jade…you and my late wife fucked this maniac. You both got a thing for hideous old pervs…is that it?"

Manning told AK to take a left.

Jade said. "At least I got paid. Your sweet little angel wife fucked him for free."

Manning broke out in laughter. "Hoo hooo…! Good one. She's right too. Hoo hoo hoo…" The bastard was almost hysterical.

Jade said. "Yeah…Fuck you too, Isaac."

I turned and made eye contact with AK. He looked like he was thinking pretty much the same as I was. How did I ever get mixed up with that woman?

We were heading towards some traffic lights. They were on red. AK eased of the accelerator and changed down. Manning spat in AK's ear. "Stop and I'll kill you both!"

We went through the red. It was after two in the morning. Nothing on the roads. I was hoping we would see a taxi or a lorry. I would have grabbed the wheel and ran us straight into it. AK glanced over again. I'm sure he was thinking the same way.

I said. "So what happened to Amber's two buddies?"

Manning said. "There were never two of them, *Mister TV*. Danker was working for me. You killed him when you fucked off with my merchandise."

He sounded mad. Good. I wanted him mad. Mad people make mistakes. I chuckled. "Good news at last! One less piece of scum in the world."

He wasn't biting. He said. "You're right. Young fucka was taking half my profits. You did me a favour Hawke." Then to AK. "Left here."

AK turned us left and suddenly we were on an unlit road with fields either side of us. I didn't like this at all. I needed to think of something quickly.

AK said. "Look, Manning…we've got your girls. How about we do a deal?"

I said. "No. Don't listen to him. We don't have any girls."

AK said. "We do and you'll never get your merchandise if you kill us now."

I punched AK's shoulder. "Shut the hell up, AK. We're not handing over any of the girls." I was sure the punch hurt me more than it hurt AK. I hit him with my sledgehammered arm. It brought tears to my eyes.

Jade said. "He's right. I've seen two of them at his place."

I heard Manning slap her face. "You still high girl? I reckon you still have a hard-on for Mr Survival here."

"I don't, Isaac. I just want you to get what you lost."

I didn't know whether she was trying to help us or she actually meant what she was saying. I didn't much care either. I continued with my act. "She's talking shit. The girls ran off. They're spread all over Cornwall as we speak. You'll never see them again."

Whack! He hit the exact same spot as before. It burned like hell! That bastard knew how to rile a guy. I wanted to shove that gun up his arse barrel first and pull the bloody trigger. Blow the bastard inside out. Boy, was I seething now!

"No, Mister fucking survival...*You'll* never see them again. You think your little act is gonna fool me? I reckon Mademoiselle Knickerless here is telling me the truth."

AK said. "She is...she is. I'll turn around right now and..."

Manning cut him off. "Turn around and you're a dead man." He pressed the pistol into the back of AK's neck. "Just keep on down this road. I'll go see if our Jade here is telling the truth. Later."

Later? That kind of creeped me out. Later, as in afterwards. After what? I glanced at AK. Where had he put that knife? Maybe I could pull it, whip around lightening fast and stab Manning right in his bloody eye. I made a cough to attract AK's attention. He didn't do the obvious thing and look my way right away. After maybe five seconds I made my left hand into a fist and made a stabbing action back and forth like I was stabbing my own thigh. Very slowly and very subtle, he moved his head from side to side. He didn't have the knife anymore. Shit! I had liked that idea. A lot.

Manning still had the pistol pressed into the back of AK's neck. He said. "Pretty soon you'll see a sign for a picnic area on the left. Take it."

I said. "Good. I'm feeling pretty peckish. You brought sandwiches?"

Nobody laughed.

I saw the little brown sign come up. AK changed down into second and a big hard ball of fear rose up in my throat. I didn't feel like making jokes anymore. I knew this place. I recognised it now. I'd been here a few years ago when I was doing some research into the erosion of our coastline. The picnic area was a large tarmac carpark with maybe fifty parking bays that overlooked the North Sea. There were a lot of higgledy-piggledy steps than ran down to a long pebbly beach. That was the only way down, other than straight over the cliff, which was maybe eighty or ninety feet. I had this awful premonition we weren't going to be taking the steps.

"Drive over there…" Manning pointed to the far corner of the carpark close to the green that ran along the cliff. On a sunny day this would be a great spot to have a picnic, walk your dog, take a walk hand in hand with your girl. I was beginning to wonder if I'd ever get the chance to do any of those things after tonight.

Manning said. "Pull up and keep your hands at ten to two."

AK did as he was told. We sat with the engine idling for maybe five seconds.

Manning shouted. "Turn the engine off and pull the handbrake."

AK said. "Can't do that with my hands at ten to two and my knob isn't that long."

It appeared I wasn't the only one who used humour to deal with fear.

Jade said. "He's right. He's kind of handicapped in that region."

AK laughed. "Yeah…and I'm gay too, right? Actually, if I had to choose between sleeping with a homo or a used up little whore like you, it'd be a no brainer. God knows what's been inside you." Then he shot me a glance. "Sorry, Brendon…I wasn't meaning you."

Jade bit. "You gonna stand for that piece of shit talking about your girlfriend that way."

I turned around in my seat. Caught Jade's eye. I said. "You're talking to that animal beside you, right?"

Her face was a picture. She really thought that she and I were still some kind of item after all I'd heard tonight. Bloody amazing!

If eyes had the power to kill then Manning had just ended my life, because he was looking at me really ugly. Having said that, I don't think he had many options with that face. He said. "You know if I had been a shrewder man I would have thought ahead, bought up some Brendon fuckin' Hawke merchandise. There's always a boom in sales after one of you celeb types kicks the bucket."

So Manning was a funny guy too. I wasn't laughing. He said. "Out. You first Mister Survival."

I was starting to get used to my new title. I was thinking I might use it if I ever get another series on TV. I was also thinking that if I get out of my car it might be the last time. I stalled. "You want to tell me where I'm going?"

Manning was really helpful. "You'll find out soon enough. Get out!"

I looked at AK. I couldn't read his face. He wasn't in a position to help, what with Manning still poking his gun in his neck. I gave a little smile. Brendon Hawke, ever the optimist!

I got out into the cold. My fleece was stuck on top of a wall at the back of Manning's place and the remnants of the lovely warm, moist manure heap now made me feel like I was wearing my clothes straight out of the wash. Apart from the smell, of course. My body tensed against the chill.

I heard Manning's voice again, but the wind was whipping over the tops of the cliff and carrying it away. Then AK got out of his side. I dared to glance across at him, but the car was between us. I couldn't catch his eye. Then Manning shouted through the window.

"Both of you start walking. Slowly."

I turned around and saw Manning was now sitting behind the wheel. My wheel. There was something just visible above the dash. It looked like a sock. A sock with a gun it. That told me that the gun wasn't just for show. It wasn't just to threaten us over the edge. Clever bastards like Manning fire their guns through socks so as not leave any gun shot residue on their hands if they get caught. It also catches the shell so no evidence is left on the ground. If he wasn't serious about shooting us then he wouldn't have bothered with the sock. I'm glad my bladder was empty. Otherwise, I'd have been emptying it around about now. In my pants.

"Turn around again Hawke and I shoot you."

The wind was wild. I thought about calling something over to AK, but I'd have to shout and the insane bastard with the gun behind me would get to hear to.

"Walk!" He just about screamed.

The one light that still worked on my X Trail illuminated the grass in front of me. I could see each blade of grass glistening with the wetness of the sea fret that was blowing in. I estimated there were maybe ten or twelve steps and then nothing. It was just blackness thereafter. From where I was standing there was no way of telling whether it was a gradual slope or a sheer drop from that point. And I wasn't overjoyed about the way I was about to find out.

I took a step forward. Followed slowly by another. In my peripheral vision I saw AK was doing the same. At times like these our brains are often numbed with panic. Once the stress response is triggered and the adrenalin floods our bloodstream, although it is designed to enable us to either fight or take flight, it often cripples us. Even with all my training and experiences in near death survival situations, I have to admit I have no super powers. I know it might be a shock to everyone, but there you go. Brendon Hawke is just as human and vulnerable and mortal as everyone else. Luckily, however, I have learned a few things over the years about staying alive.

Instead of walking directly ahead, I went off at an angle. The idea was to do three things that would help to keep us both alive. First thing was to put as much distance between the both of us as possible. It's hard to shoot two people at the same time, but it's harder still when they're a good distance apart. Secondly, walking at an angle would lead me out of the brightest light of the X Trail's one headlight beam. Again, making myself a harder target to hit. And thirdly, walking at an angle would mean I'd have to take more steps to reach the cliff edge and as I said before, I was in no rush to find out what lay beyond.

After my fifth step I was about ten feet in front of the X Trail, but instead of being directly in front, I was maybe seven feet to the left now. I dared to glance right and immediately noticed that AK had done the same thing. We'd started out at about seven feet apart and were now maybe eighteen feet apart. I suddenly felt a hell of a lot more optimistic.

I glanced back around at the X Trail. Manning was standing behind the driver's door with the gun in the sock pointed through the open window towards AK. When he saw me turn, the sock flicked towards me.

"Survival man?"

I stopped and looked back at him. My breathing was funny, awkward, laboured.

AK shouted. "Hey Manning, why don't you fight us like a real man instead of an impotent fuck who has to bully girls into having sex with him."

He was goading him. Trying to get him to change his focus back to him. It worked. Manning's gaze and his sock both switched back to AK. This was it. My one and only chance. All that adrenalin hit my legs now like rocket fuel. And boy did I take off!

As I sped away along the cliff tops like a frightened rabbit a shot decimated the silence of the night, then another and another. I ran faster than I had ever run as a teenager. Like someone possessed. Like someone running for their life. After maybe five minutes my heart felt like it might burst in my chest. My throat was burning. The air was raw. It was arctic. My lungs could take no more. I dropped to the grass and lay there like a corpse waiting for my breathing to recover.

All I could hear was the sound of my own respiration desperately trying to regain control of my body. I lay like that for several minutes and then I heard the sound of sirens. Sweat was cooling rapidly on my back and my chest and I began to shiver. But the sound of those sirens was the most wonderful sound I could have hoped for. I lifted my head and saw the flashing blue lights speeding along the same road that we had just driven along. They made the turn in to the picnic area. And then I heard more gunfire. And then I heard nothing, but the sound of the waves on the pebbled shore below.

I suddenly realized that the police were going to find my car at the picnic area. Within minutes they would trace it back to me and then within a few more minutes they would be knocking on my door. I wouldn't be there and Katerina and Anya wouldn't have a clue what to tell them. Shit! Think Brendon. Think.

I took out my mobile and rang home. It rang ten times and then went to answer phone. I hung up and rang again. And again. Finally, Katerina answered sounding very apprehensive. "Hello?"

In my mind I could see her standing in my lounge, holding my phone, her eyes as big and as bright as a child's. I shook the image away. "Katerina, it's me. Brendon."

"Oh hello, Brendon." Her voice, her accent, her pronunciation sounded even more seductive over the phone.

My teeth were chattering. My jaw stiff with the cold. I wondered if that would make me sound seductive too. No, probably not. I said. "I want you ring nine nine nine after I hang up and tell the police that some one has stolen the car."

"Someone has stolen the car?" She sounded shocked. I nearly corrected her, but stopped myself.

"Yes, that's right. Tell them it was parked in the drive and then you heard a noise and when you looked outside it had gone. Can you do that for me, Katerina?"

I figured since I had risked life and limb to save her from a life of prostitution in Manning's Mansion, then asking her to lie for me was a fair request.

"Okay, Brendon. Where are you?"

Good question. But what should I tell her? I hesitated; trying to think of some kind of alibi should the police think I had been connected with what ever happened back there at the picnic area after I ran. Oh, yes, there was the small matter of the guy AK had stabbed back in Hendon too. This would be a lot easier if I knew AK was safe and had made his escape in the same way I had.

"Gotya!"

"Jesus!" Then. "Am I glad to see you!"

I couldn't believe it. It was AK.

"How d'ya find me?" I was lying in the grass in the middle of the night, maybe a mile from where we last parted company and somehow AK had found me.

In a voice belonging to a BBC nature documentary, AK said. "Years of hunting every quarry known to mankind has taught me how to track, using nothing but the senses God provided me with."

I said. "You saw the light on my phone, didn't you?"

AK said. "Might have."

"Years of hunting…" I chuckled.

AK said. "So who you speaking to?"

"Shit!" I'd gotten sidetracked what with AK arriving. I put the phone back to my ear again. "Hello, Katerina?"

"Yes?"

"Sorry, about that. It was just AK. Listen, the police will give you a crime reference number. Write it down. If they ask who owns the vehicle tell them my name. If they want to speak to me, tell them I'm out."

She said. "Where are you?"

I wasn't happy about lying to the girl, but it was best she knew as little as possible about the truth and then she couldn't get into trouble herself. I said. "AK and I are out hunting rabbits. If the police ask just tell them that, okay?"

"Okay."

"We'll be back breakfast time. Have a good night's sleep and we'll see you then, okay?"

"Okay."

"Goodnight."

"Goodnight, Brendon."

I shut my phone and put it back in my pocket. AK said. "What now?"

I looked back along the coast. There were still lights shining. A blue flashing one and several headlights. "I say we put as much distance between that man and us as possible."

AK said. "It must be what…twenty two, twenty three miles back to your place. Is that enough for you?"

I patted his shoulder and set off. "Come on, if we cut across the fields and walk as directly in a straight line as possible, I reckon we can cut it down to less than eighteen."

AK kept pace beside me. "Just a bit of a stroll then?"

"Hmm."

Chapter Thirty One

We got back just before eight, the sun was up, but the thick grey cloud was doing its best to disguise the fact. The girls were still in bed, so I stripped and went to bed myself. AK hit the settee. Everyone got up about eleven when the police came knocking. Since I was out 'hunting' most of the night, they asked Katerina where the car had been parked and she showed them, just in front of my garage. After taking a brief statement and a look around my garden, they left. No mention of whether the X Trail had been found or not. No awkward questions about whether I knew a man named Isaac Manning or not. I saw the relief on AK's face when they drove off and we both blew out a long, satisfying sigh. We all ate breakfast together. AK kept the girls entertained whilst I scanned the internet for any news.

By two in the afternoon there was news of a fatal stabbing in Sunderland and a Mr I. Manning, a Sunderland businessman, was helping police with their enquiries. By ten that evening, just after we had all eaten a Chinese take out from Chesters, a North East News bulletin on the TV reported that a Mr Isaac Manning had been charged with the murder of one of his employees, a Mr. P. Havelock. He was also found in possession of a stolen car in which a hunting knife was found with Havelock's blood on it.

When the bulletin ended AK said. "Thank God I wiped that handle before I dropped it down the side of the driver's seat."

I said. "You think he picked it up maybe and got his prints on it."

AK cracked open his fourth Bud of the night and chuckled. "Let's hope so."

I lay back in my armchair and sipped at the cold lager in my hand. "I'll drink to that." I said.

AK raised his can to me and we drank.

After a few minutes my mood dipped and I felt more than a little melancholic. The radio was playing through the TV and Marvin Gaye was asking 'What's going on?' I turned to AK and said. "How do feel about everything?"

AK put his can down and looked at me pensively. "Let's see…" His eyes turned to the ceiling. "It looks as though Manning is gonna go away for murder; he has three less buddies to do his dirty work; we're home and safe drinking damn good beer and just through that door there…" With his foot he indicated the room where Anya and Katerina were sleeping. "Are two of the most delectable young ladies I have ever laid my eyes on."

He brought his can to his lips again and finished his beer. "How do I feel about everything?" He said with a grin forming at his lips. "I never felt better, that's how I feel. I never felt better."

I smiled with him and another can washed some of that melancholy away and pretty soon I drifted off into a coma-like state, which was just what my body needed to recover from that eighteen mile hike.

When Amber woke it was just gone half past ten in the morning. She'd been asleep almost twelve hours. When she looked at her watch she jumped out of bed like it was on fire. Her head thumped like pistons on a steam engine.

"Shit! Shit! Shit!" She swore out loud as she saw the time on the purple wall clock, pulling on her shoes and racing out of the room. When she got to the bottom of the stairs Lenny was standing by the door, his arm outstretched with his hand flat against the jamb supporting him. It meant he was blocking the door. Amber stopped and put her hands on her hips.

"I have to leave."

"You've had a really bad head injury and frankly you're lucky to be alive. I'd rather you didn't." He said it straight faced with little emotion, but the underlying message was clear. He wasn't moving.

Amber stood her ground, her mind spinning on trying to think of her next move. She let her shoulders drop and took her hands from her hips, flicking her hair back and leaning against the wall. She was trying for cool and she came pretty close, standing like she could care less. "Yeah. You're right, Len. Sorry. I woke up and didn't know where I was."

Lenny appeared to relax also, dropping his arm and standing up straight. "You want some breakfast…some bagels, cereal, orange juice?"

Amber liked the sound of that. It would buy her five minutes. "Sounds lovely Lenny."

"Sure. You go back up to bed if you like and I'll bring it up."

"Okay. Thanks Lenny."

Amber turned and plodded back up the stairs heavily. As she climbed she heard Lenny go through into the kitchen, followed by the sounds of someone busy in a kitchen, the rattle of the cutlery drawer, the bang of a cupboard door shutting, the sound of Lenny whistling something unrecognisable. She stood absolutely still at the top stair for maybe three seconds. When she was sure his attention would be fully engaged making her breakfast, she padded silently back down the stairs and slipped out the front door whisper quiet.

Lenny kept his keys on a set of three hooks just inside the front porch. The house keys were hanging there, a set of smaller shed or garage keys and the familiar large fob of a set of car keys. Amber grabbed them and headed for Lenny's Jag.

"Determined little bugger, aren't we?" Lenny said walking across the garden towards her with a black plastic bag in one hand.

Amber didn't break her stride, but she stopped when she reached the driver's door. "I'll bring it back, Lenny. I just need to be somewhere."

"Lenny stopped when he got to his wheelie bin. He opened the lid and dropped the black plastic bag inside. Then he continued walking until he met Amber at his car. "Ah ha…I can't let you go, Amber. You had a concussion. It's a wonder you didn't fracture your skull." He held out his hand. "Now, hand me the keys."

Amber's shoulders slumped noticeably. She let herself fall against the car door and blew out a long, heavy, frustrated sigh of defeat. She raised her arm as though it was a steel girder and reluctantly handed Lenny his keys.

Lenny pressed a button on the fob, unlocking the doors and the interior of the Jag lit up. "Get in. The other side. I'll drive you wherever you like. It obviously means a lot to you."

Amber kissed her own fingers and then placed those same fingers on Lenny's cheek. "You're a good friend, Lenny."

"Just get in."

Amber smiled. "No, now I know you'll take me we can have that breakfast. There's no rush. I don't need to be there until five."

They went back inside and had breakfast. Breakfast turned into brunch as Amber finished her bagels and started on the bacon sandwich Lenny prepared for her. Then they did the dishes together and shared the morning paper. It was all very civilised. At quarter to one Lenny suggested he take Amber into town to buy something nice to wear.

"I don't have much money, Lenny. I can't afford to waste it on clothes I don't need."

Lenny took a wad of notes out of his wallet and threw it into Amber's lap. "I don't have anyone to spend my money on and you need to look good for Brendon."

Amber protested. "God, no Lenny…this is too much."

"I've lost more than that in the casino in Newcastle in one night. Please spend it. At least you'll see something for it."

Lenny drove Amber into the centre of Carlisle and left her to shop for an hour. When he picked her up she had three large bags from three different shops. When they got back to Lenny's, Lenny made tea whilst Amber showered and changed. When she came back down she was dressed in an animal print jumper dress, all browns, blacks, golds and creams. It was short and figure hugging and she looked amazing. Her legs were painted a light tan by a pair of silky leggings, which disappeared into calf length brown leather boots. Her hair was tousled and bounced with every step. Lenny stared at her open-mouthed as she entered the kitchen.

"Here, I got you this." Amber held up a black embroidered shirt. It was casual, but smart. Like something you could wear to the restaurant, but also the beach café.

"I didn't give you the money to spend on me."

Amber held out her other hand and dropped a couple of twenties onto the bench. "There's a little left. I really appreciate it, Lenny."

"I only gave you two hundred. Did you shoplift that stuff? You look like you spent a thousand."

Amber smiled coyly and reached out for one of the mugs Lenny had just filled. Lenny lifted the other mug to his lips, but his eyes never left Amber, his head shaking slowly in appreciation.

Amber did the coy smile thing again. "Stop it. You'll make me blush."

Lenny gestured to the door with his mug of tea. "I think we better finish these and get going before I change my mind and decide to keep you for myself."

Five minutes later, Amber was in Lenny's car wrapping her arms around herself against the cold interior of the Jaguar. Lenny had gone back in the house. He was a minute, maybe ninety seconds and then he came back out, got in and they drove off.

"What's this?" Amber said clutching the used Cooperative shopping bag that Lenny had placed on her lap as he had got in.

"We're going back to Burnside. Right?"

Amber nodded and smiled apologetically.

"Well, that's a good hour there and a good hour back and God knows how long in between."

Amber waited for the rest of it, her eyebrows rising and staying there.

"Well, if you don't get peckish. I know I will."

Amber nodded and placed the bag in the foot well behind her. Lenny put the radio on to fill the awkwardness of silence, but apart from one station playing punk and another playing a sixties medley on a Hammond organ, every other station was full of tedious chat. On one station a man was ringing in arguing the merits of taking natural remedies for combating impotence over Viagra and on another station two lesbians were discussing various uses for used rubber gloves. When one of them suggested that straight women could recycle their Marigolds by cutting the fingers off and using them as condoms if they were unlucky enough to have husbands that would fit them, Lenny reached over and turned the damn thing off. They exchanged a glance then, both smiling at the banality of talk radio. It seemed to ease the tension.

Lenny thought this was as good a time as any to ask some questions, awkward as it might be. "Who was that girl at Brendon's?"

"I thought you saw her. It was Jade."

"Jade?"

Amber gave him a puzzled face. "You know Jade don't you?"

Lenny shook his head. "I've heard the name mentioned I guess. Would that be the same Jade who was your friend when you and Brendon first met?

"We've been friends since I was sixteen. I thought you'd met her."

"No."

Amber let Lenny focus on the road as he pulled out from the lane from his house and onto the A69 heading east. He gave way to a two-trailer articulated lorry and it hurtled past shaking the Jag as they sat stationary at the junction. And then Lenny accelerated quickly, caught it up and overtook it before settling back down to an easy and quiet seventy miles an hour with an empty road ahead.

"She hit me. Jade. She didn't even speak. She just hit me. Hard!" Amber told him, fingering the wound on the top of her head.

"Leave it. You don't want it to start bleeding again."

Amber dropped her hand into her lap and picked the nails of her other hand, then bringing her fingers to her mouth to bite off the remaining nails, chewing them smooth.

"Why would she do that?" Lenny tried.

"I was hoping you could tell me."

Lenny shook his head. "Like I said, I've never met the girl. Brendon keeps his love life to himself these days."

"So *it was* Jade in the photographs?"

Lenny's head snapped left catching Amber's eyes. "What? No...I mean..." He was struggling to say the right thing.

"It's okay, Lenny. I kind of guessed, anyway."

"What photographs are you talking about?"

Amber knew they had about sixty miles ahead of them. It would take an hour, easy. She started from the beginning, her alcoholic mother, Manning, his club, their relationship, meeting Jade, running away, meeting Brendon, Manning finding her and blackmailing her, her faked death, what she'd been doing these last two years. She told him pretty much everything. When she finished, Lenny stopped the car on the side of the road at the opening to a field, undid his seatbelt and wrapped his arms around her. Tight. They sat like that hugging each other for maybe thirty seconds until Lenny finally pulled back.

"If I don't move now..." He said rather robotically. "There's a good chance I'll stay in this position, like forever...I think my spine just seized."

"Oargh...Lenny." Amber sympathised, but then added. "But hey! You give good hugs for an oldie."

Lenny shuffled back into his seat and pulled his belt back around. "Thanks. It must be that knock to your head. It's affecting your eyesight. I'm only twenty five really."

"Well, if you were I'd probably have to fight them off for a hug like that."

Lenny pulled back onto the road and quickly got up to speed. "Never mind you'd *probably* have to fight them off…you'd definitely! I had my moments back in the day."

Amber chuckled. "Didn't you and Mrs Hawke once have something?"

"Something?" Lenny said, but it sounded rhetorical the way he said it. "I think it was mostly wishful thinking on my part, Amber. She was too good for…the likes of me." He put on an amusing voice for the last four words, as if that might make it less of a big deal, somehow. It had the opposite effect.

"I'm sure you're wrong. She never married again after Brendon's Dad died. I don't think it had anything to do with you. She was just, you know…devoted."

"Maybe."

Amber patted his knee. "No, really. Sometimes it's like that. You meet 'The One' and nobody else could ever compare."

Lenny wasn't comfortable with all the focus on him. He turned it back around to Amber. "And you…what if you can't have your Brendon. What if your friend Jade has taken his heart in your absence?"

Amber didn't answer him. She turned her head to look out of her window. They were bypassing Hexham. The road was quiet for mid afternoon.

"Sorry…that was insensitive." Lenny slowed for the roundabout that gives you the option of going into Hexham. He accelerated coming off it, bypassing Hexham and settled at seventy again.

Amber didn't answer. Lenny tried again. "What's your plan when we get to wherever we're going?"

Amber sighed heavily. "I thought I knew…I thought maybe…" She sighed again and this time she deflated so much she almost dissolved into the fabric of the seat.

Lenny said. "I'm sorry, Amber."

"No…this is all me. I screwed my whole life up. I'm sorry I ever met than man."

'Brendon?"

"No! Jesus…No. *Manning.* If only I had kept away from the bastard."

"You were sixteen…you said yourself – you had nobody that cared a damn about you. You were vulnerable."

"I was stupid. Stupid, stupid, bloody stupid. And now I have to pay for it for the rest of my life." Amber said, close to tears.

Lenny said. "So you made one stupid mistake. You think I never made any mistakes? You think Brendon didn't? You didn't kill anybody. You didn't hurt anybody. You were just a young vulnerable girl who needed some love in her life. Some happiness. So you fell for this Manning's charms. For a little slice of time…that's all. You didn't stay with him. You saw sense and you got out of there. I say good on yer…shows me what kind of person you really are…And if I can see that…" Lenny let out a long, full breath. "If I can see you're a good woman, Amber…then so will Brendon."

Chapter Thirty Two

I got home about four in the afternoon after visiting my mother. I didn't just feel down, I felt like I'd just found her dead. She wasn't. She looked well actually. But she didn't have a clue who the hell I was. It hurt like no pain I ever felt before.

I took a long, hot shower, got a four pack from the fridge and settled in a seat in my conservatory. I've never considered myself as the depressive type, but I guess everyone has their moments. The rain pelted the glass in front of me. Hundreds of tiny streams heading south to the sill. The biggest delta in the world, right there on my conservatory window. I stared unblinking. Hypnotised.

"Brendon, it's five to five." AK broke the spell. I gave him a nod, walked through to the hall and pulled my waterproof on. My chest felt tight. My lungs had shrunk. Either that or my intercostals had just atrophied all of a sudden. I left my coat zipped halfway in case it made my breathing worse. Glancing back through the lounge I caught AK's eye. He smiled the kind of smile your mother smiles just before you go into to see the dentist. The kind of smile that says 'good luck'. The kind of smile that's meant to make things better. It didn't.

I walked out into the cold and the rain and made my way around the house to the footpath down the valley. It had been a beautiful, Spring day that first time Amber and I had taken this very walk. We had held hands, squinting into the sun, chatting like we had known each other for years. We'd happened across this footpath by accident after walking for miles and getting too tired to walk the same way back. It was meant to be a short cut. We were trying to cut the walk short. But then Amber had needed to pee and so we ducked into the old barn so she could relieve herself. I had watched as she had squatted and then looked out at the woods as she did what she had to do. And then when I heard her finish I turned around just in time to see her pulling up her panties tight over her perfect bottom. They never made it all the way.

I was twenty seven years old, then. But I swear to God that was the day I lost my virginity. We didn't just make love. We fused. Melted into each other. I became part of her and she, part of me.

She told me I was her first. I believed her. She was twenty. Why wouldn't I? And now here I was walking down to meet the love of my life after she has been dead two years. *Two years!* I should have been ecstatic. On top of the world. Like a kid at Christmas.

It was like waking up Christmas morning, full of the anticipation and excitement that you've stored up for so long, only to remember that your grandmother died a week earlier. It was bitter sweet. I wasn't smiling and I didn't feel like opening any presents.

By the time I got to the valley floor it was nearly dark. Not dusk. Darker. The sky was a heavy, murky blanket that pressed down on the earth. The half-bare trees the only thing from stopping it from crushing me. When I reached the barn it was merely a silhouette. Shades of grey were all I could see, with the wide opening at the front of the barn appearing to be an interminable black hole. Was she there already? Was she even coming at all? Or had I been dreaming these last few days?

I walked into the gloom of the barn and immediately I saw her. My eyes were busy adjusting to the low light, but there was no mistaking the image before me. It was like some weird psychosis. She looked like Amber. But not. Her hair was different. Shorter. Lighter maybe. Her face had changed. Thinner. Her eyes…I took a step forward. Another. I stopped breathing. It was Amber. There was no doubt, now.

I said. "You can go back to your life and forget about Manning. The bastard won't be bothering you anymore."

She was still in the shadows. She said. "You killed him?"

I repeated. "I said he won't be bothering you anymore, didn't I?"

Her voice was all breathy and nervous. She said. "Did you find the two guys he abducted? Thrash and…"

I jumped in. "No."

"You haven't found…"

"I said no didn't I?" I might have been a little tense. I emptied my lungs pretty much all the way and started again. "Your pal Danny or Darren…or whatever…was never your pal. He worked for Manning. Anyway, he also won't be bothering you anymore."

She cleared her throat and pushed out a fast, heavy breath. "And my friend, Thrash?"

"Friend?"

She stepped forward. "Brendon, he was just a friend, we never..."

"Shut up! I don't want to hear it. I've no idea where your friend is. We never found him, so..." I think I was going to say something cutting like, 'so you'll have to go find some other guy to shag'. But I didn't. I managed to control myself.

We stood facing each other, breathing out clouds of cold air into the darkness between us. For me, it signified the feelings between us. I looked into the eyes of the woman who had stolen my heart, filled it to bursting point, and then shattered it. She blinked a glossy film of tears over them over and over again and then I saw them pool, heavy on her bottom lids. She breathed in deep and her chest rose, her breasts pressing firm against the material of her jacket. As she let it out slow, her breath hissing softly between her teeth, tears fell from her left eye and then seconds later, from her right also. But she never looked away.

To describe the emotions I was feeling right then, right there would take a book in itself. And then some. Immense feelings of longing and relief were clashing violently with stabs of anger and absolute outrage that were threatening to pour out at any moment.

We stood like that, our eyes locked on each other's; still as the air in a vacuum and if a week had passed I wouldn't be surprised. Finally, I felt something break in my throat. A word. I had spoken without even thinking. It just broke free from my lips like a caged animal. Not a cute, little furry animal. Something sinister and likely to bite.

"Why?"

I think she must have prepared her words, rehearsed them even. She took a deep breath and began. "I was young, Brendon. I was alone in the world. You know how my mother was. She never gave a damn about me. I had no real friends at school. I had no one. So yes, I went along with..." She paused, not wanting to use his name. Her eyes fell to the floor and she sighed loudly. "I went along with *it*. It felt good for a little while. To think that someone was interested in me. To think that someone cared about me. I wanted that. I wanted to have fun. I wanted to be liked and to be loved."

"Puh!"

Amber continued. Her eyes full and red around the edges. Wet. "I didn't know what love was, Brendon. Until you showed me. I thought that because he bought me stuff, took me to nice places…"

"Strip clubs? Fuckin'brothels?" Oh yes, I was pretty mad. I couldn't stop myself even if I wanted to. The words just spilled out.

"I didn't know that then. I hadn't been anywhere in my life. It seemed glamorous, exciting. Somebody was trying to please me…to make me happy…"

"So you enjoyed it? Being in his club. Being in his company…" I had rounds and rounds of ammunition that were just dying to be fired. "He made you happy, eh?" Oh yes, I was trigger-happy now.

"Not like that! Don't be disgusting."

"Me disgusting?" I threw my arms up in the air, glared at her, then looked away sickened. "You were attracted to that life. Taking your clothes off in front of a bunch of perverts for some easy money." I was spitting the words out like bullets from a magazine. And my gun was set to repeat. "What kind of girl *wants* to work in a strip club? What kind of girl *wants* to shag strangers for…"

She stepped forward and struck me hard on the side of my face. I never saw it coming. It hurt. A lot. "I *never* did that! I would never *ever* do that. Who do you think I…"

"How would I ever know? Why should I believe you? Why should I believe one of Manning's…"

She hit me again. Same cheek. Damn! She couldn't half slap hard. But still, the bullets kept on flying. "How can I ever trust you again? You're not the person I thought I married." I was angry. I was hurting. Maybe the anger and the hurt should have been directed at Manning, but Manning wasn't standing in front of me. Amber was.

She gave me a look that would melt even a serial killer's heart. "You *know* the real me, Brendon. You're the only man that has ever loved me, made love to me, pleased me, given me real happiness. You *can* trust me."

My heart wasn't melting any. I said. "Trust is like a mirror, Amber. If it's broken you can fix it. But you will always see the cracks."

She was still giving me the eyes. As she spoke a succession of tears ran down her left cheek. "But the mirror was never broken,

Brendon. You always saw the real me, the true image of me. I didn't cheat on you."

I heard her words. But I wasn't listening. I said. "You can't change what happened, what you did. You can't undo it. Losing your cherry to that bastard." I wasn't shouting any more. I'd fitted a silencer, but the bullets I fired were just as lethal. "He didn't have to *rape* you. You *gave* yourself to that monster. Willingly…. like one of his whores."

This time I saw the hand come up fast. I leaned back out of its path. Now *she* was angry. She said. "I was sixteen! *Sixteen!* I thought that's what a girl was supposed to do to get someone to love her. I thought…"

"So it's all true. Everything he said about you. The photograph of you and him…" Acid rose up in my throat as I thought about them. "Doing it like fuckin' animals!"

She squinted her eyes in repulsion. "What photograph? And stop swearing. You never used to swear."

I ignored her. "He sent me one of you with him - the fuckin' ugly bastard - in the throes of…" I tried to think of the worst possible way of putting it. To say it like it was. Disgusting. Shameful. Sick.

"Stop it! Stop it! Just stop it!" She turned around and walked away from me. She stopped when she got to the back wall. I could see her shoulders hitching. She sat on a bail of silage, sobbing. I wanted to hold her. I wanted to make it better. I wanted to take it all away. But I couldn't do any of that. I was too busy festering, picking at this wound. Making it more painful. More ugly.

"If there were photographs, then I never knew. I would never have allowed that. It wasn't like you're saying. It was *never* like us." She spoke quietly and she was facing the wall. I had to step forward to hear her better.

I said. "You're damn right it wasn't! I *loved* you. I *made love* to you. I didn't fuck you like some whore the way Manning did!" Ouch! The lid was off now and the anger just poured like blood from an open wound. A fresh wound that lay agape while I threw salt at it, over and over again.

She made her eyes into slits again. "Yes…we had sex. It was just sex. Plain, straight forward, unloving, unremarkable sex. Not sexy. Not fun. Not loving. Not how it's supposed to feel at all!"

"So bad you did it again and again." Sarcasm. Never clever, but I said it anyway.

"Do you want the facts? The truth? Or what some sick old man told you?"

I shrugged, turned my back on her and looked away to the trees outside, like I didn't care either way. Whatever. I knew how it would have been anyway, no matter what she had to say, right? She couldn't fool me.

"I went for a hot chocolate in a café the first time he took me out. He had a posh car. He bought me a cake and hot chocolate in a café in Newcastle. I had never done that in my life. It was a treat. He was a friend of my mother's. I thought, how could that be a bad thing, right?"

I twisted my mouth like Elvis might if he ever had a stroke. It didn't sound like a first date to me. It sounded like an uncle taking his niece out. A sick paedophile uncle. *Uncle Isaac!*

"The next time we went to the coast. He got me a huge ice cream with a flake in it. I had never had an ice cream with a flake in it. I was nearly sixteen and I had never had a ninety nine!"

I could hear her more clearly now. She must have turned from the wall to face me. She might have walked a few steps my way. I continued to look out at the rain; the trees swaying haphazardly in the wind.

"It was like that for a few weeks. A hot chocolate here. A Pepsi there. We went to MacDonalds once. Then one day he kissed me. Nobody had ever kissed me. I think my Dad used to, sometimes, before I went to bed. But that had been years previously. Other than that, nobody had ever kissed me. No boy. No man. It wasn't like you and me. It wasn't sexy or passionate or..."

She let out a heavy sigh. "I let it happen. I felt...important. Wanted. I was being taken out of that house, away from my mother and that was a good thing. I needed to have fun. To be loved. To be taken care of. So yes, things progressed over the next few weeks. I thought that's what I was supposed to do. I thought that's what you do when you have a man and want to keep him. And no, I didn't think of him as attractive or anything like that. But who was *I*? Nobody had ever taken any notice of *me*. I thought that that must be what was meant to be. I had found someone and so I went along with it. And it could have been worse. He wasn't a pig. He didn't mistreat me. He was kind. He took me places. He said I was pretty. He took me to his club. I was impressed. He was rich and he knew all these important people."

"Puh!" *Pornstars? Perverts? Pimps?*

"I thought they were important *then.* I was *sixteen!*" She was standing behind me now. I could hear her breathing and her feet moving around in the dirt, trying to keep warm. Part of me wanted to turn around and grab hold of her, squeeze her tight and never let her go. Even in the damp and cold of the barn I could smell her scent. Not a perfume or deodorant. Just her scent. The unique fragrance of Amber.

"The girls at the club came over to me. They wanted to know me. They brought me drinks and snacks and one even took me back stage to see all of her costumes. I was impressed. They were like the showgirls I'd seen on the TV. It was like being at the Miss World show. Live. Every girl was beautiful. Their faces, their bodies, their costumes, the way they walked, everything. Beautiful."

"They were his whor…"

"Shut up!" She shouted in my ear. I shut up.

"He took me there most Friday nights. I would drink Babycham and wear the sparkling silver dress he bought me and the diamante drop earrings. I felt like a princess. I was naïve."

I heard her feet scrape the earth and then something heavier. I turned and saw her dragging a small square bail out towards me. When she got within a few feet she stopped, sat on one end and pulled me down by the arm of my jacket, forcing me to sit next to her.

"It went on like that for maybe a month. After the show, people would dance. Girls mainly, but men took their jackets off and danced too. I thought it looked romantic. I never knew what was really happening. I never knew the girls were paid to dance."

I let out a long, heavy sigh. But I kept my mouth shut.

"One night after he'd taken me home he came in for a cuppa. Mam was out. God knows where. That was when it progressed further."

It was her turn with the heavy sigh now and then she was silent. I could feel her heat inches from my side. It was raining steady outside. There was no guttering and the drops fell heavily in front of the opening, but I could still hear her breathing. It was jaggered, uneven, laboured. I could have stopped her there. There was no need for her to tell me any more. But I needed to hear all of it. No matter how much it killed me.

Without looking up from the muddy floor in front of me, nonchalantly, I said. "Go on."

"It didn't happen that first time. It started to, but then…I think he must have drunk too much or something. Nothing happened."

She paused again. A minute passed. All the time the voice in my head was telling me to stop her going on. I'd heard enough. I didn't need to hear the details. I ignored the voice.

She continued. "The next week, it happened. I insisted on him wearing protection. They'd drummed it into us at school, so at least I knew that he had to use something." She raised her voice. "It *wasn't* loving. It *wasn't* passionate. It was over fast. It was nothing. It meant nothing. It wasn't intimate or…"

She'd pushed a button. "It wasn't intimate?"

"No."

"You can't get more intimate than intercourse for Christ's sake!" I was shouting. The anger swelled again.

"You can. That was nothing. What *you* did…what *we* did…*that* was intimate. You made love to me. We became one person. I took part of you inside me and you have been inside me ever since…*You*…Nobody but *you*."

"You lay naked with a monster for fuck's sake!"

Amber's face was red. I could see that even in the dim light of dusk. "Maybe a dozen times or so…it meant nothing. I did nothing but lie there."

"So who else? How many others were there?"

She pushed my shoulder with the heel of her hand. It knocked me off balance. "You know I'm not like that!"

"I know nothing about you. And why the hell should I believe you anyway?"

She shouted. "I am telling you the truth. It was one man. It was crap! It happened maybe a dozen times. I was sixteen. I was naïve. I wanted to be loved and instead I got used. If I could take it all back I would. I hate myself for ever meeting that shit of man. I ran away from him when he wanted me to work in his club. I realized then what he was about…what the other girls did. I wasn't like that. I ran away…I ran away!"

"So you said."

"I made a life for myself. Nobody helped me. I went to college. I got a job. I managed my own money and made my own meals and I *never* kissed another man until I met you."

She was shouting, but she was crying too. My heart had grown a hard shell around it. Nothing and nobody was going to hurt it ever again. I said. "If it was nothing. If it was as little as you say…then why keep it from me? Why go to the length of faking your own death and letting me believe you drowned?"

She got down on her knees in front of me and held my knees firm in her grip. "Cos, I knew you would be like this. I knew you wouldn't want me. I knew it would hurt you. And if he had gone to the media like he threatened, then he would hurt you even more. You know how the tabloids work…they would make it sound like I was some kind of prostitute or something. I couldn't do that to you."

"So you paid the bastard!"

"Yes…at first I paid him…thirty thousand. I'm sorry. I had to."

"Why didn't you just tell me? I could have handled it."

She rose up on her knees, her face inches from mine. "Like you're handling it now?"

Tears were filling my eyes now. "I would have handled it better than I handled losing you."

"I'm sorry, Brendon. I was ashamed. I couldn't stand for you to know about him. I hated myself so much. I didn't want you to hate me too."

I looked into her eyes, blinking the tears away, but they ran down my cheeks unchecked. "You've been dead these last two years…What do think that has done to me? I am not the man you left."

"I'm so sorry, Brendon. I'm so sorry." She cried into my chest, her hands finding mine and squeezing my fingers.

"Let me fix us, Brendon. I love you so much."

I had dreamt moments like this many times. When your wife dies you fantasise about it being a lie. A cruel mistake. You fantasise about her walking in one day and saying 'It was just a silly mistake…here I am. I never died after all.' You find yourself praying to God to bring her back to you. You would do anything just to see her face one more time. You know it's impossible. You know miracles don't exist like that. Dead is dead and nothing can bring back the dead. And yet you still have those crazy, stupid fantasies. And yet here we were, Amber in the flesh, pleading with me, holding me, breathing the same air as me.

I stood up and looked down at her in the dirt. "You say you've told me the truth?"

She stared up at me with the eyes of a puppy. A puppy with tears in its eyes, pleading to be saved from being put to sleep. "Yes, Brendon. I swear."

I swear. She said I swear. I looked at her with absolute rage filling my heart. I was hurting more than ever. I said. "So who the fuck was that skinny, blonde guy mauling your naked body in your flat in Porthtowan?"

The expression on her face told me the truth. The hesitation confirmed it. " Th...that was Thrash…my friend. He's still missing. Christ, Brendon…He might be dead by now. He never mauled me. I…I can explain…"

I started walking. She clung to my pants, her fingers digging in to my legs. I walked on, trailing her out through the opening into the rain and the mud.

"Brendon? I never did anything with Thrash…I never did. I swear to you…I…"

"Yeah! Well, Manning thought he meant something to you or he wouldn't have grabbed him." I forced my legs forward and powered on with the weight of her hanging onto my pants. She cried and wailed and slid about my feet in the muddy field.

"He means nothing to me. Brendon, I swear…"

I said. "He means nothing to me either."

I carried on robotically with the full weight of her hanging on my legs. This woman had caused me immeasurable pain when I believed she'd drowned. My very soul had been tortured since finding out about her past. I could take no more.

"And neither do you!" As I uttered my last words to her she lost her grip and fell in the mud behind me. I never looked back. And I promised myself there, in that moment that I would never look back again.

Chapter Thirty Three

Eighteen months later

I woke up with a fog over my head. Katerina's birthday celebrations had gone on until two in the morning. The nightlife in Padstow was pretty low key, but that doesn't prevent a bunch of friends going out and getting smashed. I had bought her a new dress for her twenty eighth birthday. She was still wearing it, lying on her belly, flat out beside me on our bed. Even with last night's make up smudged across her pillow and her raven locks spread across her shoulders and back like unruly clematis, she still looked amazing. Last night, in the restaurant, with the candlelight illuminating her skin and the wine putting even more brightness into her eyes, she was quite simply the epitome of perfect beauty.

She opened her eyes and immediately her plump, rose lips formed that incredible smile of hers. I don't remember what I ever did to deserve such a woman. We had been too intoxicated when we got back last night to even contemplate making love, but now she wanted her 'belated birthday bonk', as she put it.

Breakfast always tastes better after morning sex and it tastes even better on a balcony overlooking a turquoise sea. It was AK and Anya's first anniversary and Katerina had asked them to visit us in my new home in Cornwall. AK had come down alone when I first bought the place. He helped me renovate the woodwork of the old clapperboard house. A couple of months later he was down again helping me film my new series for Channel Four called 'Life's a beach'. It's about surviving on nothing but the fruits of the sea and is due to be screened in the summer. AK wanted to join me down here permanently, but his new wife, Anya had only just started a new job in Durham. After the events of 2010, I had to get away from the north east and although AK initially thought Cornwall a strange choice, what with everything that happened down here nearly eighteen months ago, he eventually agreed that there was nothing here to worry me anymore. No mad men smuggling young Russian girls in. No reincarnations of dead wives. Nothing to fear, but the English weather. And this morning it was nothing short of perfect.

I sat on the balcony chewing on my bacon sandwich and watching the waves crash in on Treyarnon Bay and further over into Constantine Bay too. I've been to the south of France, the Balearics, South America and Africa and I've seen some fantastic coastline in my life. But there's just something unique about the Cornish Coast and there was no better example than the length of coast I can see from my balcony.

"What you do today, Brendon…after I leave?" Katerina asked with her mouth full of muesli. She would cook me bacon and eat muesli herself, that's just how she was. I guess I was going to miss her this next fortnight. She was flying home today to visit her family in the Ukraine. She hadn't been back since arriving here eighteen months ago.

I said. "Well, I was thinking I might sit on this balcony and watch the waves. Then I might read the paper and have another cuppa. Then chicken and bacon pasta for lunch sounds great. And then I might take a walk along the beach over to Constantine and Booby. After a nap on that sun lounger out there…" I nodded towards the garden below. "I might think about getting the barbie going and sticking on those rib-eyes that we got yesterday. Or maybe I'll have those big twelve inch pizzas we got. By then it should be just about Bud time and I might just invite AK and Anya over for some great food and a bit crack."

She looked at me and smirked. "Brendon Hawke, if you carry on this way…you will be the laziest man ever."

I put my tea down and said. "That's what I'm aiming for."

The day pretty much went as I planned. I saw Katerina off at Newquay Airport, drove back with some very unsettling feelings about her leaving, then sat and read the paper, like I said I would, but I fell asleep outside in the garden so the walk got postponed. When I woke, the weather had changed so I decided against the barbeque. AK came over for a beer about six, just on his own. Anya had gone into Padstow to get some shopping.

"God, life's good, isn't it?" He said sitting on my balcony, feet up on the wall with a slice of pizza in one hand and a beer in the other.

I said. "Sure is."

AK continued. "I can't believe it's a year since I married that gorgeous woman."

I nodded with my can at my lips. After one slice of pizza, I'd passed the plate to AK, suddenly feeling more thirsty than hungry. Thirsty for beer, anyway.

"You're okay with being back down here, yeah?"

I said. "You're kidding right? It's perfect."

AK stood and looked over the bay. The dark clouds had now blown inland leaving the grass barely damp and now the sky was orange, red, lilac and purple. It seemed ablaze above the boiling sea, which reflected all of its glory.

AK finished off my pizza and I finished another Bud. I pulled two more up from the bucket of ice at my feet. We both pulled back the ring pulls and sank another mouthful down, harmonising when we sighed after that first taste. My bare feet were up on the plastic table and AK had his sandals resting on one of the spare plastic seats. The beer was doing what it was supposed to do and I don't think I ever felt more chilled.

Then AK had to go and spoil things. "Think you'll ever get hitched again?"

I carried on pouring lager down my throat. It was good and cold. "I'm not you, AK. You kind of fell in love right away. You were ready…you know?"

AK sipped at his can. Then he said. "Aren't you?"

I opened yet another Bud.

After a while AK said. "You still think about…"

I stopped him. "No. Never."

We sat and watched the sun dip into the cool blue of the Atlantic until the sky was on fire and the last surfers left the bay. Finally AK said. "You know, we're two of the most lucky guys I ever knew. I know how everything happened was kinda crazy and people died and stuff, but…"

I said. "People didn't die AK. Monsters maybe, but not people."

AK said. "I'll drink to that." Then. "I wish that bastard Manning had died too when the police shot him."

I shrugged and reminded him. "He got twenty five years for firing at those policemen. Getting the blame for your knife-work was rather satisfying too, don't you think? And six Hungarian girls are back home with their families after the vice squad found them in probably the only room you didn't get to see in that den of iniquity he liked to call, Manning's Mansion. He might not be dead, AK. But at the age he is now, he's never gonna get out, is he?"

"Yeah, but the bastard never got his comeuppance for murdering that surfer kid, did he? What was his name again? Lash? Slash?"

"You mean Thrash. Yeah, that was clever dumping him off St. Agnes with a broken board and a broken neck. Surfers die all the time…nobody suspected a thing. But like I said…he's in a high security prison now with no hope of parole before he's seventy something. I can live with that."

AK said. "Nah…I'd prefer it if he was dead."

The beer had obviously mellowed me. I was feeling more philosophical about the whole thing than I usually would. "Whatever. He's dead to me now anyway."

AK said. "And Amber? Is she still dead to you?"

I gave him a look that made him look away.

He said. "People do change you know."

I gave him the look again. "I don't think so."

AK supped at his Bud then held it against his forehead like he had a headache or something. He dropped it back down to his knee and held it there and stared at it. "You are wrong, my friend. We are not the sum of all of our experiences in our lives. We are not defined by every little thing we do. If our souls start out good and pure, then they will remain so. Always."

I rolled my eyes. "Jesus! How many beers you had?"

He continued. "It's true that we can change and we can learn, but our core remains the same. When I was a boy I wanted to fit in with the lads on our estate, so I stole a fiver from my Mam's purse. I told them what I'd done and they were impressed. We bought cider and cigarettes and we had a good time. But I would strike you down if you called me a thief."

I looked at him and he was still staring at his beer. I don't think I'd ever seen him look so serious, so genuine and so resolute. Scary!

He must have felt my eyes on him. He lifted his head and we exchanged a look. He continued. "I am not and I have *never* been a thief. I did what I thought I was supposed to do at that time to comply. When my Mam gave me my pocket money that week and the following week, I sneaked it back into her purse both times. She never knew the wrong that I did. And she never knew the right that I did either. Now tell me…what good would it do to tell her now about this thing?"

It was my turn to stare at my beer now. I couldn't answer him. I didn't have an answer.

He said. "Would it change the way she feels about me? Or would it cause her pain? I am the same person that she has always loved. It did not scar me. It did not change me. It did not…it does not define me."

With my eyes still on the can, I said. "I think the fact that you put the money back says a lot about you AK. I think that maybe that defines you."

"Then you understand my point. What I did was despicable. But at the time it meant that I fitted in with a gang of idiots that probably would have bullied me otherwise. I had no one when we moved to that estate. I was just a weedy little kid from a broken home with no friends. Then suddenly I became AK. I had friends and places to hang out. They didn't need to know how I really felt about what I had done. It got me through a difficult time in my life is all."

I said. "You were called AK even then? I didn't think they had even invented the AK47 when you were a kid."

He said. "My name is Alan Kennedy."

I said. "They're your initials? I thought…"

He looked at me. "I like guns Hawkeye…but I'm not some nut." He shook his head, disappointed in me I guess. "I learned from it. I learned that I would never ever do it again. Why? Because I didn't enjoy it. I didn't like the way it made me feel. It was just something I did at the time. Sometimes you just do the best you can to get through your life."

I felt slightly abashed. Humbled I guess. I didn't have anything to say in reply so I kept my mouth shut.

AK added. "I think that's how it was for Amber, maybe."

Who would have thought AK would have so much wisdom? Damn him!

The sun finally disappeared over the horizon and we went inside and put some Kings of Leon on. We acted as though he had never said those words. Anya came over to pick AK up about ten and I took a bath after changing the CD to something mellower, but maybe I shouldn't have. Luther Vandross was singing one of his little known tracks: 'How do I tell her.' The lyrics hit a note with me. 'How do I tell her, I don't want to be here anymore. Nothing she did. I just don't feel the way I did before...' Wow, that Luther really knew how to affect a guy's emotions, didn't he?

I was walking alone along the beach at Constantine a few days later. It was mid July. Dusk. The sun had just dipped into the cool blue Atlantic and all these things came into my mind. This beautiful girl who had come into my life, had made me believe I could be happy again. She made me forget the stuff I needed to forget. I had known her eighteen months and I could not find a fault with her. I had made it a point never to ask about her past and she never asked about mine. I liked the way she had put it: our lives began when we met each other. I found myself wishing I had followed that principle when I had first met Amber.

Other silly stuff entered my mind. Questions. Like the one AK had asked. 'Think you'll ever get hitched again?'

The thing was, as wonderful as everything was, I couldn't shake this dreadfully distressing feeling. When I thought about these last few years I felt like I had written off my very first car, finally recovered from my injuries, watched the tow truck take my pride and joy away and then out of the blue, a brand new replacement had turned up. I should feel elated, right? Especially since the replacement wasn't anything like the original little Mazda MX5 that I thought I'd keep forever. It was more like a Porsche 911, all red and shiny and sexy as hell. And in most men's minds it was way better than the original. I should feel like the luckiest guy in the world. Shouldn't I? So why did I find myself wishing I still had that old MX5?

As strolls along beaches go, this was proving to be one of the shittiest. The sea was as wild as ever, the off shore gusts kicking up the waves sending spray up into the fog that lay heavily upon the swell. It wasn't just murky; it was turbid. The scene was depressing. The way the sky blended with the ocean seemed to play tricks with my eyes. It sucked me in; hypnotised me. As I felt my feet sink into the saturated sand, I felt my mood sink further. Somewhere off in the distance a foghorn sounded adding to eeriness and sense of isolation I was suddenly experiencing.

I came to the headland that separates Constantine from Treyarnon and sat on one of the many benches perched along the grassy coastline. I was thinking about how fast the time had flitted away. Not four years ago I was married. Happy. Ignorant, I guess. But happy, all the same. Now I lived five hundred miles away, by the sea instead of in a rural village. The girl in my bed was dark instead of blonde, Ukrainian instead of English, stunning instead of beautiful. And now, I asked myself, was I happier? Was I even happy? I should be. Any man would swap their lives for mine, I'm sure. But the feeling persisted. I was trying to work out what it was. Why was I feeling this way?

Time is a funny thing. Raging fires die down. Strong, deep-rooted beliefs eventually erode. Deep, intense and insidious feelings fade somewhat. We grow, I guess. As time goes by we see things differently. Things that mattered plenty one time seem suddenly insignificant. And sometimes, just sometimes, all that certitude and conviction disintegrates. And I was trying to clarify what had taken its place. What had all those intense feelings that had once saturated my heart been replaced with.

My eyes filled and no matter how much I tried to climb out of this awful lugubrious hole I was in I just seemed to fall deeper. Okay, I'll say it. Regret! That's what was going on here. Regret, loss and more than a little anger too. Except this time, the anger was directed at myself. What a fool I had been!

I stared out at the pallid mess that was the sky and the ocean. There was no distinction between the two. A beautiful face appeared like a perfect watercolour, painted on a grey canvas. Katerina's face. All I could see was her incredibly big, dark and unbelievably beautiful eyes. Her smile was pretty amazing too. She was always smiling. It was infectious. Her body was pin-up perfect. I could not fault her looks. She was a good person too; kind and genuine and loyal and honest. She was the brand new Porsche that every man dreams of. Shined to showroom perfection. But.

I hated that there was a but. But there was. And the but was that I didn't really want a Porsche. I think I wanted that old Mazda back.

My mood hadn't lifted much by the end of that first week alone. I tried to do some writing. Wasted my time. My mind wasn't in the right place. I tried to do some video editing, but with a deadline months off I just wasn't motivated. I'd even stopped thinking about my mother. Well, mostly. I had lost her just six months earlier, a week before Christmas. Katerina had never met her, but she had been great. She got me through a difficult time.

Then on my eighth day alone I woke up to the sound of the postman attacking my door with an angry fist. Well, at least that's how it sounded after six Buds the night before. I pulled on my robe and answered the door all bleary eyed. I'd never met my postman before, so I was rather surprised to see that it wasn't a man at all. She was a post woman. Or maybe I should say really hot girl in a uniform with a bag over her shoulder.

"I couldn't get this through your letterbox."

She had a lisp. Not a geeky, 'Yuk, she's sounds weird' kind of lisp. No, this was the sexy as hell type of lisp. She looked me up and down, probably saw the toothpaste and curry sauce stains that adorned my grubby terry towelling bathrobe, probably saw my hairy toes too, and probably thought: Yikes! Get me out of here.

I signed for the package and watched her rush away to her little red van. I suddenly felt very old and very ugly. The start of another shitty day. By the stroke of eleven I was washed and shaved and dressed and eating cereal in front of the TV. Daytime TV should be banned for people who are feeling shitty. If I'd sat there watching that crap for much longer there was a real chance I might slit my wrists.

I switched the TV off and sat on my extra large settee in front of the picture window in my lounge. It wasn't raining today, but the clouds were so low I'd have to crouch not to get my hair wet. I picked open the package that the hot post girl had brought. Oh, good! It was Ray Mears' latest DVD. Why the hell would someone send me a Ray Mears DVD? Or more to the point, who would send me a Ray Mears DVD? The man I loved to hate, almost as much as Bear bloody Grylls. I found the Amazon receipt inside which informed me my present had been ordered by no other than Lenny Jackson, AKA my agent. Thanks Lenny. He knew I was supposed to be busy editing my latest work right now and he probably thought Ray Mears would what? Inspire me? Provide me with some tips? The guy was a bleeding genius who pulled in twice the viewing figures that I did. Far from inspire me, this guy made me want to give up. I took one last look at Mears' smug face on the cover and threw the DVD behind me.

I stared out at the Atlantic and watched the bobbing heads that constantly appeared and disappeared as the swell brought in the great breaking waves they craved. Surfers! What a crazy bunch. When I stood up a letter dropped off my knee onto the floor. How had I missed that? I bent over and picked it up and then my breathing faulted.

I recognised the writing right away. Katerina. I guess I knew then what was coming. I could call it my sixth sense, but I'd be lying. It was more of a case of what Sherlock Holmes would call deduction. She hadn't rang me yet and she'd been home nearly a week, so a letter could mean only one thing. I sat down and ripped the end of the envelope. One sheet. That's all. The first line started with, 'I'm so sorry Brendon." Did I really need to read the rest?

Apparently, she'd been feeling homesick for a while and her feelings for me had changed. Wow! We must have caught the same 'This isn't working' bug. Anyway, her ex fiancée, Dmitry, the one who hit her and kept putting off the marriage and was lousy in bed. Yes, that one. Apparently, he'd been waiting for her to come on home to him and he was now a changed man, etc, etc. And well, you get the idea.

I checked her wardrobe and found it empty. Her chest of drawers. Empty. The drawer under the bed at her side. Empty. Then I remembered the two heavy suitcases I carried for her into the departure lounge at Newquay Airport. Why did I not think that odd at the time? How had I not cottoned on? And when we had made love on the morning she left, how had I not noticed then that she was different? She hadn't really been there. She had just been going through the motions. I hadn't noticed at the time. Maybe, because at the time I wasn't really there either. With my body I had gone through the motions, but now that I thought about it, my heart hadn't really been in it. In fact, it hadn't been for a long while.

It's a funny thing, but things kind of picked up after that. Even the weather. AK and Anya went back up north at the end of the next week. I didn't tell them about the letter. They'd find out eventually. Instead I embraced this new single life. I threw myself into my work. I finished editing my latest stuff and sent it to Lenny for his perusal. I bought a Tai Chi DVD from the net and started a new fitness and relaxation regime that lasted a whopping ten days. But hey, God loves a trier, right? I splashed out on a fancy new mountain bike and have been using it everyday, doing at least eighteen hundred yards. Okay, translated, that's about a mile in total there and back to the newsagents every morning, but it sounds better when I say eighteen hundred yards. The main thing is I'm doing stuff. Writing. Keeping fit. Thinking of my next adventure. I'm not dwelling on the past. Not thinking of the mistakes I've made. Not looking back. Well, that's my goal anyway. I've even given myself a new mantra to follow. 'Don't look back. Never look back. You won't see where you're going. And most likely you'll fall down.'

So far, it's working. Most of the time.

About the author:

David Blackdene works as an Occupational Therapist in the North East of England. He lives with his family and their border collie in County Durham and spends most of his spare time in the Durham Dales. Cycling and walking in the fresh air of the dales is his greatest passion. But when he's not pretending to be Bradley Wiggins on his racing bike or scaling mountains in the Lakes you'll find him sitting in front of a blazing log burner with a cold can of Bud reading a good book (or better still writing one!) Favourite authors include Lee Child, Robert Crais, Harlen Coben & Wilbur Smith.

Don't Look Back is available on Amazon Kindle and you can order in paperback at Amazon.co.uk
Alternatively quote the **ISBN 9781481168274** at your local bookstore and they will order it in for you. **RRP: £6.99**

Praise for DON'T LOOK BACK

'...a roller coaster of action and emotions...The storyline moves along at a cracking pace keeping you eagerly turning the pages. Just when you think you've seen the last twist in the plot, hold on tight, because there is always another surprise just around the corner.' G Langdale (UK Amazon customer).

'I would thoroughly recommend this book! The plot, has drama at every turn and certainly isn't for those who like a superficial read as it has a lot of depth to offer. Looking forward to the next novel.' A Milburn (UK Amazon customer).

'What a book! Couldn't put it down...Can't wait for the next book to come out! Well done!' A Gladstone (UK Amazon customer).

....

Look out for David Blackdene's next thriller: **Double Justice** – due out Spring 2013 on paperback and Kindle.

For more information and to review this book visit:
www.DavidBlackdene.com

17128464R00159

Made in the USA
Charleston, SC
27 January 2013